WAY *of the* PILGRIM

TOR BOOKS BY GORDON R. DICKSON

NOVELS

Alien Art
The Alien Way
Arcturus Landing
The Far Call
Gremlins, Go Home! (with Ben Bova)
Hoka! (with Poul Anderson)
Home from the Shore
The Last Master
Masters of Everon
Mission to Universe
Naked to the Stars
On the Run
Other
Outposter
Planet Run (with Keith Laumer)
The Pritcher Mass
Pro
Secrets of the Deep
Sleepwalker's World
The Space Swimmers
The Space Winners
Spacepaw
Spacial Delivery
Way of the Pilgrim
Wolf and Iron

THE DORSAI SERIES

Necromancer
Tactics of Mistake
Lost Dorsai: The New Dorsai Companion
Soldier, Ask Not
The Spirit of Dorsai
Dorsai!
Young Bleys
The Final Encyclopedia, vol. 1 (rev ed.)
The Final Encyclopedia, vol. 2 (rev. ed.)
The Chantry Guild

THE DRAGON SERIES

The Dragon Knight
The Dragon and the Gnarly King
The Dragon in Lyonesse

COLLECTIONS

Beyond the Dar al-Harb
Guided Tour
Love Not Human
The Man from Earth
The Man the Worlds Rejected
Steel Brother
Stranger

WAY *of the* PILGRIM

GORDON R. DICKSON

A TOM DOHERTY ASSOCIATES BOOK
NEW YORK

WAY OF THE PILGRIM

Copyright © 1987 by Gordon R. Dickson

Design by Victoria Kuskowski

A Tor Book
Published by Tom Doherty Associates, LLC
175 Fifth Avenue
New York, NY 10010

Tor Books on the World Wide Web:
www.tor.com

Tor® is a registered trademark of Tom Doherty Associates, LLC

Library of Congress Cataloging-in-Publication Data

Dickson, Gordon R.
    The way of the pilgrim / Gordon R. Dickson.—1st Tor ed.
        p.   cm.
    "A Tom Doherty Associates book."
    ISBN 0-312-86662-3 (alk. paper)
    I. Title.
PS3554.I328W39   1999   99–27540
813'.54—dc21   CIP

First Tor Edition: July 1999

Printed in the United States of America

0 9 8 7 6 5 4 3 2 1

WAY *of the* PILGRIM

ONE

IN THE SQUARE AROUND THE BRONZE STATUE OF THE CIMBRIAN BULL, the crowd was silent. The spring sky over Aalborg, Denmark, was high and blue; and on the weather-grayed red brick wall of the building before them a man was dying upon the triple blades, according to an alien law. The two invokers, judges and executioners of that law, sat their riding beasts, watching, less than two long paces from where Shane Evert stood in the crowd of humans on foot.

"My son," the older and bulkier of the two was saying to the younger in the heavy Aalaag tongue, plainly unaware that there was a human nearby who could understand him, "as I've told you repeatedly, no creature tames overnight. You've been warned that when they travel in a family the male will defend his mate, the female and male defend their young."

"But, my father," said the younger, "there was no reason. I only struck the female aside with my power-lance to keep her from being ridden down. It was a consideration I intended, not a discipline or an attack. . . ."

Their words rumbled in Shane's ears and printed themselves in his mind. Like giants in human form, medieval and out of place, the two massive Aalaag loomed beside him, the clear sunlight shining on the green and silver metal of their armor and on the red, camel-like creatures that served them as riding animals. Their concern was with their conversation and the crowd of humans they supervised in this legal deathwatch. Only slightly did they pay attention to the man they had hung on the blades.

Mercifully, for himself as well as for the humans forced to witness his death, it happened that the Dane undergoing execution had been paralyzed by the power-lance, called by the Aalaag a "long arm," before he had been thrown upon the three sharp lengths of metal protruding from the wall twelve feet above the ground. The blades had pierced him while he was still unconscious, and he had passed immediately into shock. So that he was not now aware of his own dying, or of his wife, the woman for whom he had incurred the death penalty, who lay dead at the foot of the wall below him. Now he himself was almost dead. But while he was still alive all those in the square were required by Aalaag law to observe.

". . . Nonetheless," the alien father was replying, "the male misunderstood. And when cattle make errors, the master is responsible. You are responsible for the death of this one and his female—which had to be, to show that we are never in error, never to be attacked by the native beasts we have conquered. But the responsibility is yours."

Under the bright sun the metal on the alien pair glittered as ancient and primitive as the bronze statue of the bull or the blades projecting from the homely brick wall. But the watching humans would have learned long since not to be misled by appearances.

Tradition, and something like superstition among the religionless Aalaag, preserved the weapons and armor of a time already more than fifty thousand Earth years lost and gone in their history, on whatever world had given birth to these nine-foot-tall conquerors of humanity. But their archaic dress and weaponry were only for show.

The real power of the two watching did not lie in their swords and long arms, but in the little black-and-gold rods at their belts, in the jewels of the rings on their massive fore-fingers, and in the tiny, continuously moving orifice in the pommel of each saddle, looking eternally and restlessly left and right at the crowd.

"Then it is true. The fault is mine," said the Aalaag son submissively. "I have wasted good cattle."

"It is true good cattle have been wasted," answered his father, "innocent cattle that originally had no intent to challenge our law. And for that I will pay a fine, because I am your father and it is to my blame that you made an error. But you will pay me back five times over, because your error goes deeper than mere waste of good cattle, alone.''

"Deeper, my father?"

Shane kept his head utterly still within the concealing shadow of the hood of his pilgrim's cloak. The two could have no suspicion that one of the cattle of Lyt Ahn, Aalaag Governor of all Earth, stood less than the length of a long arm from them, able to understand every word they spoke. But it would be wise not to attract their attention. An Aalaag father did not ordinarily reprimand his son in public, or in the hearing of any cattle. The heavy voices rumbled on and the blood sang in Shane's ears.

"Much deeper, my son . . ."

The sight of the figure on the blades before him sickened Shane. He had tried to screen it from himself with one of his own private imaginings—the image he had dreamed up of a human outlaw whom no Aalaag could catch or conquer. A human who went about the world anonymously, like Shane, in pilgrim's robes; but, unlike Shane, exacting vengeance from the aliens for each wrong they did to a man, woman, or child. However, in the face of the bloody reality on the wall before Shane, fantasy failed. Now, though, out of the corner of his right eye, he caught sight of something that momentarily blocked that reality from his mind and sent a thrill of unreasonable triumph running through him.

Barely four meters or so beyond and above him and the riders on the two massive beasts, the sagging branch of an oak tree pushed its tip almost into the line of vision between Shane's eyes and the bladed man. On the end of the branch, among the new green leaves of the year, was a small, cocoon-like shape, already broken. From it had just recently struggled the still crumpled shape of a butterfly that did not yet know what its wings were for.

How it had managed to survive through the winter here was beyond guessing. Theoretically, the Aalaag had exterminated all insects in towns and cities. But here it was, a butterfly of Earth being born even as a man of Earth was dying—a small life for a large. An utterly disproportionate feeling of triumph sang in Shane. Here was a life that had escaped the death sentence of the aliens and would live in spite of the Aalaag—that is, if the two now watching on their great red mounts did not notice it as it waved its wings, stiffening them for flight.

They must not notice. Unobtrusively, lost in the crowd with his rough gray pilgrim's cloak and staff, undistinguished among the other drab humans, Shane drifted right, toward the aliens, until the branch tip with its emerging butterfly hung squarely between him and the man on the wall.

It was superstition, magic . . . call it what you like, it was the only help he could give the butterfly. The chances for the small life now beginning on the branch tip should, under any cosmic justice, be insured by the larger life now ending for the man on the wall. The one should balance out the other. Shane fixed the nearer shape of the butterfly in his gaze so that it hid the farther figure of the man on the blades. He bargained with fate. I will not blink, he told himself, and the butterfly will stay invisible to the Aalaag. They will see only the man. . . .

Beside him, neither of the massive, metal-clad figures had noticed his moving. They were still talking.

". . . in battle," the father was saying, "each of us is equal to more than a thousand thousand of such as these. We would be nothing if not that. But though one be superior to so many, it does not follow that the many are without force against the one. Expect nothing, therefore, and do not be disappointed. Though they are now ours, inside themselves these new cattle still remain what they were when we conquered them. Beasts, as yet untamed to proper love of us. Do you understand me now?"

"No, my father."

There was a burning in Shane's throat, and his eyes blurred so that he could hardly see the butterfly clinging tightly to its branch and yielding at last to the instinctive urge to unfold its crumpled, damp wings and spread them to their full expanse. The wings spread, orange, brown and black—like an omen, it was that species of sub-Arctic butterfly called a "Pilgrim"—just as Shane himself was called a "pilgrim" because of the hooded robe he wore. The day three years ago at the University of Kansas rose in his mind. He remembered standing in the student union, among the mass of other students and faculty, listening to the broadcast announcing that the Earth had been conquered, even before any of them had fully grasped that beings from a far world had landed amongst them. He had not felt anything then except excitement, mixed perhaps with a not unpleasant apprehension.

"Someone's going to have to interpret for us to those aliens," he had told his friends cheerfully. "Language specialists like me—we'll be busy."

But it had been *for* the aliens rather than *to* the aliens that interpreting had needed to be done—and he was not, Shane told himself, the stuff of which underground resistance fighters were made.

Only . . . in the last two years . . .

Almost directly over him, the voice of the elder Aalaag rumbled on. "To conquer is nothing. Anyone with power can conquer. We rule—which is a greater art. We rule because eventually we change the very nature of our cattle."

"Change?" echoed the younger.

"Alter," said the older. "Over their generations we teach them to love us. We tame them into good kine. Beasts still, but broken to obedience. To this end we leave them their own laws, their religions, their customs. Only one thing we do not tolerate—the concept of defiance against our will. And in time they tame to this."

"But—always, my father?"

"Always, I say!" Restlessly, the father's huge riding animal shifted its weight on its hooves, crowding Shane a few inches sideways. He moved. But he kept his eyes on the butterfly. "When we first arrive, some fight us—and die. Only we know that it is the heart of the beast that must be broken. So we teach them first the superiority of our weapons, then of our bodies and minds; finally, that of our law. At last, with nothing of their own left to cling to, their beast-hearts crack, and they follow us unthinkingly, blindly loving and trusting us like newborn pups behind their dam, no longer able to dream of opposition to our will."

"And all is well?"

"All is well for my son, his son, and his son's son," said the father. "But until that good moment when the hearts of the cattle break, each small flicker of the flame of rebellion that erupts delays the coming of their final and utter love for us. Inadvertently here, you allowed that flame to flicker to life once more."

"I was in error. In the future I will avoid such mistakes."

"I shall expect no less," said the father. "And now the beast is dead. Let us go on."

They set their riding beasts in motion and moved off. Around them, the crowd of humans sighed with the release of tension. Up on the triple blades, the victim now hung motionless. His eyes stared as he hung there without twitch or sound. The butterfly's wings waved slowly between the dead face and Shane's. The insect lifted like a colorful shadow and fluttered away, rising into the dazzle of the sunlight above the square until it was lost to the sight of Shane. A feeling of victory exploded in him. Subtract one man, he thought half crazily. Add one butterfly—one small Pilgrim to defy the Aalaag.

About him, the crowd was dispersing. The butterfly was gone. His feverish elation over its escape cooled and he looked about the square. The Aalaag father and son were more than halfway across it, heading toward a farther exiting street. One of the few clouds in the sky moved across the face of the sun, graying and dimming the light in the square. Shane felt the coolness of a little breeze on his hands and face. Around him now, the square was almost empty. In a few seconds he would be alone with the dead man and the empty cocoon that had given up the butterfly.

He looked once more at the dead man. The face was still, but the light breeze stirred some ends of long blond hair that were hanging down.

Shane shivered in the abrupt chill from the breeze and the withdrawn sun-warmth. His spirits plunged, on a sickening elevator drop into self-doubt and fear. Now that it was all over, there was a shakiness inside him, and nausea. . . . He had seen too many of the aliens' executions these last two years. He dared not go back to Aalaag Headquarters feeling as he did now.

He might well have to inform Lyt Ahn of the incident which had delayed him in his courier duties; and in no way while telling it must he betray his natural feelings at what he had seen. The Aalaag expected their personal cattle to be like themselves—spartan, unyielding, above taking notice of pain in themselves or others. Anyone of the human cattle who allowed his emotions to become visible would be "sick," in Aalaag terms. It would reflect on the character of an Aalaag master—even if he was Governor of all Earth—if he permitted his household to contain unhealthy cattle.

Shane could end up on the blades himself, for all that Lyt Ahn had always seemed to like him, personally. He would have to get his feelings under control, and time for that was short. At best, he could steal perhaps half an hour more from his schedule in addition to what had already been spent watching the execution—and in those thirty minutes he must manage to pull himself together. He turned away, down a street behind him leading from the square, following the last of the dispersing crowd.

The street had been an avenue of small shops once, interspersed with an occasional larger store or business establishment. Physically, it had not changed. The sidewalks and the street pavement were free of cracks and litter. The windows of the stores were whole, even if the display areas behind the glass were mainly empty of goods. The Aalaag did not tolerate dirt or rubble. They had wiped out with equal efficiency and impartiality the tenement areas of large cities and the ruins of the Parthenon in Athens; but the level of living permitted to most of their human cattle was bone-bare minimal, even for those who were able to work long hours.

A block and a half from the square, Shane found and turned in at a doorway under the now dark shape of what had once been the lighted neon sign of a bar. He entered a large gloomy room hardly changed from the past, except that the back shelf behind the bar itself was bare of the multitude of liquor bottles which it had been designed to hold. Only small amounts of distilled liquors were allowed to be made, nowadays. People drank the local wine or beer.

Just now the place was crowded, with men for the most part. All of them silent after the episode in the square; and all of them drinking draft ale with swift, heavy gulps from the tall, thick-walled glasses they held in their hands. Shane worked his way down to the service area in the far corner. The bartender stood there loading trays with filled glasses for the single waitress to take to the tables and booths beyond the bar.

"One," he said.

A moment later, a full glass was placed in front of him. He paid, and leaned with his elbows on the bar, his head in his hands, staring into the depths of the brown liquid.

The memory of the dead man on the blades, with his hair stirring in the wind, came back to Shane. Surely, he thought, there must be some portent in the butterfly also being called a Pilgrim? He tried to put the image of the insect between himself and the memory of the dead man, but here, away from the blue sky and sunlight, the small shape would not take form in his mind's eye. In desperation, Shane reached again for his private mental comforter—the fantasy of the man in a hooded robe who could defy all Aalaag and pay them back for what they had done. He almost managed to evoke it. But the Avenger image would not hold in his head. It kept being pushed aside by the memory of the man on the blades. . . .

"Undskylde!" said a voice in his ear. *"Herre . . . Herre!"*

For a fraction of a second he heard the words only as foreign noises. In the emotion of the moment, he had slipped into thinking in English. Then the sounds translated. He looked up, into the face of the bartender. Beyond, the bar was already half-empty once more. Few people nowadays could spare more than a few minutes from the constant work required to keep themselves from going hungry—or, worse yet, from being forced out of their jobs and into becoming legally exterminable vagabonds.

"Excuse me," said the bartender again; and this time Shane's mind was back in Denmark with the language. "Sir. But you're not drinking."

It was true. Before Shane the glass was still full. Beyond it, the bartender's face was thin and curious, watching him with the amoral curiosity of a ferret.

"I . . ." Shane checked himself. He had almost started explaining who he was—which would not be safe. Few ordinary humans loved those of their own kind who had become servants in some Aalaag household.

"Disturbed by what you saw in the square, sir? It's understandable," said the bartender. His green eyes narrowed. He leaned closer and whispered. "Perhaps something stronger than beer? How long since you've had some schnapps?"

The sense of danger snapped awake in Shane's mind. Aalborg had once been famous for its aquavit, but that was before the Aalaag came. The bartender must have spotted him as a stranger—someone possibly with money. Then suddenly he realized he did not care what the bartender had spotted, or where he had gotten a distilled liquor. It was what Shane needed right now—something explosive to counter the violence he had just witnessed.

"It'll cost you ten," murmured the bartender.

Ten monetary units was a day's wage for a skilled carpenter—though only a small fraction of Shane's pay for the same hours. The Aalaag rewarded their household cattle well. Too well, in the minds of most other humans. That was one of the reasons Shane moved around the world on his master's errands wearing the cheap and unremarkable robe of a pilgrim.

"Yes," he said. He reached into the pouch at the cord about his waist and brought forth his money clip. The bartender drew in his breath with a little hiss.

"Sir," he said, "you don't want to flash a wad, particularly a wad like that, in here nowadays."

"Thanks. I . . ." Shane lowered the money clip below bar-top level as he peeled off a bill. "Have one with me."

"Why, yes, sir," said the bartender. His eyes glinted, like the metal of the Cimbrian bull in the sunlight. "Since you can afford it . . ."

His thin hand reached across and swallowed the bill Shane offered him. He ducked below the counter level and came up holding two of the tall glasses, each roughly one-fifth full of a colorless liquid. Holding the glasses between his body and Shane's so that they were shielded from the view of others in the bar, he passed one to Shane.

"Happier days," he said, and tilted up his glass to empty it in a swallow. Shane imitated him, and the harsh oiliness of the liquor flamed in his throat, taking his breath away. As he had suspected, it was a raw, illegally distilled, high-proof liquid with nothing in common with the earlier aquavit but the name it shared. Even after he had downed it, it continued to sear the lining of his throat like sooty fire.

Shane reached automatically for his untouched glass of beer to lave the internal burning. The bartender had already taken back their two liquor glasses and moved away down the bar to serve another customer. Shane swallowed gratefully. The thick-bodied ale was gentle as water after the rough-edged moonshine. A warmth began slowly to spread through his body. The hard corners of his mind rounded; and on the heels of that soothing, without effort this time, came his comforting, familiar daydream of the Avenger. The Avenger, he told himself, had been there unnoticed in the square during the executions, and by now he was lying in wait in a spot from which he could ambush the Aalaag father and son, and still escape before police could be called. A small black-and-gold rod, stolen from an Aalaag arsenal, was in his hand as he stood to one side of an open window, looking down a street up which two figures in green and silver armor were riding toward him . . .

"Another, sir?"

It was the bartender back again. Startled, Shane glanced at his ale glass and saw that it, too, was now empty. But another shot of that liquid dynamite? Or even another glass of the ale? He could risk neither. Just as in facing Lyt Ahn an hour or so from now he must be sure not to show any sign of emotion while reporting what he had been forced to witness in the square, so neither must he show the slightest sign of any drunkenness or dissipation. These, too, were weaknesses not permitted servants of the aliens, as the alien did not permit them in himself.

"No," he said, "I've got to go."

"One drink did it for you?" The bartender inclined his head. "You're lucky, sir. Some of us don't forget that easily."

The touch of a sneer in the bitterness of the other's voice flicked at Shane's already overtight nerves. A sudden sour fury boiled up in him. What did this man know of what it was like to live with the Aalaag, to be treated always with the indifferent affection that was below contempt—the same sort of affection a human might give a clever pet animal—and all the while to witness scenes like those in the square, not once or twice a year but weekly, perhaps daily?

"Listen—," he snapped, but checked himself. Once more, he had nearly given away what he was and what he did.

"Yes, sir?" said the bartender, after a moment of watching him. "I'm listening."

Shane thought he read suspicion in the other's voice. That reading might only be the echo of his own inner turmoil, but he could not take a chance.

"Listen," he said again, dropping his voice, "why do you think I wear this outfit?"

He indicated his pilgrim's robe.

"You took a vow." The bartender's voice was dry now, remote.

"No. You don't understand. . . ."

The unaccustomed warmth of the drink in him triggered an

inspiration. The image of the butterfly slid into—and blended with—his image of the Avenger. "You think it was just a bad accident, out there in the square just now? Well, it wasn't. Not just accidental, I mean—I shouldn't say anything."

"Not an accident?" The bartender frowned; but when he spoke again, his voice, like Shane's, was lowered to a more cautious note.

"Of course, the man ending on the blades—it wasn't planned to finish that way," muttered Shane, leaning toward him. "The Pilgrim—" Shane broke off. "You don't know about the Pilgrim?"

"The Pilgrim? What Pilgrim?" The bartender's face came close. Now they were both almost whispering.

"If you don't know, I shouldn't say—"

"You've said quite a lot already—"

Shane reached out and touched his six-foot staff of polished oak leaning against the bar beside him.

"This is one of the symbols of the Pilgrim," he said. "There're others. You'll see his mark one of these days and you'll know that attack on the Aalaag in the square didn't just happen by accident. That's all I can tell you."

It was a good note to leave on. Shane picked up the staff, turned quickly and went out. It was not until the door to the bar closed behind him that he relaxed. For a moment he stood breathing the cooler air of the street, letting his head clear. His hands, he saw, were trembling.

As his head cleared, sanity returned. A cold dampness began to make itself felt on his forehead in the outside air. What had gotten into him? Risking everything just to show off to some unknown bartender? Fairy tales like the one he had just hinted at could find their way back to Aalaag ears—specifically to the ears of Lyt Ahn. If the aliens suspected he knew something about a human resistance movement, they would want to know a great deal more from him; in which case death on the triple blades might turn out to be something he would long for, not dread.

And yet, there had been a great feeling during the few seconds he had shared his fantasy with the bartender, almost as if it were something real. Almost as great a feeling as the triumph he had felt on seeing the butterfly survive. For a couple of moments he had come alive almost, as part of a world holding a Pilgrim-Avenger who could defy the Aalaag. A Pilgrim who left his mark at the scene of each Aalaag crime as a promise of retribution to come. The Pilgrim, who in the end would rouse the world to overthrow its tyrannical, alien murderers.

He turned about and began to walk hurriedly toward the square again, and to the street beyond it that would take him to the airport where the Aalaag courier ship would pick him up. There was an empty feeling in his stomach at the prospect of facing Lyt Ahn, but at the same time his mind was seething. If only he had been born with a more athletic body and the insensitivity to danger that made a real resistance fighter. The Aalaag thought they had exterminated all cells of human resistance two years ago. The Pilgrim could be real. His role was a role any man really knowledgeable about the aliens could play—if he had absolutely no fear, no imagination to make him dream nights of what the Aalaag would do to him when, as they eventually must, they caught and unmasked him. Unhappily, Shane was not such a man. Even now, he woke sweating from nightmares in which the Aalaag had caught him in some small sin, and he was about to be punished. Some men and women, Shane among them, had a horror of deliberately inflicted pain. . . . He shuddered, grimly, fear and fury making an acid mix in his belly that shut out awareness of his surroundings.

This cauldron of inner feelings brewed an indifference to things around him that almost cost him his life. That and the fact that he had, on leaving the bar, automatically pulled the hood of his robe up over his head to hide his features, particularly from anyone who might later identify him as having been in a place where a bartender had been told about someone called "the Pilgrim." He woke from his thoughts only at the faint rasp of dirt-stiff rags scuffing on cement pavement behind him.

He checked and turned quickly. Not two meters behind, a man carrying a wooden knife and a wooden club studded with glass chips, his thin body wound thick with rags for armor, was creeping up on him.

Shane turned again, to run. But now, in the suddenly tomblike silence and emptiness of the street, two more such men, armed with clubs and stones, were coming out from between buildings on either side to block his way. He was caught between the one behind and the two ahead.

His mind was suddenly icy and brilliant. He had moved in one jump through a flash of fear into something beyond fright, into a feeling tight as a strung wire, like the reaction on nerves of a massive dose of stimulant. Automatically, the last two years of training took over. He flipped back his hood so that it could not block his peripheral vision, and grasped his staff with both hands a foot and a half apart in its middle, holding it up at a slant before him, and turning so as to try to keep them all in sight at once.

The three paused.

Clearly, they were feeling they had made a mistake. Seeing him with the hood over his head and his head down, they must have taken him for a so-called "praying pilgrim," one of those who bore staff and cloak as a token of nonviolent acceptance of the sinful state of the world which had brought all people under the alien yoke. They hesitated.

"All right, pilgrim," said a tall man with reddish hair, one of the two who had come out in front of him. "Throw us your pouch and you can go."

For a second, irony was like a bright metallic taste in Shane's mouth. The pouch at the cord around a pilgrim's waist contained most of what worldly goods he might own; but the three surrounding him now were "vagabonds"—Nonservs—individuals who either could not or would not hold the job assigned them by the aliens. Under the Aalaag rule, such outcasts had nothing to lose. Faced by three like this, almost any pilgrim, praying or not, would have given up his pouch. But Shane could not. In his pouch, besides his own possessions, were official papers of the Aalaag government that he was carrying to Lyt Ahn; and Lyt Ahn, warrior from birth and by tradition, would neither understand nor show mercy to a servant who failed to defend property he carried. Better the clubs and stones Shane faced now than the disappointment of Lyt Ahn.

"Come and get it," he said.

His voice sounded strange in his own ears. The staff he held seemed light as a bamboo pole in his grasp. Now the vagabonds were moving in on him. It was necessary to break out of the ring they were forming around him and get his back to something so that he could face them all at the same time. . . . There was a storefront to his left just beyond the short, gray-haired vagabond moving in on him from that direction.

Shane feinted at the tall, reddish-haired man to his right, then leaped left. The short-bodied vagabond struck at him with a club as Shane came close but the staff in Shane's hand brushed it aside and the staff's lower end slammed home, low down on the body of the vagabond. He went down without a sound and lay huddled up. Shane hurdled him, reached the storefront and turned about to face the other two.

As he turned, he saw something in the air, and ducked instinctively. A rock rang against the masonry at the edge of the glass store window, and glanced off. Shane took a step sideways to put the glass behind him on both sides.

The remaining two were by the curb now, facing him, still spread out enough so that they blocked his escape. The reddish-haired man was scowling a little, tossing another rock in his hand. But the expanse of breakable glass behind Shane deterred him. A dead or battered human was nothing; but broken store windows meant an immediate automatic alarm to the Aalaag police, and the Aalaag were not merciful in their elimination of Nonservs.

"Last chance," said the reddish-haired man. "Give us the pouch—"

As he spoke, he and his companion launched a simultaneous rush at Shane. Shane leaped to his left to take the man on that side first, and get out away from the window far enough to swing his stave freely. He brought its top end down in an overhand blow that parried the club blow of the vagabond and struck the man himself to the ground, where he sat, clutching at an arm smashed between elbow and shoulder.

Shane pivoted to face the reddish-haired man, who was now on tiptoes, stretched up with his own heavy club swung back in both hands over his head for a crushing down-blow.

Reflexively, Shane whirled up the bottom end of his staff, and the tough, fire-hardened tip, traveling at eye-blurring speed, smashed into the angle where the other man's lower jaw and neck met.

The vagabond tumbled, and lay still in the street, his head now bent unnaturally sideways on his neck.

Shane whirled around, panting, staff ready. But the man whose arm he had smashed was already running off down the street in the direction from which Shane had just come. The other two were still down and showed no intention of getting up.

The street was still.

Shane stood, snorting in great gasps of air, leaning on his staff. It was incredible. He had faced three armed men—armed at least in the same sense that he, himself, was armed—and he had defeated them all. He looked at the fallen bodies and could hardly believe it. All his practice with the quarterstaff . . . it had been for defense; and he had hoped never to have to use it against even one opponent. Now, here had been three . . . and he had won.

He felt strangely warm, large and sure. Perhaps, it came to him suddenly, this was the way the Aalaag felt. If so, there could be worse feelings. It was something lung-filling and spine-straightening to know yourself a fighter and a conqueror. Perhaps it was just this feeling he had needed to have, to understand the Aalaag—he had needed to conquer, powerfully, against great odds as they did. . . .

He felt close to rejecting all the bitterness and hate that had been building in him the past two years. Perhaps *might* actually could make *right.* He went forward to examine the men he had downed.

They were both dead. Shane stood looking down at them. They had appeared thin enough, bundled in their rags, but it was not until he stood directly over them that he saw how bony and narrow they actually were. They were like claw-handed skeletons.

He stood, gazing down at the last one he had killed, and slowly the fresh warmth and pride within him began to leak out. He saw the stubbled sunken cheeks, the stringy neck, and the sharp angle of the jawbone jutting through the skin of the dead face against the concrete. These features jumped at his mind. The man must have been starving—literally starving. He looked at the other dead man and thought of the one who had run away. All of them must have been starving, for some days now.

With a rush, his sense of victory went out of him, and the sickening bile of bitterness rose once more in his throat. Here he had been dreaming of himself as a warrior. A great hero—the slayer of two armed enemies. Only the weapons carried by those enemies had been sticks and stones, and the enemies themselves were half-dead men with barely the strength to use what they carried. Not Aalaag, not the powerfully armed world conquerors challenged by his imaginary Pilgrim, but humans like himself, reduced to near animals by those who thought of these and Shane, in common, as "cattle."

The sickness flooded all through Shane. Something like a ticking time bomb in him exploded. He turned and ran for the square.

When he got there, it was still deserted. Breathing deeply, he slowed to a walk and went across it, toward the now still body on the triple blades and the other body at the foot of the wall. The fury was gone out of him now, and also the sickness. He felt empty, empty of everything—even of fear. It was a strange sensation to have fear missing—to have it all over with; all the sweats and nightmares of two years, all the trembling on the brink of the precipice of action.

He could not say exactly, even now, how he had finally come to step off that precipice at last. But it did not matter. Just as he knew that the fear was not gone for good. It would return. But that did not matter, either. Nothing mattered, even the end he must almost certainly come to, now. The only thing that was important was that he had finally begun to act, to do something about a world he could no longer endure as it was.

Quite calmly he walked up to the wall below the blades holding the dead man. He glanced around to see if he was observed, but there was no sign of anyone either in the square or watching from the windows that overlooked it.

He reached into his pocket for the one piece of metal he was allowed to carry. It was the key to his personal living quarters in Lyt Ahn's Headquarters, at Minneapolis, in what had once been known as the United States of America. It was made of some special alloy developed by the Aalaag—"warded," as all such keys had to be, so that it would not set off an alarm by disturbing the field which the Aalaag had set up over every city and hamlet to warn of unauthorized metal weapons in the possession of humans. With the tip of the key, Shane scratched a rough figure on the wall below the body: the Pilgrim and his staff.

The hard tip of the metal key bit easily through the weathered surface of the brick to the original light red color underneath. Shane turned away, putting the key back into his pouch. The shadows of late afternoon had already begun to fall from the buildings to hide what he had done. And the bodies would not be removed until sunrise—this by Aalaag law. By the time the figure scratched on the brick was first seen by one of the aliens, he would be back among the "cattle" of Lyt Ahn's household, indistinguishable among them.

Indistinguishable, but different, from now on—in a way the Aalaag had yet to discover. He turned and walked swiftly away down the street that would bring him to the alien courier ship that was waiting for him. The colorful flicker of a butterfly's wings—or perhaps it was just the glint of a reflection off some high window that seemed momentarily to wink with color—caught the edge of his vision. Perhaps, the thought came suddenly and warmly, it actually was the butterfly he had seen emerge from its cocoon in the square. It was good to feel that it might be the same small, free creature.

"Enter a Pilgrim," he whispered to it triumphantly. "Fly, little brother. Fly!"

TWO

DESCENDING IN THE ICY, GRAY NOVEMBER DAWN FROM THE CROWDED bus that had brought the airline passengers from Bologna—as frequently happened in wintertime, the airport at Milan, Italy was fogged in; and the courier ship, like the commercial jets, had been forced to set down in Bologna—Shane Evert caught a glimpse out of the corner of his eye of a small stick figure, inconspicuously etched on the base of a lamp-post.

He did not dare to look at it directly, but the side glance was enough. He flagged a taxi and gave the driver the address of the Aalaag Headquarters for the city.

"E freddo, Milano," said the driver, wheeling the cab through the nearly deserted morning streets.

Shane gave him a monosyllable in a Swiss accent, by way of agreement. Milan was indeed cold in November. Cold and hard. To the south, Florence would be still soft and warm, with blue skies and sunlight. The driver was probably hoping to start a conversation and find out what brought his human passenger to an alien HQ, and that was dangerous. Ordinary humans did not love those who worked for the Aalaag. If I say nothing, Shane thought, he may be suspicious. No, on second thought, he'll just think from the Swiss accent that I'm someone with a relative in trouble in this city and who doesn't feel like conversation.

The driver spoke of the summer now past. He regretted the passing of the old days when tourists had come through.

To both these statements, Shane gave the briefest of responses. Then there was silence in the cab except for the noise of travel. Shane leaned his staff at a more comfortable angle against his right

leg and left shoulder, to better accommodate it to the small passenger compartment of the cab. He smoothed his gray robe over
his knees. The image of the stick figure he had seen still floated
in his mind. It was identical to the figure he himself had first
marked upon a wall beneath the triple hooks with the dead man
on them, in Aalborg, Denmark over half a year ago.

But he had not marked this one on the lamppost. Nor, indeed,
had he marked any of the other such figures he had glimpsed
about the world during the last eight months. One moment of
emotional rebellion had driven him to create an image that was
now apparently spawning and multiplying to fill his waking as well
as his sleeping hours with recurring nightmares. It did no good to
remind himself that no one could possibly connect him with the
original graffito. It did no good to know that all these eight months
since, he had been an impeccable servant of Lyt Ahn.

Neither fact would be of the slightest help if for some reason
Lyt Ahn, or any other Aalaag, should believe there was cause to
connect him with any one of the scratched figures.

What insane, egocentric impulse had pushed him to use his
own usual pilgrim-sect disguise as the symbol of opposition to the
aliens? Any other shape would have done as well. But he had had
the alcohol of the Danish bootleg liquor inside him; and with the
memory of the massive Aalaag father and son in the square watching the death of the man they had condemned and executed—
above all, with the memory of their conversation, which he alone
of all the humans there could understand—also burning in him,
for one brief moment reason had flown out the window of his
mind.

So, now his symbol had been taken up and had become the
symbol of what was obviously an already existent human Underground in opposition to the Aalaag, an Underground he had never
suspected. The very fact that it existed at all forecast bloody tragedy
for any human foolish enough to be related to it. By their own
standards the Aalaag were unsparingly fair. But they considered
humans as "cattle," and a cattle owner did not think in terms of
being "unfair" to a sick or potentially dangerous bull that had
become a farm problem. . . .

"Eccolo!" said the cab driver.

Shane looked as directed and saw the alien HQ. A perfectly

reflective force shield covered it like a coating of mercury. It was impossible to tell what kind of structure it had been originally. Anything from an office building to a museum was a possibility. Lyt Ahn, First Captain of Earth, in his HQ overlooking St. Anthony's Falls in what had once been the heart of Minneapolis, scorned such an obvious display of defensive strength. The gray concrete walls of his sprawling keep on Nicollet Island had nothing to protect them but the portable weapons within—though these alone were capable of leveling the surrounding metropolitan area in a few hours. Shane paid the driver, got out and went in through the main entrance of the Milan HQ.

The Interior Guards inside the big double doors and those at the desk were all human. Young for the most part, like Shane himself, but much bigger, for the largest of humans seemed frail and small to the nine-foot Aalaag. These guards wore the usual neat, but drab, black uniforms of servant police. Dwarfed beside them, in spite of his five feet eleven inches of height, Shane felt a twinge of perverse comfort at being within these walls and surrounded by these particular fellow humans. Like him, they ate at the aliens' tables; they would be committed to defend him against any non-servant humans who should threaten him. Under the roof of masters who sickened him, he was physically protected and secure.

He stopped at the duty desk and took his key from the leather pouch at his belt, leaving the documents within. The human duty officer there took the key and examined its alien metal—metal which no ordinary Earth native was allowed to own or carry—and the Mark of Lyt Ahn that was stamped on it.

"Sir," said the officer in Italian, reading the Mark. He was suddenly obliging. "Can I be of assistance?"

"I sign in, temporarily," answered Shane in Arabic, for the officer's speech echoed the influence of the throat consonants of that language. "I am the one who delivers messages for the First Captain of Earth, Lyt Ahn. I have some to deliver now to the Commander of these Headquarters."

"Your tongue is skilled," said the officer in Arabic, turning the duty book about and passing Shane a pen.

"Yes," said Shane, and signed.

"The Commander here," said the officer, "is Laa Ehon, Captain of the sixth rank. He accepts your messages."

He turned and beckoned over one of the lesser human guards. "To the outer office of Laa Ehon, with this one bearing messages for the Commander," he ordered in Italian. The guard saluted, and led Shane off. Several flights of stairs up beside an elevator which Shane would have known better than to use, even if the guard had not been with him, brought them to a corridor down which, behind another pair of large carved doors, they reached what was plainly an outer room of the private offices of the Aalaag Commander in Milan.

The guard saluted again and left. There were no other humans in the room. An Aalaag of the twenty-second rank sat at a desk in a far corner of the large, open space, reading what seemed to be reports on the sort of plastic sheets that would take and hold multiple overlays of impressions. In the wall to Shane's left was a large viewing screen, showing in three dimensions a view of what must be an adjoining office, having benches for humans to sit on. This office was empty, however, except for a dark-haired young woman, dressed in a loose, ankle-length blue robe tied tight around her narrow waist.

Where Shane was, there were no places to sit. But, accustomed as he was to close attendance on Lyt Ahn and other Aalaag of low-number rank, he was used to waiting on his feet for hours.

He stood. After perhaps twenty minutes, the Aalaag at the desk noticed him.

"Come," he said, lifting a thumb the size of a tent peg. "Tell me."

He had spoken in Aalaag, for most human servants had some understanding of the basic commands in the tongue of their overlords. But his face altered slightly as Shane answered, for there were few humans like Shane—and Shane both worked and lived with all of those few—who were capable of fluent, almost accentless response in that language.

"Untarnished sir," said Shane, coming up to the desk. "I have messages from Lyt Ahn directly to the Commander of the Milan Headquarters."

He made no move to produce the message rolls from his pouch; and the Aalaag's massive hand, which had begun to extend itself, palm up, toward him at the word "messages" was withdrawn when Shane pronounced the name of Lyt Ahn.

"You are a valuable beast," said the Aalaag. "Laa Ehon will receive your messages soon."

"Soon" could mean anything from "within minutes" to "within weeks." However, since the messages were from Lyt Ahn, and personal, it was probable that it would be only minutes. Shane went back to his corner.

The door opened, and two other Aalaag came in. They were both males in middle life, one of the twelfth, one of the sixth rank. The one of sixth rank could only be Laa Ehon. A Captain of a rank that low-numbered was actually too highly qualified to command a single HQ like this. It was unthinkable that there would be two such here.

The newcomers ignored Shane. No, he thought, as their gaze moved on, they had not merely ignored him. Their eyes had noticed, catalogued, and dismissed him in a glance. They walked together to the viewing screen; the one who must be Laa Ehon spoke in Aalaag.

"This one?"

They were examining the girl in the blue robe, who sat in the other room, unaware of their gaze.

"Yes, immaculate sir. The officer on duty in the square saw this one move away from the wall I told you of, just before he noticed the scratching on it." The Captain of the twelfth rank pointed with his thumb at the woman. "He then examined the scratching, saw it was recently made, and turned to find this one. For a moment he thought she had been lost among the herd in the square, then he caught sight of her from the back, some distance off and hurrying away. He stunned her and brought her in."

"His rank?"

"Thirty-second, immaculate sir."

"And this beast has been questioned?"

"No, sir, I waited to speak to you about procedure."

Laa Ehon stood for a moment, unanswering, gazing at the woman.

"Thirty-second, you said? Did he know this particular beast previously to seeing her in the square?"

"No, sir. But he remembered the color of her apparel. There was no other in that color nearby."

Laa Ehon turned from the window.

"I'd like to talk to him, first. Send him to me."

"Sir, he's presently on duty."

"Ah."

Shane understood Laa Ehon's momentary thoughtfulness. As Commander here, he could easily order the officer in question to be relieved from duty long enough to report to him in person. But the Aalaag nature and custom was such that only the gravest reason would allow him to justify such an order. An Aalaag on duty, regardless of rank, was almost a sacred object.

"Where?" Laa Ehon asked.

"The local airport, immaculate sir."

"I will go and speak to him at his duty post. Captain Otah On, you are ordered to accompany me."

"Yes, immaculate sir."

"Then let us move with minimal loss of time. It is unlikely that this matter has more importance than presently seems, but we must make sure of that."

He turned toward the door with Otah On behind him. Once more his eyes swept Shane. He stopped and looked over at the Aalaag behind the desk.

"What is this one?" he asked, pointing a thumb at Shane.

"Sir." The Aalaag at the desk was on his feet at once. "A courier with messages for your hand from Lyt Ahn."

Laa Ehon looked back at Shane.

"I will accept your messages in an hour, no more, once I've come back. Do you understand what I have just said to you?"

"I understand, immaculate sir," said Shane.

"Until then, remain dutiful. But be comfortable."

Laa Ehon led the way out of the room, Otah On close behind him. The Aalaag at the desk sat down again and went back to his sheets.

Shane looked once more at the solitary female figure beyond the one-way glass. She sat, unaware of what another hour would bring. They would question her using chemicals, of course, first. But after that their methods would become physical. There was no sadism in the Aalaag character. If any of the aliens had shown evidence of such, his own people would have considered it an unfitting weakness and destroyed him. But it was understood that cattle might be induced to tell whatever they knew if they were subjected to sufficient discomfort. An Aalaag, of course, was above any such persuasion. Death would come long before any degree of discomfort could change the individual alien's character enough to make him or her say what they wished to keep unsaid.

Shane felt his robe clinging to his upper body, wet with a secret sweat. The woman sat almost in profile, her dark brown hair down her shoulders, her remarkably pale-skinned face smooth and gentle-looking. She could not be more than barely into her twenties. He wanted to look away from her, so that he could stop thinking about what was awaiting her, but—as it had happened to him with the man on the triple hooks when he had first created the symbol—Shane could not make his head turn.

He knew it now for what it was—a madness in him. A madness born of his own hidden revulsion against, and private terror of, these massive humanoids who had descended to own the Earth. These were the masters he served, who kept him warm and well fed when most of the rest of humanity went cold and ate little, who patted him with condescending compliments—as if he was in fact the animal they called him, the clever house pet ready to wag his tail for a kind glance or word. The fear of death was like an ingot of cold iron inside him, when he thought of them; and the fear of a long and painful death was like that same ingot with razor edges.

But at the same time there was this madness—this madness that, if he did not control it by some small actions, would explode and bring him to throw his dispatches in some Aalaag face, to fling himself one day like a terrier against a tiger, at the throat of his Master, First Captain of Earth, Lyt Ahn.

It was a real thing, that madness. Even the Aalaag knew of its existence in their conquered peoples. There was even a word for it in their own tongue—*yowaragh*. *Yowaragh* had caused the man on the hooks a half year ago to make a hopeless attempt to defend his wife against what he had thought was an Aalaag brutality. *Yowaragh*, every day, caused one human at least somewhere in the world to cast a useless stick or stone against some shielded, untouchable conqueror, in a situation where escape was impossible and destruction was certain. *Yowaragh* had knocked at the door of Shane's brain once, less than a year ago, threatening to break out. It was knocking again.

He could not help but look at her; and he could not bear to

look at her—and the only alternative to an end for both of them was to somehow keep it from happening—Laa Ehon's return, her torture, and the *yowaragh* that would lead to his own death.

In one hour, Laa Ehon had said, he would be back. Rivulets of perspiration were trickling down Shane's naked sides under the robe. His mind had gone into high gear, racing like an uncontrolled heartbeat. What way out was there? There must be one—if he could only think of it. What was on the other side of the coin to what they would do to the girl was built on the same lack of sadism. The Aalaag would only destroy property for some purpose. If there was no purpose, they would not waste a useful beast. They would have no emotional stake in keeping her merely because she had been arrested in the first place. She was too insignificant; they were too pragmatic.

His mind was feverish. He was not sure what he planned, but all his intimate knowledge of the Aalaag in the three years he had lived closely with them was simmering and bubbling in the back of his mind. He went and stood before the Aalaag at the desk.

"Yes?" said the Aalaag after a little while, looking up at him.

"Untarnished sir, the Captain Commander said that he would be back in an hour to accept my messages, but until then I should be dutiful but comfortable."

Eyes with gray-black pupils gazed at him on a level with his own.

"You want comfort, is that it?"

"Untarnished sir, if I could sit or lie, it would be appreciated."

"Yes. Very well. The Commander has so ordered. Go find what facilities there are for such activities in the areas of our own cattle. Return in one hour."

"I am grateful to the untarnished sir."

The gray-black pupils were cast into shadow by the jet brows coming together.

"This is a matter of orders. I am not one who allows his beasts to fawn."

"Sir, I obey."

The brows relaxed.

"Better. Go."

He went out. He was moving swiftly now. As before, in Denmark, he was at last caught up in what he was doing. There was no longer any doubt, any hesitation. He went swiftly down the outside corridor, which was deserted, his ears and eyes alert for signs of anyone, but particularly one of the aliens. As he passed the elevators, he stopped, looked about him.

There was no one watching; once aboard the elevator he would be able to go from this floor down to street level or below without being seen. There would be other doors to the outside than the one by which he had come in; and on other levels, beneath the main floor, he could possibly find them. There would be portals used only by the Aalaag themselves and their most trusted servants, where they would be free to come and go without being noticed.

He punched for the elevator. After a moment it came. The two doors swung wide. As they opened he turned away and readied himself to pretend—in case there was an Aalaag aboard—that he was merely passing by. But the elevator compartment was empty.

He stepped inside and punched the button for the first basement level. The only danger remaining for him now was that some other Aalaag on a floor below might have also just punched for this elevator. If it stopped for one of the aliens and the door opened to reveal him inside, he would be trapped—doubly guilty, for being where he should not be and also for being absent from his duty, which at the present was to lie down or otherwise relax. Only Aalaag were permitted to use elevators.

For a moment he thought the one in which he was descending was going to hesitate on the first floor. In the back of his mind, plans flickered like heat lightning on a summer evening. If it did stop, if the door did open and an Aalaag walked in, he planned to throw himself at the alien's throat. Hopefully, the other would kill him out of reflex, and he would escape being held for questioning as to why he was where he was.

But the elevator did not stop. It continued moving downward, and the telltale light illuminating the floor numbers as they passed showed it was approaching the floor just below street level. Shane punched for the cage to stop. It did, the door opened and he stepped into a small, square corridor leading directly to a glass door and a flight of steps beyond, leading upward. As he had expected, he had hit on one of the alien ways out of the building.

He left the elevator and went quickly along the corridor to the door. It was locked, of course; but in his pocket he carried the Key of Lyt Ahn, or at least the key that all the special human servants of Lyt Ahn were allowed to bear. It would open any ordinary door in a building belonging to the aliens.

He tried the key now, and it worked. The door swung noiselessly open. A second later he was out of it, up the stairs and into the street above.

He went down the street, walking at a pace just short of a run, and turned right at the first crossing, searching for a market area. Four blocks on, he found a large square with many shops. A single Aalaag sat on his riding animal, towering and indifferent to the crowd about him, before a set of pillars upholding a sidewalk arcade at one end of the square. Whether the alien was on duty or simply waiting for something or someone, it was impossible to tell. But for Shane now, to use a shop on this square would not be wise.

He hurried on. A few streets farther on, he found a smaller collection of shops lining both sides of a blind alley, and one of these was a store for such simple clothing as the Aalaag allowed humans to use nowadays. He stepped inside and a small bell over the door chimed softly.

"Signore?" said a voice.

Shane's eyes adjusted to the interior dimness and saw a counter piled high with folded clothing, and behind the counter a short, dark-faced man with a knife-blade nose. Remarkably, in these days of alien occupation, this man had a small potbelly under his loose yellow smock.

"I want a full-length robe," Shane said. "Reversible."

"Of course." The proprietor began to come around the counter. "What type?"

"How much is your most expensive garment?"

"Seventy-five new lire or equivalent in trade, signore."

Shane dug into the purse hanging from the rope around his waist, and threw on the counter before him metal coins issued by the Aalaag for use as an international currency—the gold and silver rectangles with which his work as an employee of Lyt Ahn was rewarded.

The store owner checked his movement. His eyes moved to the coins, then back to Shane's face with a difference. Only humans of great power under the alien authority, or those engaged in the illegal black market, would ordinarily have such coins with which to pay their bills; and it would be seldom that such would come into a small shop like this.

He moved toward the coins. Shane covered them with his hand.

"I'll pick the robe out myself," he said. "Show me your stock."

"But of course, of course, signore."

The proprietor went past the coins and out from behind the counter. He opened a door to a back room and invited Shane in. Within were tables stacked with clothing and cloth. In one corner, under a kerosene lamp, was a tailor's worktable with scraps of cloth, tools, thread, and some pieces of blue or white chalk.

"Here are the robes, on these two tables," he said.

"Good," said Shane harshly. "Go over to the corner there and turn around. I'll pick out what I want."

The man moved swiftly, his shoulders hunched a little. If his visitor was black market, it would be unwise to argue with or irritate him.

Shane located the reversible robes among the others and pawed through them, selecting the largest one he could find that was blue on one side. The other side of it was brown. He pulled it on over his own robe, the blue side out, and drew the drawstring tight at the waist. Stepping across to the worktable, he picked up a fragment of the white chalk.

"I'll leave a hundred lire on the counter," he said to the back of the proprietor. "Don't turn around, don't come out until I've been gone for five minutes. You understand?"

"I understand."

Shane turned and went. He glanced at the counter as he passed. He had snatched coins from his purse at random and there was the equivalent of over a hundred and fifty lire in gold and silver on the counter. It would not do to make the incident look any more important to the storeman than was necessary. Shane scooped up fifty lire-equivalent and went out the door, heading back toward the square where he had seen the mounted Aalaag.

He was very conscious of the quick sliding by of time. He could not afford to be missing from the Headquarters more than the hour the officer on duty had allowed him. If the Aalaag had left the square . . .

But he had not. When Shane, sweating, once more emerged

into the square, the massive figure still sat unmoved, as indifferent as ever.

Shane, because of his duties, was allowed to carry one of the Aalaag's perpetual timepieces. It lay in his purse now, but he dared not consult it to see how much time remained. A glimpse of it by the ordinary humans around would identify him as a servant of the aliens, and win him the bitter enmity of these others; and that enmity, here and now, could be fatal.

He went quickly through the crowd swarming the square. As he got close to the Aalaag on the riding animal, the adrenaline-born courage inside him almost failed. But a memory of the prisoner back at the Headquarters rose in him, and he pushed himself on.

Deliberately, he made himself blunder directly beneath the heavy head of the riding animal, so that it jerked its nose up. Its movement was slight—only an inch or two—but it was enough to draw the attention of the Aalaag. His eyes dropped to see Shane.

Still moving, Shane kept his head down. He had pulled the cowl of his cloak down over his forehead as far as possible to hide his face from the alien's view—but it was not really that that he was counting on to preserve his anonymity. Few Aalaag could tell one human from another—even after two years of close contact, Lyt Ahn recognized Shane from the other courier-interpreters more by the times on which Shane reported than by any physical individualities.

Shane scuttled past; and the alien, indifferent to something as mere as a single one of the cattle about him, raised his eyes to infinity again, returning to his thought. Shane went on for only a few more steps, to the nearest pillar, and stopped. There, hiding his actions with his body from the alien behind him, he pulled the tailor's white chalk from his pouch and with a hand that trembled sketched on the stone of the pillar the cloaked figure with its staff.

He stepped back—and the sudden, almost inaudible moan of recognition and arrested movement in the crowd behind him drew—as he had known it would—the attention of the Aalaag. Instantly, the alien wheeled his animal about, reaching for the same sort of stunning weapon with which the woman prisoner had been captured.

But Shane was already moving. He ran into the crowd, threw

himself down so that the bodies about would shield him from the view of the Aalaag, and rolled, frantically pulling off the outer, reversible robe as he moved.

Instinctively, defensively, the other humans closed about him, hiding him from the alien, who was now—weapon in one massive hand—searching their numbers to locate him. The reversible robe stuck and bound itself under his armpits, but at last Shane got it off. Leaving it on the ground behind him, still with its blue side out, he scuttled on hands and knees farther off until, at last near the edge of the square, he risked getting to his feet and leaving as quickly as he could without drawing attention to himself.

Panting, soaked with sweat, leaving behind humans who studiously avoided looking at him, and beginning to move now among others who looked at him with entirely normal interest, Shane half ran toward the Aalaag Headquarters. Subjectively, it seemed as if at least an hour had passed since he had first stepped under the nose of the Aalaag riding animal; but reason told him that the whole business could not have taken more than a few minutes. He stopped at a fountain—bless Italy, he thought, for having fountains—to bathe his face, neck, and underarms. Officially, the Aalaag were indifferent to how their cattle stank; but in practice, they preferred those humans who were physically as much without odor as possible—though it never seemed to occur to them that they were as noisome in human noses as humans were in their own. But for Shane to return smelling strong from what had theoretically been a rest period might attract interest to the period of time he had spent out of the office.

He let himself in with his key through the same door which had given him egress; and this time took stairs, rather than the elevator, to the entrance level of the Headquarters. No one saw him emerge on the entrance level. He paused to check his timepiece and saw that he still had some twelve minutes left of his allotted hour.

THREE

HE MADE USE OF THE TWELVE MINUTES BY ASKING AN INTERIOR
Guard where the rest facilities for transient cattle were, went there
and retraced his steps from that point to the office he had waited
in before. Outside the office door, he discovered he had still four
minutes left, and stood where he was until he could enter at the
exact moment when he had been told to return.

The alien officer at the desk looked up as he came in, glanced
at the clockface over the door and returned to his papers silently.
Nonetheless, Shane felt the triumph of a minor point scored. Precise obedience was a mark in any human's favor, in Aalaag eyes.
He went back to the spot on which he had been standing before—
and stood again.

It was nearly three-quarters of an hour later when the door
opened and Laa Ehon, with Otah On, entered. With a subjected
being's acuteness of observation, reinforced by the experience
gained in his two and half years of close contact with aliens, Shane
recognized both of the officers at once. They went directly to the
wall screen to stare at the human prisoner beyond, and Shane's
heart sank in panic.

It was inconceivable that his actions in the square of an hour
before should not have been reported by this time. But it looked
as if the two senior officers were about to proceed with the young
woman as if nothing had happened. Then Laa Ehon spoke.

"The garment is indeed the same color," the Headquarters
Commander said. "There must be many of the cattle so dressed."

"Very true, immaculate sir," answered Otah On.

Laa Ehon studied the young woman for a moment longer.

"Was it at any time made aware of the specific reason it was brought here?" he asked.

"Nothing has been told it, immaculate sir."

"Yes," said Laa Ehon thoughtfully. "Well, then. It is a healthy young beast. There is no need to waste it. Let it go."

"It will be done."

Laa Ehon turned from the screen and his eyes swept over the rest of the room, stopping on Shane. He walked forward to Shane.

"You were the beast with dispatches from Lyt Ahn?"

"Yes, immaculate sir," said Shane. "I have them here for you."

He produced them from his pouch and handed them into the large grasp of the Commander. Laa Ehon took them, unfolded and read them. He passed them to Otah On.

"Execute these."

"Yes, immaculate sir."

Otah On carried the dispatches over to the desk of the duty officer and spoke to him, handing him the papers. The eyes of Laa Ehon fastened on Shane, with a glimmer of interest.

"You speak with great purity," said the Commander. "You are one of the First Captain's special group of beasts for speaking and carrying, are you not?"

"I am, immaculate sir."

"How long have you spoken the true language?"

"Two and a half years of this world, immaculate sir."

Laa Ehon stood looking at him, and a trickle of perspiration crept coldly down Shane's spine under his robe.

"You are a beast worth having," said the Commander slowly. "I did not think one such as you could be brought to speak so clearly. How are you valued?"

Shane's breath caught silently in his throat. Existence was barely endurable as one of the favored human group that was the personal property of Earth's ruling alien. The madness he feared would come quickly, if instead he should be trapped here, in this building, among the brutes that made up the Interior Guard.

"To the best of my knowledge, immaculate sir"—he dared not hesitate in his answer—"I am valued at half a possession of land—"

Otah On, who had just regained the side of his Commander, raised his black eyebrows at the voicing of this price, but Laa Ehon's face remained thoughtful.

"—and the favor of my master Lyt Ahn," said Shane.

The thoughtfulness vanished from Laa Ehon's features. Shane's heart was pounding. It was true he had prefaced his answer with the words "to the best of my knowledge," but in fact he had never officially been acquainted with the fact that part of his price involved the favor of his owner. What he knew himself to be valued at, half a possession of land—about forty miles square of what the Aalaag called "good country"—was an enormously high price in itself for any single human beast. It was roughly equivalent to what, in pre-Aalaag days, would have been the cost of a top-price, custom-made sports car, gold plated and set with jewels. But Laa Ehon had looked ready to consider even that.

It was not the first time Shane had been aware that he possessed the status of a sort of luxury toy. Only, this time, Shane had mentioned that his price included the favor of Lyt Ahn. "Favor" was a term that went beyond all price. It was a designation meaning that his master was personally interested in keeping him, and that the price of any sale could include anything at all—but probably something Lyt Ahn would favor at least as much as what he was giving up. Such "favor," involved in a sale, could in effect constitute a blank check signed by the buyer, cashable at any time in the future for goods or actions by the seller, guaranteed under the unyielding obligation code of the Aalaag.

Shane had never been told he had Lyt Ahn's favor. He had only overheard Lyt Ahn once say to his Chief of Staff that he must get around to extending his favor over all the beasts of that special group to which Shane belonged. If Laa Ehon should check with Lyt Ahn, and this had never been done, then Shane was doomed as an untrustworthy and lying beast. Even if the favor had been extended, Lyt Ahn might question how Shane had come to know of it.

And then again, the First Captain, busy as he was with much more weighty affairs of Aalaag government, might simply conclude that he had mentioned it at some time to Shane and since forgotten the fact. Claiming it now was one of the gambles necessary to human daily existence in the midst of the aliens.

"Give him his receipt," said Laa Ehon.

Otah On passed Shane a receipt for the dispatches, made out a moment before by the duty officer. Shane put it in his pouch.

"You return directly to Lyt Ahn?" Laa Ehon said.

"Yes, immaculate sir."

"My courtesies to the First Captain."

"I will deliver them."

"Then you may go."

Shane turned and left. As the door closed behind him, he drew a deep breath and went quickly to the stairs, then down to the entrance floor and the entrance itself.

"I'm returning to the residence of the First Captain," he told the officer of the Interior Guards who was in charge at the entrance. It was the same man with the Arabic influence noticeable in his spoken Italian. "Will you get me space on the necessary aircraft? I've priority, of course."

"It's already taken care of," said the officer. "You're to travel with one of the Masters on courier duty; in a military small craft, leaving in two hours. Shall I order transportation to the airfield?"

"No," said Shane briefly. He did not have to give the reasons for his actions to this uniformed lackey. "I'll get myself there."

He thought he caught a hint of admiration in the officer's steady gaze. But then, if the other ever thought of walking the Milan streets alone, it would be in his regular uniform, which he was never permitted to discard. Someone like this officer would never be able to imagine the freedom of Shane in going about, ostensibly as one of them, among the ordinary humans of the city— nor could he imagine how necessary these few moments of illusory freedom were to Shane.

"Very well," said the officer. "The one who will carry you is Am Mehon. The Masters' desk at the air terminal will direct you to the ship when you get there."

"Thank you," said Shane.

"You are entirely welcome."

They had both picked up, inevitably, Shane thought bitterly, the very courtesies and intonations of their owners. . . .

He went out through the heavy, right-hand door of the pair that made up the entrance, and down the steps. There were no taxis in sight—of course. No human without need to be there would hang around the alien Headquarters. He turned up the same street he had followed to find the square.

He walked a block away from the Headquarters and chose a

corner to wait on. Some little time went by and no taxi passed. He was beginning to think of walking farther from the Aalaag stronghold when a taxi finally passed him, cruising slowly. He hailed it, and it pulled over to the curb.

"To the airport," he said to the driver, looking at the thin, overcoated man behind the wheel as his fingers automatically opened the cab door. He stepped inside—and tripped over something on the floor as he got in.

The door slammed, the cab took off with a rush. He found himself held, pinioned by two men who had risen from crouching positions on the floor of the cab's back seat. He felt something sharp against his throat.

He looked down and saw a so-called glass knife, actually a dagger made by a sliver of glass held between two bound-together halves of a wooden dagger. The glass formed the cutting edge and could be—as this one had been—sandpapered to razorlike sharpness.

"Lie still!" growled one of the men in Italian.

Shane lay still. He smelled the rank, old stink of dirty clothing from both of the two who held him. The taxi whirled him away through unknown streets to an unguessable destination.

They rode for at least twenty minutes, though how much of this was necessary distance to reach their goal and how much was to mislead Shane in any attempt to estimate the length of the trip was impossible to guess. At length the taxi turned, bumped over some very uneven pavement, and passed under the shadow of an arch. Then it stopped, and the two men hustled Shane out of the vehicle.

He had just a glimpse of a dark and not too clean courtyard surrounded by buildings, before he was pushed up two steps, through a door and into a long, narrow corridor thick with cooking odors.

Shane was herded along, more numb than frightened. Inside him there was a feeling of something like fatalistic acceptance. He had lived for two and a half years with the thought that someday ordinary humans would identify him as one of those who worked for the aliens; and when they did, they would then use him as an object for the bitter fear and hatred they all felt for their conquerors, but dared not show directly. In his imagination, he had lived through this scene many times. It was nonetheless hideous now for finally having become real, but it was a situation on which his emotions had worn themselves out. At the end, it was almost a relief to have the days of his masquerade over, to be discovered for what he really was.

The two men stopped suddenly. Shane was shoved through a door on his right, into a room glaringly lit by a single powerful light bulb. The contrast with the shadowed courtyard outside, and the even dimmer hallway, made the sudden light blinding for a second. When his eyes adjusted, he saw that he was standing in front of a round table and that the room was large and high-ceilinged, with old, grimy paint on the walls and a single tall window which, however, had a blackout blind drawn tightly down over it. The cord from the light bulb ran not into the ceiling, but across the face of it, past a capped gas outlet, and down the farther wall and to a bicycle generator. A young man with long black hair sat on the bicycle part of the generator, and whenever the light from the ceiling bulb began to fade, he would pump energetically on his pedals until it brightened again and held its brightness.

There were several other men standing around the room, and two more at the table with the only woman to be seen. She was, he recognized, the prisoner he had seen in the screen. Her eyes met his now with the look of a complete stranger, and even in his numbness he felt strange that he should recognize her with such strong emotional identification and she should not know him at all.

"Where's that clothing store owner?" said one of the men at the table with her, speaking to the room at large in a northern Italian underlaid with London English. He was young—as young in appearance as Shane himself; but, unlike Shane, spare and athletic-looking with a straight nose, strong square jaw, thin mouth and blond hair cut very short.

"Outside, in the supply room," said a voice, speaking the same northern Italian, but without accent.

"Get him in here, then!" said the man with the short hair. The other man beside him at the table said nothing. He was round-bodied and hard-fat, in his forties, wearing a worn leather jacket. In his mouth was stuck a short-stemmed pipe. His face was round. He looked entirely Italian.

The door opened and closed behind Shane. A minute later it

opened and closed again, and a blindfolded man Shane recognized as the proprietor of the store where he had bought the reversible cloak was brought forward and turned around to face Shane. His blindfold was jerked off.

"Well?" demanded the short-haired young man.

The shopkeeper blinked under the unshaded electric light. His eyes focused on Shane, then slid away.

"What is it you want, signore?" he asked. His voice was almost a whisper in the stark room.

"Didn't anyone tell you? Him!" said the short-haired man impatiently. "Look at him. Do you recognize him? Where did you see him last?"

The store proprietor licked his lips and raised his eyes.

"Earlier today, signore," he said. "He came into my shop and bought a reversible cloak."

"This cloak?" The short-haired individual made a gesture. One of the men standing in the back of the room came forward to shove a bundled mass of cloth into the hands of the proprietor, who slowly unfolded it and looked at it.

"This is mine," he said, still faintly. "Yes. This was the one he bought."

"All right, you can go then. Keep the cloak. You two—don't forget to blindfold him." The short-haired man turned his attention to the young man slouching on the bicycle seat of the electric generator. "How about it, Carlo? Is he the one you followed?"

Carlo nodded. He had a toothpick in one corner of his mouth. Through his numbness, Shane watched Carlo with fascination, for the toothpick seemed to give him a rakish, infallible look.

"He left the Square of San Marco and went straight back to the alien HQ," Carlo said. "As fast as possible."

"That's it, then," said the short-haired man. He looked at Shane. "Well, do you want to tell us now what the Aalaag had you up to? Or do we have to wait while Carlo works you over a bit?"

Suddenly, Shane was weary to the point of sickness—weary of the whole matter of human subjects and alien overlords. Unexpected fury boiled up in him.

"You damn fool!" he shouted at the short-haired man. "I was saving her!"

And he pointed at the woman, who stared back at him, her gaze frowning and intent.

"You idiots!" Shane spat. "You stupid morons with your Resistance games! Don't you know what they'd have done to her? Don't you know where you'd all be, right now, if I hadn't given them a reason to think it was someone else? How long do you think she could keep from telling them all about you? I'll tell you, because I've seen it—forty minutes is the average!"

They all looked at the woman.

"He's lying," she said in a thin voice. "They didn't offer to do a thing to me. They just made me wait awhile and then turned me loose for lack of evidence."

"They turned you loose because I gave them enough reason to doubt you were the one who made the mark!" The fury was carrying Shane away like a dark, inexorable tide. "They let you go because you're young and healthy and they don't waste valuable beasts without reason. Lack of evidence! Do you still think you're dealing with humans?"

"All right," said the short-haired man. His voice was hard and flat. "This is all very pretty, but suppose you tell us where you learned our mark."

"Learned it?" Shane laughed, a laughed that was close to a sob of long-throttled rage. "You clown! I invented it. Me—myself! I carved it on a brick wall in Aalborg, half a year ago, for the first time. Learn about it! How did you learn about it? How did the Aalaag learn about it? By seeing it marked up in places, of course!"

There was a moment of silence in the room after Shane's voice ceased to ring out.

"He's crazy, then," said the hard-fat man with the pipe.

"Crazy!" echoed Shane, and laughed again.

"Wait a minute," said the woman. She came around and faced him. "Who are you? What do you do with the Aalaag?"

"I'm a translator, a courier," said Shane. "I'm owned by Lyt Ahn, the First Captain of the Aalaag—me and about thirty men and women like me."

"Maria—," began the short-haired man.

"Wait, Peter." She held up her hand briefly and went on without taking her eyes off Shane. "All right. You tell us what happened."

"I was delivering special communications to Laa Ehon—you know your local Commander, I suppose—"

"We know Laa Ehon," said Peter harshly. "Keep talking."

"I had special communications to deliver. I looked through a viewing screen showing the room you were in and saw you—" He was looking at Maria. "I knew what they'd do to you. Laa Ehon was talking to one of his officers about you. All that had been spotted was some human wearing a blue robe. There was just a chance that if they had another report of a human in a blue robe making that mark it would make them doubtful enough so they wouldn't want to waste a healthy young beast like you. So I ducked out and tried giving them that other report. It worked."

"Why did you do it?" She was looking penetratingly at him.

"Just a minute, Maria," said Peter. "Let me ask a few questions. What's your name, you?"

"Shane Evert."

"And you said you heard Laa Ehon talking to one of his officers. How did you happen to be there?"

"I was waiting to deliver my communications."

"And Laa Ehon just discussed it all in front of you—that's what you're trying to tell us?"

"They don't see us, or hear us, unless they want us," said Shane bitterly. "We're furniture—pets."

"So you say," said Peter. "What language did Laa Ehon speak in?"

"Aalaag, of course."

"And you understood him so well that you could tell there was a chance to make them think that the human they wanted was someone else than Maria?"

"I told you." A dull weariness was again beginning to take Shane over as the fury died. "I'm a translator. I'm one of Lyt Ahn's special group of human translators."

"No human can really speak or understand the Aalaag tongue," said the man with the pipe, in Basque.

"Most can't" answered Shane, also in Basque. The weariness was beginning to numb him so that he was hardly aware of changing languages. "I tell you I'm one of a very special group belonging to Lyt Ahn."

"What was that? What did you say, Georges—and what did he

45

say?" Peter was looking from one to the other.

"He speaks Basque," said Georges, staring at Shane.

"How well?"

"Good . . ." Georges made an effort. "He speaks . . . very good Basque."

Peter turned on Shane.

"How many languages do you speak?" he asked.

"How many?" Shane said dully. "I don't know. Eighty or ninety, maybe, I speak . . . well. A lot of others, I speak a few words of."

"And you speak Aalaag just like one of them?"

Shane laughed.

"No," he said. "I speak it well—for a human."

"Also, you travel all over the world as a courier—" Peter turned to Maria and Georges. "Are you listening?"

Maria ignored him.

"Why did you do it? Why did you try to rescue me?" She held him with her eyes.

There was a new silence.

"Yowaragh," he said dully.

"What?"

"It's their word for it," he said. "The Aalaag word for when a beast suddenly goes crazy and fights back against one of them. It was like that first time in Aalborg, when I snapped and put the Pilgrim mark on the wall under the man they'd thrown on the hooks."

"You don't really expect us to believe you were the one who invented the symbol of resistance to the aliens?"

"You can go to hell," Shane told him in English.

"What did you say?" said Peter quickly, in Italian.

"You know what I said," Shane told him savagely, still in English, and in the exact accent of the London area in which the other had grown up. "I don't care whether you believe me or not. Just give up trying to pretend you can speak Italian."

A small dark flush came to Peter's cheeks and for a second his eyes glinted. Shane had read him clearly. He was one of those who could learn to speak another language just well enough to delude himself that he was accentless—but he did not speak it like a native. Shane had touched one of his vulnerabilities.

But then Peter laughed, and both flush and glint were gone.

"Caught me, by God! You caught me!" he said in English. "That's really very good! Magnificent!"

And you'll never forgive me for it, thought Shane, watching him.

"Look now, tell me—" Peter seized one of the straight-backed chairs and pushed it forward. "Sit down and let's talk. Tell me, you must have some sort of credentials that let you pass freely through any inspection or check by the ordinary sort of Aalaag?"

"What I carry," said Shane, suddenly wary, "are my credentials. Communications from the First Captain of Earth will pass a courier anywhere."

"Of course!" said Peter. "Now sit down—"

He urged Shane to the chair; Shane, suddenly conscious of the weariness of his legs, dropped into it. He felt something being put into his hands and, looking, saw that it was a glass tumbler one-third full of a light brown liquid. He put it to his lips and smelled brandy—not very good brandy. For some reason, this reassured him. If they had been planning to drug him, he thought, they surely would have put the drug in something better than this.

The burn of the liquor on his tongue woke him from that state of mind in which he had been caught ever since he had stepped into the taxi and found himself kidnapped. He recognized suddenly that he had now moved away from the threat involved in his original capture. These people had been thinking of him originally only as one of the human jackals of the Aalaag. Now they seemed to have become aware of his abilities and advantages; and clearly Peter, at least, was thinking of somehow putting these to use in their Resistance movement.

But the situation was still tricky and could go either way. All that was necessary was for him to slip, and by word or action imply that he might still be a danger to them; and then their determination to destroy him could return, redoubled in urgency.

For the moment the important thing was that Peter, who seemed to be the dominant of their group, appeared to be determined to make use of him. On his part, Shane was finding, now that his first recklessness of despair was over, that he wanted to live. But he did not want to be used. Much more clearly than these people around him, he knew how hopeless their dream of successful resistance to the Aalaag was, and how certain and ugly the end toward which they were headed, if they continued.

Let them dig their own graves if they wanted, he thought savagely. All he wanted was to get safely out of here and in the future to stay clear of such people. Too late, now that he had answered their questions, he realized how much leverage against himself he had given them, in telling them his true name and the nature of his work with the Aalaag. Above all, he thought now, he must keep the secret of Lyt Ahn's key. They would sell their souls for something that would unlock most alien doors—doors to warehouses, to armories, to communication and transportation equipment. And the use of the key by them would be a certain route to his association with them being discovered by the Aalaag. He had been making himself far too attractive to them, thought Shane grimly. It was time to take the glamour off.

"I've got thirty minutes, no more," he said, "to get to the airport and meet the Aalaag officer who's flying me back to Lyt Ahn's Headquarters. If I'm not there on time, it won't matter how many languages I can speak."

There was silence in the room. He could see them looking at each other—in particular, Peter, Georges, and Maria consulting each other with their gazes.

"Get the car," said Maria in Italian, when Peter still hesitated. "Get him there on time."

Peter jerked suddenly into movement, as if Maria's words had wakened him from a dream so powerful it had held him prisoner. He turned on Carlo.

"Get the car," he said. "You drive. Maria, you'll go with me and Shane. Georges—"

He spoke just in time to cut short the beginnings of a protest from the man with the pipe.

"—I want you to close this place up. Bury it! We may end up wanting better security on this than we ever have had on anything until now. Then get out of sight, yourself. We'll find you. You follow me?"

"All right," said Georges. "Don't take too long to come calling."

"A day or two. That's all. Carlo—" He looked around.

"Carlo's gone for the car," said Maria. "Let's move, Peter.

We'll barely make it to the airport as it is."

Shane followed them back through the hall by which he had entered. Crammed in the back seat of the taxi between Maria and Peter, with Carlo driving up front, he had a sudden feeling of ridiculousness, as if they were all engaged in some wild, slapstick movie.

"Tell me," said Peter in English, in a voice that was friendlier than any he had used until now, "just how it happened you made that first mark in—where did you say it was?"

"Denmark," answered Shane in English. "The city of Aalborg. I was delivering messages there; and on my way back from that I saw two of the aliens, a father and a son, mounted on their riding animals, crossing the square there that has the statue of the Cimbrian bull—"

It came back to him, as he told them. The son, using the haft of his power-lance to knock aside a woman who otherwise would have been trampled by his riding animal. The husband of the woman, suddenly mad with *yowaragh*, attacking the son barehanded and being easily knocked unconscious.

Remembering, Shane felt the inner center of his body grow icy with the recalled horror and the near approach of his own madness. He told how he had gone on to the bar, drunk the bootleg rotgut, and been set upon by the three vagabonds. He had not intended to tell it all, but somehow, once he started talking, he could not help himself. He told how, once more crossing the now empty square, on impulse he had scratched the mark of the Pilgrim beneath the body on the hooks before returning to the airport.

"I believe you," said Peter.

Shane said nothing. Crowded together as they were, he was conscious of the softness of Maria's thigh, pressed against his; and the warmth of her seemed also to press in upon the iciness within him, melting it as if he were someone lost and frozen in a snowstorm who was now getting back life and heat from the living temperature of another human being.

He felt a sudden, desperate longing for her as a woman. Beasts were encouraged by the Aalaag to breed—particularly valuable cattle like those special human courier-translators of Lyt Ahn; but living continually under the observations of the aliens as Shane and his colleagues did had cultured paranoia in all of them. They all knew too well the innumerable ways that could bring them to destruction at the hands of their masters; and when their duties were completed, their instinct was to draw apart, to creep separately into their solitary beds and lock their individual doors against each other, for fear that close contact with another could put their survival too completely in another's power.

In any case, Shane did not want to breed. He wanted love—if only for a moment; and love was the one thing the highly paid human servants of the First Captain of Earth could not afford. Suddenly, the warmth of Maria drew him like a dream of peace. . . .

He jerked himself out of his thoughts. Peter was looking at him curiously. What had the man just been saying—that he believed Shane?

"Get someone to check Aalborg and ask people there what happened. The mark I made might still be there, if the Aalaag haven't erased it."

"I don't need to," said Peter. "What you say explains how the mark could spread around the world the way it already has. It would have to take someone who can move around as you can to get it known everywhere as the symbol of resistance. I always thought there must have been someone at the root of the legend."

Shane let the first part of Peter's comment pass without answer. The other man obviously did not understand what Shane had learned in his travels—the speed with which rumor of any kind could travel in a subject population. Shane had been present at the origin of rumors in Paris which he had heard again in this city of Milan less than a week later. Also, Peter seemed to be giving him credit for continuing to spread the mark around, himself; and that, too, was probably a matter on which it was better not to correct the other.

"But I think you ought to face something," Peter said, leaning hard against him for a second as Carlo whipped the taxi around a corner. "It's time to move on from just being a legend, time to set up an organization with practical goals of resistance against the aliens, looking forward to the day when we can kill them all, or drive them off the Earth entirely."

Shane looked sideways at him. It was incredible that this man could be saying such things in all seriousness. But of course, Peter had not seen what Shane had, up close, of the power of the Aalaag.

Mice might as well dream of killing or driving off lions. He was about to say this bluntly when the instinct for survival cautioned him to go carefully, still. Avoiding a direct answer, he fastened on something else.

"That's the second time you've mentioned a legend," he said. "What legend?"

"You don't know?" There was a note of triumph in Peter's voice. He did not offer to explain.

"There's talk all the marks are made by one person," said Maria, also in English now. She had only a trace of an Italian accent—it was Venetian. "By someone called only the Pilgrim, who has the ability to come and go without the Aalaag being able to stop or catch whoever it is."

"And you, all of you, have been helping this Pilgrim, is that it?" said Shane, raising his voice.

"The point is," Peter interrupted, "that it's time the Pilgrim was associated with a solid organization. Don't you think?"

Shane felt a return of the weariness that had deadened him when he had first been abducted by these people.

"If you can find your Pilgrim, ask him," he said. "I'm not him, and I've got no opinions."

Peter watched him for a moment.

"Whether you're the Pilgrim or not is beside the point," he said. "The point still is, you could help us and we need you. The world needs you. Just from what you've told us, it's plain you could be invaluable just acting as liaison between Resistance groups."

Shane laughed grimly.

"Not on the best day in the year," he said.

"You aren't even stopping to think about it," Peter said. "What makes you so positive you don't want to do it?"

"I've been trying to tell you ever since you kidnapped me," said Shane. "You're the one who doesn't listen. You don't know the Aalaag. I do. Because you don't know them, you can fool yourself that you've got a chance with this Resistance of yours. I know better. They've been taking over worlds like this and turning the native populations into their servants for thousands of years. Did you think this was the first planet they'd ever tried it on? There's nothing you can come up with by way of attacking them that they haven't seen before and don't know how to deal with. But even if you could come up with something new, you still couldn't win."

"Why not?" Peter's head leaned close.

"Because they're just what they say they are—born conquerors who could never be dominated or defeated themselves. You can't torture an Aalaag and get information out of him. You can't point a weapon at one of them—even out of armor—and force him to back off or surrender. All you can do is kill him—if you're lucky. But they've got so much power, so much military power, that even that'd only work if you killed them all in the same moment. If even one escaped and had warning, you'd have lost."

"Why?"

"Because with any warning at all, any one of them could make himself or herself invulnerable, and then take all the time he needed to wipe out whole cities and sections of Earth, one by one; until the other humans who were left served you up on a platter, and anyone else who had been fighting the Aalaag, to stop the killing."

"What good would it do just one Aalaag, to do all that," Peter said, "if he was the last one on Earth?"

"You don't think all the Aalaag in the universe are here, do you?" said Shane. "Earth, with only one Aalaag left alive on it, would only represent that much new homesteading territory for the surplus Aalaag population elsewhere. In a year or less, you'd have as many Aalaag here as before; and the only result would be the humans who'd died, the slagged areas of Earth, and the fact that the Aalaag would then set up an even stricter control system to make sure no one like you rose against them again."

There was silence in the car. Carlo whipped them around another corner and Shane could see a sign beside the highway announcing that the airport was now only one kilometer distant. The warmth of Maria's body penetrated his, and he could smell the harsh, clean odor of the all-purpose soap with which she must just this morning have washed her hair.

"Then you won't lift a finger to help us?" said Peter.

"No," said Shane.

Carlo turned the car onto an off-ramp leading up to the airport road.

"Isn't anybody willing to do anything?" burst out Maria suddenly. "Not anybody? Nobody at all?"

An icy, electric shock jarred all through Shane. It was as if a sword had been plunged clear through him, a sword he had been expecting, but a sword to take his life nonetheless. It cut to his instinctive roots, to the ancient racial and sexual reflexes from which *yowaragh* sprang. The words were nothing, the cry was everything.

He sat for a numb moment.

"All right," he said softly. "Let me think about it then."

He heard his own voice far off, remote.

"You're never going to get anywhere the way you've been acting so far," he said numbly. "You're doing all the wrong things because you don't understand the Aalaag. I do. Maybe I could tell you what to do—but you'd have to let me tell you, not just try to pick my brains, or it won't work. Would you do it that way? Otherwise it's no use."

"Yes!" Maria said.

There was a slight pause.

"All right," said Peter. Shane turned to stare at him.

"If you don't, it won't work."

"We'll do anything to hit at the Aalaag," said Peter; and this time his answer came immediately.

"All right," said Shane emptily. "I'll still have to think about it. How do I get in touch with you?"

"We can find you, if we know what city you're coming into," said Peter. "Can you arrange to put an ad in the local paper before you come—"

"I don't have that much warning before I'm sent places," said Shane. "Why don't I go into a shop in the center of a city when I first get there, and buy a pilgrim robe—a reversible one like the one I bought—and pay for it in a silver or gold Aalaag coin. You can have the shopkeepers warn you if anyone does that. If the description fits me, you watch the local Aalaag HQ and pick me up coming or going."

"All right," said Peter.

"One other thing," Shane said. They were almost to the terminal building of the airport. He looked directly into Peter's eyes. "I've seen the Aalaag questioning humans and I know what I'm talking about. If they suspect me they'll question me. If they question me, they'll find out everything I know. You have to understand that. If everything else fails, they have drugs that just start you talking and you talk until you die. They don't like to use them because they're not efficient. Someone has to wade through hours of nonsense to get the answers they want. But they use them when they have to. You understand? Anyone they question is going to tell them everything. Not just me—anyone. That's one of the things you're going to have to work with."

"All right," said Peter.

"What it means as far as I'm concerned is that I don't want anyone who doesn't already know about me to know I exist."

He held Peter's eye, glanced meaningfully at Carlo and back to Peter.

"And those who aren't going to have something to do with me in the future—if I decide to have anything to do with you in the future—should believe that I get out of this car now and none of you ever see me again."

"I understand," said Peter. He nodded. "Don't worry."

Shane laughed harshly.

"I always worry," he said. "I'd be insane not to. I'm worrying about myself right now. I need my head examined for even thinking about this."

The taxi pulled up to the long concrete walk fronting the airline terminal and stopped. Peter, on the curb side of the car, opened the door beside him and got out to let Shane out. Shane started to follow him, hesitated, and turned for a second back to Maria.

"I really will think about it," he said to her. "I'll do whatever I can, the best I can."

In the relative shadow of the corner of the taxi's back seat, her face was unreadable. She reached out a hand to him. He took and held it for a second. Her fingers were as icy as Milan itself had been this morning.

"I'll think about it," he said again, squeezed her fingers and scrambled out. On the walk, he stood for a second facing the other man.

"If you don't hear from me in six months, forget me," he said.

Peter's lips opened. He appeared about to say something, then his lips closed again.

He nodded.

Shane turned and went swiftly into the terminal. Just inside the entrance doors, he spotted a terminal policeman and swung on him, taking the key from his purse and exposing it for a second in the palm of his hand to the other's gaze.

"This is the Key of Lyt Ahn, First Captain of Earth," he said in rapid Italian. "I'm one of his special couriers, and I need transport to the Masters' section of the field, fast. Fast! Emergency! But do it without attracting attention!"

The officer snapped upright, jerked the phone from his belt and spoke into it. There was no more than a thirty-second wait before an electric car came sliding through the crowd on its air cushion. Shane jumped into one of the passenger seats behind the driver, glancing at his watch.

"The hangars for smaller military craft!" he said. He hesitated, then made up his mind. "Use your siren."

The driver cranked up his siren, the crowd parted before him as he swung the car around and drove at it. They slid swiftly across the polished floor, out through a vehicle passway by the entrance to the field itself.

Once on the field, the car lifted higher on its cushion of air and went swiftly. They swung around two sides of the field and approached the heavily guarded silver hangars housing the military atmosphere ships of the Aalaag. They slowed at the guard gate of the entrance to this area. Shane showed his Key and explained his errand to the human Special Guard on duty there.

"We've been warned to expect you," said the Guard. "Hangar Three. The courier ship is piloted by the untarnished Am Mehon, who is of the twenty-eighth rank."

Shane nodded and the driver of the car, having heard, moved them off without any further need for orders.

In the hangar, the slim, dumbbell shape of the courier sat dwarfed by the large fighter ships of the Aalaag on either side of her. Yet, as Shane knew, even these seemingly larger ships were themselves small as Aalaag warships went. The true fighting vessels of the Aalaag never touched planetary surface, but hung in continuous orbit and readiness—as far as he could gather, not so much for reasons of principle as for the fact that there was no air or spaceport on Earth where they could have set down without causing massive damage to themselves as well as the place where they touched surface.

He jumped from the car as it paused by the open port of the courier vessel and ran up the steps of the port, stepping into the cramped interior. It need not have been so cramped, but even this ship, designed for carrying dispatches, was heavy with armament.

The massive back of an Aalaag showed itself above one of the seats at the control panel in the front of the ship. Shane walked up to just behind the seat and stood waiting. This was not only his duty, but all that was necessary, even if the pilot had not heard him come in. This close to the other, he smelled the typical Aalaag body odor plainly, and the pilot was as surely scenting him. After a moment the pilot spoke.

"Take the seat farther back, beast." It was the voice of an adult Aalaag female. "I have two other stops to make before I bring you to the House of the First Captain."

Shane went back and sat down. After only a couple of minutes, the courier ship lifted and hovered lightly perhaps ten feet off the floor of the hangar. It slid out into the late daylight of the field, turned and went softly to a blast pad. At the pad it stopped. Shane let the air out of his lungs and laid his arms in the hollows of the armrests on either side of his chair.

For a second there was neither sound nor movement. Then there was something like a clap of thunder, and a great weight crushing him into the seat so that he could not move for a long moment—followed by a sudden freedom and lightness, so that he felt almost as if he could float out of the chair. Actually, the feeling was exaggerated. He was still within gravity. It was the contrast with the pressure of takeoff that created the illusion of lightness.

He looked at the viewing screen in the back of the seat before him and saw the surface of the Earth below, a curving horizon and a general mottling of clouds. Nothing else. The memory of Maria's face with no expression on it, in the moment he had left her, came so clearly back into his imagination that it was as if it floated before him in the air. He felt the coldness of her fingers against his fingers, and her voice rang, re-echoing in memory—

"Isn't anybody willing to do anything? Not anybody? Nobody at all?"

They were all insane, those Resistance people. He shivered. He had been wise to play along and pretend to consider their suggestion that he involve himself in their charade of resistance that could only lead to torture and death at Aalaag hands. They had no chance. None. If he had seriously considered joining them, he would have been as insane as they were.

His heart beat heavily. The cold touch of Maria's fingers that lingered in his fingers seemed to spread up his arms and all through him. No, he was lying to himself. It was no use. It made no difference that they were insane.

There was no real choice for him. There never had been from the moment he first saw her in the viewing screen. Something within him left him no choice, even though he knew what helping them would mean. He would do it even knowing it would mean his death in the end. He would seek them out again and go back to them. Join them. . . .

FOUR

THE DUMBBELL SHAPE OF THE AALAAG COURIER SHIP IN WHICH SHANE was being transported dropped suddenly like an extremely swift elevator. Shane's stomach floated within him, making physical the uneasiness that had ridden with him all the way from Milan.

Then his body adjusted and he felt himself weightless, held in place solely by the restraining arms of his seat. The control board viewing screen was all but hidden by the massive, white-uniformed shoulders of the nine-foot Aalaag female who was his pilot. But the same view was displayed in the screen on the back of the seat ahead of him, so he had a telescopic November view of the Twin Cities— Minneapolis and St. Paul.

In summer these cities, chief population centers of what had once been Minnesota, one of the former United States of America, would have been only partly visible like this, from above. Thick-treed avenues and streets would then have given the illusion of nothing more than two small, separate downtown business centers surrounded by heavy forest. But now, in the final months of the dying year, the full extent of buildings in both cities and their sub-urbs lay revealed among the piled up leaves stripped from their branches by the winds of early winter. It was as if winter, too, was a servant of the Aalaag and had cleared all that was soft and gentle from the scene.

Even snow would have relieved some of the uncompromising harshness from what he looked at now, but no snow was yet on the ground to soften what the fallen leaves had uncovered. Shane looked down into the empty-seeming thoroughfares. Under Aalaag rule they would be as clean as, but colder than, those he had just left in Milan of northern Italy; particularly clean, here around the Headquarters of all the alien power on Earth, that building placed above the headwaters of navigation on the Mississippi River. That destination to which Shane now, without choice, returned.

The body odor of his pilot forced itself once more on his attention. It was inescapable in the close confines of the small vessel—as no doubt his human smell was to her. Though as an Aalaag she would never have lowered herself to admit noticing such a fact. The scent of her in his nostrils was hardly agreeable, but not specifically disagreeable, either.

It was the smell of a different animal, only. Something like the reek of a horse or cow barn, only with that slightly acid tinge which identified a meat-eater. For the Aalaag, though they required that Earthly foodstuffs be reconstituted for their different digestive systems, were, like humanity, omnivores who made a certain portion of their diet out of flesh—though of Earthly creatures other than human.

That exception of human flesh from the Aalaag diet might be merely policy on the part of the aliens. Or it might not, thought Shane. Even after nearly three years of living here at the very heart and center of the Aalaag Command on Earth, in many cases like this he had no way of knowing what their real reasons were, or whether what he believed might be merely a false assumption on his part. . . .

He forced his mind to stop playing with the question of the aliens' diet. It was unimportant, as unimportant as the differences in appearance of the Twin Cities between June and November. Both thoughts were straw men thrown up by his subconscious as excuses to avoid thinking of the situation which would be facing him momentarily.

In only a few minutes he would be once more in the House of his Master, reporting to him—to Lyt Ahn, First Captain and Commander of all the Aalaag on this captive and subject Earth. And this time, for the first time, he would face that all-powerful ruler, knowing himself to be doubly guilty of what to these Aalaag was a capital crime among themselves, let alone in one of their servants. It was not merely that he had violated an order, but he had violated it while he was on duty, as a courier and translator for the First Captain.

It was ironic. He had clung to the thought, these last few years, of himself as someone well able to endure existence under the domination of the alien rulers. He had gone on believing this until just a few hours ago. But now he had to face the fact that there was one area in which he was just as vulnerable as any of the rest of his race.

As a member of the Courier-Translator Corps belonging to the First Captain of Earth, he was well fed, well housed, well paid—unbelievably so by comparison with the overwhelming mass of his fellow humans. As a result, he had come to believe in his own ability to avoid trouble with their overlords. But in spite of all this, twice now, *yowaragh* had overtaken him, just as if he had been one of the ordinary, starveling mass of Earth's population. Even though no alien knew it, he had now twice defied them.

Further, during the hours just past, he had revealed his existence and his identity to several members, at least, of the human Resistance group in Milan.

Now, on the return trip to his Master's Headquarters, he faced the fact that he was no different from all the rest of the race of humans. Like them, he walked a razor's edge between the absolute laws and power of his rulers and a possibility that at any moment an uncontrollable inner explosion might drive him to do something that would bring his hatred of them to their attention.

It was strange, he thought, that this should only now be striking home to him, more than three years after the Aalaag had landed and taken over Earth in one swift and effortless moment. Squarely, he faced the fact that he was terrified of what the consequences could be of another such bout of madness in him. He had seen Aalaag interrogation and disciplines at work. He knew, as the Resistance people like those in Milan did not, that there was literally no hope of a successful revolt against the military power of the aliens. Anyone attempting to act against the Aalaag was courting certain and painful death—as an object lesson to other humans who might also be tempted to revolt.

And this would be as true for him as for any other human, in spite of the value of his work to the aliens and the kindness with which Lyt Ahn had always seemed to regard him.

But at the same time the logical front of his mind was reading him this lesson, the back of it was playing with the notion of finding ways around his situation and avoiding any such future risks that might trigger off the *yowaragh* reaction in him. He remembered how simple it would be to contact the Resistance people again. All he had to do was buy himself the pilgrim's gown of two different colors with the gold that only an alien-employed human like himself would be carrying. The dream of revolt, even to him, was an unbelievably seductive one—in the years before the coming of the Aalaag, he could never have imagined how seductive. He checked the thought. He must never forget how hopeless and false it was. He must remember he lived with one goal and one goal only—his personal survival. That was all that the Aalaag had left him.

So he must hold himself under tight control and continue to chart his way cool-headedly among the reefs of Aalaag behavior that surrounded him. Some things to protect himself, he could do.

To begin with, as soon as he got the ear of Lyt Ahn, he must set up excuses against the two crimes he had just committed in Milan. The lie to Laa Ehon about his worth must be covered; and there was still deep danger in the fact that he had helped to rescue Maria. For a moment the thought of her brought back an inexpressible longing. If he had only had the chance to at least get to know her. . . . He forced his mind back to immediate problems. The Aalaag, if they should ever actually come to suspect him, had devices which could, like mechanical bloodhounds, sniff out his having left the Milanese Headquarters building without permission.

That was the most dangerous of the two crimes he had just committed in Aalaag terms—crimes, as they would be seen by Aalaag eyes. The lesser crime, that he had lied to Laa Ehon about the price Lyt Ahn had placed upon him, was the more likely of the two to come to light.

The ship he rode in was almost to its landing place now.

A lying beast, in Aalaag eyes, was an untrustworthy beast, and should therefore be destroyed. Somehow, this statement of his to Laa Ehon must be handled—but at the moment he had no idea how to do it. Perhaps, if he put it deliberately out of his mind, a solution would come to him naturally. . . .

He made a conscious effort to do so, and out of habit his thoughts drifted off once more into his fantasy of the Pilgrim, who, like himself, lived under the cover of being a courier-translator for Lyt Ahn, and who was also superior to all Aalaag, as they were superior to humans.

The Pilgrim, he dreamed, would wear the same anonymous garb in which Shane himself came and went among his fellow humans; who, otherwise, catching him alone and away from Aalaag or the Interior Guard who policed them, would have torn him apart if they had known that he was one of those favored and employed by their masters.

The Pilgrim would be uncatchable and uncontrollable by the Aalaag. He would set their laws and their might at defiance. He would rescue humans who had been trapped by those same alien rules and laws—as Shane had, by sheer luck more than anything else, managed to get Maria out of the clutches of the Milanese garrison.

Above all, the Pilgrim would bring home to the aliens the fact that they were not the masters of Earth that they thought themselves to be. . . .

For the few minutes in which the courier ship dropped to its destination, he let himself indulge in that dream, seeing himself as the Pilgrim with a power that put him above even Lyt Ahn, to say nothing of all the other alien masters who made his insides go hollow every time they so much as looked at him.

Then he roused himself and shook it off. It was all right as a means to keep him sane; but it was dangerous, indulged in when under alien observation, as he was about to be within seconds. Besides, he could afford to put it aside for the moment. Five minutes from now he would be in the small cubicle that was his living quarters and he could think what he liked, including how to protect himself against Lyt Ahn's discovery of either of his recent crimes.

The courier ship was now right over its destination. The landing spot to which it dropped was only a couple of hundred meters below, the rooftop of an enormous construction with only some twenty stories or so above ground but as many below, and covering several acres. Like all structures now taken over or built by the Aalaag, it gleamed; in this chill, thin November sunlight looking as if liquid mercury had been poured over it. That shining surface was a defensive screen or coating—Shane had never been able to discover which, since the Aalaag took it so for granted that they never spoke of it. Once in place, apparently, it needed neither renewal nor maintenance; although the First Captain often turned it off.

Just as it seemed their ship must crash into the rooftop, a space of the silver surface vanished. Revealed were a flat, gray surface and a platoon of the oversized humans recruited as Interior Guards to the aliens. These stood, fully armed, under the command of an Aalaag officer who towered in full, white armor above the tallest of them. The officer was a male, Shane saw, the fact betrayed by the narrowness of his lower-body armor.

As the ship touched down, its port opened and Shane's pilot stepped out. The Interior Guards at once fell back, leaving the Aalaag to come forward alone and meet the pilot. Shane, lost behind her powerful shape, had followed her out.

"Am Mehon, twenty-eighth rank," the pilot introduced herself. "I return one of the First Captain's cattle, at his orders—"

She half turned to indicate, with the massive thumb of her left hand, Shane, who was standing a respectful two paces behind her and to her left.

"Aral Te Kinn," the Aalaag on guard introduced himself. "Thirty-second rank . . ."

His armored head bent slightly, acknowledging the fact that the courier pilot outranked him by four degrees. But it would have bent no farther for the First Captain himself.

Theoretically all Aalaag were equal; and the lowest of them, when on duty, could give orders to the highest, if the other was not. Here, on the roof landing space of the House of Weapons, as the First Captain's residence and Headquarters were always called, the officer on guard, being in control of the area, was therefore in authority. Only courtesy dictated the slight inclination of his head.

"This beast is to report itself to the First Captain immediately," he went on now. His helmet turned slightly, bringing its viewing slit to focus on Shane. "You heard me, beast?"

Shane felt a sudden, sickening emptiness in his stomach. Surely it was impossible that what he had done in Milan could have been found out and reported to the First Captain this quickly? He shook off the sudden weakness. Of course it was impossible. But even with the sudden fear gone, he felt robbed of the anticipated peace and quiet of his cubicle, the chance to think and plan he had been looking forward to. However, there could be no delay in obeying the order.

"I heard, untarnished sir," answered Shane in Aalaag, bending his own head in a considerably deeper bow.

He walked past the pilot and Aral Te Kinn toward the shedlike structure containing the drop-pad that would lower him to his meeting with Lyt Ahn. The tall humans who were the Interior Guards gazed down at him with faint contempt as their ranks parted to let him through. But Shane was by now so used to their attitude to such as himself that he hardly noticed.

". . . I had heard there were a rare few among these cattle who could speak the actual language as a real person does," he could hear the pilot saying to Aral Te Kinn behind him, "but I had not believed it until now. If it were not for the squeakiness of its high voice—"

Shane shut the door to the shed on the rest of her words and on the scene behind him as he entered the structure. He stepped onto the round green disk of the drop-pad.

"Sub-floor twenty," he told it, and the alien-built elevator obeyed, dropping him swiftly toward his destination, twenty floors beneath the surface of the surrounding city.

Its fall stopped with equal suddenness, and his knees bent under a deceleration that would not have been noticed by an Aalaag. He stepped forward into a wide corridor with black-and-white tiles on its polished floor, and both walls and ceiling of a hard, uniformly gray material.

A male Aalaag officer sat on the solid block that was his seat, at the duty desk opposite the elevator, engaged in conversation with someone in the communications screen set in the surface of the desk before him. Shane had halted at once after his first step out of the drop-pad and stood motionless. Eventually, the talk was ended and the Aalaag cut the connection, looking up at him.

"I am Shane Evert, courier-translator for the First Captain, untarnished sir," said Shane, as the pale, heavy-boned and expressionless, humanlike face, under its mane of pure white hair, considered him. This particular alien had seen him at least a couple of hundred times previously, but like most Aalaag, was not good at distinguishing one human from another, even if the two were of opposite sexes.

The Aalaag continued to stare, waiting.

"I have returned from a courier run," Shane went on, "and the untarnished sir on duty at the roof parking area said I was ordered to report immediately to the First Captain."

The desk officer looked down and spoke again into his communications screen—checking, of course, on what Shane had said. Ordinarily, the movements of a single human would be of little concern to any Aalaag, but entrance to the apartments of the First Captain, along the corridor to Shane's right, was a matter of unique security. Shane glanced briefly along the corridor in the opposite direction, to his left, and toward his own distant quarters, with those of the other translators, and such other private servants of Lyt Ahn, or his mate-consort, the female Adtha Or Ain.

Shane had been continuously on duty and in the presence of Aalaag for three days, culminating in that disastrous, if still secret, act of insanity he had given way to in Milan. His desire to return to his own quarters, to be alone, was like a living hunger in him, a desperate hunger to lock himself away in a place that for a moment would be closed off, away from all the daily terrors and orders; a place where he could at last put aside his constant fears and lick his wounds in peace.

"You may report as instructed."

The voice of the Aalaag on duty behind the desk cut across his thoughts.

"I obey, untarnished sir," he answered.

He turned to his right and went away down the long hall, hearing the clicking of his heels on the hard tiles underfoot echoing back from the unyielding walls. Along those walls at intervals of what would be not more than half a dozen strides for an Aalaag hung long arms—equivalents of human rifles—armed and ready for use. But for all their real deadliness, they were there for show only, a part of the militaristic Aalaag culture pattern that justified the name of House of Weapons for this abode of Lyt Ahn.

A house of weapons it was indeed; but its military potency lay not in the awesomely destructive, by human standards, devices on its walls. Behind the silver protective screen that covered the building were larger, portable devices capable of leveling to slagged ruin the Earth surrounding, to and beyond the horizon in all directions. For a moment Shane was reminded of what he had not thought of for years, of those human military units that in the first days of the Aalaag landing on Earth had been foolish enough to try resisting the alien invasion. They had been destroyed almost without thought on the invaders' part, like hills of ants trodden underfoot by giants.

To all destructive devices known to human science and technology, including the nuclear ones, even a single Aalaag in full battle armor was invulnerable. Against the least weapon carried by an individual Aalaag, no human army could, in the end, survive. Nor would an Aalaag weapon work in the hands of any but one of the aliens. It was not merely a matter of humans understanding how to activate it. There was also some built-in recognition by the weapon itself that it was not in Aalaag hands, which in others' hands turned it into no more than a dead piece of heavy material; at most, a weighty club.

Walking down the wide, high-ceilinged, solitary corridor where no other figures, human or alien, were to be seen, Shane felt coming over him once again the sense of shrinking that always took him over in this place.

It was a feeling like that which Swift's hero, Lemuel Gulliver, had described in *Gulliver's Travels*, as happening when he had found himself in the land of the giant Brobdingnagians. Like Gulliver, then, each time Shane found himself in this place, a time would come when he would begin to feel that it was the Aalaag and all their artifacts which were normal in size, while he, like all other humans and human creations, was shrunk to the scale of pygmies. Shrunk, not only in a physical sense, but in all other senses as well; in mind and spirit and courage and wisdom, in all those things that could make one race into something more than mere "cattle" to another.

He checked abruptly, passing a door that was uncharacteristically human-sized in one wall of that overlarge hall, and turned in through it to one of the few rooms on this corridor equipped to dispose of human waste. There was no telling how long he might be in the presence of Lyt Ahn, and there would be no excusing himself then for physical or personal needs. No Aalaag would have dreamed of so excusing himself while on duty, and therefore no human servant might.

He stood before a urinal, emptying his bladder with a momentary sense of stolen freedom, only secondary to that which he yearned for in his own quarters. Here, too, for the moment, in theory he was free of Aalaag observation and rules, and the Gulliver-like sensation lifted, briefly.

But the moment passed. A minute later he was toy-sized again, back outside in the corridor, walking ever nearer to the entrance of Lyt Ahn's private office.

He stopped at last before great double doors of bronze-colored material. With the tip of the index finger of his right hand, he lightly touched the smooth surface of the panel closest to him.

There was a pause. He could not hear, but he knew that within the office a sensor had recorded his touch as being that of a human, and a mechanical voice was announcing that *"a beast desires admittance."*

"Who?" came an Aalaag voice from the ceiling. Unusually, it was not that of an Aalaag secretary or aide—but of Lyt Ahn himself.

"One of your cattle, most immaculate sir," answered Shane. "Shane-beast, reporting as ordered, following a courier run to the immaculate sir in command at Milan, Italy."

The right-hand door swung open and Shane walked through it, into the office. Under a white ceiling as lofty as that of the hall, and large enough for a small ballroom by human standards, the gray-colored desk was a surface afloat in midair, the chairs, the couches standing on the rugless floor of the same black-and-white tiles, were all simple blocks, with no back rests. Also, they were all built to the scale of the nine-foot aliens. There was no padding or upholstery on any of them, but the material of which they were made was resilient.

Lyt Ahn was indeed alone; seated, looming behind his desk, which held in its surface a screen like that in the desk of the officer in the corridor, plus a scattering of some small artifacts, each tiny enough to be encompassed in Shane's merely human hand, but showing no recognizable shapes or purposes. In a like situation, on a human desk, they might have been miniature sculptures. But the Aalaag owned no art, nor showed interest in any. What they really were, and their purpose in being there, was still an unsolved puzzle to Shane. On the wall to his right as Shane entered was a larger screen, now unlit, some three-by-two meters in area. In the left wall was an Aalaag-sized single door that led to Lyt Ahn's private apartments.

Lyt Ahn raised his head to look at Shane as the human stepped through the doorway, taking one pace and then halting.

"Come here," the alien Commander said; and, both permitted and ordered—for the two words were one in Aalaag—Shane came up to the far side of the desk.

The First Captain of all Earth gazed at him. Just as Aalaag had difficulty distinguishing between individual humans, so most humans, aside from the fact that they saw their overlords most commonly in armor and therefore faceless, were not adept at telling one Aalaag from another. Shane gazed back. He had been in close contact with the alien Commander since Lyt Ahn had formed his corps of human interpreters, nearly three years before. Shane not only recognized the First Captain, he had become expert at studying the other for small clues to his master's momentary mood. Like all humans nowadays he was dependent; in this case, dependent upon the First Captain not only for food and shelter but for a continuance of life itself. He studied his master daily, as a lamb might study the lion with which it was required to lie down each night; and just at the moment, he thought now that he read fatigue and a deep-seated worry, plus something else he could not identify, in the visage of the towering individual before him.

"Laa Ehon, of the sixth rank and Commander of the Milan garrison has received your sending, most immaculate sir, and sends his courtesies to the First Captain," said Shane. "He returned no message by me."

"Did he not, little Shane-beast?" said Lyt Ahn. Shane's name was uttered in what was as close to an affectionate diminutive as the alien language possessed; but the words were obviously spoken more to Lyt Ahn, himself, than to the human.

Shane's heart took an upward leap. Lyt Ahn was clearly in as warm and confidential a mood as it was possible for an Aalaag to be—and more so than Shane had ever seen any other alien permit himself. Nonetheless, there was also in the other that impression of worry and concern with some problem that Shane had noted on first entering the room; and he continued covertly to study the heavy-boned face opposite. There was a greater impression of age about his master than he had ever seen before, although the face was barely lined, and there was no way that age could have made the hair of the Earth's Supreme Commander any whiter than that of any other adult Aalaag. It would have been yellowish at birth, but purely snow-colored by puberty, which in the aliens seemed to come about the age of eighteen to twenty-five Earth years.

Nor was there anything else different about the grayish eyes in the pale Aalaag skin that never appeared to tan. With its great, sharp bones and colorlessness it gave the impression of being carved out of a soft, gray-white stone. But still, somehow, it also managed to give Shane not only the impression of great age, but of that same weariness and emotion that currently seemed to be at work in the First Captain.

As Shane watched, the massive figure got slowly to its feet, walked around from behind its desk and sat down on one of the long blocks that did duty as couches. The change of position was a signal that the meeting had now become informal. Lyt Ahn was dressed in black boots and a white, single-piece suit, like any other alien on duty. Shane turned as the other moved, in order to keep facing his master, and, after a moment, saw the eyes that had been looking more through him than otherwise focus directly upon him.

"Come here, Shane-beast," said Lyt Ahn.

Shane moved forward until he stood one alien-sized step from the seated alien. Lyt Ahn studied him for a long moment. Their heads were on a level. Then, reaching out, he cupped an enormous hand gently, for a moment, over Shane's head.

Shane checked his body from tensing just in time. Physical contact was almost unknown amongst the Aalaag themselves, and unheard of between Aalaag and human; but Shane had learned over the last two years that Lyt Ahn permitted himself freedoms beyond those generally used by those lesser in rank than himself. The large hand that could easily have crushed the bones of Shane's skull rested lightly for a moment on Shane's head and then was withdrawn.

"Little Shane-beast," said Lyt Ahn—and unless it was his imagination it seemed to Shane that he heard in the Aalaag voice the same tiredness he had suspected in the First Captain's face—"are you contented?"

There was no word in the Aalaag language for "happy." "Contented" or "very interested" were the closest possible expressions of it. Shane felt a sudden fear of an unknown trap in the question, and for a second he debated telling Lyt Ahn that he was, indeed, contented. But Aalaag could accept nothing but truth, and the First Captain had always allowed his human interpreters a freedom of opinion no other Aalaag permitted.

"No, most immaculate sir," Shane answered. "I would be contented only if this world was as it was before the untarnished race came among us."

Lyt Ahn did not sigh. But Shane, used to the First Captain, and having studied him as only children, animals and slaves have always studied those who hold their life and every freedom in their hands, received the clear impression that the other would have sighed if he had only been physiologically and psychologically capable of doing so.

"Yes," said the First Captain, absently looking through him once more, "your race makes unhappy cattle, true enough."

Fear came back to Shane and chilled him to the bone. He told himself that Lyt Ahn could by no means have discovered this soon what he had done illegally in Milan, but the words the alien Supreme Commander had just now used came too close to his knowledge of guilt not to cause him to stiffen internally.

For a second he debated trying to entice Lyt Ahn to be more explicit about whatever had caused him to make such a remark. Ordinarily, a human did not speak unless ordered to do so. But the First Captain had always allowed Shane and the other translators unusual freedom in that respect. Shane checked, however, at the thought, for two reasons. One, his uncertainty of how such a question could be phrased without offense; and two, a fear that if Lyt Ahn did indeed suspect him of some violation of proper conduct, any such asking would only confirm the suspicion.

He stood silent, therefore, and simply waited, in the helplessness of the totally dependent. Either Lyt Ahn would speak further, or the First Captain would dismiss him; and neither of these things could Shane control.

"Do you find your fellow cattle in any way different these days, Shane-beast?" asked Lyt Ahn.

FIVE

SHANE'S HEART JUMPED. HE THOUGHT INVOLUNTARILY OF THE LARGE, grimy, tenement room in Milan to which he had been kidnapped.

"No, most immaculate sir," he answered, and felt the danger of his lie like a heavy weight in his chest.

There was another pause that could have been a sigh from Lyt Ahn.

"No," said the alien Commander, "perhaps . . . perhaps even if there were, it would not be such as you they would admit their feelings to. Your fellow cattle do not love those who work for us, do they, little Shane-beast?"

"No," said Shane, truthfully and bitterly.

It was that very fact that required him to wear the pilgrim's cloak and carry the pilgrim's staff when he moved about the Earth on Lyt Ahn's business—as Lyt Ahn knew well. The First Captain was in a strange mood today, with his mind off on some problem which at this moment was still unclear to Shane, but which had plainly directed his attention elsewhere than at Shane himself. It occurred to Shane suddenly that now might be an opportunity to cover his tracks in regard to the lesser matter of his having lied to Laa Ehon when that alien had asked him what price Lyt Ahn might put upon him.

"If the most immaculate sir pleases," Shane said, "this beast was asked a question by the sir who is called Laa Ehon. The question was what price my master might put upon me."

"So," replied Lyt Ahn, his thoughts clearly still occupied with that primary concern Shane had noted in him. The First Captain's response was in fact no response at all, merely an acknowledgement of the fact that he had heard what Shane had said. Shane allowed himself to hope.

"I answered," said Shane, "that to the best of my knowledge, the most immaculate sir had valued all of his translator-beasts at half a possession of land—" Shane tried to keep his voice unchanged but for a fraction of a second his breath caught in his throat—"and the favor of my master."

"So," said Lyt Ahn, still in the same tone of voice.

He had heard, but clearly he had not heard. Internally, Shane felt the weakness of relief. He had gambled that the First Captain would not remember whether he had or not—and the gamble had now paid off.

A single musical note from the door leading to the private apartments of the First Captain interrupted the thoughts of both Shane and Lyt Ahn.

The door swung open to let in a second Aalaag. But this one was a female—and Shane recognized her with something close to panic. She was Adtha Or Ain, the consort of Lyt Ahn; and the panic arose from the fact that Shane was, for the first time in a long time, encountering a situation involving Aalaag mores with which he was not familiar. When, on rare occasions before this, he had anything to do with the consort of the First Captain, it had been with her alone, when he had been sent about the planet with one of her private messages.

His encounters with her had been purely formal and conducted entirely within the known code of behavior between Aalaag and human beast. On the other hand his private meetings with Lyt Ahn had, like this one, largely come to be informal. There was no way of telling how she would react to the informality he was used to being permitted by Lyt Ahn. On the other hand, it would raise the question of his disobeying Lyt Ahn's authority if he suddenly reverted to the formal mode, after Lyt Ahn, by sitting down on the couch, had, in effect, ordered him to abandon it. There was no way for him to tell whether, if either should address him, he should respond in the formal or the informal mode. Either mode could be a response that would offend either Lyt Ahn or Adtha Or Ain.

Shane stood motionless and silent, praying that he would be ignored by both aliens. He studied Adtha Or Ain as he had studied Lyt Ahn earlier—and for the same reasons. There was something like a bitterness that he had always noted in her, but it had always seemed to be hard-held under control. In this moment, however, that control seemed to have loosened.

For the moment, his luck seemed to be holding. Lyt Ahn had risen from the couch and gone to meet Adtha Or Ain. They stopped, facing each other, an Aalaag arm's length apart, looking into each other's faces.

Adtha Or Ain was slightly the taller of the two, but, aside from that, if Shane had not come to recognize the slight sexual differences in Aalaag bodies, it would have been hard to tell the two apart. Their dress was identical. Only the slight individuality of their features, that individuality which Shane had finally taught himself to look for over these past years, and the individual difference of their voices, marked them apart. Adult Aalaag females, like human ones, tended to speak in somewhat higher voices than the males of their race—although the difference was nowhere near as marked as in humans—particularly in the case of an older Aalaag female like Adtha Or Ain, whose voice had deepened with age.

Now, the two stood facing each other. There was a tension between them, that Shane sensed strongly, and with that feeling came another wave of relief. If these two would just stay completely concerned with each other, he would in effect be invisible—of no more importance to them than the furniture in the room, and the chances of either requiring an answer from him would be almost nil. For the first time, Shane dared to look on them as an observer might, rather than as a potential victim of their meeting.

They did not touch. Nonetheless, Shane's experience with the Aalaag, and elsewhere, let him read into their confrontation a closeness—love was a word that did not exist in the Aalaag language—which implied that, had they been humans, they might have touched. At the same time, however, Shane felt a sadness and an anger in Adtha Or Ain and a sort of helpless pity in Lyt Ahn.

The two ignored him.

"Perhaps," said Lyt Ahn, "you should rest."

"No," said Adtha Or Ain. "Rest is no rest to me, at times like this."

"You make yourself suffer unnecessarily."

She turned aside and walked around the First Captain. He turned also to look after her. She went to the wall bearing the large screen; and although Shane could not see her make any motion to turn it on, it woke to light and image before her, the starkness of what it showed dominating the room.

The three-dimensional shape on it was the last that Shane could have imagined. It was of an adult male Aalaag, without armor, but carrying all personal weapons and encased in a block of something brownishly translucent, like an insect in amber.

It was only after he got past his first shock of seeing it and began to examine it in detail that he noticed two unusual things. One was that there was a faintish yellow tinge to the ends of the white hair on the head of the encased Aalaag; and the second—it was unbelievable, but the Aalaag shown was alive, if completely helpless.

He could see the pupils of the gray eyes move minutely, as he watched. They were focused on something that seemed to be outside the scene imaged on the screen. Other expression there was none—nor probably could be any, since the face, like all the rest of the body, seemed imprisoned and held immobile by the enclosing material.

"No," said Lyt Ahn behind him.

Shane's ears, sharpened by two and a half years of servitude, heard that rare thing, a note of emotion in an Aalaag voice; and, faint as it was, he read it clearly as a note of pain. Those years of attuning himself to the moods of the First Captain had finally created a bond that was all but empathic between them; and his own emotions felt Lyt Ahn's in this moment without uncertainty.

"I must look at it," said Adtha Or Ain, standing before the screen.

Lyt Ahn took three steps forward, moving up behind her. His two great hands reached out part way toward her shoulders and then fell back to his sides.

"It's only a conception," he said. "A mock-up. You've no reason for assuming it represents reality. Almost certainly no such thing has happened. Undoubtedly he and his team are dead, destroyed utterly."

"But perhaps he is like this," said Adtha Or Ain, without turning her head from the screen. "Maybe they have him so, and will keep him so for thousands of lifetimes. I will have no more children. I had only this one, and perhaps this is how he is now."

Lyt Ahn stood, saying nothing. She turned to face him.

"You let him go," she said.

"You know—as I know," he answered. "Some of us must keep watch on the Inner Race who stole our homes, in case they move again and the movement is in this direction. He was my son—my son as well as yours—and he wanted to be one of those to go and check."

"You could have denied him. I asked you to order him to stay. You did not."

"How could I?"

"By speaking."

Shane had never before seen emotion at this level between two of the normally expressionless Aalaag, and he felt like someone tossed about in a hurricane. He could not leave, but to stay and listen was all but unbearable. Against his will, the empathic response he had so painstakingly developed to the feelings of Lyt Ahn was at him now with a pain he felt at second hand, pain he could not understand or do anything about.

"In a thousand lifetimes," she said, "a thousand lifetimes and more, they've made no sign of moving again. They only wanted our worlds, our homes, and once they had them they were content enough. We all know that. Why send our children back to what's theirs now—so that they can catch them and make toys for themselves of our flesh and blood—make a toy and a thing of my son?"

"There was no choice," said Lyt Ahn. "Could I protect my son before others—when he'd asked to go?"

"He was a child. He didn't know."

"It was his duty. It was my duty—and your duty—to let him go. So the Aalaag survive. You know your duty. And I tell you again, you've no way of knowing he's not at peace, safely dead and destroyed. You make yourself a nightmare of the one most unlikely thing that could happen."

"Prove it to me," Adtha Or Ain said. "Send an expedition to find out."

"You know I can't. Not yet. We've only held this world three of its years. It's not properly tamed yet. The crew, the needs for the expedition you want aren't to spare."

"You promised me."

"I promised to send an expedition as soon as team and materials were to spare."

"And it's been three years, and still you say there're none."

"None, for only a possibility—none for what may be nothing more than a nightmare grown in your own mind. As soon as I can in duty and honor spare people for something of that level, the expedition will go. I promise you. It will bring back the truth of what happened to our son. But not yet."

She turned from him.

"Three years," she said.

"These beasts are not like some on other worlds we've taken. I've done with this planet as much as I might, given the force I had to work with. No one could do more. You are unfair, Adtha Or Ain."

Silently, she turned, crossed the room once more and passed back through the doorway by which she had entered. Its doors closed behind her.

Lyt Ahn stood for a moment, then looked at the screen. It went blank and gray once more. He turned and went to sit down again at his desk, touching the smaller screen inset in it and apparently returning to the work he had been doing when Shane had come in.

Shane continued to stand, unmoving. He stood, and the minutes went by. It was not unusual that a human should have to hold his place indefinitely, waiting for the attention of an Aalaag; Shane was trained to it. But this time his mind was a seething, bewildered mass. He longed for the First Captain to remember he was there and do something about him.

A very long time later, it seemed, Lyt Ahn did lift his head from his screen and his eyes took notice of Shane's presence.

"You may go," he said. His gaze was back on the desk screen before the words had left his lips.

Shane turned and left.

He went back down the long corridor, past the Aalaag officer still on duty at the desk and after some distance, to the door of his own cubicle. Opening that door at last, he saw, seated in the room's single armchair by the narrow bed, a human figure. It was one of the other translators, a brown-haired young woman named Sylvie Onjin.

"I heard you were back," she told him.

He made himself smile at her. How she had heard did not matter. There was an informational grapevine among all humans in the House of Weapons that operated entirely without reference to whether the giver and receiver of information were personally on good terms. It was to the benefit of all humans in the House that as much as possible be known about the activities of both Aalaag and humans there.

Probably, word of his return had been passed through the ranks of the Interior Guards, either directly to the corps of translators, or by way of one of the other groups of human specialists personally owned and used by the First Captain.

What did matter was that now, of all times, was not a moment in which he wanted to see her—or anyone. The need for privacy was so strong in him that he felt ready to break down emotionally and mentally if he did not have it. But he could not easily tell her to go.

The humans owned by Lyt Ahn, being picked beasts and therefore of good quality, were encouraged to intermingle, and even to mate and have young if they wished. Although Aalaag mores stood in the way of the aliens' making any specific command or order that they do so. Only the Interior Guard welcomed the idea of being parents under these conditions. None of those in the translator ranks had any desire to perpetuate their kind as slaves of the aliens. But still, sheer physical and emotional hungers drew individuals together.

Sylvie Onjin and Shane had been two so drawn. They had no real lust or love for each other, in the ordinary senses of those words. Only, they found each other slightly more compatible than either found others of the human opposite sex in the House of Weapons. In the world as it had been before the Aalaag came, Shane thought now, if they two had met they would almost undoubtedly have parted again immediately with no great desire to see more of each other. But in this place they clung instinctively together.

But the thought of Sylvie's company now, when his mind was

in turmoil and his emotions had just been stretched to a breaking point, was more than Shane could face. At best, it was only an act he and she played together, a pretense that erected a small, flimsy and temporary private existence for them both, away from the alien-dominated world that held their lives and daily actions in its indifferent hand. Also, now, after Shane's encounter with the other young woman, the one called Maria, there was something about Sylvie that almost repelled him, the way a tamed animal might suffer in comparison with one still wild, but free.

But the narrow face of Sylvie smiled confidently back up at him. Her smile was her best feature; and in the days before the Aalaag she might have emphasized her other good features with makeup to the point where she could have been considered attractive, if not seductive. The aliens, however, classed lipstick and all such other beauty aids with that uncleanliness they were so adamant about erasing from any world they owned. To an Aalaag, a woman with makeup on had merely dirtied her face. Ordinary humans, in private, might indulge in such actions, but not those human servants which the Aalaag saw daily.

So Sylvie's face was starkly clean, pale-looking under her close-cropped, ordinary brown hair. It was a small-boned face. She was a woman of one hundred and thirty-four centimeters in height—barely over five feet, a corner of Shane's western mind automatically calculated—and narrow-bodied even for that height. Her figure was unremarkable, but not bad for a woman in her early twenties. Like Shane himself she had been a graduate student when the Aalaag landed.

She sat now with her legs crossed, the skirt of the black taffeta cocktail dress she had put on lifted by the action to reveal her knees. In her lap was a heavy-looking, cylindrical object about ten inches long wrapped in white documentary paper, held in place by a narrow strip of such paper wrapped around its neck, formed into a bow and colored red, apparently by some homemade substance, since such a thing as red tape—let alone the red ribbon the paper strip was evidently intended to mimic—was not something which the Aalaag would find any reason for permitting to be manufactured.

"Happy homecoming!" She held it out to him.

He stepped forward automatically and took it, making himself smile back at her. He could feel through the paper that it was a full bottle of something. He hardly drank, as she knew—there was too much danger of making some mistake in front of their owners if some unexpected call to duty should come—but it was about the only gift available for any of them to give each other. He held it, feeling how obvious the falseness of his smile must be. The image of Maria was still between them—but then suddenly it cleared and it was as if he saw Sylvie unexpectedly wiped clean of all artifice, naked in her hopes and fears as in the pretensions with which she strove to battle those fears.

His heart turned suddenly within him. It was a physical feeling like a palpable lurch in his chest. He saw her clearly for the first time and understood that he could never betray her, could never deny help to her in this or any like moment. For all that there was not even the shadow of real love between them, he felt his smile become genuine and tender as he looked down at her; and he felt—not the actual love for which she yearned, or even the pretense of it, for which she was willing to settle—but a literal affection that was based in the fact that they were simply two humans together in this alien house.

Not understanding the reasons for it, but instinctively recognizing the emotion that had come into him, she rose suddenly and came into his arms; and he felt a strong gush of tenderness, such as he had never felt before in his long months in this place of weapons, that made him hold her tight to him.

Later, lying on his back in the darkness, the slight body of Sylvie sleeping contentedly beside him, he was assaulted by an unexpected tidal wave of loneliness and emptiness that washed over him, and threatened to drown him.

His father and mother had died when he had been so young that he barely remembered them. He had been raised after that by an aunt and uncle, who were well off and had given him everything that could physically and socially be expected; but they had made no real effort to hide the fact that they considered raising him a duty rather than a matter of affection. Left to themselves, they would have preferred not to have been bothered with children.

He had escaped them with relief as soon as he was old enough to go to college; but he had never been able to escape the feeling that there was no real place for him among other people. Deeply, he envied Sylvie's ability to find satisfaction and relief in these brief encounters of theirs. Outside of a moment's forgetfulness of the world that held them prisoner, and a rare burst of emotion such as the one he had felt earlier when he had seen her as naked in her hopes and fears, his inner feeling of valuelessness had him by the throat once more.

He wrestled with the despondency in him, fought it off, and after a while he, too, slept.

He was roused from deep slumber by the burring of his bedside phone. He reached out toward it and the action triggered to life the light over the nightstand where the square screen of the phone sat. He touched the screen and the face of an Aalaag above the collar of a duty officer appeared in it.

"You are ordered to attend the First Captain, beast," said the officer's deep, remote voice. "Report to him in the Council Conference Room."

"I hear and obey, untarnished sir," Shane heard his own voice, still thick with sleep, answering.

The screen went blank, leaving a flat, silvery gray surface. Shane rose and dressed, a sick feeling growing inside him. Whatever reason there could be for the unheard-of action of calling a beast into a Conference of the Council made up of the Area Commanders among the Aalaag, it could mean nothing good for the beast. Sylvie was already gone and the chronometer by his bed showed that the hour was barely past dawn.

Twenty minutes later, shaven, clean and dressed, he touched the bronze surface of the door to the Council Conference Room.

"Come," said the voice of Lyt Ahn.

The door opened itself and he entered to find twelve Aalaag, five males and seven females, seated around the floating, shimmering surface that served them as a table. Lyt Ahn sat at the far end. On his right was Laa Ehon, the Commander whom Shane had only just left in Milan. A dryness tightened Shane's throat as he remembered his secret crimes against that officer and his command. He told himself no such august assemblage would be convened only to deal with the criminal acts of a simple beast; but his throat remained tight. He looked down the table surface toward the First Captain and waited for orders. He had halted, from custom, two paces inside the open door, and the twelve powerful alien faces were studying him as lions might study some small animal that had wandered into the midst of their pride.

SIX

"THIS IS THE ONE YOU SPOKE OF?" ASKED THE FEMALE AALAAG CLOS-
est on Lyt Ahn's left and second down the table from him.

Her voice had the depth of age and it came to Shane that she—
in fact, all the aliens here—would be Captains of no lower than
the ninth rank, not to be easily satisfied with quickly dreamed-up
explanations. He wondered what District the speaker commanded.
She was no alien he recognized.

"It is the one I call Shane-beast," said Lyt Ahn. "It is the one
I sent only the day before yesterday to Laa Ehon with communications."

He turned to look at the Commander of the Milanese area.

"I'm still uncertain as to how you think its presence here can
contribute to the discussion," he went on to Laa Ehon.

So, it was Laa Ehon who was responsible for his presence here.
The sick feeling in Shane expanded. His mind raced.

"Order it to speak," Laa Ehon replied to Lyt Ahn.

"Identify yourself and your work," Lyt Ahn said to Shane.

"By your command, immaculate sir," said Shane clearly. "I am
a translator and courier of your staff and have been so for nearly
three of our planet's years."

There was a moment's silence around the table.

"Remarkable," said the female Aalaag on Lyt Ahn's left who
had spoken earlier.

"Exactly," put in Laa Ehon. "Notice how perfectly it speaks
the true language—all of you who are so used to the limited
mouthings of your beasts, when they can be brought to attempt to
communicate in real speech at all."

"It's one of a special, limited corps of the creatures, all of whom have been selected for special ability in this regard," said Lyt Ahn. "I'm still waiting to hear how you think, Laa Ehon, that its presence here can contribute to our discussion."

" 'Special,' " echoed Laa Ehon. The single sound of the word in the Aalaag tongue was completely without emphasis.

"As I said," replied Lyt Ahn.

Laa Ehon turned his head to the First Captain, inclined it in a brief gesture of respect, and then turned back to look around the table at the others there.

"Let's return to the matter at hand, then," Laa Ehon said. "I asked for this meeting because it's been over three local years since our Expedition to this world first sat down upon it. That length of time has now passed and certain signs of adjustments to our presence here, in the attitudes of the local dominant race, that should by now be showing themselves have not done so—"

"The incidence of *yowaragh* among the beasts," interrupted the female who had spoken before, "isn't that much above the norm for such a period. Granted, no two situations on any two acquired worlds are ever the same—"

"Granted exactly that," Laa Ehon interrupted in his turn, "it is not *yowaragh* with which I am primarily concerned, but a general failure on the part of the cattle to keep production levels as expected. Past Expeditions on other worlds have often found such a slump in production in their early years, but always it's turned out in the end to be caused by depression in the beasts at finding themselves governed—even though that governing has resulted for them in a safer, cleaner world, as it has here. On this world, however, it is something much more like silent defiance than depression with which we seem to be dealing. I repeat, it is this, not incidents of *yowaragh*, with which I am concerned."

A cold shiver threatened to emerge from its hiding place in the center of Shane's body and betray itself as a visible tremor. With a great effort, he held it under control, reminding himself that the aliens here were not watching him. For the moment, once more, he had become invisible, in the same sense that the furniture and the walls of the room about them were invisible.

"It is"—Laa Ehon's voice drew Shane's attention back to what the Milanese Commander was saying to the rest of the table—"a matter of hard statistics. May I remind the untarnished and immaculate officers here assembled that the preliminary survey of this world, carried on over several decades of the planet's time, gave no intimation of such an attitude or such a potential falling off of production. The projection gave us instead every reason to believe that the local dominant race should be tamable and useful in a high degree; especially when faced with the alternative of giving up the level of civilization they had so far achieved, and on which, in so many ways, they had become dependent. Remember, they were given a free choice and they chose the merciful alternative."

"I've never been quite sure, Laa Ehon," put in Lyt Ahn from the head of the table, "about the accuracy of the adjective for the alternative. It doesn't seem to me that I can bring to mind a single incidence in which a race of conquered cattle believed the alternative they had chosen to be one deserving of the word 'merciful.' "

"It was clear they understood at the time of takeover, First Captain," said Laa Ehon, "even if your corps of translators had not yet been established. I remember there was no doubt that they understood that their choice was between accepting the true race as their masters, or having all their cities and technology reduced to rubble, leaving them at their original level of stone-chipping savages. How can that alternative not have been merciful when they also clearly understood that we also had the power to eradicate each and every one of them from the face of their planet, but chose not to use it?"

"Well, well," said Lyt Ahn, "perhaps you're right. In any case, let's avoid side issues. Please get to whatever point you were going to make."

"Of course, First Captain," said Laa Ehon.

The words were said mildly enough, but for the first time there exploded in Shane's mind what he suddenly realized he should have sensed from the first: that there was a power struggle going on in this room, at this table.

And the antagonists were Laa Ehon and Lyt Ahn.

As soon as the realization was born in him, his mind was ready with excuses for its not being obvious to him minutes before. Even six weeks ago, he told himself, he would not have recognized the

subtle signals of such a conflict, blinded by an unquestioning assumption that his master's supreme position among the Aalaag was
unquestioned and unassailable. But now those same signals leaped
out at him. After all, the others were theoretically the equals of Lyt
Ahn. They had only elected him to leadership and could remove
him by majority vote, if necessary.

Yes, now that Shane was aware of them, the signs of conflict
were everywhere, in the tone of the voices of those speaking, in the
attitudes with which the various officers sat in their places about
the table—in the very fact Laa Ehon could request that Lyt Ahn
have Shane himself brought here; and then delay this long in giving his full reasons why he had requested it.

Shane had not read the implications of those signals before
this because he had let himself become too secure in his belief in
Lyt Ahn's authority. Only now, he realized how the curious small
freedoms allowed him by the First Captain, as well as the momentary Aalaag-uncharacteristic confidences and transient betrayals of
emotion on the part of that ruling officer should have prepared
him for this moment of understanding, but had not.

Lyt Ahn, he suddenly realized, was vulnerable. The First Captain had to be vulnerable in this sense. Shane had come to understand how the Aalaag lived by tradition and the mores developed
by that tradition. Tradition and those mores had been developed
to put survival of the race first, the individual Aalaag second. They
could not have failed to provide means for removing a Supreme
Commander who became incapable or proved himself inept. Just
how such a procedure would work, Shane as yet had no idea. But
of this he was suddenly, utterly convinced. Lyt Ahn was under attack here and now; and Laa Ehon was either the attacker or the
spearhead of that attack.

As for the others present . . . Shane was reminded of the social
patterns of wolf pack. All those there would follow unquestioningly
the Alpha leader—who was Lyt Ahn—right up until the moment
when his leadership was seriously brought into question. Then, if
that question was not effectively answered, they would turn to follow the questioner and aid him in rending their former leader.
But, if the question was effectively answered, then the questioner
would lose all support from the others—until the next instance of

questioning arose. It was that moment of doubt in which the other Captains would swing about to support the questioner that Lyt Ahn must foresee and avoid.

". . . I have requested this meeting," Laa Ehon was saying, "primarily because of my own difficulties in meeting production estimates with the cattle of my Area; and hoping that my fellow senior officers could suggest ways by which I might improve the situation. I must admit, however, that it begins to appear to me lately that the problems I notice are not restricted to my District alone, but reflect a general problem of attitude which is worldwide—and may even be growing—among the subject beasts."

"It seems to me," broke in a thick-chested male Aalaag halfway down the table on Lyt Ahn's right, "that what you say almost approaches insult to the rest of us. Laa Ehon, are you saying we others have failed to notice something that you've clearly seen?"

"I did not say, or imply, that I had seen anything with particular clearness," said Laa Ehon. "I'm only attempting to point to the importance of something you must all have already noticed— the discrepancy between the original estimates of beast-adjustment to our presence in the time since our landing, and the actuality of that adjustment. I believe there's cause for concern in that discrepancy."

"We've been following the patterns established by successful subjugations on other worlds in the past," said another of the female Aalaag, one whose face showed the hollowness of age beneath her cheekbones. "It is true, as Maa Alyn just said, that each world is different, each race of beasts different—"

"And some, a rare few such races, have even turned out to be failures," said Laa Ehon.

A feeling of shock permeated the conference, perceptible to Shane where it might not have been to any other human, even another one of the special handful of humans employed by Lyt Ahn; the expressions of the Aalaag officers there had not changed at Laa Ehon's last words. There had been only an unnaturally prolonged moment of unnatural silence; but Shane was sure he had read it correctly.

"It seems to me, Laa Ehon," said Lyt Ahn, finally breaking that silence, his heavy voice sounding strangely loud in the room, "that you're holding back something it's in your mind to tell us. Did you ask for this conference merely to air a concern, or have you some special suggestion for us?"

"I have a suggestion," said Laa Ehon.

He turned to look again at Shane, and the eyes of the others at the table followed the changed angle of his gaze.

"I suggest that the situation here—insofar as it reflects a delay in beast-adjustment to our presence—calls for some actions which must necessarily break to some small extent with the patterns of successful subjugation mentioned by Maa Alyn—"

He glanced toward and inclined his head slightly toward the elderly Aalaag female who had recently spoken.

"I suggest," he went on, "that we vary that pattern—oh, in no large way, but experimentally, by attempting to counter this marking on walls we've all been seeing in our Districts, this evidence of some rebellious feeling among a few of these beasts—"

A chill passed through Shane. Clearly now, Laa Ehon was talking of the activities of foolish and doomed Underground groups like Maria's in Milan; and the marking was equally clearly his sketch of the Pilgrim figure.

"Such things," said the thick-chested Aalaag, "are familiar, even expected, during the early years of the subjugation of any race of beasts. Such defacements cease as succeeding generations adapt to serving our purposes, and forget the resentments of their forebears. This is far too soon to see a problem in a few rogue creatures."

"I beg to disagree," said Laa Ehon. "We know that of course the beasts communicate among themselves. This one standing before us now may be aware of more discontent among its race than we suspect—"

"You suggest we put it to the question?" inquired the female Aalaag called Maa Alyn, who had been the first to reply to Laa Ehon; and the chill within Shane became a solid iciness of fear.

"If I may interrupt," said the heavy voice of Lyt Ahn, almost sardonically, "the beast in question is my property. Moreover, it is an extremely valuable beast, as are all the talented small handful like it that I keep and use. I would not agree to its being questioned, and possibly damaged, if not destroyed, without adequate proof of need."

"Of course I don't suggest the damaging of such a valuable

beast, particularly one which is the property of the First Captain, and which I myself have seen to be so useful." Laa Ehon turned back to face Lyt Ahn. "In fact, quite the contrary. I only asked that the beast be produced in order to illustrate a point I think is important to us all. With all due respect, First Captain, I've yet to be convinced that what this beast does can't also be done by at least a large number of its fellow beasts, if not most of them. Certainly, if they have the physical vocal apparatus which can correctly approximate the sounds of the true speech—or even approach those sounds understandably—and their minds have the ability to organize that speech in coherent and usable fashion, one almost has to assume the potential to be a property common to their species as a whole."

"I can only assure you," said Lyt Ahn, with a touch of formality in his voice, "that this isn't the case. There seems to be something more necessary—a conceptual ability, rare among them. At my orders many such cattle were tested and only the handful I use here were found capable on a level with this one you see before you. In fact, this particular beast is the most capable of all those I own. None speak as clearly as this one."

"Far be it from me to differ with you, First Captain and immaculate sir," said Laa Ehon. "You are informed on this subject and I'm not. Nevertheless, as I have pointed out, faced as we are with a problem of adjustment on the part of this species—"

"As you have continued to point out to us, untarnished sir," said the thick-chested Aalaag, "almost to the point of weariness since we first sat down together here."

"If I have overemphasized the point," said Laa Ehon, "I apologize for that to the immaculate persons here assembled. It merely seemed to me that enunciating the point is necessary as a preamble to stating my personal belief; and that is that under the circumstances it's worth exploring even some unorthodox solutions to the problem, since it threatens to diminish worldwide production by these beasts. A production, which I don't need remind any of us, that is important, not merely to us on this planet, but to all our true people, on all the worlds we have taken over; not only for our present survival, but for the protection of the Immaculate People as a whole in case the Inner Race, which stole our home worlds originally, should make another move, this time in this direction."

"As you say," murmured the voice of Lyt Ahn, "you don't need to remind us of that. What exactly is this suggestion of yours, then?"

"Simply," said Laa Ehon, "I propose we depart slightly from past procedure and set up specific beasts as Governors in our respective Districts, holding them responsible for the production of the cattle in their Districts; and allowing them to use other cattle as subsidiary officers to set up their own structures of authority to guarantee such production."

"Absolutely against standard operations!" said the thick-chested officer.

"Indeed," said Maa Alyn, leaning her body slightly forward to stare down the tabletop directly at Laa Ehon, "those who've gone before us have found by hard experience that the best way to handle native cattle is to give them all possible freedoms of custom and society according to that which they have been used to, but never to allow individuals among them power as intermediaries between ourselves and the rest of the beasts. Whenever we've set up intermediaries of their own race like that, between us and them, corruption on the part of their officials has almost invariably occurred. Moreover, resentment is born among the general mass of the cattle; and this, in the end, costs us more than the original gains achieved by using intermediaries."

"I seem to remember something just said, however," answered Laa Ehon, "about each world and each race upon it being a different and unique problem. The recalcitrance shown by the local cattle as a whole on this particular world of ours, as demonstrated by the statistics, is of an order above those shown on any previous world we have taken over. It's true there's been no show of overt antagonism on the part of the general mass of cattle—yet, at least. But on the other hand, it would be hard to show any except our directly used beasts, such as those in the Interior Guard, or this Courier-Translator Corps of the First Captain, who can be said sincerely to have made a full and proper adaptation to us, as their owners and rulers."

"That doesn't mean your proposal is the correct solution to the problem," put in a male Aalaag who had not spoken before. He sat little more than a meter from Shane's right hand, at the extreme far end of the table from Lyt Ahn.

"Of course," answered Laa Ehon. "I recognize the danger of making any large changes—let alone ones that go against established procedure—without having adequate data first. Therefore, what I'm actually suggesting is that certain measures be put into effect on a trial basis."

He tapped the tabletop before him and screens alight with data in the Aalaag script appeared in the surface before each alien there.

"I've had surveys made," he went on, "and you see the results of them on the screens before you. I've also had hard copies delivered to your offices by available underofficers of mine. You'll note my survey turned up three Districts best suited to the putting into effect of temporary test procedures to see if my estimations are correct. Two were islands areas; one being what the cattle formerly called the Japanese Islands, the other called the British Islands. There are advantages of homogeneity and diversity in each case. Of these two, the British Islands seems the better prospect—"

"These islands, of course, are within my District," said Maa Alyn stiffly. "But you also mentioned, I think, three—not two— areas as being possibly suitable as testing areas?"

"I did," said Laa Ehon. "However, the third area, according to my surveys, would be this one surrounding the House of Weapons, and I didn't think we'd want to make any experiments that close to our prime seat of authority, even if the First Captain would give permission . . . as, of course, I would expect to wait upon your permission, Maa Alyn, before proposing to experiment in the area of the British Isles."

There was a murmur around the table that seemed to Shane to express diverse opinions.

"So," went on Laa Ehon, ignoring the sound, "what I would like to suggest, with the concurrence of this Council and everyone concerned, is to set up a temporary governing structure such as I described earlier; monitored directly by us, with a few officers of the true race supervising and working in parallel with each individual beast who is in a position of intermediate authority as Governor."

There was a moment's silence.

"I see a great many difficulties . . . ," began Maa Alyn.

"Frankly, I do myself," said Laa Ehon. "This is unknown territory to all of us. For one thing, as has been pointed out, any tendencies for the beast-governor and his staff to take advantage of their positions over their fellow cattle would be difficult for us to see and check promptly. This, however, it has recently occurred to me—and this was why I asked our First Captain to send for the beast who stands before us now—could be greatly helped by requiring all beast-governor staff to have contact with their supervisory numbers of the true race in the real language."

"But such a condition would require that the beast-governor, to say nothing of his staff, be not merely adequate, but fluent, in the true language—" The thick-chested Aalaag broke off suddenly. "Are you proposing that the First Captain lend his corps of translators to this task? If so, that immaculate sir would of course have to volunteer them for the duty. There is no way in honor this Council could suggest—"

"Not at all—not at all," said Laa Ehon. "I was merely about to suggest that the beasts chosen to be Governor and staff be put first through an intensive course of teaching, to make them fluent in the true language, using as teachers—if the First Captain agrees—some of his translators such as the beast before us—and, of course, provided that my overall suggestion meets with the approval of the Council. The intent would be to produce cattle who would be able to explain themselves clearly to their own kind while still being clear and understandable in their reports to us, thereby making for a strong, plain link of understanding between us and the mass of cattle in general."

"I have already said," put in Lyt Ahn, "that it is only the rare beast that can be taught to speak with such adequate clearness. The evidence for this is in the efforts I mentioned, to which I was put in staffing this particular corps of beast translators and couriers, to which you refer and of which the beast now present is an example."

"It seems to me we lose nothing by trying," said Laa Ehon.

"We stand to lose something by trying," said Lyt Ahn, "if what we are trying is foredoomed to a failure that may make us look ridiculous in the eyes of our beasts."

"Of course," said Laa Ehon, "but at the same time I find it hard to believe that what this handful you use as translators can do, others of their kind can't also be brought to do. The idea flies in the face of logic and reason. What is hypothesized to be missing from those who, according to your experience, are incapable of being taught to use the true language clearly?"

"Exactly what the blocking factor is, we've never been able to discover," answered Lyt Ahn. "Would you care to question the beast we have present?"

"Ask a beast?" said Laa Ehon; and experience made Shane perceptive enough to catch the evidence of shock and surprise, not only in Laa Ehon, but in the others about the table.

"As you have said," replied Lyt Ahn, "it'll do no harm to explore any and all possibilities; and this beast might, indeed, be able to provide you with some information or insight."

"The suggestion is a—" Laa Ehon hesitated, obviously searching for a way of putting what he wanted to say in words that would not fall into the category of insult to his First Captain, but would still express his reaction to such a suggestion. "—far-fetched idea."

"What have you to lose?" said Lyt Ahn; and a murmur of agreement ran around the table. Laa Ehon's expression showed no change, but Shane guessed that the Milanese Commander was seething with anger. He turned and his eyes met Shane's.

"Beast," he said, "can you offer any information as to why a majority of your species cannot be taught to speak the true language as well as you, yourself, have come to speak it?"

"Immaculate sirs and dames—" Shane's voice sounded high-pitched and strange in his own ears after the deep tones of those around the table, "it is a characteristic of our species that during our first few years of life, at a time when our pups are learning how to speak, that their capability for so learning is very great. In the years just before the untarnished race came among us, it had been established that our young could learn as many as four or five different variants of our tongue, simultaneously, but that this facility was lost for most beasts by the time these young were five to eight years of age. Only a fortunate few of us keep that ability; and it's been from such fortunate few that the First Captain's corps of courier-translators has been drawn."

There was a moment of silence—a long moment.

"I don't think I'm completely ready to believe this without independent substantiation," said Laa Ehon. "It's well known that, unlike ourselves, these subject races use the lie quite commonly.

Moreover, even when they do not consciously lie, they can be ignorant or subject to superstitions. The point this beast has just made, that the language-learning ability of his race is largely lost after the first five to eight years of their life may be a lie, the result of ignorance, or simply belief in a superstition that has no real basis in fact."

"I," said Lyt Ahn heavily from the far end of the table, "am inclined to believe this Shane-beast—such being its name. I've had much contact with it over the last two years and always found it truthful, as well as remarkably lacking in ignorance for one of its species, and not superstitious . . . even in the meaning of that term as understood by our own race."

"If what the beast says is true, however," put in Maa Alyn, "there'd be no point in trying your experiment, Laa Ehon."

Laa Ehon turned toward her.

"When were the plans of the untarnished race ever made or changed upon the basis of input from one of the subject species?" he said. "I mean no disrespect to the First Captain; but the fact remains the beast here may be mistaken, or may not know what we are talking about. We should hardly make any decision here on an unsupported faith in its possible correctness."

"True enough," murmured another female, who had not spoken before. "True enough."

"What's been said here does suggest one thing, however," said Laa Ehon, "and that's that we should begin immediately, on the chance that the beast is correct, to expose some of the young beasts to the true language. Then, if this one is correct, we may breed up a generation which takes advantage of this early language ability of theirs, if such actually exists. Certainly, nothing can be lost by trying."

A mutter of agreement sounded around the table, interrupted once more by the heavy voice of Lyt Ahn.

"Am I correct then?" the First Captain said, looking around the table. "At least a number of you are agreeable to taking young beasts into your households and keeping them continually with you?"

There was a silence.

"A nurse-beast, of course," said Laa Ehon, "could be detailed to take care of each young creature. The young one would no more be in the way, then, under such circumstances, than the adult beasts are when we use them for various duties. The only requirement would be that the nurse-beast keep the infant creature in position to overhear as much of our speech as possible."

"I think Laa Ehon may have the answer," Maa Alyn said.

"I can't see any flaws in his reasoning."

"Nor can I—but I am a member of the true race," said Lyt Ahn. "However, perhaps it would be wise for the untarnished and immaculate individuals here assembled to check first with the representative of the beasts we have with us at the moment—in case there might be some unseen flaw in this course. It's always possible that there are pitfalls in it perceptible to one of the species, but which none of us have observed."

Once more, Shane found the eyes of all the Aalaag there turned upon him.

"Beast," said Maa Alyn, "we have been discussing the possibilities of raising some of your young with early exposure to the true language, assuming this theory of yours for early aptitude for the learning of it is a fact—"

"You need not recap, Maa Alyn," interrupted Lyt Ahn. "I can assure you that this Shane-beast has heard and understood all we've been saying."

There was a strange, almost startled silence around the table. Almost as if it had been suggested that there was a spy in their midst. Shane realized that, with the exception of Lyt Ahn, all those there had until that moment not really made the connection between his knowledge of their language and the fact that he would be able not only to follow but to understand all that they had been saying to each other. Comprehension of that fact clashed violently with their habit of ignoring the underraces.

"Well then, Shane-beast, since the First Captain assures us that's your name," said Laa Ehon after a second, "have you any comment on our plan to raise some young of your species where they can overhear the true language being spoken, during their receptive years of growth?"

"Only," answered Shane, "if the immaculate sir pleases, that I believe if you follow the plan as you have outlined it, the result will be that these young of my species will understand Aalaag, but not necessarily be able to speak it."

He hesitated. He had been given no order to volunteer information. To do so would be greatly daring. But that lack was almost immediately remedied.

"Go on, Shane-beast," said Lyt Ahn from the head of the table. "If you have any suggestions to make, make them."

"Yes, make them," said Laa Ehon, his black eyes glittering on Shane. "The most immaculate First Captain seems to feel there may be a flaw in our reasoning which you might have discerned."

"I might merely suggest," said Shane, picking his way as carefully through the alien vocabulary as through a mine field, in search of words which would at once be absolutely truthful but at the same time carry his meaning without implying any pretense to equality, or possible offense, "a danger could lie in the fact that you have the young of my species merely listening to the true language as it's correctly spoken. As I say, it might be that the young referred to would learn to understand, but not to speak, the true language, since they would have no opportunity to speak it."

He hesitated. There was a dangerous silence around the table.

"What I am trying to say," he said, "is that perhaps the untarnished or immaculate individuals dealing with these young beasts should consider speaking to and allowing themselves to be answered by these young ones in the true tongue. It would have to be understood that, being so young still, the small beasts would not yet have acquired a knowledge of polite response, and might inadvertently fail to show the proper respect . . ."

The shock around the table this time was a palpable thing, and the pause was longer than at any time since Shane had entered the room.

"You are suggesting," said Maa Alyn finally, "almost that we treat these young of your species as if they were young of the true race."

"I am afraid that is my meaning, immaculate dame," said Shane.

There was a further silence, broken at last by Maa Alyn.

"The suggestion is disgusting," she said. "Moreover, even more than any other suggestion put forward here today, this flies in the face of all the rules evolved from the experience of the true race with their underspecies over many worlds and many centuries. There must be some other way.''

There was a general noise of concurrence from those gathered around the table.

SEVEN

FOR A MOMENT, SHANE WAS SURE THAT WHILE LAA EHON HAD LOST his point about introducing humans into Aalaag inner households, he had come dangerously close to gathering the leadership of the Council to him. He saw that all eyes had now turned sharply to the First Captain, as if waiting for some magical, alternate solution from him.

Then he spoke; and with the first words, Shane realized his master had seized the most propitious moment for forestalling Laa Ehon's bid for power and regaining his own position of Alpha leader in the Council.

"I fully realize the distastefulness of the suggestion," said Lyt Ahn. "Nonetheless, I'm going to ask all those around this table to take this matter of bringing human young into their households into consideration, and think about it seriously between now and our next meeting. It is true that we're at variance with the prognosis and the estimates originally made for our settling of this particular world; and recently there has been an outbreak of what can only be regarded as an attitude inimical to the true race in these drawings that appear in the cities from time to time—and, I believe, more frequently lately."

"Clearly they are of a beast, wearing what they call 'pilgrim' clothing," said Maa Alyn. She stumbled badly in her attempt to pronounce the English word. "Has the First Captain considered ordering that no such clothing be worn in the future?"

"It's hard to see what that would accomplish at this date, immaculate dame," answered Lyt Ahn. "The symbol has already been established. In fact, we would be dignifying it by paying that much attention to it. The beasts might consider that we actually saw the drawing as a threat—which is what those who put them up undoubtedly want."

"True enough." Maa Alyn nodded.

"On the other hand, something undoubtedly must be done; and the immaculate sir who is our Commander in Milan has at least come up with a proposal, which is more than anyone else has done. I suggest in addition to considering the taking of beast children into our households, we put Laa Ehon's other suggestion to trial. I therefore authorize him—hopefully, Maa Alyn will not object—to set up a trial Governor Unit in the British Isles Area, with whatever beast-staff is necessary; and I will temporarily lend to the Project one of my translators to ensure communication between Governor and the true race to commence with."

"I do not object." It was very nearly a growl from Maa Alyn.

"If I might have this Shane-beast as translator, then—," Laa Ehon was beginning, and Shane chilled. But Lyt Ahn interrupted the other.

"Shane-beast, I have special uses of my own for," said the First Captain. "I will, however, provide you with a beast adequate to your needs. I will permit this much—that Shane-beast be available to you as liaison on this project to keep me informed of its progress and such special advices as you wish to pass on to me by courier."

"If you wish, and as you wish, of course, First Captain," said Laa Ehon smoothly, but his eyes flashed for a moment on Shane with something cold in them.

"That being settled," said Lyt Ahn, "shall we close this meeting?"

There were sounds of agreement in which the Milanese Commander joined. A moment later, Shane found himself outside the room, in the corridor, hurrying to match Lyt Ahn's long-legged strides back toward the First Captain's private offices. Shane had been given no orders to follow. On the other hand he had not been dismissed, so he hurried along, half a pace behind his master, waiting for orders.

These were not forthcoming even after they had passed into the office. Perhaps the orders would have come, but when Lyt Ahn and Shane stepped inside the heavy doors, they found Adtha Or Ain. She was standing once more before the large screen, which was again showing the figure of their son in whatever it was that encased him. She turned as they entered, and spoke to Lyt Ahn.

"It went well—the meeting?"

The First Captain looked at her soberly.

"Not well," he said. "I have broken slightly with custom to allow Laa Ehon to make a trial of interposing native Governors between ourselves and the cattle, using the British Isles as an experimental area."

He turned to Shane.

"I will lend him a translator to help. Shane-beast here, however, will act as my liaison with the Project, and as my own private eyes and ears upon its progress."

His eyes were steady on Shane.

"You understand, Shane-beast?" he said. "You will observe everything carefully, and I will question you equally carefully each time you return from there."

"So, it did not go well," repeated Adtha Or Ain, as much to herself as to the First Captain.

"No, how could you expect it to?" said Lyt Ahn. He seemed to become suddenly conscious of the image in the large screen. "Put that away."

"I need to look at it," responded Adtha Or Ain.

"You mean you need it to use as a club against me," said Lyt Ahn. He made no visible gesture that Shane could see, except a small jerk of the head; but the image disappeared from the screen, leaving it pearly gray, flat and blank.

"It doesn't matter if you take it from me," said Adtha Or Ain. "I can see it just as well with the screen off. I see it night and day. Now, more than ever."

"Why, now more than ever?"

"Because I can't avoid seeing what's coming."

Adtha Or Ain turned from the empty screen to face Lyt Ahn.

"What do you mean?" There was a note of demand in Lyt Ahn's voice.

"No expedition will go to look for my son."

"Why do you say that? I've promised you—," began Lyt Ahn.

"Your promise is only as good as your authority," said Adtha Or Ain, "and your authority . . ."

She did not finish.

"I was elected by the senior officers of this Expedition. I hold my rank by that authority, which remains with me," answered Lyt Ahn in a steady voice, "and that rank can only be taken from me by popular vote of those same officers—which will never happen."

"No," said Adtha Or Ain. "But you could resign it on your own decision, as other First Captains on other New World Expeditions have occasionally done before you."

"I have no intention of resigning."

"What does that matter? You will resign," said Adtha Or Ain. "It's as much a certainty as that screen on the wall before us—the screen you do not want me to use; and once you are no longer First Captain, whoever holds that rank will have no interest in sending an expedition to find out what happened to my son."

"You talk in impossibilities," said Lyt Ahn. "Even if I could spare the officers and materiel for such an expedition now, who would lead it?"

"I would, of course," said Adtha Or Ain. "I'm of fourth rank—or had you forgotten that?"

"I can't spare you," retorted Lyt Ahn. "The consort of the First Captain belongs with the First Captain."

"Particularly when the position of that First Captain may become questionable," said Adtha Or Ain.

"There is no *may*. My position is not questionable, and it is not going to become questionable."

The attitude of Adtha Or Ain changed subtly, although the signs of that change were so slight that only Shane's long experience with her allowed him to note them. But some of the tension went out of her. She seemed to soften and went to Lyt Ahn, close enough to touch him, standing to one side of him and looking very slightly down into his eyes.

"In all things I am your consort," she said in a lower voice. "Also, in all things I am the mother of your son. I must see clearly, even if you refuse to. Laa Ehon intends to replace you as First Captain. Let that, at least, be out in the open between us."

"I have no intention," said Lyt Ahn, "of abandoning the First Captaincy to Laa Ehon, or anyone else."

"Consider the situation honestly," said Adtha Or Ain. "The possibility is there. The possibility means that no expedition would ever be sent to find my son; and not only that, it means I would lose you as well, since I think you would not merely accept duties under another's command."

"That much is true," said Lyt Ahn. "If it were shown to me that I was no longer worthy of the post of First Captain, I would consider myself excess to our effort here and make sure that the Expedition was no longer burdened by my presence."

Shane felt a new sense of shock. This was the first intimation he had had that something like honorable suicide was practiced among the Aalaag. But the fact that there was such a practice made sense. It made very good sense for this race of male and female warriors. He thought of Laa Ehon in the post of First Captain of Earth; and, if anything, his inner fears increased.

His own life was just barely endurable now under Lyt Ahn. It could become literally unbearable under Laa Ehon; and if it became literally unbearable, sooner rather than later a fit of *yowaragh* would take him again and he would do something that would lead to his own end. The best he could hope for under those circumstances would be that it would lead him to a quick and relatively painless end, though, considering his own post, there was less reason to expect it might, than that it would not.

"You may go, Shane-beast," said Lyt Ahn.

Shane went. The next two days were a blur of duties in attendance on Lyt Ahn, during one of the periodic twice-yearly internal inspections of all services housed within the House of Weapons. On the third day, however, he was summoned back to Lyt Ahn's office, where an assistant Aalaag officer handed him a hard copy message to be hand-delivered to Laa Ehon. Laa Ehon, he was told by Lyt Ahn, had already set himself up in London with the staff of the project he had described to the Council.

". . . I deduce from this, small Shane-beast," said Lyt Ahn, once the underofficer had left and they two were alone in the office together, "that the immaculate Commander of Milan had already picked and trained the individuals he would need for his project before mentioning his plan to the Council. You will find his offices already in place and staffed. I would desire you to take particular notice of what kind of humans he uses. You will be in a better position to judge your own kind than myself or any of the true race. Also, report to me anything else you think I might find of interest. I'll want to know, of course, about the general arrangement. I have the plans on record, of course, but that is not the same thing as receiving a direct observation report from a trustworthy pair of eyes."

"I will do as the First Captain orders," said Shane.

"You may go."

"I thank the immaculate sir."

Two hours later, once more in a courier ship and headed toward London, Shane watched from the window beside his seat as the vessel lifted until the world's horizon was a perceptible curve and the sky overhead was black with the airlessness of space. Curiously, now that he was on his way, for the first time he had a moment in which to think, and to his surprise, he found himself strangely clearheaded.

It was remarkable—remarkable almost to the point of bitter humor. After the episode in Milan he had yearned for the sanctuary of his small cubicle in the House of Weapons, as a retreat where he could sit down and take stock of what had happened, and was happening, to him. Then that imagined oasis of peace had ceased to be an oasis, when he found Sylvie Onjin waiting for him there.

In the end, in the House of Weapons, he had found no time— no moment of personal freedom at all in which to try and think of some way of avoiding what seemed to be a greased slide to inevitable self-destruction. Now, here, in the last place he would have looked for it, he had found it. He was on duty. Therefore the eyes of the Aalaag were momentarily off him, and he was free at last to stand back and consider his position, to think his own thoughts for a small while before they touched down in the British Isles.

It was freedom-on-duty. There was no human word for it, but there was an Aalaag one, *alleinen.* It meant the supreme authority and freedom of being under orders—one's own master or mistress within strictly specified limits.

He pronounced it now, silently in his mind—*alleinen*—and smiled grimly to himself. For of course he did not pronounce it correctly, in the strict sense. The truth was he did not speak Aalaag as well as even his masters gave him credit for doing. Certain sounds were physical impossibilities to his human throat and tongue.

The actual truth was that he, like the other successful linguists in Lyt Ahn's corps of courier-translators, cheated in all his Aalaag-speaking. The alien word that had just come to his mind should properly be pronounced with something like a deep bass cough, in the middle syllable; and that deep bass cough, which was so much a part of many Aalaag words, was simply beyond his capabilities. He had always gotten away with pronouncing it without the cough, however, because he was able to hide behind the fact that his voice was too high-pitched to manage the sound. He had learned to pronounce words containing such a sound as the similarly high voice of a very young Aalaag child would say them; and while the ears of such as Lyt Ahn, and even of Laa Ehon and others, consciously noted the lack, they unconsciously excused him for not making it, because of the otherwise excellence of his pronunciation—and because the word as heard resembled what they had heard so many times from the high voices of their own children.

So, in just such a manner, humans had always excused, and with familiarity become ear-blind to, the mispronunciations of their very young children, foreign-born friends and acquaintances. The Aalaag, he thought now, were indeed humanoid. Or humans were Aalaagoid? In any case, similar physical environments on similar worlds during the emergence of both races had shaped them not only physically, but psychologically and emotionally, in remarkably similar ways. Yet they were not really like humans in the fine points—any more than, for example, the average human was nine feet tall. In the fine points, they differed. They had to differ. One race could not catch the other race's disease, for example.

There had been a time when he had dreamed of a plague on Earth that would decimate the aliens but leave the humans untouched—a sudden plague that would wipe out the conquerors before those conquerors had time to pass, to their own kind on other worlds, the word that they were dying. Of course, such a plague had never come; and probably, long ago, the Aalaag had devised medical protections against any such happening. He pulled his mind away from such wool-gathering. The important problem was finding a solution to his own situation. In the silence of the hurtling courier ship, caught between the blue and white of Earth below and the black of space above, he forced himself to face that question squarely, now, while there was a chance.

Leaving Milan, several days earlier, headed back to the House of Weapons, he had faced the fact that *yowaragh* had twice driven him to do foolishly desperate things against the Aalaag regime; and that therefore, it was only a matter of time until he would be drawn back—for powerful emotional reasons with which the last words of Maria had been connected—into contact with this human Resistance, this Underground that he knew, if those in it did not, was doomed to certain discovery and destruction at Aalaag hands.

He had faced the fact then that, given sufficient provocation, he would not be able to help himself; as he had not been able to help himself earlier this year, when the urge had driven him to draw that first Pilgrim symbol. As he had not been able to stop himself when he had seen, through the viewing screen in Laa Ehon's office, Maria awaiting questioning.

Normal human cattle, according to the way the Aalaag thought, were not supposed to have such reactions as *yowaragh*. But for one of them to have it was not a deliberate fault in them when they did, only a weakness in the one afflicted. But of course one who showed signs of it was obviously untrustworthy and sick, and must be disposed of.

Even when they were as valuable as Shane-beast.

Therefore, leaving Milan, he had finally faced the fact that what had happened twice would happen again. Eventually, a third attack of *yowaragh* would catch him in a visible situation where either he had no choice but to appear openly as one of the Resistance people and share their fate, or else he would simply make some wild, personal attack upon one of the aliens, which would result in his death. He did not want either of those fates—as he did not want Maria to share either one of them with him.

Maria had moved him, and the thought of her moved him now, in memory, as nothing had ever done since his mother had died.

But there seemed no way of avoiding one or the other of these probable ends, and it was this dilemma he had carried back with him to the House of Weapons, with a desperate need to study the situation for some kind of solution.

But now, out of nowhere, events pushed by Laa Ehon's ambition seemed to have offered him a possible way out. The basic situation had not changed; but just now, sitting here in his first moment of *alleinen* peace, for the first time, unexpectedly, he saw the glimmer of a hope that there might be something with which he could bargain for his own life and possibly that of Maria as well. It was a wild hope, a crazy hope, but it was nonetheless a hope where before there had been none.

As he considered it, the small glimmer of that hope suddenly expanded into a glare like that from a doorway suddenly opened to outer sunlight. It would be a matter of setting two dragons to destroy each other, of using one evil to eat the other up.

The operative factor behind it all was the fact that even after three years together, the two races did not understand each other. Humans did not understand Aalaag and the Aalaag did not understand humans.

Basically, the obvious solution to Shane's problem was no less than the destruction of Laa Ehon. It was a far-fetched thought, like that of a mouse deciding to destroy a giant. On the face of it, ridiculous; but he had one advantage which even Lyt Ahn—who was even more of a giant than Laa Ehon—did not have. He, Shane, was not restricted by the Aalaag mores. In fact, he was restricted by no mores at all, alien or human; but only by his own need to survive and, if possible, to save Maria.

The operative factor was that the two races did not really understand each other. He repeated that to himself. Humans did not understand the Aalaag, with whom they had never had any real chance to have contact on what might be called a person-to-person basis; and the Aalaag could not possibly understand humans, walled in as they were by the armor of their own alien attitudes and traditions.

This was why what had been planned at the Council table would not work. The theory of bringing up the children in the Aalaag households would never turn out as Laa Ehon and the others hoped. Shane thought of the human babies to be used this way and his stomach curled up inside him. He remembered his own loveless upbringing and the difference in human and alien emotional responses.

The bitter part of it would be that the scheme would actually seem to work at first, as the human youngsters began to pick up the Aalaag tongue and get responses that would seem at least friendly, if not loving, from these large creatures who sheltered and fed them. The children would respond automatically with affection, which would last up until that devastating moment when they were rebuked by the large creatures for not realizing that they were only beasts. In that discovery, as the children matured and began to have minds of their own, was more fertile ground for *yowaragh* than in anything else the Aalaag had done on Earth since their arrival; and it would be *yowaragh* by humans who knew the overlords, and the weaknesses of those overlords, better than these had ever been known before by any of the underraces.

For a similar reason, Laa Ehon's plan to set up human Governors would not work. The Aalaag, who lived under unquestioned authority among themselves, could never really understand that a human Governor would be no more palatable to most other humans than an alien one would—perhaps even less so. The Governor would simply be included in the detestation in which the mass of humanity already held all servants of the Aalaag, such as the Interior Guards and translators like Shane, himself. Noncooperation would be the order of the day, automatically. Unless . . .

It was in exactly this area that he might be able to do something—at least for himself and Maria. For the rest—he owed nothing to the Resistance groups, he told himself once more. They had no hope of success—no hope at all, though it would be impossible to tell them that. Inevitably they would be caught and executed by the Aalaag. He shuddered, thinking of what would happen to them. But he reminded himself that that happening was unavoidable, no matter what he might do or not do. Meanwhile, they could be the instrument which would save him; and, possibly even more important, aid Maria and himself, in destroying Laa Ehon, at one and the same time.

He looked more closely at the plan that had just begun to take shape in his mind.

It would be risky. It would necessitate his achieving some sort of dominance over the humans Laa Ehon had picked to make his Governors' Project work. At the same time, he would have to appear to lend his aid to the Resistance groups; and without letting Lyt Ahn suspect. For Lyt Ahn would never countenance what Shane was planning, although he might well concur with what Shane had done, once Laa Ehon had been frustrated as a result of the translator's efforts.

It would also be necessary for Shane to keep his identity as secret as possible from the Resistance people themselves. Those few who had captured him in Milan already had some idea of who he was. But if it could be done, they should remain the only ones. That would be difficult because he would have to do more than just join them; he would have to effectively take charge of their movement, as well as dominating the humans in Laa Ehon's plan.

This could be possible with the Resistance people, however, since he knew more about their enemy than they did themselves. His scheme itself was simple in the extreme. It would merely be a matter of coordinating all the Resistance groups—and there must be some in at least every large city and they must know each other, already, even if they were not already part of one overall organization. With their help he could cause an apparent cooperation to take place with the governorship organizations by the ordinary human public; so that to the Aalaag in general these would seem to be an unqualified success. While, at the same time, the organization of the Resistance into a single coordinating unit could appear to the humans involved to make possible a plan for a worldwide uprising against the aliens everywhere; which was what people everywhere dreamed of.

Only he, of course, would know that such a revolt could stand no chance of success. In fact, it would almost certainly never reach the point of taking place. Long before it was ready to explode, he would have pulled the plug of the cooperation that had been given the Governors; and Laa Ehon's plan—in which by this time the Aalaag would have invested deeply—would reveal itself as a total failure. For which Laa Ehon could only take the blame.

And, if some sort of honorable suicide was indeed part of the Aalaag tradition, Laa Ehon might thereupon remove himself. Even if he did not, his power within the Council and his presence as a threat to succeed Lyt Ahn would be destroyed. Shane could then allow Lyt Ahn to understand how at least part of all this was due to Shane's efforts, and with luck a grateful First Captain would aid him in bringing Maria into the Courier-Translator Corps, or some similar position of relative safety.

Meanwhile, of course, the other Resistance members, who by this time would have exposed themselves, or become easily identifiable, would be rounded up and disposed of by the other Aalaag. Shane set his thoughts against the mental picture of what that would mean, reminding himself fiercely that he had a right to think

8

of his own survival first; and, again, that there had never been any
hope for such fools, in any case.

It was a purely selfish and heartless plan. It had no justification
beyond the fact that its success might save him—and Maria. Just at
the moment he was not sure just how her rescue should be worked;
but the beginnings of some ideas were working in the back of his
mind, all of them dependent upon the claim he would have on Lyt
Ahn's good graces after Laa Ehon was taken care of.

One immediately necessary matter would be to get the Resistance's agreement to Maria's helping him personally. Later on,
therefore, to Lyt Ahn, he could credit part of his success to her
association with him, which he would make appear to be a willing
and informed one.

The strange thing, he found himself thinking, was that he
should be contemplating doing what he had earlier been deathly
afraid of doing—associating with those who were subversive to the
aliens. The equation of life and death for him in any association
like that had not changed; and yet he found himself now feeling
good, almost buoyant, about the plans he had just considered. He
felt in fact more alive than he had felt since word had first come
of the Aalaag landings on Earth.

A feeling very close to that of triumph possessed him. He was
still engrossed in it when a slight jolt announced the landing of the
aircraft.

"Out, beast!" said the pilot.

He gathered up his small travel bag and left the ship to find
himself in the special airport for Aalaag use only which the aliens
had blasted out of the heart of London. Walking out of here even
in the business suit he was wearing could attract unwelcome attention to him. He went looking for the human in charge of Maintenance and Supply, and found him—a young man with a lower
Alabama accent, a round, almost childish face, but a steady, cold
stare that would have done credit to an Aalaag.

"I'm on special duty for the First Captain," said Shane, showing his credentials as a courier-translator. "I'll need to get out of
here without being seen. Have you got some kind of a closed car
or truck just about to leave I could ride in, out of sight?"

The M. and S. Head considered him for a moment.

"We've got a load of dirty laundry going out in a van," he said.

"You can ride with that. Where you want to go to? I can tell the driver."

"Just have him drop me where I ask him to," said Shane.

"Fine. You come along with me, now."

"This'll do," said Shane to the driver of the laundry van some ten minutes later. The van stopped, he got out, and watched it out of sight. Then he walked two blocks and hailed the first open taxi that came along.

"Sheldon Arms Hotel," he said to its driver. "Do you know where that is?"

"I know it," said the driver, putting his cab in movement. The hotel, in fact, was less than five minutes away.

"Wait for me," said Shane, giving the driver a couple of ten-pound notes. "I've got to register, but as soon as I do that I've got an errand to run, then back here again."

"Right." The tone of the driver's voice had become a good deal more friendly with the appearance of the ten-pound notes. Shane went inside.

"Shane Evert," said Shane to the desk clerk. The amount of money he slid unobtrusively across the desk to the clerk was considerably more than he had given the taxi driver. "I don't have a reservation, but I've been here once before. I'm particularly fond of Room 221. Do you suppose I could have that again?"

The clerk glanced at the money on the desk. Shane added another bill.

"I think that could be arranged, sir," said the clerk, sweeping up the money with a gesture that suggested he was brushing some small untidiness off the desktop. "It'll take a few minutes, perhaps twenty minutes. . . ."

"Good," said Shane, turning away. "I've got to go out for a bit anyway. I'll register now, but bring my luggage back when I come again."

"Of course, sir."

Shane signed the registration book and returned to the waiting cab.

"There's something I need to buy," he told the driver.

They sought out a shop selling secondhand clothing.

"I need a two-color pilgrim's robe," Shane told the small, middle-aged man behind the counter at the store. "Blue on one side, brown on the other." He opened his hand over the counter-top and this time it was a pair of gold oblongs he laid down, the currency in which the Corps members and those of a few others were paid by the Aalaag. He saw the eyes of the little man fasten on them.

"I'll have to take them into the back room to make change," he said to Shane.

"Of course," said Shane.

Such gold tabs saw their way into ordinary human monetary channels only through the hands of those who worked for the aliens or those who dealt in the black market that sold special luxuries to those who so worked. The word of his purchase would reach local Resistance headquarters quickly.

The small man disappeared through a door behind the counter. He was gone perhaps four or five minutes, to return with a robe fitting Shane's description and a handful of notes and coins.

"Will that do, sir?" he said, putting this all on the counter in front of Shane.

"Perfectly," said Shane. "Wrap the robe for me, will you? Could you deliver it to Room 221 at the Sheldon Arms Hotel this afternoon for me?"

"It'd be a pleasure, sir."

Shane left the shop and regained the taxi.

"Back to the Sheldon Arms," he told the driver. In his room at the hotel, which showed some sign of having been hastily cleared of a previous occupant, Shane ordered up a meal, ate, and then lay on the bed, thinking and waiting.

It was only a little over two hours before there was a knock at the door of his room.

"Delivery for you, sir," said a voice beyond the door.

He was on his feet instantly and as silently as he was able to move. He stepped across to the darkest corner of the room and stood there with his back to the window. He pulled up his pilgrim's hood over his head, drawing the sides of the hood in, so that his face was hidden in deep shadow. He said nothing.

He had expected at least one more knock at the door, but there was a sudden splintering crash as the lock gave and two very large men erupted into the room. They stared at the empty bed and around them, for a moment plainly not identifying him as a human figure in his stillness and the shadow of the corner. In that moment a third man moved into the room from behind them. It was the man called Peter who spoke Italian with an English accent and who had been in charge of the group that had kidnapped Shane in Milan.

"I *thought* this was your home ground," Shane said to him.

At the sound of Shane's voice they saw him. Before they could move, he went on. "I am the Pilgrim. I'll talk to you, Peter, and you only. Get the others out."

There was a moment in which it seemed anything might happen. The two large men glanced back at Peter.

"All right," said Peter, after a moment's hesitation. "Outside, both of you, and put the door back in place. But wait right outside it, there."

He looked directly at Shane.

"But what you've got to say better be worthwhile," he added.

"It is," said Shane. "I'm going to help you. I know the Aalaag and what their weaknesses are. I can tell you how to fight them." Having said this much, the rest came easily to his lips. "I may even be able to tell you how to get rid of them altogether. But you're the only one who ought to hear what I've got to say, or know who I am."

Peter stared at him for a long, blank-faced moment. Then he turned to the two men, who were lifting the door back into place in its opening.

"On second thought, wait down the hall," he said. "That's an order."

He turned back and smiled at Shane. It was a smile of pure relief.

"It's good to have you with us," he said. "You don't know how good it is."

EIGHT

THERE WERE FOURTEEN OF THEM, GATHERED IN THE SMALL ROOM OF an empty warehouse about a table made of two smaller tables pushed together.

They were the greater London area Resistance leaders, according to what the man Shane knew only as Peter had claimed. Privately, Shane had doubts about that. Peter himself was obviously in command here, as he had been the obvious dominant figure—even though he did not appear to be the local leader—of the group in Milan, Italy that had kidnapped Shane after he had rescued Maria from the Aalaag. Maria—whom he somehow hoped to save from exactly this sort of thing—wasn't there.

The light in this room came not from electricity provided by a bicycle generator, but from kerosene lamps, spaced on a long metal worktable, lamps whose mantles hissed and glowed whitely inside their glass chimneys. The illumination they gave seemed hardly less than the same number of hundred watt electric bulbs would have given, and Shane drew the edges of the cowl to his cloak close together before his face.

The rest, even Peter, were already seated in chairs at the table. Shane remained the only one standing in the room. He had never done this sort of thing before in his life and he was hollow within at the moment with the empty sense of isolation that had been with him as long as he had been aware of other people.

"It's up to you to convince them," Peter had said while driving them both to this meeting.

But this sort of confrontation was not what he was good at. He knew so, instinctively. His way had always been to avoid crowds and gatherings. He was a loner; and while he could be effective in con-versation or even argument, one on one, he had never had the desire to address a number of people at once. It was ironic, to be in this position, given his instinct always to avoid groups and or-ganizations. Events had seemed to contrive to draw him away from that instinct ever since the moment he had drawn the figure of the Pilgrim on the wall in Aalborg.

His only hope now, he thought, looking at their faces, was to be himself, let the words in him come as they would, and not try to hide his sense of being different. He could never be one of them, so there was no point in trying. It had never worked all through the years of his boyhood and his school days; and it would not work now. Perhaps at least some of them, too, would know what it was to be different and apart from the general mass of people everywhere.

". . . We're perfectly safe here," Peter was saying, speaking from his own chair at the far end of the makeshift conference table, looking down its long length at Shane, who stood at the other end. "You can take off that hood now, and let the rest of them here have a look at you. And sit down."

"No," said Shane.

The negative had been reflexive—almost instinctive in its pro-tectiveness. But the moment it left his lips he had no doubt about why he had said it.

He saw them all staring at him.

"If I could find some way of doing it," he said, speaking spe-cifically and directly to Peter as he remained standing, "I'd erase what I look like from your memory, too. I know the Aalaag better than any of you ever will. You can either believe that or not—that's up to you. If you believe it, you'll realize you've got everything to gain by dealing with me; but I've got everything to lose if one of you ends up being able to identify me, later on. So you'll deal with me with my face hidden, or not at all."

"What is it we're going to do together, then?" asked Peter. "That's what we're all waiting to hear."

Seated at the far end of the table, Peter looked an unlikely person to hold authority over these others around him, some of whom had reached into the second half of life's century and many of whom looked more like leaders than he did. He was boyishly

113

round-faced and round-skulled, with his short, straight blond hair on top of the skull. His appearance was that of a man in no more than his early twenties, but he must be older than that to have the authority he appeared to have over these people and those Shane had seen him with in Milan.

"I'm going to give you a plan for getting rid of the Aalaag," Shane answered. "The same thing you and others like you have been trying to do ever since the aliens landed, but without succeeding in anything much more than sitting around and talking about it, or marking on walls—"

There was a murmur that was half a growl from those around the table. Their faces were not friendly.

"Like it or not, it's a fact," Shane said. "I repeat, I know the Aalaag. With my help you've got some hope. Without me, you've got no more than you ever had—and that's nothing at all. Your attitude here isn't encouraging. I did a lot of thinking before I decided to get back in touch with you people."

He paused. None of them said anything.

"I want you to be completely clear about this," he said. "I can help you—but I'm putting my own life on the line to do it. I know. The rest of you are all doing that, too. But you've made your choice. For me to work with you means my taking chances none of you have to take; and whether I do that depends on you. It depends, in fact, on whether we can agree to work together on my terms."

He paused again.

"You could be a spy for the aliens," said a man in his forties with a heavy jaw, halfway down the table to Shane's left. Shane laughed; and he did not have to exaggerate the bitterness of that laughter. It came up like an acid bubble from his stomach into his throat.

"Now, there's a perfect example of why you've never succeeded in doing anything large against the Aalaag by yourselves, and never will," he said. "That's exactly the attitude that leaves you helpless where they're concerned. You can't help thinking of yourself as equal to them, with the only difference between you and them the fact that they've got a massive edge in technology over anything we humans ever came up with. You think of them basically as equals under their armor and without their weapons—"

"Well, aren't they?" interrupted the man with the heavy jaw. "Those things; and a little more height and some extra muscle. That's all the difference; and they act like they're gods and we're dirt!"

"Maybe." Shane shook his head. "The point isn't," he said, "whether you're actually their equals or not, but that you think you are. As a result, you take it for granted they think of you the same way; which is so far from their way of thinking that they'd have trouble believing you could imagine something like that."

He paused. Was he getting through to them at all? He went on.

"To you," he said, "it might make sense to send a spy among troublemakers of a subjugated race. To them . . . would you send a laboratory mouse to spy upon other mice? Can a mouse be a spy? And if it could, what could it report back to you, other than that others of its own kind were there in the walls—and you knew that already. Sooner or later, with poison and traps, you'll get rid of them anyway; so why this nonsense of sending a beast just like them to 'spy' on them?"

Shane stopped speaking. The others around the table stared back at him and said nothing for a long moment. Then Peter spoke.

"My apologies, fellow Resistance fighters," he said. "I brought you here to meet this man who calls himself Pilgrim because I thought he could be useful to our own efforts. I still think so. Very useful. But I had no idea he'd start out by insulting us. In fact, I don't see the reason and the sense of his doing it, even now. Why, Pilgrim?"

"Because there's no use in our talking unless I can get through to you on a level where your minds have been closed from the start," Shane answered. "You've got to face some facts and get rid of some illusions; and the first of those is the dream that someday you're going to be able to fight them and beat them. Get it into your heads that if there was only one Aalaag on Earth, short of surrounding him or her with a wall of living human flesh renewed as fast as the alien killed those who made it up, you couldn't even contain him, let alone conquer him."

"Even if there was only one, it'd be worth doing," shouted a small man with a face like a dried apple, farther down the table than the heavy-jawed man.

"That's right," said a thick-bodied, thick-faced woman.

"He'd have to run out of power for his weapons sooner or later."

"Do you know he'd run out—or do you just assume that?" retorted Shane. "You see? That's a human-type assumption. I've lived with the Aalaag for over two years and I'll tell you I wouldn't take it for granted that he'd run out of *anything*. No, in fact, what I'd assume would be that his power would last beyond the point where the last person on Earth was dead."

"What are you trying to tell us then?" said the heavy-jawed man. "That we can't win?"

"Not in any face-to-face, stand-up fight with them, no. Never," said Shane. "You can never destroy the Aalaag. But, what you might be able to do is trick them into leaving this planet and going some-place else."

"Go someplace else? Go where?" The female voice came from close to Shane on his right, and by the time he had pulled his gaze back from the heavy-jawed man, there was no way he could tell which of the three women seated close to him on that side of the table had spoken.

"Who knows?" Shane said. "Somewhere where they'd find an-other race to subjugate, one more profitable to own than we are."

The heavy-jawed man snorted and leaned back in his chair, tilting it on its two back legs.

"Just ask them to go away, I suppose?" he said.

"No," said Shane. "A lot more than that. There'll be a lot more to do to get that done, and work a lot more difficult and a lot more painful than that."

He paused and looked down the table at each in turn.

"Tell me this, then," he said slowly. "You've been ready to give your lives to fight the Aalaag if some kind of workable plan could be made. Are you still ready to do that?"

There was silence, but the expressions on the faces were answer enough.

"All right," Shane said. "Now I come along. All I have to offer is something that might not work. But it also might work—which is more than you or anyone you know has been able to come up with in two and a half years or more. And I tell you that to get a chance to use it you have to take me as I am—without questions about myself—and believe what I tell you about the Aalaag. Isn't it worth your accepting that for the chance—even just the chance—of doing what you've been trying to do so long without success?"

Silence, then the voice of the heavy-jawed man.

"You've got to give us some reason to go along with you."

"All right," said Shane. "I'll say this much. You haven't been able to fight the Aalaag on your own. But if you listen to me I think I can show you how to make them fight themselves, by taking advantage of the way they really are, and what they really think."

No one said anything.

"Well?" asked Shane after a moment. "Does that give you reason enough to try to believe what I'll tell you?"

Peter also said nothing, at the far end of the table. He only sat, a little sideways in his chair as if his legs were crossed to one side, just clear of the overhang. He seemed, not so much to be smiling, as to be about to smile.

"All right," said the heavy-jawed man at last. "I'll listen. If I can believe you, I'll go with you."

Slowly, one by one, the mutter of an assent sounded about the table.

"Anyone still not ready to listen and give me credit for knowing what I'm talking about?" asked Shane.

No one moved or spoke.

"All right," said Shane. "Then I'll go back to what I said in the beginning. From the start you've thought of the Aalaag as equals and assumed they thought of you as equals. They don't. They call you beasts, and they not only don't think of you as anything but beasts, they'd find it unbelievable to think of you as anything else. Now, contrary to what you believe, the things that make them think that way aren't their superiority in weapons and armor at all—they take those things for granted, as the sort of advantage that superior beings like themselves would naturally have."

He paused, smiling.

"Don't any of you have any idea why they think so little of you? So little, in fact, that they've never really made a serious effort to get rid of those like you, here, who meet to plan how you'd fight against them?''

"Now wait a minute," said the thick-bodied woman, "you can't tell us they aren't out to get rid of us Resistance people!"

"Of course they are, when they stumble across you marking on a wall or breaking one of their laws. But they know—which you don't—that there's no way you can do them any real harm. So most of your secrecy and your organizational mumbo-jumbo isn't necessary. The Aalaag destroy you when they find you, not because they think of you as dangerous, but because they consider anyone who doesn't obey the law as insane; and insane animals should be destroyed before they infect others of their kind. That's all.''

He paused to give them another chance to object. No one spoke up.

"Let's get back then to why the Aalaag simply take it for granted you're an inferior race of beasts. All the evidence, from their point of view, points to that. Before they came, crime was common in all parts of our race. To an Aalaag, any crime—even the telling of the smallest lie—is unthinkable. Do you know why?''

"We don't know they don't lie," put in Peter.

"I do; and you'd better take my word for it I'm right," said Shane. "To lie, to disobey an order, to do anything that's been established as forbidden is unthinkable to them, because it would be contrary to the survival of their race. And it's that survival, not the survival of any individual one of them, that's the first concern of each one of them. Where we humans have an instinct for individual self-preservation, they've got a reflex for race-preservation.''

"You call ours an instinct, theirs a reflex?" said Peter.

"That's right. Because theirs is something they've only developed over the last few thousands of years in order to survive. I think there was probably a time when they didn't have it. But that was before they were driven from their own worlds by some race with either numbers or powers superior even to theirs.''

"Who were they?" asked the heavy-jawed man.

"I don't know," answered Shane. "I haven't been able to learn the whole story. I get the impression they were more like a swarm of bees than an animal-type race. But that's just an impression. From what I can gather, the Aalaag fought back hard at that time, with pretty much the weapons they have now—but they lost, because at that time they were a people as varied in occupation as we are. Only a handful of them then were trained fighters—though they all had to fight before they were finally forced to turn and run for it. They've been something like interstellar gypsies ever since; and in that process they've given up every profession but one. Now, every individual among them's a fighter, and as a race they live under the fear of being followed and attacked again by whoever it was that drove them from their home worlds in the first place."

"Given this as all true," said Peter, "how does knowing it help us? It seems to me you've just made a case for the aliens being less vulnerable, rather than more."

"No," said Shane, "because in making themselves over into a race in which everyone was a warrior, they were left without people to fill the support jobs and positions. They solved that problem by finding and taking over worlds, each of which had a race which had developed some technology but was not by Aalaag terms 'civilized.' Our world, for example. These subject races filled the support vacuum. They could be made to supply the needs not only of themselves, but of a certain number of Aalaag overlords. That way the problem was solved."

"As Peter says," spoke up the female voice Shane had failed to identify before—he turned his head quickly enough this time to see her now, still speaking. She was a tall, dark-haired young woman only three chairs from him on his right. "How does that make them vulnerable?"

"Why," said Shane, "because to control a subjugated race like ours and make it produce for them means that a large proportion of the Aalaag here have to spend all or most of their time making sure the individuals of that race do what needs to be done, from the Aalaag point of view. If you like—call it an economics of power. So much in the way of supplies for the Aalaag requires so much time and effort spent in maintaining control over us."

"But what can we do about it?" asked the heavy-jawed man.

"Make it too expensive to maintain that control," said Shane.

"How?"

Shane drew a deep breath.

"That," he said, "is what I'll tell you only after I'm sure you understand the Aalaag and me; and after a worldwide structure of Resistance members has been set up, so that we can act all together and at the same time—as we'll have to when the time comes. What I've just told you is all I'll tell you for now.''

"You can't leave us like that,'' said the thick-bodied woman. "You've still given us no proof of any kind, no real reason to believe you.''

Shane hesitated.

"All right,'' he said. "I'll tell you this much that you don't know. Right now, in this city, a pilot program is being set up by the Aalaag, which involves the establishment of a human Governor for Britain, Ireland and the islands around them; a Governor who with his staff will be responsible to the Aalaag for all production from this Area, and who'll have the powers of the Aalaag behind him to enforce any rules or laws he cares to make. I'll be heading directly to that Governor's new headquarters now, when I leave you.''

There was a long silence as those around the table stared at each other.

"It'll never get off the ground,'' said the heavy-jawed man. "We'll make sure nothing about that Governor arrangement works.''

"No, you won't,'' Shane said. "Just the opposite. You'll cooperate in every way—if you're going to be part of what I have in mind. What we want to do is gain control of that organization—which we can do, because it's to be human-staffed—and use it, not destroy it. For now, if you'll just get used to believing the fact that you can never win by going against the Aalaag in any head-on fashion, we'll have taken the first step together. I'll leave you to think that over for now. Remember, the only way is to make the Aalaag defeat themselves.''

Shane stopped talking and took a step back from the table.

"Peter,'' he said, looking directly down at the other man, "you and I need to talk, privately.''

Peter was already on his feet and coming toward him, up around the table, behind those there, who were also on their feet but had fallen into a buzz of conversations with their near neighbors.

"Have you got a vehicle of some kind?'' Shane asked quietly as the other came up to him.

"My car's outside. Yes,'' said Peter. He grinned. "And I've not only got a permit to have it on the streets, but a full tank of gas."

"Then you can drive me where I need to go and we can talk on the way," said Shane. "I've got to report in at this Governor Unit I told everyone about. I'll give you the address."

Once in the car and proceeding down streets that were already beginning to shine oilily under a fresh, light rain, Shane looked at Peter's profile outlined against the street-lit, wet window beside him.

"Well?" Shane asked. "Did I convince them?"

"You left them with damned little choice," said Peter. "As for telling them anything specific, you didn't."

"What do you expect, when you introduce me to a room full of people who work for you and tell me they're the heads of independent cells in the Resistance?" Shane replied.

"And you didn't think they were?" Peter's tone was guarded.

"I knew what they weren't. First, they all gave in to you and waited for you to lead things; secondly, you couldn't get together a group of your equals that quickly—to listen to someone they knew nothing about and about whom you hardly knew more."

"I might," murmured Peter, "be somewhat more important than you think, in certain circles."

"Even if you were—but let's not waste time on that," said Shane. "I've got two things to talk to you about. What other languages does Maria—that girl in Milan I saved—speak besides her native Italian?"

Peter glanced sharply at him.

"I don't know certainly," he said slowly. "What most educated Europeans speak, I'd expect. English, with an accent. In her case also almost certainly good French, German of God-knows-what quality, and as many other languages as well or as badly as may be. Why?"

"I'm going to need someone to work with me who's a Resistance member, and it has to be one of those who've already seen my face, to keep the number knowing it down to as few as possible; and I'm going to try to get her accepted into the Courier-Translator Corps as someone with an unusual aptitude for language. Of all those who got a look at my face in Milan only you and she fit the bill, and I'll give you this much credit—you're too important to play second fiddle to me."

"Thank you oh so very much," murmured Peter, guiding the small car expertly down the almost deserted, but slippery wet streets. "I don't know that Milan would want to let her go. For that matter, I don't know if she'd be willing to work with you."

"She'd better and they'd better," said Shane. "Now, on this other matter. In addition to someone to work directly with me, I'm going to need a liaison to the Resistance's Supreme Council, or whatever it'll end up being called. I want you for that."

"Thank you again."

"Don't bother. You just happened to be the first Resistance leader I met; and you've got the same qualification Maria has, you've already seen what I look like. But I eventually want you to run that particular Supreme Council, or whatever, so that between the two of us, you and I, we can make decisions and act on them without putting everything to a vote and getting bogged down in argument over details."

"I see," said Peter. Almost absentmindedly, he wheeled the car smoothly around a corner.

Silently watching the other man out of the corner of his eyes, Shane felt a sense of relief. He had guessed that Peter was ambitious. His reaction now seemed to support that idea.

"The first thing I'll need you to do," said Shane, "is to get together a meeting of all those in other nations who could be called leaders of the Resistance—"

Something very close to a splutter from Peter interrupted him.

"Are you insane?" Peter exploded. "Do you think you've stumbled onto a worldwide organization already set up on strict military lines? Resistance is a game anyone can play—"

"I know what I've stumbled onto," Shane interrupted. "But something pretty close to that sort of organization is what I'm going to need before I'm done; and you're going to help me get it. Now, if there's no such thing as national leaders to the Resistance groups here and across Europe, who is available, if we try to get a congregation of European leaders together? Because that's what we're going to need."

"For what?"

"Eventually, for putting the unified pressure on the Aalaag that'll be needed to get them to leave this world."

"You know," said Peter, glancing sideways at him for a second, "you're talking nonsense. It may have been all right for those people back there. But you've got to tell me something to convince me first you aren't either mad or some kind of con man."

"That's a ridiculous statement," said Shane. "It implies a question you'd already answered for yourself when you asked me to get in touch with you again, back in Milan—nevermind the fact that just now I was able to tell you and the others about something happening in your own territory that you ought to have known about, but didn't—all about the new Governor set-up. I'm your pipeline to Aalaag Headquarters—something so rare and valuable to you, you never even dreamed of having anything like it. You know it. I know it. That's why you'll take me on my terms or not at all. Besides, you're not unintelligent. When I tell you that I act and talk this way to you because I understand the Aalaag a few orders of magnitude better than any of the rest of you, you ought to be able to see why I'm telling the truth—and take me on faith until you've got some further evidence to judge me by."

"But you want us all to follow you blindly," said Peter.

"That's right. It's the only safe way for me; so those are my terms, to start off with at least," answered Shane, losing patience. "Now look, if there's nothing resembling an international organization of the Resistance, you still must know people of authority on the Continent I could talk to. Am I right, or wrong?"

"Well," said Peter slowly. "Every large city has its important Resistance figure. Anna ten Drinke in Amsterdam, Albert Desoules in Paris, and so forth. We can invite them to get together with us, but—"

"Good. You take care of that," said Shane. "I want them here for a meeting on a date no more than two weeks from now."

"Two weeks! It'll take most of a week just to contact them. It can't be done in as short a time as that—"

"It better," said Shane grimly. "I'm only supposed to be here for three weeks; and even at that something could come up that would make the First Captain call me back early. If there's to be any margin for unavoidable delays, two weeks is the most we can give any of them to get here."

"Next," said Peter, equally grimly, "who says they'll come?

There's no reason for any of them to risk the trip. They don't know you from Adam. I can invite them, but if any show up, it'll be a miracle."

"It's up to you to convince them to come," said Shane. "If they're the kind of people to deserve their reputations, they ought to be smart enough to see the advantages of having someone like me on their side—just as you did. I think if you tell them about how I can get them information from Aalaag Headquarters—but don't tell them anything else you know or think you've guessed about me, if you don't mind—I think you can get some of them here. Those who don't come will just have to regret that they didn't and hope to hop on the bandwagon later on. Now, about Maria, how soon can you get her here?"

Peter did not answer immediately.

"I don't think you really need her," he said finally.

"As it happens, I do," said Shane. "My needing her isn't a debatable point."

"Well," said Peter, "I can't just whistle and get her here. The situation in her case is the same as it is with the leader types you want me to call in. I can send her a message, say you want her and ask her to come. I don't know that she'll want to come. I don't know that her people in Milan are going to approve of her coming. It'll take three days at least to get a message to her, too. We don't trust the mails—"

"No, you wouldn't," said Shane wearily. "For what it's worth, the mails are as safe as any courier's pouch. The Aalaag haven't the time or the interest—you remember my telling your people just now about the mice in the walls—to monitor all the mail that's written in the hope of catching a few Resistance people or other insane beasts. But, do it your way."

"We pass messages from hand to hand, then to small boats crossing the Channel to the Continent and so on," said Peter with a touch of stubbornness in his voice. "At any rate it'll take three days."

"Just so she comes; and you better do your best to get her here," said Shane. "I've got to have her. We've got to have her—"

"We're here," interrupted Peter, putting his foot on the brake of the car.

"Keep going!" said Shane swiftly. He glanced at the structure Peter had indicated with the wave of one hand. It was a large, brick building, with an entrance to what seemed a courtyard through which could be seen some ordinary human vehicles parked. "Turn a corner and drop me off out of sight, so I can walk back."

"What's up?" demanded Peter, accelerating nonetheless. "The most they can guess if they see you is that you came here in one of the free-lance cabs. There's lots of those nowadays. Anybody with the gas to burn who needs money for something on the black market—"

"It's not me, it's you," said Shane. "One of the Interior Guardsmen they'll be sure to have there might just be watching; and he just might be someone who recognizes you as a member of the Resistance."

"Me?" Peter hooted. "If one of those bastards in the Interior Guard'd suspected me, I'd have been picked up by them months ago—years ago."

"There's another example of ignorance of how the Aalaag, and those who serve them, work," said Shane. "Any Interior Guardsman with any experience makes it a point to find someone arrestable and then keep that information tucked away until he needs it, either to gain points with his superiors or to balance off some infringement of the rules they've caught him at. It doesn't always pay off for them, but most older Guardsmen have the equivalent of a whole pocketful of bits of information like that. You can let me out here."

They were around the corner. Peter pulled the car to a halt beside the wet curb. Shane got out.

"Remember," he said before closing the car door, "get that message to Maria off right now, and by the fastest way you know."

"I'll do it," answered Peter. "But as I told you, it's the most I can do."

"Just do your part—and hope, for your sake as well as mine, and for everyone else's, that she's here in time for me to take back to Aalaag Headquarters with me," said Shane. He pulled his staff from the rear seat where he had put it on getting into the car, jerked his hood more fully over his head and ran through the still falling light rain toward the corner.

He turned in at the courtyard entrance, finding some small

shelter from the rain, and hurried across the open space, past half
a dozen human cars and two of the Aalaag mercury-shining vehicles, then up a flight of half a dozen stone steps to a heavy door,
which opened automatically before him. He stepped inside to find
himself standing between two young fresh-faced giants of Interior
Guard enlisted men.

Neither of them made any move either to stop or acknowledge
him. The door here would be controlled by Aalaag equipment and
it would not have opened to him if that equipment had not somehow recognized his right to enter. A few steps farther on brought
him through a sort of small cloakroom or anteroom into a larger
foyer with a marble floor and dark woodwork on the walls. A desk
with an Interior Guard lieutenant was at his right, and ahead to
his left a wide oak staircase led up a flight of steps to the floor
above. An elevator for Aalaag use had its door inset in the wall
opposite the staircase. The lieutenant at the desk looked up as
Shane stopped before him.

"Shane Evert?" asked the officer automatically, reading the
name off the screen inset in the surface of his desk.

"Yes," said Shane. The question and the answer would be recorded as password and countersign, for future reference by their
masters and the machinery at their masters' disposal.

"We've been expecting you." The lieutenant was as tall, but of
slighter build than the two enlisted Guards at the door and looked
if anything younger than they did. "If you'll take a seat over
there"—he nodded at some benches against the wall opposite his
desk—"someone will be down in a moment to take care of you."

The English accent, the situation, was all so normal and pre-
Aalaag in what was being said and done that Shane was briefly
moved, almost to tears, for what once had been.

"Thank you," he said, and sat down on the bench.

Less than five minutes later, a colonel of the Interior Guard, a
tall, bony, narrow-faced man in his forties with neatly combed,
straight gray hair, descended the staircase and greeted Shane.

"I'm Colonel Rymer," he said, extending his hand for Shane
to shake. "We're glad to have you here. The immaculate sir Laa
Ehon has been interested in seeing you as soon as possible."

"Right now, you mean?" Shane asked—for it was not unheard
of for him to be ushered in to see one of the aliens immediately

on arrival, for all that he was usually made to wait at least an hour or so.

"If you're presentable." Colonel Rymer ran his eye over Shane's cloak and staff. "I don't know enough about that outfit. Are you?"

"Presentable enough to be let in to see the First Captain back at Headquarters," said Shane.

"You should be all right here, then," said Rymer.

"Laa Ehon makes a point of appearance?" Shane asked. "I only met him once before and he didn't say anything to me about it."

"Perhaps you were lucky. Perhaps you were all right," said Rymer. "But he likes things correct."

"Thanks for telling me," Shane said.

Rymer shrugged.

"You asked."

They had reached the top of the stairs. They made a right turn into a corridor that had been enlarged to Aalaag-comfortable dimensions, and followed it to a door at its far end.

Rymer touched the door with his index finger.

"Come," said an Aalaag voice.

They stepped into a room not so large as the office of Lyt Ahn, with which Shane was familiar, but nonetheless a good-sized office, with its windows blacked out and largely covered by wall viewing screens. An Aalaag officer of the twelfth rank sat at a desk to one side of the entrance. Straight ahead, behind an exactly equivalent desk, sat Laa Ehon.

"This is the courier-beast?" Laa Ehon asked Rymer.

"Yes, immaculate sir," answered Rymer.

"You also may stay for the moment. Courier-beast—what is it the First Captain calls you? Shane-beast, you may come to the desk, here."

Shane walked forward until he was only the regulation two paces of distance—Aalaag paces—from the front edge of Laa Ehon's desk. The large, white face, lean by Aalaag standards, examined him.

"Yes," said Laa Ehon after a moment, "I might almost recognize you. You stand with an attitude a little different from that of other beasts I have seen. Do you know if your dam or sire was

127

known for any noticeably different way of standing?''

"I do not, immaculate sir,'' said Shane.

"It does not matter. But it will be convenient for me to recognize you on sight. I have an eye for beasts and can often tell one from the other. You've met the Colonel Rymer-beast; and you will be having to do with Mela Ky, of the twelfth rank, who is my adjutant and shares this office with me.''

Shane turned his head to meet the black-eyed gaze of the alien at the other desk.

"I am honored to encounter the untarnished sir,'' he said.

Mela Ky neither answered nor changed expression. He went back to his work.

Laa Ehon put a hand to the belt at his waist, and then hesitated.

"I will speak with this beast privately,'' he said to the other Aalaag. "Do you have a privacy tool with you, Mela Ky?''

"I have, immaculate sir.'' The adjutant got up from his own desk, came over to that of Laa Ehon and took from his own belt a small, flat rectangle of what seemed to be metal, which he handed to Laa Ehon. In the big fingers of the Aalaag, it looked like a business card as it changed hands, though it would have filled Shane's hand to hold it. Mela Ky returned to his desk. Laa Ehon touched the device with one finger of his other hand and a silvery sphere seemed to enclose him, his desk and Shane.

Shane had experienced this sort of thing before. The privacy tool, so-called, evidently set up a field that acted as a lens to bend light around the field, so that anyone looking at it saw not the field itself but what was on the other side of it, no matter from what angle it was looked at. As Laa Ehon took it into one of his hands there was a flash of silver that Shane knew only he and Laa Ehon could see, and for a fraction of a second it enclosed Shane and Laa Ehon in what seemed like a glistening, egg-shaped space. Then this cleared and he saw the office around him once more—but knew that he and Laa Ehon were now invisible and inaudible to Rymer and Mela Ky.

"The First Captain,'' said Laa Ehon, "has expressed a wish that you act as liaison between him and me. He also informs me he has asked you to observe and report on the beasts making up this controlling staff with which we are experimenting here. With my concurrence, of course. I am happy to concur with the First Captain in this. In a moment, when we are alone, I will be giving you a private command of which you will say nothing to anyone. I wish it to be thought that if any private information passed to you from me, it did so during this moment we are unobserved by the sir Mela Ky and Rymer-beast. If questioned at any future time, I would like you to give the impression that it was at this moment I said all I had to say that was private to you. Do you understand?"

"Yes, immaculate sir," said Shane.

There was another flash of silver and Laa Ehon laid the privacy tool down on the top of his desk. Shane knew they were visible once more to the other two occupants of the room.

"The Colonel Rymer-beast will introduce you to the cattle of the staff, from the beast who is Governor on down," Laa Ehon said. "Thereafter you may observe them as you will—avoiding as much as possible any interference with their work. You may also observe, but of course not interfere with, the activities of the Colonel Rymer-beast and his company of Interior Guards in their duties. In the case of any questions, you will come to me. In fact, we will be talking regularly. In my absence, you will treat the sir Mela Ky as myself."

Silently, Shane took this last piece of information with a measured amount of skepticism, born of his experience at the First Captain's Headquarters. In the momentary, transient relationships of most humans to their alien masters, such a statement could be taken literally. But in a situation like this where contact between specific individuals of the two races was not only close but continuing, it was not always exactly true that one Aalaag could be counted on to act as another. The aliens had individual personalities, and the human who had to live closely with them quickly learned who to ask and for what.

But he said nothing. Again, no verbal reaction had been called for from him.

"That much disposed of," said Laa Ehon, "I am interested in talking to you now on various matters. Colonel Rymer-beast, you may now wait for Shane-beast outside. Mela Ky, would you be so kind as to go prepare the Governor-cattle to be of use and cooperative with this liaison?"

"Gladly, immaculate sir," said Mela Ky, getting to his feet behind his desk. Two long strides took him to the door and out. Colonel Rymer followed him.

"Now we will talk," said Laa Ehon. His eyes were unmoving on Shane. "While you are of course a beast of the First Captain, here you are also under my command; and I have a duty for you."

These words, of course, did require an answer from Shane; and there was only one which could be given.

"I am honored, immaculate sir," said Shane.

"My understanding," said Laa Ehon, "is that you will report back to the First Captain regarding the success of this experimental project, and also on the beasts who are being used to staff it, so that he may make his best estimate of the Project's future success. To the best of your knowledge, that is your duty here for the immaculate sir, Lyt Ahn, is it not?"

"Yes, immaculate sir."

"I am extremely interested," said Laa Ehon. "This seems to me to be very useful information and information that I would do well to have myself. I have no wish, of course, to know what you will report to the First Captain, but I have decided that in addition to examining the situation and the cattle connected with this project for Lyt Ahn, you will also examine these things and report separately on them to me."

He paused.

"It will be an honor to do so, immaculate sir," said Shane.

"Good. Such understanding in a beast is most desirable. I have been very interested in you, in any case. You are clearly a valuable beast. I would have concluded as much, even if I had not learned of the high price set upon you by the First Captain. What is your rank?"

Shane was caught unawares. Everything, to the Aalaag, was ranked—according to usefulness, according to value, according to desirability. As a result, even he and the others in the Courier-Translator Corps had been assigned ranks; but as these had no real purpose or use to the humans, they were referred to so seldom he had almost forgotten his. If he had forgotten, it would have been necessary to guess at his rank, hoping that Laa Ehon would not check to see that he had told the truth. But luckily, in that moment, his memory was with him.

"I am of ninth rank in the Courier-Translator Corps."

"Of ninth? You might be interested to know that at our last meeting of senior officers, the First Captain gave us all to understand you were one of his most valuable, if not the most valuable, of your Corps of cattle—"

It was typical, thought Shane, that while Laa Ehon undoubtedly remembered that he had been frustrated at that same meeting by Shane's protest that the human children brought up in alien households might learn to understand but not speak the alien language, his Aalaag social blindness to the understanding of beasts had caused him to overlook the fact that Shane would also have heard and understood what Lyt Ahn had said about Shane's value, at the meeting.

"—and on the basis of what I have seen of you so far," Laa Ehon was going on, "that confidence of the immaculate sir does not seem to have been misplaced. Indeed, if your value had not been so great in Lyt Ahn's mind, I might have bought you to start my own crops of translators."

"I am honored, immaculate sir," said Shane through stiff lips.

"In which case, I might well have ranked you of no less than third rank. However, it now seems unlikely—"

Laa Ehon paused to stare at the plain gray expanse of one of the large viewing screens on the wall to his right. As his eyes fastened on it, it cleared to give a view of the London outside the building. The clouds had brought the darkness of evening down promptly upon the city, and the rain still fell.

"—that I will be purchasing you," finished Laa Ehon, looking away from the screen, which immediately became blank again, and fixing his gaze once more on Shane. "However, I think you might not despair of reaching the second rank, eventually—that is, if my early opinion of you is borne out."

Shane felt an ugly chill within him.

"Thank you, immaculate sir."

"I think that is all, for the moment," said Laa Ehon. "You will find the Colonel Rymer-beast outside and inform him it is my order that he take you to, and make you acquainted with, the Governor staff cattle. You may go."

"Immaculate sir." Shane bent his head in a gesture of understanding, and took a step backward before turning and going to the door to let himself out. In the hall, Colonel Rymer stood a little to one side of the doorway, patiently waiting.

"Done in there, are you?" said Rymer as Shane emerged. "It'll be my job to introduce you to our fellow-humans now. Come along."

NINE

"I HOPE YOU LIKE THIS PLACE," SAID THE GOVERNOR, AS THE HUMAN executive officer of the governing unit was apparently to be called. "It's black market, of course—I mean, it can serve the food and drink it does, and charge the way it does, because here's where a good number of the people in the black market come to do business over a meal. Perhaps I should say gray market—our alien masters haven't really left us the freedom to indulge in anything really black."

It was a small place, with what seemed to Shane to be tables which were proportionately smaller, but meticulously tableclothed and set with attractive china and silverware. The table where the four of them sat was one of the largest in the place, tucked back into a corner so that they had some privacy for conversation. The ceiling was high, the walls were light-colored panelled woodwork, and the reddish blue carpet underfoot was deep and soft. The Governor was a powerful-appearing, square-faced man in his late forties, and while large rather than overweight, seemed as if he might be the kind to like his food.

"From the look of things here the meal ought to be good," said Shane.

He was not someone who enjoyed dining out, or someone who dined out gracefully. Nor could the present gathering honestly be called a happy one. There was an air around the table of businesslike cheer underlaid by an armed neutrality and watchfulness. With these, unlike his experience with the London Resistance people, he felt some confidence. These three would have points in common with other human servants of the Aalaag he had dealt with everywhere, but particularly in the House of Weapons.

"No point in having the staff wait, just so you could look them over tonight," the Governor went on. "I always think it's best to start off with a small, cozy dinner, anyway—and of course we'd have been taking you out to feed you tonight, no matter what. But it's much more relaxing with just you, me, Walter and Jack."

Walter, Shane had learned, was Rymer, who sat at Shane's left. The Governor—what was his name again, Tom Aldwell? Jack was the Lieutenant Governor, a large, balding, silent man past his thirties and apparently in the Governor's shadow, in that he spoke only when called upon to do so by Aldwell. Since Rymer also was clearly not strong on making conversation, this had left the conversation pretty much a dialogue between Shane and the Governor—who seemed to enjoy talking, with the zest and ease of a politician.

"I'll have another drink," said Rymer, wagging one finger at a passing waiter. "You, Shane?"

"No thanks," said Shane. "I've still got a way to go with this one yet."

The past two years had conditioned him to the dangers of the relaxation that alcohol brings, to the point where he really did not enjoy drinking; although he pretended to for people like Sylvie and his other fellow translators on their rare social occasions together. Here was another cause for pretense. Either his companions did like their alcohol, or they were out to get him drunk in hopes of learning things from him that he would not tell them sober.

"Well, I think I'll have another, too," said the Governor.

The waiter, an older man with a bushy mustache and a slight limp, who had seemed to ignore Rymer's original signal, was now coming back to them with an agreeable smile on his face. "How about you, Jack?"

"I'm not quite ready—but, yes," said the Lieutenant Governor. Jack was short for some longer first name, which at the moment, along with the surname it belonged to, had slipped Shane's mind completely—ah, he had it. Jackson Wilson. Wilson had lost most of his hair in front, which gave his long face an egg-shaped look; and his name seemed an awkward one for someone who was not a physically impressive individual to begin with.

"Are you sure you won't, Shane—?" said the Governor. The Governor's first name, Shane remembered, was Tom. All this use of given names on such short acquaintance made Shane uncomfortable. This was England, after all, where a certain amount of formality on first acquaintance certainly ought to be expected. He wondered if they were deliberately using first names because he was North American. He shook his head.

"Just the three of us, then," said the Governor to the waiter, who went off.

I suppose, thought Shane, I should call him Tom Aldwell in my own mind, rather than Governor, just to get used to doing it. He had been unable to bring himself to use the first names aloud, and so far had successfully avoided using any.

"This is an important occasion, after all," Tom said to him, in a tone that was almost confidential. "With you here, as far as I'm concerned, this—which is a human bit of business, really—is officially under way. I don't mean to downrate Laa Ehon's part in it, or any of the parts other aliens have contributed; but after all, in this, they're proposing to depend on us to do for them what they haven't been able to do successfully for themselves."

"You might want to amend that and say, 'haven't been able to do to their satisfaction,' Tom," Rymer said. "We don't actually know they were in any kind of a bind and that that was what led to this program's being tried."

"Oh, of course not," said Tom. "Nonetheless, it's the first time on record of their depending on humans—on the four of us right here, in particular."

This was going a little too far.

"You'd better make that the three of you," demurred Shane. "I'm only liaison—an observer for the First Captain."

"No one doubts it! No one doubts it a moment!" cried Tom. "Still, you're human and a vital piece of the machinery, so I don't see how you can dodge at least part of the credit."

The menus came and were studied. Wine was ordered. Shane allowed himself to be prevailed upon to take a second drink. He pulled the new glass in front of him, pushing aside his first, now half-empty glass of Scotch and water as if what was left in it was mainly melted ice; and the waiter obligingly carried it away.

"Do you know London?" Rymer asked Shane somewhat later, as the meat course arrived and the second bottle of wine was opened. Whatever had been hoped for by the others in the effect of the drinks upon Shane, these were undeniably having an effect upon the rest of them. While none of them was very drunk, to Shane's more sober eye they had all relaxed considerably.

"No," answered Shane. "I've been here more than a hundred times in the last two years, but it's always been a case of my going directly from the Aalaag courier ship that brought me to whatever Aalaag official I've got things to deliver to."

"If you're going to come in regularly, we'll have to set you up in some place halfway decent," said Tom. "A good flat with service, or a suite in one of the better hotels. Where are you now?"

Shane told them the name of his hotel.

"Never heard of it," said Tom. "You, Walt? Jack? No, I thought not. We can do you a great deal better than that, I think."

"Thanks, I think I'll stay where I am," said Shane. "As the rest of you know from working closely with the Aalaag, it pays people like us to be anonymous."

This reference to the attitude of the general populace toward those who worked for the aliens caused a sudden, uncomfortable silence around the table. They were all in civilian clothes, including Shane and Rymer; Tom in a suit, the rest in the less formal jacket and slacks of everyday business wear. They had driven themselves here from their headquarters building, but they had been preceded and followed by two other cars, each filled with Interior Guardsmen also in civilian clothes but fully armed with the latest and best in easily portable weapons of human invention, which was all the Aalaag allowed them to carry. Further, Shane had no doubt that at least some of the other diners in the restaurant were also either members of the Interior Guard, or belonged to some London police service with whom the Governor Unit had connections.

After a long moment, Tom broke the silence.

"Crackpots are always with us," he said with something like a sigh. Shane felt a moment's ironic humor, imagining the reaction of Peter and the other Resistance members to the idea that they were 'crackpots.' "Wise to play safe, of course."

That apparently settled the matter of Shane's housing. However, the attitude around the table had changed. The air of determined cheerfulness underlaid by an armed neutrality and watchfulness had returned. No, it was more than that now, thought Shane. In the mixture that confronted him now, in the attitudes of the other three was a combination of uneasy contempt and concern.

He was far and away the youngest one at the table. Tom was close to fifty. Rymer might well be. The closest to Shane in age was Jack, who could be anywhere from his mid-thirties to his early forties. From the standpoint of age and experience, to say nothing of the fact that they were on their home ground and he was an intruder, they all tended to look down on him. At the same time, he came from the First Captain, and his personal power over their fortunes was an unknown quantity.

"Only trying to do the best for you we can, of course," said Rymer.

"Yes, as a matter of fact," said Jack, unexpectedly taking the initiative, "what exactly is it you're going to want? The word came down from Laa Ehon through Mela Ky that you were to be given anything you asked for. But that's all we've had to go on. What, precisely, is your brief with this project of ours, Shane?"

"Just to observe and report," answered Shane, in as casual a voice as he could manage.

"Stand around the offices and watch—that sort of thing?" said Jack, who had suddenly become the spokesman for the rest of them. "How about reports, orders, written paperwork in general?"

"Essentially," Shane said, "I'll want to look at everything."

There was a short silence.

"That goes pretty far," said Tom.

"I'm afraid so. In fact, it goes anywhere I want it to go," said Shane, smiling at Tom to take some of the impact out of his words. "You have to remember this is all for the First Captain."

Another short silence followed. He had confirmed their worst fears, he saw; and they were appalled. Not only their work, but they, themselves, were to be passed for judgment through the hands of this youngster at the table with them.

"This doesn't mean—what does it mean?" demanded Jack.

"Only," said Shane, looking from Tom back at him, "that the First Captain has a deep interest in this project."

"In its success? Or in its failure?" said Rymer bluntly.

"I don't know how any Aalaag thinks. Do you?" answered Shane. "But since the Project's being tried I assume all the aliens have an open mind about its chances and they all hope it works."

The waiter came to see if any of their plates needed clearing away. He was allowed to take them all in a suddenly thoughtful pause in which no one seemed to have much to say.

"Well, I can give you the background of the Project, of course," said Jack. "I mean I can give you all the hard copy on it you'd care for and I can also give you a quick rundown on it right now. Stop me if I'm telling you things you already know. But I believe Tom was contacted by the aliens on behalf of Laa Ehon about five months ago, through the alien Headquarters for these islands, to handle an executive position with regard to the supply of goods produced generally from this Area. That's about it in a nutshell, isn't it, Tom?"

There was a grunt from the chair where Tom sat.

"He was asked to supply a list of possible first assistants from which one could be picked for him. He did that—and the aliens chose me. Walter here was simply assigned to command the Interior Guard unit detailed to protect us. I don't think he has any idea why he was picked. Is that right, Walter?"

"The aliens tell my commanders what but not why, when they want something; and my commanders very seldom tell me why, even when they know," said Rymer with a slightly sour smile. "In this case there was no explanation, only orders."

"So you can see," said Jack, "we've all rather been conscripted."

"Not that I'm not enthusiastic about the idea," said Tom. "I really think that for the first time the aliens have come up with something that could have them and humans working together for the first time. But, as Jack says, we weren't so much asked as told."

"Of course," said Shane. The distinction these three were making was a meaningless one as far as the Aalaag were concerned. No one ever stopped to ask a horse if he was agreeable to carrying a rider. At the same time, a new understanding came to him. He found himself appreciating more fully what it must mean to these essentially middle-aged men, raised and trained in a different sort of world entirely and conditioned by it, to be in the power of someone of his age and with his connection to Aalaag high authority. A moment's animosity on Shane's part—even a momentary blunder— and they had no way of knowing that Shane could be trusted not to blunder—and any one of the three could find themselves in very bad trouble with their alien masters.

He realized now he had underestimated the basis of their fears. Their distrust of him and their apprehension that he might not understand could cause them to try to hide things from him and bring on the very trouble they were seeking to avoid. Not only that, but what he needed to do with them and their organization would depend upon their accepting some suggestions he would later be making; and in the present atmosphere, any such acceptance stood little chance.

"In a way," he said, "I'm glad to hear that—" He was interrupted by the waiter handing out small booklets covered in what seemed to be midnight blue velvet, that turned out to list the dessert choices.

"No dessert." He handed his booklet back to the waiter—and with a sudden impulse to improve the situation, added, "Just cognac, if you don't mind."

"Excellent idea," said Tom heartily. "I get far too little exercise for all these rich desserts nowadays, anyway. I'll just have cognac, too."

Jack and Rymer also took cognac.

There were a few brief moments of self-congratulatory talk on their virtuousness in skipping dessert, a few more moments of discussion on the need for more frequent exercise, then the waiter appeared with four snifter glasses.

"You were saying . . . ," said Rymer to Shane as the waiter left them alone again.

Turning to face the other, Shane felt himself caught by the undeviating gaze of the dark brown eyes in the long-boned face. For the first time it struck him that Rymer could be a bad enemy. As commander of the local Interior Guard contingent, he had the people and the tools to do away with an unwelcome intruder quietly and effectively.

It was true that Shane was a particularly valuable servant of the First Captain—more valuable, in fact, than the three here with him were ever likely to appreciate. But it was known to the Aalaag as well as to everyone else that things could happen to those humans who worked for them, as these went to and fro among their own race, where collaborators were not loved. The Aalaag minds, long untuned to crime among themselves, were normally content to let the Interior Guard investigate anything like the death of a human courier, and accept the explanation given by the Guard without question.

In short, Shane's death could happen. It would be regrettable to Lyt Ahn, but probably not sufficiently so to trigger an investigation by the Aalaag with their own devices—which would otherwise inevitably uncover the truth. Most likely, it would simply be considered to have happened; and the only concern in the First Captain's mind would be how to replace a particularly useful and well-liked servant.

"Oh," said Shane, twirling the stem of his glass between thumb and forefinger without lifting it from the table, "I was just saying I'm glad in a way to hear that you were drafted into this job, too."

He could almost see the ears prick up about the table.

"Drafted? You?" demanded Tom.

"Essentially. You see, my actual job as a courier-translator keeps me on the go all the time. This is just an added duty. The less time it takes, the more I'm going to like it. If all of you were handpicked by the Aalaag, that makes them responsible, not you. It also relieves me of a good deal of responsibility, since I'm not here to report on the Aalaag concerned, only on the humans. I don't mean to suggest you can just sit back and think you can fail safely—"

"Good God, who wants to fail!" burst out Tom. "We all want to see this work. We want it to be a galloping success!"

"Of course," said Shane. "But I'm still glad to hear that responsibility is with the Aalaags. That being the situation, I can just ride along with things as they happen here. In fact, if all goes well, I may even find myself in the position of being able to drop you a useful hint from time to time on how the Project's being viewed by our masters; and maybe even suggest directions you might want to go in."

He smiled at them again and sat back with his glass of cognac in hand. The other three had taken a moment to absorb what he had said. It was Tom who recovered most quickly.

"That *will* make it easier for you, won't it?" he said. "A shame you don't share our enthusiasm for what this work could mean in human-alien relations, but maybe that'll come with time. We'll be very grateful for any information or opinions you can give us, naturally."

It was a masterful job of covering up what Shane suspected was undiluted joy at their discovery that he had a minimum of interest in the Project and their personal actions. The other two spoke right behind Tom.

"And we'll try to spare you as much of the nonsense as we can," drawled Rymer.

"In fact," said Jack, "if you just let me know the sort of information you'll want for your reports, I may be able to have most of it ready and waiting for you, each time you get here."

"That'll be good of you," said Shane.

"Good? Not at all," said Jack. "It'll make it easier for me, too. What's the sort of matter you'll be wanting to know?"

"I don't have a clear idea, just yet," answered Shane.

He smiled at them once again. They had tasted the sugar coating. Now for the pill beneath it.

"I won't have until I get an overall picture of the Project, as you've set it up," he said. "I'm required to know what's been planned so far and the backgrounds of everyone connected with it. You might start out tomorrow by giving me that much—say, a rundown in print of the way things are going to be done by you and your staff; together with all relevant statistics and personal dossiers—including your own, of course."

"I'll be glad to do that," said Jack. "We can make you up a book with everything in it, first thing tomorrow—do you really want to wade through all those dossiers, though? The First Captain certainly can't be very interested in the backgrounds of mere humans."

"He won't be," said Shane. "But he'll be expecting me to be interested, and to know everything there is to know in case he asks. Don't worry, I'll be spreading the cloak of professional confidentiality over everything I read."

"Now, now," said Tom. "Of course we trust you to do the responsible thing. Let's all have another cognac, shall we? Walter, would you try catching that waiter's eye? You seem to be better at it than I am. Shane, forgive me for sounding like a worn-out record, but have you really thought this thing through—stopped to think of the marvelous things this project could lead to? It could lead eventually to what would amount to joint government of the world, by Aalaag and humans working together."

"You think that, do you?" said Shane. The level of cognac in his glass had hardly been lowered, but he made no objection to having a second one ordered for him, and no one else at the table commented on the redundancy.

"I'm sure of it." Tom leaned toward him earnestly. "Things would have to go well, of course; and you can't rule out the fact that conditions would have to play along with us—that's why it's excellent news to find someone like you working with us in this liaison position—but it could be the germ from which we grow a whole structure of worldwide government, perhaps overseen by the aliens, but effectively administered and operated by humans."

"And all without that bloodshed advocated by those same people who'd hang us to a lamppost for collaborating with the aliens," put in Jack.

There was an emotional sincerity in the voices of both men that caught Shane's attention. If they did not believe what they were saying, at least they had talked themselves into a passable imitation of belief in it. He had not, in fact, ever stopped to consider what Laa Ehon had suggested, except as a political move on the part of that Aalaag Commander, a move doomed to failure as governmental machinery where humans were concerned, but possibly of some use in advancing Laa Ehon's personal rank among the Aalaag. It would be ironic if, after all, this project did, indeed, offer some kind of a bloodless solution to the human-Aalaag situation on Earth.

His immediate reaction, the result of all the experience he had gained by living closely with the First Captain and other Aalaag, was that anything like such a solution was far too simplistic to work. But what if he was wrong and there was something to Tom's idea?

"Well, it's an interesting thought, at least," he said, sitting back in his chair and twirling the stem of his glass once more between his fingers.

There was a moment in which the other three said nothing. Clearly, they were giving him time to think over what had been said. Then the waiter reappeared and there was a further moment of thinking time in which the added cognac was ordered. When the waiter left again, Shane had his reaction ready.

"What makes you think anything like that could come out of it?" he asked Tom.

"Isn't it obvious? We're being set up as a piece of administrative machinery to make sure the aliens get the production they want in this District. That's really all they want—the production. Give them that, and they won't care about how we part our hair, otherwise. All right," said Tom energetically, "let's say we do it—give them the production they want from the British Isles and Ireland. If it works here, they'll want to try it elsewhere, wouldn't you imagine?"

"Yes," said Shane dryly, remembering Laa Ehon at the Council meeting describing this as a pilot project to his fellow officers.

"All right, for every new place they set up, they're going to need cadre, some old experienced hands to help get the new offices off the ground. Where are cadre like that to come from, but from us, once we've got our machinery working here and know what operates and what doesn't? In other words," said Tom, "while the aliens don't have to think ahead in this respect, we do. I do, particularly, since I'm the administrative head."

"Not only that—" Jack broke off. "Sorry, Tom, I imagine you were about to explain it to him."

"Yes. In addition to the responsibilities involved in looking ahead this way, there's a unique chance in it—the chance that we could have no little influence on the way newer stations are set up. Which of course means that in the long run we could have an influence on the whole intermediate government that's finally set up. It could be sculptured to a great extent by what was wanted by we humans who knew how it worked. That could mean more autonomy—eventually even a chance to deal with the Aalaag as equals; or at least the way a strong labor union might be able to deal with the management that controls its working conditions."

"I see," said Shane.

And indeed he did see. The sort of integrated, worldwide organization Tom was suggesting would have to have overall managers—individuals in positions of tremendous power. Individuals with ambition. He looked about the table at the three faces closely studying his reactions.

"The possibilities are tremendous," said Tom.

"I can understand that," said Shane.

"Of course," Tom went on, "it all depends on our making this first project go. But I think we can do that, one way or another.

Our only blind side was the one where the aliens sat; and providentially, here you are, in a position to relate our goals to that, too."

"Or relate it to your goals," murmured Shane.

"That too, if possible." Tom waved a generous hand.

Shane let them sit and wait a moment. Then he sighed.

"You know," he said, "you've given me a lot more to think about than I expected."

To himself he was thinking that indeed they had.

TEN

IT WAS ON THE FIFTH DAY AFTER THE DINNER THAT SHANE CAME BACK to his hotel room and found a note shoved under his door that said merely, "Kensington Gardens. 4:00 pm."

Since it was already eighteen minutes past six in the evening, Shane angrily tore up the piece of paper and dropped it in the wastebasket beside the tiny desk with which his room was furnished. He had just had dinner downstairs in the hotel. He dropped into the room's one easy chair and opened the first of the dossiers he had brought back with him from the office they had assigned to him at Unit Headquarters.

The pattern of the Government Unit had turned out in practice to be little more than one of requiring reports and setting quotas for human government offices that already had had a responsibility for getting goods produced to the requirements of the Aalaag. Nonetheless, it took Shane most of the next four days to read and comprehend it all. The dossiers on the staff members, whom he had met in person the morning following his dinner with Tom, Jack and Rymer, held no particular surprises—including those on the three heads of staff.

Shane was used to finding at least a touch of self-interest obvious in almost all those who seemed to find authority comfortable under the Aalaag; and this was certainly so with two out of the three in question.

The exception might be Walter Edwin Rymer, who had been a captain in the British Air Force and had been drafted by the Aalaag for the Interior Guard because of his height. He was enough taller than Shane for Shane to be unable to guess that height closely; but certainly Rymer was more than six feet four inches and most likely six feet six or better. Which raised a curiosity in Shane's mind. He had had a notion that the British military forces, like the U.S. ones, had maximum height limits as well as minimums for those who wore their uniforms. It had never occurred to him before, but most of those now in the Aalaag's Interior Guard must have been overheight for the military services of most nations before the Aalaag came.

At any rate, Rymer had been given no choice about becoming an Interior Guard—although his rise in rank from captain in that body to full colonel in two years was suspiciously rapid for someone who did not find some reason for self-interest in his occupation.

Thomas James Aldwell and Jackson Orwell Wilson, on the other hand, had both effectively volunteered to work for their alien masters, Tom as a member of a Consultation Committee to the Aalaag, made up of former Members of Parliament—one of which Tom had been at the time of the Aalaag conquest—and Jack as a volunteer accountant, when the Aalaag had passed down through that same Consultation Committee a requirement for members of that profession to work in the human administrative units they were setting up.

Not only had both men volunteered—although there could always have been good and unselfish reasons for that—but both had, like Rymer, risen swiftly ever since in rank and importance under the Aalaag. The pattern of their lives in the brief time since the Aalaag had come, in other words, agreed well with the ambition that Shane felt both had betrayed to him at the close of their dinner together.

He settled down now to reread both their dossiers. He had discovered that in his case multiple readings of such documents tended to generate not only more accurate conclusions, but also inspired guesses, which more often than not later helped to fill out his understanding of the individuals concerned. He was a third of the way through Tom's dossier when a faint rustle of paper made him raise his head and see another note being shoved under his hotel room door.

He threw the dossier onto the soft surface of the bed, jumped noiselessly to his feet and took three long, silent steps to the door, jerking it open as he reached it.

But he was too late. The corridor without was empty. He bent, picked up the note that had just been left, closed the door, and went back to his easy chair to read it.

"Trafalgar Square, nine pm," this one said.

He was at Trafalgar Square at the appointed time. It was a cold night but not wet, for which he was thankful—an umbrella went awkwardly with his pilgrim garb; and he did not want to advertise himself by the fact that, thanks to a minor touch of Aalaag technology, this particular robe, which he had brought with him from the House of Weapons, would shed any water falling on it.

No particular meeting point in Trafalgar Square had been specified by the note; so as much to avoid whatever notice he would attract by obviously standing still and waiting, he began to stroll around the circumference of the square. He was less than a third of the way around when Peter appeared and joined him.

"This way," said Peter, leading him away from the square. A minute later, a car pulled to the curb beside them, stopped, and a back door was opened. Peter pushed him in and followed. The door closed, the car took off.

"Why in Christ's name," snapped Shane, "didn't you just call me, instead of going through this cloak and dagger routine of slipping notes under hotel doors?"

"Your phone might be bugged," said Peter.

Shane burst into laughter.

"I mean it," said Peter, angry in his turn. "That Interior Guard unit you've got working with you would only have to pass the word to the proper branch of the police here to have a phone tapped; and of all the easy phones to tap, one in a hotel room leads the list."

"You don't understand," said Shane, sobering. "The Interior Guard at the Project might be ready to give anything you could name to tap my phone; but its commander—a colonel named Walter Rymer, by the way, I've met him—would have to know better than to try. Anything he did, Laa Ehon would eventually be responsible for; and not only wouldn't the Aalaag think in terms of such spying, it would be a direct insult by Laa Ehon to Lyt Ahn. In effect, it would be Laa Ehon spying upon Lyt Ahn. I explained to you that they just don't violate their own laws, rules and mores. They die first."

"How can you be so sure your Colonel Rymer knows that?"

"If he's been an officer in the Interior Guard for two years—and he has," said Shane, "he must have learned the first rule of survival as a kept beast—never to do anything that might be construed as interfering between two Aalaag. He knows, all right. You can call me at that hotel room safely, any time you want to. I'm in no danger."

Peter was quiet for a long moment.

"I think," he said in a lower, calmer voice, "you may be forgetting something. It may be all right for you to ignore what other humans, and other human organizations, can do to you; but the rest of us aren't in your position as a servant of the First Captain, or of any alien, for that matter. Maybe you've forgotten, but nowadays the human police forces are committed to enforcing the Aalaag laws; and that makes us in the Resistance fair game for any London police officer who has reason to suspect we are what we are. Maybe you can forget that fact. We can't."

Shane found himself unexpectedly ashamed.

"I'm sorry," he said. "I am sorry. I do forget what it's like to be without the protection of my master."

"And I wish," said Peter, angry once more, "you wouldn't keep referring to them as masters, and particularly to Lyt Ahn as your master. It's that very attitude we're fighting."

"That," answered Shane a little grimly, "I won't apologize for. You can't take time to tailor your speech when you live cheek to cheek with the Aalaag. You have to think the right way, so that when you're required to answer with no time to think, you say the right thing. But since we're getting into mutual irritations, how about you and the rest calling them by their real name, instead of always referring to them as 'aliens' as if they were something just landed from outer space, dripping slime?"

"It's not an easy name to say."

"Try it anyway."

"Lull . . . ull . . ." Peter tried to get the second syllable properly into the back of his throat, gargled, and then literally gagged with the effort.

"All right," said Shane more soberly, "I stand corrected a second time. But a native English speaker should have the easiest time with it. I can teach you how to say it—or rather approximate it—

if you're willing to practice; and it may help you someday to be able to say it properly. The Aalaag tend to rate the intelligence of humans according to how they're able to speak the Aalaag tongue; and to value the humans according to their intelligence—which to them means trainability. Let's forget all that for now, though. What did you want to see me about? Have you heard from the Resistance leaders on the Continent, any of them?"

"Just from Anna ten Drinke in Amsterdam. She'll come," said Peter. "There really hasn't been time to get an answer back from the others. But I've got some large news for you. It turned out there was someone going directly all the way to Milan the day after you spoke to me. Maria Casana not only answered your letter, she answered it in person. She came. She's here now."

"Maria Casana? Is Casana her last name? You say she's here now?"

"I have to admit I didn't expect it myself," said Peter. "Apparently you had a strong effect on her. Yes, it's Casana. Anyway, we're taking you to where we're putting her up."

Where they were putting her up turned out to be a flat occupied by a young male member of the Resistance with a wife and two children, one still of cradle size. As the husband of this family let them in the front door, Shane could hear women's voices coming from farther back in the flat, one of which he recognized as Maria's voice. Casana, he thought, it was a strange-sounding name, now that he thought of it. It reminded him that he still did not know Peter's last name.

He listened to the voices with part of his attention as he was introduced to the Resistance member who had let them in. Maria spoke English, as Peter had said, with fair fluency but a recognizable accent. That, however, would not be the major problem, except as to what it might indicate about her aptitude for learning new languages.

Maria, the wife and the older child came into the front room of the flat.

"My wife," the younger Resistance man was saying, "and you already know Maria Casana."

Shane acknowledged the introductions hardly knowing what he was saying. His eyes were on Maria. She was as he remembered her, slim, dark-haired, brown-eyed and with something remarkably alive about her. The sight of her stirred him more deeply than he had had any expectation of being stirred; and he forced himself not to stare at her.

"Look," he said, turning to Peter as soon as the introductions were over. "I've got a lot to do with Maria and only a few days to do it in. We haven't got even minutes to waste. I need a place to talk to her alone—some restaurant, preferably. Someplace where no one, not even your Resistance people, are going to recognize us."

"Well," said Peter, "there's no lack of places. We could—"

"Not we," said Shane. "What I've got to go into with Maria is something for just the two of us. It'd only be dangerous for anyone else to know—and that particularly includes you."

"I see," said Peter. His tone was stiff. "In that case, you can take the car and get the driver to drop you where you want, or simply step outside and start walking. But if you don't want to be conspicuous, you did the wrong thing coming out in your pilgrim getup. Even here in London, in any restaurant good enough to give you some privacy, the sight of a pilgrim at dinner with a good-looking girl having an Italian accent, or the two of you talking in some foreign language like Italian, is going to be remembered by the waiter and anyone nearby who's looking around him at all."

"Don't worry about that," said Shane. "I've been wearing ordinary business clothes to the Project Headquarters. I just put my robe on over them when I came out tonight because I didn't know what I might run into. I can leave my staff and robe here—"

He paused.

"I'm afraid I'll have to ask everyone but Maria and Peter to leave the room," he said.

He had half expected objections from the husband and wife owning the flat. He had certainly expected some resentment at being ordered out this way. But the two went without protest, disappearing around the corner of the entrance to the hall that ran the length of the flat. He heard a door close a second later.

He laid his staff against the overstuffed chair beside him and pulled his robe off over his head, dumping it on the same chair. Maria laughed.

"Your hair," she said.

There was a rectangular mirror hanging on the wall across the room. Shane glanced at himself in it and saw his own brown hair standing up like a clump of wild autumn grass, upright but already killed by the first frosts.

"Um," he said, and tried to smooth it down with his hands.

"Just a second," Maria told him.

She went out of the room for a moment and came back with a comb, with which he finally put his hair in order. The mirror showed him an unremarkable man in blue coat and gray slacks with a dark blue tie on a light blue shirt.

"All right?" he said, turning to Peter.

"You'll show up less this way, I'll give you that much," said Peter, somewhat grudgingly.

"We'll take the car," Shane said. "You tell the driver someplace to take us. He can leave us there and forget about us. We'll take taxis home afterward."

In the car, Maria was silent—agreeably silent, but no source of words. Shane was both grateful for this, which was probably a learned precaution on the part of a Resistance member such as she was, and made self-conscious by it.

He felt very much at a loss. In the case of other women he had known, the cause that had brought them together had been open and obvious. Something that he knew could be taken for granted, if not immediately referred to. Something, at any rate, that he could be honest about. Also, by and large, he realized for the first time, he had always been in this position before with women like Sylvie, who had taken the initiative in bringing them together.

Here, neither condition held. Much of what he would be telling Maria this evening would not be the truth. In fact, it would add up to the sort of lie she would not stand for if she knew the truth. Secondly, it was his initiative, not hers, which had brought them together; and he found he did not know what to do first.

There was that feeling of difference and isolation in him, the same feeling he had lived with all his life, except that it was particularly present and painful in this moment. He wanted to reach out to Maria, to make her smile, laugh. He wanted to touch her . . . and he had no idea how to go about any of these things, even if they had been part of the order of business for the occasion— which they were not.

He had survived under the Aalaag until now because he had

been able to take refuge in the fact that he stood alone and apart from even his fellow courier-translators. He had found safety and comfort of a sort in being alone with his emptiness. Now he was proposing to bridge the space around him to one particular other human being; and he was full of fear and self-doubts at the prospect.

He told himself that it would be easier once they were away from the driver of the car and privately at table in the restaurant. But the feeling inside him did not abate once they were seated in the restaurant. His generous bribe to the headwaiter had given them an excellent table semi-detached from the other tables in the restaurant's one large room, which was enclosed on two sides and had a window on a third. Immersed in himself he almost forgot the ritual of pre-dinner drinks and remembered it only just in time. Predictably, Maria took a glass of white wine. He ordered whisky and soda without bothering to wonder why he chose that, rather than some other drink.

"You surprised Peter by simply arriving, instead of just writing back to his letter," he said to her in Italian, when they were alone with the drinks.

"So I noticed," she answered in the same language—and she did smile. "But you weren't surprised, were you?"

"I expected you here, eventually, but not quite so fast," he said.

Her face became serious.

"The letter said you had a use for me. You do have a use for me, haven't you?"

"Oh yes," he said. "It's critical to have you with me."

Her face grew even more serious.

"I hope you don't expect too much from me," she said. "I'm not a remarkable person."

"I don't think I expect too much," he said. "We'll have to find that out. Your coming without asking what for was a good sign, a great sign."

She looked him directly in the eyes.

"I know what you did for me," she answered. "I know what would have happened to me if you hadn't got me out of that alien Headquarters. You gave me my life. It's yours to use now, if you've a real need of it. I did a lot of thinking about what you did, and what you told all of us after we had you picked up and brought in. I believe everything you said then was the truth, including being the one who invented the Pilgrim symbol. I also believe that you can do things for us no one else can do."

He felt pinned by her gaze as a specimen butterfly might be pinned in a case.

"I'm not superhuman," he said awkwardly. "I just have the advantage of knowing something more than others about the Aalaag, and I've got some physical advantages by being a sort of special servant of theirs. That's all."

"That's everything," Maria leaned forward toward him. Her eyes still held him. "Peter told me after I got here what you told him and the English fighters—that your plan is to make the aliens drive themselves away from here, off this planet completely. I know you don't dare tell us how, yet, but I believe you can do it. I think if anyone can, you can."

He was cut adrift by her belief in him. It made the fact that he was planning to betray everyone she knew and everything she presently believed in, to achieve his planned end, a dozen times more painful a secret. But it remained just that: a secret that must be kept, even from her, until it was too late for her or anyone else to do anything about it. Once more he thought of the Resistance members and what would happen to them when his plan worked, and the thought was like a deep inward pain, almost too great to hide. It was only by reminding himself that they would face their fate anyway, no matter what he did—and that she would be one of them if his plan did not work, that he brought himself back under control. At least, he would have snatched this one brand from the burning.

"I can tell you more than I told Peter," he said to her. He lowered his voice and glanced around to make sure there was no one close enough to overhear. "Because you'll need to know more. In fact, you'll need to know more than anyone else except me. But it's all going to depend on your being able to do some things. How many languages do you speak?"

"Besides my own?" she said. "French—and my English is passable. So is my Romanian—we have Romanian relatives I used to visit occasionally when I was a little girl. My German is not good and other languages—languages of Europe—I know only a few words, like a tourist. And that's all."

He nodded.

"All right," he said. "The next question, then. How old are you?"

She frowned a little at him.

"Twenty-three," she answered. "Does my age matter a great deal?"

"I want to try to pass you off as about sixteen," he said. "Do you think you could dress and perhaps act that age? Fooling the Aalaag isn't any problem. But there'll be other humans who'll also have to believe you're sixteen. Particularly, there'll be other women."

She laughed.

"Sixteen wasn't so long ago that I've forgotten what it was like being that age," she said. "I think I can convince men, and probably women, even those my own age, as well. With the women I'll simply be a little innocent, stupid and dowdy . . . and not too successful with the men."

"You won't have too much to do with other men," he said. "Just me."

She looked at him calculatingly.

"Then it might not be so easy after all, if any of the women you talk about are interested in you," she said. "You're attractive."

"I am?"

He was genuinely startled. What women, like Sylvie, had come his way he had assumed had done so because of his tendency to yield to their desires and do what they wanted. If anything, he had assumed they had only put up with his looks, which had seemed to him a dull average, at best.

"Let me think about it," she said. "There should be ways of making me seem harmless, even at that. Why am I going to be mostly with you?"

"I need someone alongside who can both go into the Aalaag areas and be accepted by Resistance people," he told her.

She paled.

"Go into alien areas? Like the Headquarters in Milan where you first saw me?"

"Yes," he said. "They're not that different or that terrible, if you have a right to be there. I'll tell you more about that in a minute. But the first problem is a language one."

"What language is that?"

"Aalaag," he said.

A little of the color that had left her face a second earlier had come back. Now it went again.

"But humans can't possibly talk like the aliens!"

"Yes, they can," he said. "Well, to be strictly truthful, no, they can't. Not actually like the Aalaag, but close enough so that even the Aalaag understand them and find their speaking and understanding of it acceptable. That's my job, after all. . . ."

He told her a little about Lyt Ahn's original drafting and testing of humans to act as translators and couriers, as well as other servants who would work directly with the Aalaag.

"Outside of translators like myself," he said, "most human servants only have to understand a few Aalaag words—which isn't hard. There're a few commands that go along with any job done for them and these can be recognized and told apart fairly quickly by anyone who isn't literally ear-blind. Speaking's a different matter—and that's where you're technically right. Of course we can't speak just the way they do. We don't have the vocal apparatus for it. Our vocal apparatuses are almost identical to theirs, but not quite, and there's the difference in physical size."

"You don't make it sound easier," she said. She had not moved, that he had noticed, and yet she seemed to have huddled in on herself. "You make it sound harder."

"The point is—and those of us who were natural linguists and got picked for Lyt Ahn's translator group found it out almost immediately, I suppose because we were used to experimenting with sounds—that the trick is to approximate the sounds the Aalaag make when they speak. Luckily for us, there's a model for us to work to. The Aalaag children have high voices and trouble with some—not all, just some—of the same sounds we do. By playing to that difference, it's possible to convince an adult Aalaag ear that they're hearing their own tongue spoken passably well. Of course, it helps that since they consider us beasts, they expect the least from us and they're happy to find any success in us at all."

"Would I be actually living in one of their Headquarters?" Maria asked.

"You would. In Lyt Ahn's—the Headquarters of the First Captain."

"And all those aliens there would expect me to understand them and speak to them?"

He laughed deliberately, to counteract her fears.

"It's nowhere near as bad as that," he said. "But we're putting the cart five kilometers in front of the horse. First, let's see what you can do. I said there were a number of Aalaag sounds that their very young children have trouble pronouncing and we can get away with mispronouncing ourselves. Unfortunately, their name—Aalaag—doesn't have any of these particular sounds in it; and it's also the one word by which they make a snap judgment of the intelligence of any human pronouncing it. Let's hear you try to say it . . . 'Aalaag.' "

She stared across the table at him for a long moment, opened her mouth, sat a moment without making a sound, then closed her mouth again.

"I can't say it the way you say it," she said. "I just can't."

"Try it anyway. 'Aalaag.' "

She looked at him for a long moment, drew a deep breath like a child about to blow out the candles on a birthday cake and spoke—but not rapidly as Peter had done. She spoke carefully and precisely as if she would imitate each twist his mouth had made as he had pronounced the word.

"Ahh . . . yaa . . . h'ag," she said.

He stared at her.

"Good!" he said—then checked himself. "I don't mean you said it just the way it should be, just yet, but you're on the track of saying it right. Shorten up that first sound; and on the second sound—you're right, it is something like 'yaa' but actually it's closer to an 'l' sound. Think of a double 'l.' Let your tongue vibrate—tremble—once against the roof of your mouth as you say it. Try it again."

"Ah . . . yawl . . . ag," she said, and checked herself. "No, I was even worse."

"You're trying too hard. And you were right the first time when you ended up with 'h'ag.' It's not precisely that. That's the part of the name where the adult Aalaag goes back deeper into his throat than any human can do. The young ones use a sort of breathy cough to fill in. Try something like that yourself. Try a voiceless 'h'; say 'hah' under your breath.''

She did.

"Now try putting it all together once more. . . .''

They went on practicing. Maria improved for a while, then began to get worse.

"You're tiring,'' he said. "Let's leave it for now. What I want to do in the next two weeks I'm here is spend every moment I can working with you; not only to get that word down pat, but several phrases I want you to be able to reel off when you need to. Also, you're going to have to learn to understand some Aalaag. We'll practice with me saying certain set phrases to you, for you to answer.''

"But how am I going to use all this?''

"Oh,'' he said. "I'm sorry. Now I'm the one who's gone and put the cart before the horse. I want to try and get Lyt Ahn to accept you as a young girl I've run across, who by natural talent only has picked up some of the Aalaag language, and have him agree to take you into the translator corps to be my personal assistant on this liaison business.''

He saw by her face she did not understand, and spoke before she could open her mouth.

"Sorry again,'' he said. "I forget how little I've told Peter and the rest and how much you have to know. Did Peter tell you I told the local Resistance people that a new Aalaag project here is a government unit staffed by humans but directly under Aalaag control, being set up to improve production in these islands?''

She nodded.

"All right,'' he said, "what I didn't tell Peter is that I'm sent as a liaison for Lyt Ahn—who you'll need to start thinking of, even in your dreams, by his title of First Captain''—he repeated the title for her in Aalaag—"to Laa Ehon, whose idea the Project was and under whose control it is—''

"But Laa Ehon's Commander of our Milanese District.''

"He is. But he's this, too. The whole thing is experimental, and involved in what I'd call Aalaag politics, if the word politics wasn't misleading where the Aalaag are concerned. At any rate, I'm to report to Lyt Ahn on what I see of the human element of that project. It's to Laa Ehon's advantage that the Project work. Probably—but not certainly—to Lyt Ahn's advantage if it fails; and to our human advantage if it works. We want it to work so other such governing units will be set up elsewhere in the world and so the Aalaag'll become dependent on them for the goods they need produced by the economy of our world. Then, hopefully, the day will come when by destroying the effectiveness of the governing units we can make Earth seem unreliable enough in its production so that the Aalaag will look for other worlds to colonize. So they'll go away and leave us alone. Do you follow me?"

"I understand what you tell me," she said. "But I don't see how it's going to work."

"Most of that I'll have to explain later. The point is I need to be liaison to all this whole governing system, and I'll need help— as I say, someone who's in both the Courier-Translator Corps and the Resistance at the same time. It also has to be one of the few people who already know what I look like, so as to cut down on the number of people who could identify me if they were caught and questioned by the Aalaag. Finally, it has to be someone who I think has the intelligence and the other capabilities to do what they'll have to do. That limited the field to those of you who saw my face in Milan; and of those only you or Peter were the sort I could hope to get accepted among the translators of the Corps. Peter, I've a need for in another capacity."

He stopped speaking and gazed at her.

"You can say no to all this, you know," he said. "I can only use you if you want to work with me, if you want to help."

"But I do," she said. "You scare me. I'm frightened to death by all this you talk about so casually, like living in an Aalaag Headquarters. But I want to do it."

"Good," he said. "I think you're being braver than I'd be in the same situation, where you don't actually know what you're getting into."

He looked around for a waiter. "Let's order our meal," he said. "I've got a lot to tell you. More, in fact, than we'll have time for tonight."

They ordered, the meal came, and he did tell her. Privately, he was astonished and dismayed to find that her ignorance of the Aalaag was even greater than he had suspected even the Resistance members of having. He talked steadily about the organization of

Aalaag society, the place in it of people like Lyt Ahn and Laa Ehon, the Aalaag rules and mores and outlook on life. He tried to describe how the Aalaag were individuals and the kind of thing that made one different from another; and how important it was for any human owned by one of them to know the personality of his or her master and be able to predict even the small reactions of the Aalaag to ordinary, daily happenings.

He tried to give her some idea of how uncompromising the difference was between what was acceptable to an Aalaag—and therefore to any human they controlled—and what was unacceptable. Finally, he tried to make this information real for her by showing how all these elements had helped produce the kind of world they had presently and the specific laws the Aalaag had set up for humans to make it work.

By the time dinner was over, he was not quite hoarse but close to it. The back of his neck ached a little from the rigidity with which he had held himself in making the effort to bring her to a better understanding. When he finally fell silent, he became suddenly aware of exhaustion all through him like a deep stain.

He sat back in his chair and, in an action unusual for him, drained the glass holding the wine he had, for her, ordered with the meal.

She smiled a little wistfully at him.

"Yes," she said. "You wear an invisible cloak and carry a staff, even when you're dressed like this."

"Oh—," he said. "I'm sorry. I should have introduced myself again. My name is Shane Evert. You'll have to know that to talk about me to the other humans in the Courier-Translator Corps and at Headquarters where I'm known."

"I remembered your name," she said. As if on an impulse, she reached out and gently touched his cheek with her fingertips. "But for me the only right name for you is Pilgrim."

ELEVEN

"BEAST," SAID LAA EHON, SIX DAYS LATER, "YOU HAVE NOW HAD TEN days in which to observe the cattle at work on this project. Give me your report on them."

Enclosed with the Aalaag by a privacy sphere, Shane stood before the desk at which Laa Ehon sat in the latter's office. Shane was not quite standing at attention, but there was a large difference between this situation and the more relaxed conditions under which he normally reported to Lyt Ahn.

As usual, whenever he had to deal with an Aalaag, there had been that first rush of fear, escalating swiftly to a tension so tight that all emotion was lost in the intense concentration of giving answers that would be at once satisfactory and safe. He had thought in the past that what he felt at these times must be something like what a high-wire artist in a circus must go through just before, and once he had stepped upon, the thin, taut strand of metal on which his life depended.

"When I arrived here," Shane answered, "there were twenty-five cattle on the staff of this project. That number has since increased to thirty-two—"

"You need not tell me what I already know," interrupted Laa Ehon. "I'm interested in your opinion of these beasts, only."

"I am corrected, immaculate sir," said Shane. "My opinion of those who have joined the staff since my arrival lacks the benefit of the time I have been able to give to observing those who were here when I came. Nonetheless, all seem trainable, some more so than others, of course, but all are of a level of ability which seems to be adequate to the tasks at which they are set, or about to be set."

"I expected no less," said Laa Ehon. "Are there any in which you find possible weaknesses or inadequacies which might prove a source of problems later?"

"I have observed none, immaculate sir," said Shane. "This is not to say that such may not exist in certain cases. There are two possible sources of future problems that might be mentioned to the immaculate sir. Since the Project is so new and the staff has been together such a short time, it has not yet had time—"

He hesitated.

"Why do you not go on?" said Laa Ehon.

"I am searching for a word to describe something to the immaculate sir, since it is a characteristic of us cattle which the true race does not have and I know of no word for it in the true tongue."

"I understand," said Laa Ehon, which surprised Shane. "Take your time and describe it as best you can."

"One of the characteristics of us who are cattle," said Shane, "is that our relationships, one with the other, change over a period of acquaintanceship—"

"There is indeed a word in the true tongue which describes such a process," said Laa Ehon. "It is an archaic word, seldom used. Nonetheless, I am interested to find that one of Lyt Ahn's celebrated translators lacks knowledge of it. The word is—"

The sounds he gave Shane, Shane translated in his own mind into the term 'familiarity.'

"I thank the immaculate sir. They lack, then, familiarity, which will build as time passes and they spend more of it working with each other. This familiarity may improve their working together, or in some cases, it may impede it. Only time will tell. But if I am to estimate which, I would say that my belief is that generally it will improve this group of cattle, although in a body of this number, it is almost inevitable that one or several individuals might later turn out to be beasts better replaced by others."

"Good," said Laa Ehon. "That, now, is the sort of information I want from you. Since I expressed my interest in the fact that you did not know the term 'familiarity,' I will also mention that I am also interested—favorably—in the correctness with which you pronounce it, after having heard it only once from me. So, at present the staff is satisfactory—as far as you can ascertain at this time— but as familiarity takes place within it, some beasts may need to be replaced. But you mentioned a second possible source of future problems."

"Yes, immaculate sir. The second is that, as you know, we cattle are prone to weaknesses which those of the true race do not share. One is that, given authority and over a period of time having become accustomed to having it, the temptation may occasionally occur to one individual beast or another to overuse that authority; perhaps even to put it to work to satisfy some personal desire, or protect it against a work failure on its own part from discovery by the cattle in authority over it, or even by one of the true race. But again, this is something that it will be necessary to wait to find out."

"I find what you say interesting indeed," said Laa Ehon. "I am pleased with your lack of hesitation in telling me of possible flaws in the staff members which would be the product of flaws you freely admit are common to your kind. I am to assume, am I not, that you also share the possibility of being hampered by these flaws?"

"I am obligated to admit so, immaculate sir," said Shane. "However, my lot has been cast as a servant of one of the true race and I find in the true race much of what I would like to find in myself. To yield to such flaws as I have described would put me beyond achieving an imitation of what I have seen in those of immaculate and untarnished nature. Therefore I am very unlikely to find myself tempted to so yield."

There was a slight pause.

"For a beast," said Laa Ehon, "you speak with unusual boldness in saying you desire to model your conduct on that of the true race. I would caution you, in speaking to me, that you do not allow that boldness to be confused with license to go beyond what should properly be said by one of the cattle to one of the true race."

Back to Shane's mind came the junior Aalaag officer at Laa Ehon's Headquarters in Milan saying: "I am not one of those who allows his beasts to fawn on him."

"I will remember the words of the immaculate sir and keep them in mind at all times hencefoward," said Shane.

"Good. Now, I am particularly interested in those three beasts who are in authority—Tom-beast, Walter-beast and Jack-beast. What have you, if anything, to report to me about them?"

"They seem singularly able, immaculate sir," said Shane. "Beyond this, the immaculate sir might find interest in the fact that Tom-beast in particular is unusually happy to have been given this work to do. He foresees a result of it in which we cattle may much more efficiently serve our masters."

"So that particular beast has given me to understand," said Laa Ehon.

He rose to his feet suddenly, towering over Shane, with only the width of the desk between them—a width that abruptly seemed to have shrunk.

"I leave immediately for my District of Milan," said Laa Ehon. "I will be gone at least three days and in that time Mela Ky will speak my words."

Shane's spirits leaped. He had calculated during his trip to London that Laa Ehon, no matter what his interest in this project, could not afford to be absent from his post of main responsibility in Milan for a full, uninterrupted two weeks. Shane had been waiting for word that the other would need to leave London, even if only for part of a day, listening to all the Aalaag conversation he could overhear, reading all Aalaag hard copy that he could come close enough to read. Still, it was not surprising that he had been unable to find out the time of Laa Ehon's leaving until now. Laa Ehon himself might have made up his mind to go only a matter of a few hours or minutes before.

"This beast will listen to the untarnished sir Mela Ky in all things," Shane said.

"Good. You may go."

The privacy sphere disappeared from around them.

Shane went out. A little more than twenty minutes later, he saw Laa Ehon leave for his personal courier ship, which was kept in a cradle on the roof of their building; and fifteen minutes after that he was at the door in the basement that was the entrance to a room, the name of which translated from the Aalaag to a place that was at once a museum and an arms locker.

There were three other Aalaag on the premises—the nucleus of the alien staff to come later. They were Mela Ky and two others. The three took shifts of being available for Laa Ehon's orders and running the Aalaag end of the office. Mela Ky, as senior officer and the commanding officer's direct assistant, took the main, daytime shift with Laa Ehon. The other two took, respectively, the evening and the early morning shift, so that at all times there was an Aalaag awake on the premises.

Right now, the one on duty was Mela Ky; but with Laa Ehon's leaving he was now in Laa Ehon's position of responsibility, which meant he had moved directly to his desk in the office he shared with his commanding officer the moment Laa Ehon had flown his courier ship out of the cradle overhead and up toward airlessness. The other two Aalaag would be in their rooms.

Shane made a tour of the premises to make sure that this was indeed where they were. But it was so; and nothing to be surprised at. The Aalaag when off duty spent nearly all their time in their quarters. They seemed to have three primary activities besides work and exercise, of which they also did a great deal in their officially off-duty hours. The primary off-duty activity was viewing on their wall screens which seemed to be from the thousands of years past when they had lived on their native worlds—and this was close to being, if it was not in fact so, a religious exercise. Of the other two activities, one was sleeping—for the aliens apparently needed something like ten hours' sleep out of the twenty-four; and the last was the playing of some incomprehensible game that could be two-handed or played by a single individual. It involved a screen set flat in the surface of a desk and a bank of lights that formed shapes both in the screen and in the air above it, as controls were pressed by the players.

The two off duty would not be playing against each other now, however, because the one who would take the early morning shift would necessarily be sleeping in preparation for that. The other, left to himself, would be either viewing the past, working, or playing one-handed with the game screen in his room.

That meant that Shane had at least a fair chance of getting into the arms locker without being caught at it. Laa Ehon might have known that Lyt Ahn had supplied his human courier-translators with keys that opened most ordinary doors that were locked to those who were not Aalaag. It was almost certain, however, that his subordinates did not; unless the Milanese Commander had specifically warned them of the fact—and there had been no reason to give them such a warning. Not only did crime not exist among the Aalaag; anything they considered of any importance—such as weapons—would not operate except when handled by an Aalaag.

Also, it was an almost inconceivable possibility that a beast might possess an Aalaag key. Only the unique nature of the duties to which the courier-translators were assigned, which made it occasionally necessary for them to use routes through Aalaag Headquarters and elsewhere that were normally restricted only to the aliens themselves, had made keys available to such as Shane.

Facing the door of the arms locker—which looked like a simple slab of wood, but which he knew to be far more than that—Shane took from his pocket the rectangle of dull material that was the key and touched the end of it he was not holding to the door.

The door dissolved, first to a brown mist, then into nothingness, before him. He stepped through the opening that had appeared and looked back. The door was once again solid and closed behind him. He looked forward again.

The arms locker was more spacious than might have been suspected from the ordinary appearance of the door. It gave the impression of a large room carved out of white plastic or snow-colored rock, cut into innumerable niches and crannies, most of which held a single item as if it was on display. A soft, white light flooded the area, seeming to come from nowhere in particular but be everywhere equally. Underfoot, the uncarpeted flooring was soft—softer than any floor of Aalaag construction that Shane had walked on, except in the arms locker at Lyt Ahn's Headquarters, which was a many times larger duplicate of this place he was in now.

The single items, each displayed in its own niche, were all weapons. Every Aalaag had his personal weapons that were, in effect, heirlooms, having been passed down from generation to generation since the time they had been carried against those who had driven the Aalaag from their home worlds. Others, duplicates of these arms, were carried when ordinary use required, such as when mounting guard, either in a Headquarters or when on display or patrol of the cities of Earth they had conquered.

The originals, these precious inheritances, were taken from their niches only for ceremonies of the highest importance, and immediately thereafter returned to them. Where the individual Aalaag went, his or her ancestral weapons went. They were seldom touched; but, like all arms possessed by the aliens, they were charged and ready for use at all times.

Still, they were symbolic rather than real. In the final essential, the only enemy the Aalaag really feared was the race that had dispossessed them of their original homes; and if that race should come this way, hand weapons such as these would be of little use—like lighting matches in the face of a blizzard. But symbolically, they were everything.

Each of the four Aalaag connected with the Project had his private area in the arms locker. In the case of the subordinate three officers these were filled with all their weapons. In the case of Laa Ehon, by only a token few; since most of the Commander's heirloom arms would be still in Milan. Shane, about to move toward the back of the locker, paused for a moment to gaze at the long arm—the weapon that was closest in likeness to a human rifle—that Laa Ehon would carry if he rode abroad on one of the riding beasts that to the aliens were almost as symbolic as the weapons. The long arm lay dark against the white nest that held its narrow, two-meter length.

He had seen such weapons many times before. Not only were those like this one hung on the walls of Lyt Ahn's Headquarters, the House of Weapons, but he had also seen them in the arms locker there. He had even seen the equivalent long arm of Lyt Ahn, himself, on one of those occasions when he had been sent to fetch something from that arms locker. What he had been sent for had been something of small importance and nonmilitary, always. Humans—beasts—were never allowed to touch Aalaag weapons. In fact, to do so incurred an automatic death penalty for any one of them—even one such as Shane. Not because of the danger involved—for there was the fact that no weapon would discharge in the hands of any not an Aalaag—but because the touch of a lesser being was to the aliens like a stain upon any such weapon.

For a second, Shane was swept by an overwhelming urge to lift Laa Ehon's long arm from its niche and hold it. A mixture of feelings had him in its grasp. Partly it was made up of defiance of the rule that said he should never touch such a thing. In part it was also a wild urge to test for himself the truth of the belief that the weapon would not work for a human. But overlaying all this was a fascination of which he was half-ashamed but which he could not help feeling.

He had been, he discovered, around the Aalaag long enough to have become at least in some small part affected by the mystique about their weapons. Some buried part of him wished to hold the long arm, as a child or savage might yearn to hold an object reputed to possess great magic, to see if some of that magic and—face it—the courage and single-mindedness of the Aalaag, might not flow from it into him.

He made himself turn away without touching the long arm and went toward the back of the locker. As he went, he passed in turn each of the sections given to the cherished, inherited weapons of each officer in this building, then passed the weapons for everyday use, racked all of one kind together, since none of them had a specific owner. Finally he came to what he was searching for, the area that held what had brought him here. It was the section that held clothing and other lesser items, such as those he had been permitted to carry or fetch for Lyt Ahn in the House of Weapons.

These, a beast might touch. These, hopefully, would work for a beast. At least, some of them had, when he had been left alone in the arms locker at the House of Weapons long enough to try some of them out. He had had time then to experiment with nearly a couple of dozen items, picked at random; for they had been like adult toys in the sorcerous results they produced when properly activated . . . and yet they were nothing but the simplest of everyday tools to the Aalaag.

The first item he searched for now was a device that would lift him up the clock tower at the north end of the Houses of Parliament, to the face of Big Ben itself, the clock there; and after a moment he did find such an item, an exact duplicate of the one he had experimented with in the House of Weapons' arms locker. It was a ring made for an Aalaag finger, which made it far too big for both his thumbs placed together, with a smaller ring which could be slid around it.

He put the device loosely on his middle finger, held it there by closing his fist and slowly tried sliding the smaller ring a tiny distance around the curve of the larger. For a second it seemed that he felt no difference, and then he was aware that his feet were not pressing upon the floor with the weight they had pressed before. Cautiously, he moved the smaller, controlling ring farther, and felt himself float free of the floor entirely and start to ascend ceilingward. Hastily, he pushed the controlling ring back to its original position and put the device in the right-hand pocket of his pants.

The next item was one of the privacy tools. To locate this called for a longer search; and he was on the point of giving up when finally he found it. Seen up close, it was a thin box-shape, apparently of metal and as large as his hand. A sliding stud was set in the center of one of the faces of the box. Once more he cautiously advanced the control stud while holding the device.

For a moment, again, he thought that nothing had happened. Then, very quickly, the silvery sphere appeared around him. He sighed with relief, returned the control to its original position and put this into his jacket pocket. It made a noticeable bulge there, and, after a moment, he changed it instead to his left pants' pocket. Here it also bulged, but the overhang of his jacket disguised the sharp outlines of its shape as seen through the cloth.

Hastily, he used his key again and left the arms locker, with its door apparently undisturbed behind him. His intention was to get away from the building as quickly as possible. But as he was reaching for the front door, the Interior Guardsman on duty at the desk in the lobby checked him with a message.

"Governor said to tell you he'd like to see you," said the guard.

Shane hesitated, thinking of the bulges in his pockets, and then decided that he could brazen out any curiosity about them by standing on his rights as an independent observer of the Project. He turned and went back, up the stairs and to the office of Tom Aldwell.

He found all three of them there—Aldwell behind his desk, Rymer and the Lieutenant Governor, Jack Wilson, in easy chairs facing him. They made pleased noises at seeing him and Jack brought forward a similar chair, so that he found himself seated as part of their circle.

"We've been saying how well things have been going," said Tom, beaming at him. "It'll be interesting to see how much Laa Ehon is actually required, how much we miss him during the few days he's gone. My guess is that it's going to be little."

"Very little," said Jack.

"Or not at all," put in Rymer.

Shane looked around at their faces.

"His job's only to see that you do your job," he said. "I wouldn't expect he'd be needed, as you put it. The guard on the front door said you wanted to talk to me, Tom."

"Oh, that." Tom waved a hand. "Nothing too important. It's just that we understand you were talking to Laa Ehon about us just before he left, just now."

"What gives you that idea?" Shane asked.

"Well . . ." Tom touched a button inset in a panel of such buttons on the top of his desk. Instantly, the sound of two speakers conversing in Aalaag filled the office. One voice was that of an Aalaag, the other was that of a human speaking the alien language—Shane's voice.

Shane exploded out of his chair.

"Are you insane?" he shouted at Tom. "Shut that off!"

Tom smiled indulgently, but reached out and touched the button. The sound of the voices ceased abruptly. Shane sank back in his chair.

"Haven't you learned anything about the Aalaag?" he said. He turned to Rymer. "Walt, you at least ought to know what it means to bug any room belonging to one of the masters!"

"Calm yourself," said Rymer harshly. "We haven't bugged anything. This place used to belong to one of those African consulates and they had it wired from basement to attic. We didn't do a thing but find their system, chart it, and hook into it here and there."

"Do you think that makes any difference?" Shane blazed at him. "It's the intent to overhear that'll hang you on the hooks if the Aalaag find out."

"No reason why they should find out," said Tom. "In any case, this use of it was more or less an experiment. If you feel that strongly about it, we won't do it anymore. It's merely interesting that we should have happened to overhear you talking to Laa Ehon about the three of us."

"Happen" was undoubtedly not the word, thought Shane grimly; but there was no point in pursuing that now. And to think that he had spoken with such assurance to Peter about the local police or Interior Guard not daring to bug the phone conversation of a servant of the Aalaag like himself; and here they had actually gone and secretly recorded their own master in conversation. It just showed that it paid to remember that there were always idiots who would dare anything.

"Interesting?" he said. "Why?"

"Well, one always likes to know what's being said about one," said Tom, spreading his hands on the desktop reasonably, "and as you know, we weren't able to understand what was being said—just recognize the sound of our own names when they came up in conversation. We hoped you could tell us what you and our alien master had to say about us."

"No," said Shane. "I could, but I won't. That'd make me almost as guilty as the rest of you for listening. Forget there ever was a conversation of that kind—and destroy that recording."

"You may not be willing to admit what you said," spoke up Jack, "and perhaps the three of us here can't understand it, but there're linguists not owned by the aliens who may not be able to speak the lingo, but given time to work with that tape could do a pretty good job of puzzling out what was said."

"No, no," said Tom hastily, "Shane, here, knows the aliens much better than we do. We'll destroy the tape; and forget all about the conversation. You see to that, Jack. I can count on you to take care of the tape, can't I?"

"If you say so, Tom," said Jack.

"In any case," Tom went on, "we all know Shane well enough to know that he wouldn't say anything to our discredit—unless of course there was something to our discredit to say—"

He broke into a smile which included them all.

"And I, for one, don't believe there is," he wound up. He held up a hand. "No, Shane, and I'm not asking for a hint from you as to how you talked about us. I have full trust in your good sense and honesty."

"Thanks," said Shane.

"No need for thanks. Now—on another subject. It seems we're about to get one of your coworkers as permanent translator attached to this project and on loan from Lyt Ahn. A man named Hjalmar Jansen. He's due in tomorrow. I thought you could perhaps give us some idea of what he's like and what he'd prefer in working with us—just any information you feel free to give, information in confidence, of course."

Shane had become too schooled at hiding his feelings in the past couple of years to raise his eyebrows at the name of Hjalmar Jansen. It was not that out of the whole Courier-Translator Corps there were not more unlikely choices; it was simply the irony involved in the choice of Hjalmar. He was a big young man—big enough to have qualified for the Interior Guard, if it had not been that his linguistic skills were so much more valuable; and powerful in proportion to his size—but so mild and soft of manner that some people got an impression of him as being almost boneless. The irony lay in the fact that under that extraordinarily soft exterior he was probably the most stubborn human being that Shane had ever met. Once Hjalmar had made up his mind about something there was no point in discussing it with him, because he simply did not hear you. It would be interesting to see how he and Tom would rub along together.

"Hjalmar's about my age," said Shane. "Swedish, originally, and a very good linguist—good with Aalaag, also. He's pleasant, easy to get along with"—mentally, Shane crossed his fingers behind his back—"and you'll find him something more of a drinker than I am."

"How very nice!" said Tom. "I don't mean that he should prefer the fleshpots more than you do, Shane. It's just that it's pleasant to hear a good report of someone we're going to be working with so closely. Well—look, we won't keep you. I apologize for asking you about what you said about us to Laa Ehon; and, don't worry, we'll destroy the tape of the conversation you heard."

"Right, then." Shane got to his feet. "It's time I was on my way back to my hotel room. I'll see you all tomorrow."

"Certainly, certainly," said Tom, and the other two murmured agreement.

Shane went out. So they'd destroy the tape, would they, he thought to himself. Like hell they would! They would continue to hang on to it in hopes of finding it useful until something scared them bad enough to make them destroy it.

He left the building and a few blocks away from it caught a taxi, giving it the address not of his hotel, but of the restaurant at which he had arranged to meet Peter at this time.

TWELVE

As he rode to the restaurant Shane found himself unexpectedly depressed and churned by a mix of other feelings. He had never imagined that his adventure into association with the Resistance people and Maria would affect him so.

The growing darkness of the streets through which he passed depressed him further. He had needed to talk to Peter, and Peter, surprisingly, had claimed to need to talk to him. He had impressed on Peter the necessity of a place to eat where no one else in the Resistance would go, so that there was no danger of Peter's being recognized by someone who would later also remember what Shane looked like. Clearly, Peter had acted accordingly. The route on which the cab took Shane was into a part of London he did not recognize. The streets were full of old, tall row houses with their stone front steps leading almost directly up from the curbside, so narrow was the sidewalk before them.

The fact that a light snow had fallen earlier should have hidden some of the ugliness; but by this time, everywhere the snow had been underfoot it had either been obliterated or churned to a black mush, making the neighborhood especially dirty and dreary.

Shane found himself noting the obvious poverty of the foot travelers they passed. The scenes framed by the car windows could have been out of the last century, the way those on foot were bundled and muffled in anything at all that would keep them warm. In fact, the general picture was of a sad, poverty-stricken populace.

The sight of these people stirred Shane's feelings in areas he had avoided for a long time. Over more than the past two years he had lived either with the Aalaag or in hotels or other establishments that were at least clean and tried to be inviting; and he had gradually all but forgotten the effect of the Aalaag's original edict that all but a very few humans should live at a single uniform level—as they, the Aalaag, did, regardless of rank.

That edict had resulted in some improvement for those in the worst slums and deprived areas of the countrysides or overcrowded cities. But for those in the rest of the world the sudden drop in the conditions of their existence had left them scrambling to survive. Shane had recognized this fact academically before this. He felt it now in his guts. The very taxi he was in was a gypsy cab—the private car of a driver who had a gasoline allotment but could not afford to burn gas for his own use, so was putting it to use to earn supplementary income after his regular work hours were over.

The truth was that the Aalaag had not just evened out income. They had evened it out on the basis of what was left over after they had taken their own tax on the world's production. Not only foodstuffs and minerals, but many other things for which most humans could see no use, were regularly taken either for the consumption of the occupying Aalaag or for shipment off to other worlds where the aliens ruled. To be processed there by native beings longer in servitude to the Aalaag, and apparently more trained and trusted in turning raw material into whatever the Aalaag needed, from space warships on down. Shane had no idea what proportion of the world's production was drained away in this manner, but he had guessed it could be as high as a third.

In theory, the Aalaag believed in disturbing the society and customs of the beasts they conquered and ruled as little as possible. But the practice of their occupation made a mockery of that theory.

Shane caught himself, wondering why he should start to question the order of things under the Aalaag now, of all times? The answer came all too swiftly and easily to him—Maria.

She had come to him of her own choice, and the strongest effect of having her around had been to peel from him the comfortable layer of insulation he had let build up over the years, leaving him naked to an awareness of what the Aalaag had really done to his planet.

And now, his awareness of what they had done was making decisions he had expected to be straightforward surprisingly complex.

His original idea had seemed such a simple and easy one. The Resistance people, he had known, longed for a chance to revolt. All he had to do, he had told himself, was to give them an excuse, fully aware as he did so that such a revolt would be hopeless, but that he could use the putting down of it to his own advantage, to gain security for himself and Maria . . . and possibly one or two others worth saving, like Peter.

The thought of including Peter and possibly others in those he might be able to save was one of those complexities that now seemed to crop up all too freely. The idea stopped his thoughts dead for the moment. But before he could examine it further, the cab was drawing up to the curb.

It halted. Shane got out and paid the driver. The place he had been brought to was a basement of one of the tall old row houses, the sign of which was a painted board illuminated by a single incandescent light bulb, given a rosy cast by some scraps of translucent red plastic that had been glued together around it to form a globe. He went down the stairs to its entrance and opened the door there to enter a small, shabby room with what looked like very old tablecloths of various colors over card tables. Each table was supplied with a tall, homemade candle, of which the only ones lit were those at occupied tables. To his right he almost stumbled over a chalkboard on which had been listed the two choices for dinner—curried lamb and chicken pie. Wine by the glass was noted as being available.

The lamb would be mutton, he knew, and the curry designed to cover up any off-taste in the meat or in the rest of the dinner. The chicken pie would have very little chicken meat in it and a great deal of flour and water thickening. The "wine" would simply be that—whatever they had on hand at the moment. White or red was not specified.

Looking across the room, he saw Peter already at a table in one corner, isolated by surrounding empty tables from the other diners in the room. Peter beckoned him over.

There was no place to leave his coat and hat. Shane took them off as he approached the table. They would have to be draped over the back of his chair—unless the very evident chilliness of the room forced him to put them back on again, as some of the other diners had already done to stay reasonably warm.

He reached Peter's table. There was a large glass of red wine in front of the other man that looked as if it had hardly been touched. There was a second glass of wine in front of the chair opposite. Shane sat down there and laid his coat and hat on the floor between his chair and the wall. He picked up the wine in front of him and tasted it. It was raw and almost undrinkable.

"Been here long?" Shane asked.

"Since the place opened for dinner," said Peter. The tone of his voice was light, but had an edge to it. "Don't worry. I've watched everyone who's come in. There's been no one I know, and that makes it pretty certain there's no one here who knows me."

"Good," said Shane. He picked up the menu on the plate before him and glanced at it. "I'll have the curried lamb. You do all the ordering."

"When the waitress gets here," said Peter evenly.

"What's the latest count of people who've shown up from across the Channel?" Shane asked.

"Eight," said Peter. "Anna ten Drinke came in from Amsterdam and Georges Marrotta from Milan—you remember him, the man who spoke to you in Basque? Albert Desoules of Paris was already here, and Wilhelm Herner, so we've got the big four."

"I'm surprised at—who did you say they were—ten Drinke and Marrotta?" Shane said. "Amsterdam's so close and Marrotta knows who I am and knows about Maria's being here. I'd have thought they two would have been among the first to show up. Does it mean anything, do you suppose, that they took this long to come?"

"I wouldn't know their reasons," said Peter. "Some of the less well known names might have come just for the trip to London— this call of yours makes a good excuse. Marrotta and ten Drinke don't need excuses. No more do Desoules and Herner, so they probably decided to take as short a time off from ordinary business as they could get by with."

"I see," said Shane.

"Meanwhile," said Peter, "they're growing impatient—understandably so—to meet you, now they're here. I've told them about the new Governor Unit project and your connection with it, and given them the idea that it wasn't easy for you to get away from it safely, and that that's what's been holding you back from meeting them. But they're getting restless, just the same."

"They can see me tomorrow afternoon—" Shane interrupted himself as a heavy, middle-aged waitress passed by their table too close.

". . . In fact," he went on, "it's most important they see me tomorrow. But they won't be able to talk to me, just see me, until evening."

Peter gazed steadily across the table at him in the dim light.

"What do you mean?"

"I mean that in the day I'm going to put on a show for them in a public place; and I want you to see they're there to take it all in. But they mustn't make any attempt to speak to me there, or get close to me."

"I see," said Peter, "and you're going to need our help to put on this show, too, of course?"

Shane looked back across the table at him and saw a perfectly expressionless face except for a particular stoniness of gaze.

"That's right," he said gently. "Something wrong with that?"

"There could be," answered Peter. "This isn't Denmark or Milan. This is my ground; and what you do on it hits me directly. You told me you wanted to meet for dinner to talk to me about something. Now you have. And now it's my turn to talk to you, as I said I'd need to."

Shane studied the other man for a moment. There was something here he had not seen in Peter before; or if he had seen it, he had not paid proper attention to it.

"Your turn?" he said. "All right. Go ahead."

"I'll do that," said Peter. "I know what involves every one of the people you saw at that meeting I brought you to when you first got here—I know why each one of them's in the Resistance. There wasn't one of them there who hadn't lost someone close—relative or friend—to the aliens; either directly killed by them or their human troops, or dead because of some change the aliens made. So answer me this. You've got a lot of personal freedom, money and just about everything anyone could want, the situation being what it is. As far as I can find out you've no relatives or friends outside the other collaborators who work with the aliens. So, tell me. What exactly was it that made you mark the sign of the Pilgrim, that first time, on the wall in Denmark?"

Shane stared at him. The question called for so complicated

an answer that he did not know where to start. Finally, he managed to say something.

"The Aalaag have a word for it," he said. "*Yowaragh.*"

"*Eeyah* . . . what?" said Peter.

"Don't try to pronounce it," said Shane. "It's one of the more impossible words for a human to say properly. *Yowaragh.* It means beasts who suddenly go insane to the point where they try a perfectly hopeless physical attack on an Aalaag."

Peter looked at him narrowly.

"*You* did this?"

"No, no." Shane shook his head. "Not me. Remember the Dane I told you about after you, shall we say, escorted me to your hiding place in Milan? The one who attacked the Aalaag who accidentally killed the man's wife?"

"I remember," Peter said. "But it's still not clear to me what that has to do with your joining us now."

Shane had told, at that first meeting in Milan, about the execution in the square he had been made to watch, about getting drunk in the tavern and being attacked outside by the Nonservs, but he had not told about the butterfly.

Now, he tried to explain to Peter why the Aalaag had felt they had to execute the man publicly, on the hooks, how they would not tolerate anything but obedience. And he tried to explain about the tension he always felt, living close to them all the time and knowing as he did how uncompromising they were in their rules and laws, even when their own children were involved. He told Peter about the father Aalaag solemnly bringing his son to task for being responsible for the deaths of two valuable beasts. How the son had defended himself saying it was an accident, he was only trying to save the woman from being trampled by the riding beast, and how the father scorned all excuses. He tried again to explain the term *yowaragh*, the craziness that overcame him at times and made him want to strike out, no matter what the consequences.

"There was a—" Shane broke off. He found these words hard to come by.

"It was spring," he said. "There was a butterfly on a branch of a tree there, just coming out of the chrysalis. You know how the Aalaag've cleared all insects and wild creatures of any kind out of the cities? These two didn't see the butterfly; and so . . . this won't make any sense to you, but it seemed to me that if the butterfly could just last long enough to get its wings working and escape, then we'd have gained a life—even if it was only the life of a butterfly—for the two they'd just taken from us. I know this doesn't make sense. . . ."

Peter was looking at him oddly.

"Nevermind," said Peter. "Go on."

"So I concentrated on the butterfly. Kept my eyes on it. And it got away. The man died. Then all of us who'd been required to stand and watch were free to go; and I found the tavern not far away. The barman sold me some illegal homemade liquor. I got a little drunk and I was still all shaken up by what I'd had to watch. I left and right away I was jumped by the three Nonservs who wanted to rob me. I beat them off with my staff—killed two of them, actually; and ended up thinking what a great warrior I was, until I saw how they were nothing but skin and bones—they'd been starving to death."

He stopped.

"Go on," said Peter.

"On my way back, I had to pass through the square again. There was no one in it but the dead man and his wife. I had to do something—it was *yowaragh*, as the Aalaag say. All I could think of doing was making some kind of protest where people could see it— putting some kind of mark there to say, even if only to myself, that they may have killed the man and woman but the butterfly lived. Something lived . . . that's all there is to it."

He said no more and Peter was silent for a long minute or two.

"So," he said, "you still didn't do anything about the Aalaag until you were in Milan, the time we picked you up."

"I could see Maria there through one of the vision screens they have in their offices. Just waiting . . . it was Aalborg all over again. I thought if I could only make sure she lived, save one life. It was the way it had been with the butterfly. . . ."

He ran down.

"Well," said Peter after a bit. He had been staring off across the room at nothing in particular; now he brought his gaze back to Shane. "That answers me."

Shane took a deep breath and drank some of the god-awful wine.

"I'm glad," he said.

"So am I," said Peter.

"And now," said Shane, gathering strength, "now that I've told you all about me, how about telling me about you? I don't know a thing about you. Who you are, or what you do. Your turn to tell me."

"I'm a solicitor," said Peter, staring moodily at his wineglass. He lifted it to his lips, but at the first taste set it quickly down again.

"A lawyer?"

Peter opened his mouth to answer and closed it again as the heavy-bodied, middle-aged waitress, with a wisp of hair dangling down on a forehead shiny with sweat, came to their table and took their orders.

"One kind of lawyer," he said when she was gone. "You know we've got barristers, who actually appear in court, and solicitors—"

"I do know. I'm sorry," said Shane. "It's not an important point. Go on about yourself."

"Well, that's all there is about me, really." Peter frowned at the tablecloth, on which he was drawing lines with the tines of his fork. "I've got a little independent income; but I try to get into the office fairly regularly to look busy to the aliens and the police, if nothing else."

"Why are you in the Resistance?" asked Shane bluntly.

"Well, there isn't much choice, is there?" said Peter. "I can't say I and those close to me have been directly and personally misused by the aliens. Though it was a result of their occupation that my father and mother are dead now. They were old, you see. I was an only child and a late child. They had all sorts of little things wrong with their health; and the way they had to live after the aliens came was fairly hard on my father. He died about a year after the aliens took over and my mother only about six months after that. But I can't say I'm out for revenge, anything like that."

"Oh?" Shane looked at him. Peter's eyes were still on the marks he was making in the tablecloth. "What is it that made you an Aalaag-fighter then?"

Peter raised his gaze and looked straight at Shane.

"I suppose you could call it some kind of duty," he answered. "As I said, this is my ground. In fact, this is my world. If a thief comes and sets up camp in your house, you do something about it, don't you? You don't just sit there and let him use the silver and empty the refrigerator. You do whatever has to be done to get rid of him."

"Including facing what the Aalaag will do to you when they catch you?"

"More of the *if* and less of the *when*, if you don't mind," said Peter. "Of course. Whatever's necessary. There'd hardly be much point in living, otherwise."

Shane looked down at the lines in the tablecloth, at a loss for something to say. Peter, seeing his eyes upon the fork tines, laid the fork down.

"I expect everybody has their own reason," he said with unexpected gentleness.

Shane shook his head. "I guess there's nothing we can do about ourselves, anyway," he said. "Well, shall I tell you what I've got in mind to show the visiting firemen?"

"Firemen?"

"The visitors here from the Continent to see me," said Shane.

"All right, then. What is it?"

"I want you to get all of them into positions—separate positions—close to the Houses of Parliament, so that they've got as close a view as is safe, of Big Ben, at just a little after noontime, tomorrow. There's an Aalaag on his riding beast always on duty around the Houses of Parliament—"

"I know," interrupted Peter.

"I know you know," said Shane. "I'm trying to tell you something. Please listen. He rides from position to position around the building, sits his riding beast a short while at each position, then moves on. He usually stops just before the clock tower at noon, or a little after. Tell your people that when they see him ride into position there and stop, to start watching the face of Big Ben. They may have to wait some minutes before they see anything, but they're to keep their eyes on the clockface until they do, or they'll miss what I want them to see."

"And what is it they're going to see?" demanded Peter.

"Let me finish telling you what I'll need, first," said Shane. "Now, I want you, personally—"

He broke off as the waitress once again approached their table, this time with filled plates. He waited until she had gone again, then picked up where he had left off.

". . . I'll need you standing out about twenty yards beyond the Aalaag on his riding beast; and you'll have a car either parked, or driving around close enough by so that you can get me into it and away in the shortest possible time. There's nothing about that that'll be difficult to arrange, is there?"

"No," said Peter. "Go on. What's all this for?"

"A show for the visitors, as I said. One to make sure they don't doubt my *bona fides* as the Pilgrim," Shane went on. "Most of them are probably going to be coming in with strong doubts—"

"You can count on that," said Peter.

"I am. This should put their doubts to rest. I haven't got time to go around convincing them all individually. Let me go on—I want you standing by ready to guide me to that car, or to where it can pick me up. Our visitors who're observing will have to see to getting themselves out of the area and meeting us somewhere else later. They can be given instructions on what to do and where to go. I'll be wearing my pilgrim outfit, of course, with the hood pulled together in front, just as I will when I talk to them that evening. I suppose you've warned them about the fact I've got to preserve my anonymity; and they've agreed to go along with that?"

Peter nodded.

"Right," he said. "Now—and no more nonsense about it—what is it you're planning to do?"

Shane took a deep breath.

"Mark a Pilgrim symbol on the face of the clock," he answered, "while the Aalaag on duty's right there—and walk away under his nose while all our friends watch."

THIRTEEN

PETER STARED.

"You're out of your head! With the alien there on his riding beast at the same time?"

"With luck, he won't see me until I'm back on the ground," said Shane. "Even if he does, I'm just another beast who was working up in the clock tower and left a sort of smudge or mark on it. But the chances are he won't even look up. Why should he?"

"Why shouldn't he—when he sees you up there on the clock-face?"

"I tell you, he shouldn't see me. If he did, why should he be interested? His job is to ride around the Houses of Parliament, and, of course, to react to any crimes against Aalaag law that happen right under his nose."

"Putting the Pilgrim mark anywhere is a crime."

"He'll only see it's a Pilgrim symbol if (a) he notices it at all and if (b) he takes a very close look at it. It'll take a good pair of human eyes—and the Aalaag vision isn't any better than ours—to make out what the mark is from the ground unless you really look closely at it. He might decide to do that, but meanwhile I'll be walking away. I've got a few Aalaag-type tricks up my sleeve he won't be expecting from a human. Now—that's all I'm going to say about it, even to you. Did you change those gold pieces I gave you into ordinary money?"

Peter reached into his inside coat pocket and took out an envelope, which he handed to Shane.

"Thanks," said Shane. "The gold's useful sometimes, but most of the time now, I'd rather not attract attention to myself; and after tomorrow, I particularly won't want to attract attention when I'm wearing the pilgrim robe. Oh, I'll get myself to the Houses of Parliament to begin with, by the way."

"I assumed you had something like that in mind; otherwise you'd have asked me for transportation there at the start," said Peter drily.

They talked of nothing more that had to do with tomorrow during the rest of their meal together. Shane did not offer any more information and Peter did not ask questions, for which Shane was grateful. He was coming to like Peter, almost against his will. More and more, he was convinced of the wisdom of his first reaction on seeing those Resistance people whom Peter had got together to meet him on his first arrival in London. It would be much safer to be disliked than liked by those he met who had dedicated themselves to fighting against the Aalaag. To say nothing of the fact that it would help his conscience to sleep nights.

By a natural progression from that thought he found himself thinking again of Maria; and he was still thinking of her as he took a taxi home from the restaurant where he had eaten with Peter. With their need for spending as much time as possible together to practice on her speaking and understanding of Aalaag, it had been effectively necessary that they move into the same quarters. He was too aware of the advantages of anonymity which a hotel offered to take the flat which Peter suggested. Instead he had moved to a larger hotel and changed his single room for a two-bedroom suite.

The hotel he had chosen was a British edition of one of the chain hotels from the U.S., and he was careful to speak to anyone on the premises there, when he had to speak at all, with a North American accent. Maria, speaking English with an Italian accent, was unremarkable enough so that they could be taken for a visiting couple from the States.

As the taxi moved him through the darkened streets, he found himself wound up by the same feelings that he wrestled with each time he returned to the hotel and Maria.

He could not wait to get back to her—and that feeling was a dangerous indulgence. He had faced the fact, shortly after they had moved into the new hotel, that she meant more to him than anyone else ever had; and that was the one thing she must never be allowed to suspect. It would be hard enough on her, when the time came that he delivered up the rest of the Resistance people to the Aalaag, without her knowing that she alone was in a position of safety because he had come to value her so highly.

She would hate him, of course, when she found out what he was doing. If, in addition to hating him, she should ever tell herself that it had all happened because of the way he felt about her, and because he had wanted to keep her, her alone, alive—if that ever happened, her hate would be mixed with guilt. Nevermind that she had no responsibility for what had happened. She would see only those that were dead and blame herself for being the cause of those deaths.

And the end result would be that she would give up her own life to ease her conscience. She would go to the Aalaag and denounce herself as a Resistance member. She would also tell them all about him—but if it came to that point, what happened to him would hardly matter. He could not make the prospect of it matter to him even now, thinking about it. All he could think of was Maria and the absurd joy he felt in the fact that soon he would be with her again . . . and with all this, he had never even touched her.

He smiled a little in the darkness of the cab's rear seat. That puzzled her, he knew. What she felt for him was an entirely overblown sense of gratitude, plus something that could hardly be described otherwise than as hero worship. She had not hidden it, nor had she hidden the fact that she would not have been averse to being physically close to him. But he dared not. He could never have made his lie continue to work, the lie that he was concerned only with her usefulness to him, once physical intimacy had been established.

He stiffened his resolve, therefore, paid off the cab at the hotel from the envelope Peter had handed him in the restaurant, and climbed the five flights of stairs to let himself into the sitting room of their hotel suite.

She was seated on the sofa there, with some pages of a part of a routine Aalaag order he had surreptitiously copied for her to study, spread out on the low coffee table before her. She jumped up on seeing him and came forward.

"I did not order you to move," he said in Aalaag.

They had fallen into a practice of speaking that language, in which he played the part of an Aalaag and she tried to respond as a human would be expected to respond.

She checked her forward motion.

"Forgive this beast," she said in Aalaag, not too awkwardly— but then it was a routine phrase that she had been drilling on steadily. "This beast was only—"

She broke off.

"You never taught me the word for 'happy,' " she said in English. "I was going to say 'happy to see you.' "

"There is no such word," he told her, also in English. "The closest you could come to 'happy' is 'very interested.' You might say 'this beast is very interested to see you,'—except that such a thing is never said. It would be presumptuous on the part of a beast, even if such a reaction on the part of a beast would make any sense to an Aalaag. But it wouldn't."

"It wouldn't?" She stared at him.

"No. Why should a beast have any reaction other than a willingness to obey when it sees its master? Anything else suggests some kind of unwholesome relationship between master and beast—unwholesome to the Aalaag mind, that is."

"But you told me that Lyt Ahn had sometimes been considerate and even kind to you—and you're a beast to him."

"The First Captain has different needs and purposes stemming from his responsibility to govern. . . ." She had been answering him in English and unthinkingly he had slipped also into that language. He switched back to Italian now, to make sure she understood. He repeated his first words, in that language. ". . . That is, the First Captain may have reasons or purposes for doing many things that even other Aalaag don't understand; and as long as he's First Captain, they don't inquire why he does them or judge his doing of them."

"Then I could say to the First Captain that I was very interested to see him?" she asked in Italian.

"No," said Shane. "For two reasons. One, because it's at odds with Aalaag psychology; and two, because he can do what he wants, but that doesn't mean that you can."

"This beast understands," she said, returning to Aalaag.

"It's all right," Shane went on, still in Italian, "work's over for the day. I've got a lot to tell you and it's probably better done in Italian. Let's sit down."

He seated himself deliberately in one of the armchairs, rather than on the couch, and she went to the armchair opposite to sit down facing him. But she passed by him so close she all but brushed against him, and his senses were full of the awareness of her body as she passed. There was a sad ache within him, at having her so close and yet so untouchable.

"Have you eaten something?" she asked.

"Yes—yes, I had dinner with Peter," he said. "He told me, by the way, that Anna ten Drinke and Georges Marrotta are here, finally, so I'm going to put on a sort of demonstration I'd had planned for these visiting leaders to see. I told Peter to have them in position before the clock tower of the Parliament buildings, so they can see what happens to the clock there—it's called Big Ben—"

"I know about it," she said gravely, in Italian. "Someday I'd like to see it, and the Parliament buildings themselves, and other things here."

"Perhaps we can take a few hours off, after tomorrow night," he said. "The point is, I want these European visitors to see at noon tomorrow what the Pilgrim can do. Then tomorrow night, I'll talk to them all and explain why we need to support this Governor Project here in London, and other projects like it as they're set up; and why at the same time we've got to build a tight, unified working structure that includes all Resistance members."

"Good," she said. "What am I supposed to do?"

"Nothing," he said. "I mean I don't want you there at the clock tower. You wait here, and if I'm not back before 2:00 pm or if no one else, like Peter, has shown up by that time with some kind of news about me or how things went, then I want you to get out of this hotel. Don't check out. Don't take anything more than you'd carry if you were just stepping out for an hour or so; but get completely clear of the hotel, fast. Find someone in Peter's local Resistance group and get word from them of how things went at the tower."

He paused.

"You understand?"

She nodded.

"But what are you going to do at this clock tower?" she asked. Her face had tightened. "What is it that's so dangerous?"

"I'm not going to do anything, as myself. But the Pilgrim is going to make his mark on the face of the clock there, not only so everybody can see it, but so that everyone there who's watching— as all these visitors of ours should be—can see him as he does it."

"How will you—how will he get away afterward?"

"I'll walk away. Peter will meet me and take me to a car that'll be nearby. That's all. There'll be nothing to it."

She looked at him penetratingly.

"Didn't you tell me something about an Aalaag on one of their riding beasts who has a regular post of duty that has him patroling about the Houses of Parliament?"

"Yes, that's right. There is." Mentally, he snarled at himself for having mentioned it.

"What if he's there at the time?"

"I want him there," he said. "I've timed the thing for noon so as to be sure he'll be there. But he won't do anything."

"He won't?" Disbelief rang like a hammer on an anvil in her voice.

"No. His primary job is a symbolic one, to establish the supremacy of the Aalaag over the government that still sits in the Houses of Parliament. It's only his secondary duty to enforce any of the Aalaag laws he sees being broken. But there's no Aalaag law against a human coming down from the clock tower and walking off. There'll have been no reason for him or her to look up before he sees me, near the ground, and no reason to see the sign I've marked on the clockface. To anyone with good eyesight, or any kind of binoculars or a telescope, it'll be plain what that sign is, but to anyone just glancing up there it'll look like a small damage or dirty spot on the clockface. However, the Aalaag'll have no need even to look, so he won't; and there'll be no reason to stop me from leaving, so he won't do that either. There's no Aalaag law against a human coming down the tower and walking away, so why should an Aalaag concern himself with a beast who does?"

"It can't be that easy. It won't be that easy!" she said vehemently. "You're not telling me something."

"But it is that easy," he said soothingly. "I even have the help of Aalaag technology. Look . . ."

He reached into his pockets to pull out the ring device and then the privacy tool. He demonstrated both for her.

"You see," he said, "I can be both invisible and independent of gravity when I do it. How can there be any problems?"

She stared at the two things. He let her take them and examine them. Reluctantly she yielded them back to him when he reached for them again.

"You're still not convinced?" he said.

"No." She shook her head firmly.

"Well, you should be," he said, as quietly and calmly as he could. "In most of what we're going to be doing together, you and I, you're going to have to trust me when I say certain things will work. They'll work because that's the way the Aalaag are; and, knowing how they are, I'm as safe doing something like this as I would be climbing a deserted tower out someplace in a wilderness."

"When you tell me only what you want to tell me," she said, "I can't argue with you, because I don't know what I need to know to argue intelligently."

The understanding that he was lying to her, by implication if not in outright words, was plain in her eyes as he sat watching her now. But wasn't his whole association with her a lie? The more barriers between them the better, he told himself harshly, and the less likely that in a moment of weakness he might give in and try to reach out to her.

The next day he was at the Project early and set himself up in the office that had been assigned to him, strewing the desktop with papers and building as complete as possible a picture of being immersed in some large piece of work. Just after eleven in the morning, he waited until there was no sound of anyone coming and going in the corridor outside his door, then took off his shoes, put on his robe and opened the door enough to let him look out.

The corridor was deserted.

Carrying his shoes in his right hand, he reached in through a slit in his robe to the left side pocket of the jacket he was wearing underneath, and touched the stud on the privacy tool. Now invisible, he slipped out, into the corridor, heading toward the stairs and the front door.

His office was on the third floor. He made it to the stairs and down them without a sound and without encountering anyone. An Interior Guard corporal sat at the desk by the front door with the sign-out book open on the table in front of him and a pen handy. But in the relative dimness of the building's interior even the shield's illusion of heat waves in still air was not visible. He did not even glance up as Shane slipped by him.

At the door, however, Shane was forced to wait. He stepped back into a dimmer corner of the lobby beside the door and composed himself to patience. The minutes slipped by and nothing happened. Then, so suddenly it was almost like an explosion on the quiet of the lobby, came the sound of shoes briskly ascending the steps outside to the door, the door was flung open and a young, blond-headed staff member named Julian Ammerseth came in carrying a large manila envelope under his arm.

"Back again—," he said cheerfully to the corporal, approaching the desk to sign in; but that was all Shane heard, for he had caught the door from closing with an invisible hand behind the other's back and slipped through to the outside.

He paused just at the bottom of the outside steps to put his shoes on; but he kept himself invisible until he was well away from the Project headquarters and could find a niche of an alleyway not overlooked by windows, into which he could step long enough to let himself become visible again.

Visible, he pinched the hood of his robe together and continued down the street on foot until he could hire a cab and have it take him within a few blocks of the Houses of Parliament.

It was fortunate he had allowed himself some extra time. It took him some minutes to walk around the Parliament buildings until he had found the Aalaag sentry and made sure that he was more or less on his regular schedule, which should put him before the clock tower at noon or shortly thereafter. The actual time of his arrival there could only be guessed at, since the officer—it was a male, this time, Shane noted from the armor shape—would ride to a point, sit there a while, then ride on to another point at which he would pause; and both points and length of pause were apparently chosen at random.

Having found the alien, he returned to the base of the clock tower. The time was seven minutes to twelve. There was no lack of people going to and fro, or standing and talking to each other in the walks on this side of the tower. He did not see Peter; and the Resistance leaders from the Continent, of course, were unrecognizable to him. He continued around a corner of the tower, hunting for a place where he could safely turn himself invisible. But there was none.

In desperation, he settled for a moment when none of those around him seemed to be looking in his direction and pushed over the stud of the privacy tool in his left jacket pocket. There was the momentary flash of silver surrounding him, and, invisible, he returned to the tower below the clock, activated the ring device and let its powers lift him slowly up the face of the tower to the clock.

He had not taken into account the effect of apparently standing in midair on nothing, some stories off the ground. He was not ordinarily affected by heights, but now he had to fight down an irrational feeling of panic that began to rise in him as he himself ascended toward the clockface.

He reached it and, playing with the ring device, managed to halt himself opposite the hub from which the two hands of the clock were pivoted. He looked down. The Aalaag was nowhere in sight.

Invisible, suspended in air, he waited and scanned the walks below for some sign of Peter. At just two minutes to twelve, he located him, standing in apparent conversation with a short, round-hatted man at the distance Shane had told him to be beyond the tower.

Time slowly passed. The minute hand of the clock was so large that by watching it, he could see the slow creep of its tip around the dial. It reached noon and the Aalaag had not yet appeared. It moved on, past five minutes after twelve, past ten minutes after twelve . . .

At a little more than fourteen minutes after twelve, the massive figure in shining armor rode its huge, bull-like beast around a corner of the tower, and moved to a position roughly opposite the middle of it before stopping. To Shane's relief, the rider had brought his beast to a halt facing outward, so that he, too, looked away from the clock. Shane reached a perspiration-slippery hand in through the slit on the left side of his robe and turned off his invisibility.

There was the silver flash and, looking down he saw his robe and shoes against the face of the clock. Within him the urge was overwhelming to make his mark on the clockface and start his descent; but he had calculated beforehand that he would have to hold a visible position where he was for at least sixty seconds, to make sure everyone who should be watching for him had noticed him; and as many others, except the Aalaag, as possible. He hung there, accordingly, with the sweat rolling down his body under the robe and waited for the huge minute hand to move forward one full minute.

Finally it touched the black mark toward which it had been progressing. Shane reached in under his robe and brought out a stoppered vial of paint and an inch-wide paintbrush. He poured the paint onto the brush and applied the brush end to the clock-face beside him, making the sketch of the cloaked figure with staff in hand. Then he put vial and paintbrush back in under the robe, heedless of what the paint would do to the jacket he was wearing, and touched the ring device to let himself begin a slow drift down the face of the tower. Out beyond him, on the ground, he could see faces, a number of faces now, turned up to watch him. At any moment he expected the Aalaag also to turn, to see what was attracting the attention of the humans. He had counted on the Aalaag indifference to beasts to cause this one to ignore the curiosity of the surrounding people, as something beneath the notice of a master.

But luck was not with him. Before he had reached the ground, the riding beast swung about, on some signal from its rider, and that rider looked up.

In a second the viewing slit in the silver protective screen over the helmet would be in line with the tower and he would be discovered. There was no hope the rider would ignore a human descending slowly through the air as Shane was. Humans did not have the technology to make that sort of descent; and it was expressly forbidden for humans to make use of Aalaag tools anywhere but in the Headquarters buildings themselves, and then by special permission. The rider would have to investigate and the first step in any investigation would be rendering Shane paralyzed or unconscious.

Hastily fumbling under his robe, Shane turned himself back into privacy mode again. There was the familiar silver flash and he was now invisible to the watching humans. But the privacy tool was not perfect in its bending of light around an object. It left a slight shimmer like heat waves in the air where the hidden object was; and the Aalaag would recognize that shimmer immediately for what it was if he looked directly as it, as he was now starting to do, as the riding beast under him completed its turn.

Shane stopped breathing. But then, without warning, a miracle occurred. The slit of the sentry's helmet tilted upward. He was staring, not at Shane, but at what all the human eyes were fixed upon now that Shane had disappeared—the face of the clock.

In that moment, Shane reached the ground and made himself once more visible. No one seemed to notice. He began to walk at an unhurried pace directly toward the sentry, who had now put his riding beast in motion and was moving toward the tower to look more closely at the clockface. Whether the eyes behind that slit in the helmet had already identified the mark Shane had drawn as an illegal one, Shane did not know. But he knew that if the Aalaag looked long enough, he could not fail to recognize what was up there.

Shane and the great pair of alien figures approached each other steadily. They drew level. At any moment, Shane expected to hear the deep Aalaag voice behind him, commanding him to halt; or perhaps he would simply without warning feel the stunning blow of the officer's long arm, on the theory of a sentinel like this that a nonservant human would not understand even a simple order in Aalaag to stop.

He and the Aalaag passed each other.

Peter was only about twenty feet away. At the same steady pace, Shane walked toward him; and just before Shane reached him Peter turned and began to move away, walking some ten feet before Shane.

Shane followed him.

Behind him he had no idea what was happening. But none of the humans he passed spoke to him or turned toward him, although every one of those he went by in the first minute or so glanced surreptitiously at him. He continued following Peter until they turned a corner and were passed by a group of some four or five men walking in the opposite direction and talking animatedly, who blocked them from the view of those by the tower, but paid no attention to either of them, lost in conversation as they went.

Peter glanced back over his shoulder briefly, then nodded and beckoned. He sped up, his walk becoming a very fast walk indeed. Shane increased his own pace to keep up. They were moving alongside a street now, down which there was a flow of traffic, and a moment later a car pulled to the curb just ahead of them.

Peter reached it first, opened the door for him and stood aside. Shane ducked in. Peter followed. The door slammed and the car accelerated away from the curb once more. A moment later they were lost in traffic.

FOURTEEN

"YOU CAN DROP ME AT THE GOVERNMENT UNIT," SAID SHANE, ONCE the car was well on its way. "I've got to get back as soon as I can. They think I'm there now."

"Look," said Peter. They were sitting together in the rear seat of the small, private vehicle. An anonymous driver was up front, giving Shane nothing more than a view of the back of her head. "You can spare another hour, can't you? I told all the visitors we'd meet right after the demonstration. Just so you could say a word or two to them—the real talk from you comes tonight, exactly as you planned."

Shane glared at him.

"I can't take the time now," he said. "If someone at the Unit calls for me or goes looking for me—"

"Just an hour."

"An hour could be an hour too long."

"Now, look here," said Peter, "you wouldn't have taken off like this unless you felt pretty safe doing it. An hour's no time at all; and it's important to say a word to these people while they're still in shock from seeing you paint the Pilgrim sign right under the nose of an alien and get away with it."

"You don't understand—," began Shane, and checked himself. Of course, Peter did not understand, but explaining to him would take too much time and trouble, even if it could be done successfully. Moreover, the other man was right about a word said right away after the demonstration.

Not only that, Shane thought, the fact that he only had time for a word or two with the visitors now would give him a chance to dodge any awkward questions; and he would have the hours between then and tonight's scheduled meeting to consider how such questions should be answered.

"All right," he said. "But I've got to be at the Government Unit an hour from now."

"You will," said Peter. "The place I told them all to meet is close by here."

It was, indeed, close. It was barely more than a couple of minutes more before the car pulled up before a block of flats and two minutes after that Shane was in the sitting room of a small flat belonging to one of Peter's contacts, a young couple who might or might not be Resistance members themselves.

There was a knock at the door five minutes later and Shane prudently moved out of sight, into the flat's one bedroom, where he waited with his only company, the couple's year-old baby. In a few minutes, Peter joined him.

"Guess who was first in?" said Peter. "Georges Marrotta. You remember the man who spoke to you in Basque when we picked you up in Milan?"

Shane nodded. He had a clear mental picture of the thick-bodied man in the leather jacket, with the short, black hair and the pipe in the teeth of his round, hard face.

By the time another ten minutes had gone by, the flat had been entered eight more times and Shane was beginning to grow restless.

"What time is it?" he asked Peter.

"One-forty pm," answered Peter.

"Aren't they all here yet? I've got to get going," Shane said.

"We're still missing two," answered Peter.

But Shane had made up his mind.

"I can't wait any longer. The new Aalaag Officer of the Day'll be coming on duty in thirty minutes. He might have some reason to want to see me. Those who aren't here now are just going to have to catch up with me this evening."

He pulled the edges of the cowl on his cloak close together before his face.

"Let's go in," he said. "You said Maria's one of the ones already there?"

"Yes."

"Good," said Shane. "Let's go."

They went into the sitting room, which, being of a size with the flat it belonged to, was overcrowded with the twelve people now in it, now that Shane and Peter had arrived. Windows had been opened on the cold December afternoon to counteract the stifling heat caused by so many bodies crowded into so small a space.

Shane found himself wedged into one corner of the room, so that he could face all of them at once. His audience was perched on everything from sofa backs to cushions on the floor.

Peter began by introducing to him everyone there but Maria. Out of the sudden spate of names, only a few managed to stick in Shane's mind. Anna ten Drinke would have stood out in any crowd. She was a short, large-boned, powerful woman of about fifty with a square face and an uncompromising attitude. Wilhelm Herner was a slim, gentlemanly looking individual in no less than his sixties, neatly suited and neck-tied. The only other woman—from Madrid—looked no older than Maria; and a late arrival from Warsaw looked like a boy in his teens, with a stiff brush of black hair and a smiling face.

"I'm sorry," Shane said to them, turning his head from right to left so that he could look at them all in turn through the narrow vertical opening of his closed hood. "But any real talk will have to wait for our scheduled meeting tonight. Peter can tell you after I'm gone—if he hasn't yet—what I told the people here in London. Meanwhile, to give you the essentials briefly, I know the Aalaag better than any other human you're going to find—for reasons that, for safety's sake, like everything else about me, I can't tell you. I invented the Pilgrim symbol, and it's to be a rallying symbol for those ready to act in opposition to the aliens. I'll be coming to your cities—Peter, again, will tell you how I make contact when I do that. If you want to work with me, help me to do the same sort of thing you saw me do today, then fine. If not, I'll work without you. If you're with me, you'll start immediately to form a tight, international organization, and recruit people to it who're ready to act against the Aalaag."

He paused.

"Now," he said, "I've got to leave in a minute or two. Quickly and briefly, any questions?"

Their faces were not the faces of the Londoners Peter had introduced him to originally. These were, for the most part, harder, older faces, more used to command. They would possibly also be more intelligent than Peter's people, as a group, Shane thought.

"I saw you come partway down from the clock tower, but then you disappeared," said a gray-haired man with a young face, but a thickened body. He was sitting with two others on the room's only couch. He spoke in North American English with a midwestern accent that was almost faultless, but Shane's linguist's ear guessed him to be a native speaker of North African French. "I saw you again on the ground. You walked right past the Aalaag, who didn't stop you. How did you get up to the clockface without anyone seeing you? I was there a good fifteen minutes before noon, watching, and if you climbed that tower you must have done it somehow from the inside."

"The answer," said Shane, "is—I'm sorry, but again that's something I'm not going to tell you. You can like it, or not. My survival depends on not telling much about myself. Go on."

"Did you deliberately wait until the Aalaag"—he pronounced the alien name very well, thought Shane, for someone not of Lyt Ahn's special corps—"was there to do what you did, because you wanted him to see you? Or perhaps did you wait so that we could see him seeing you?"

"The latter," said Shane. "As I say, I'm going to be repeating that sort of performance in some of your cities. The purpose is to show that the Pilgrim can do things right under the Aalaag's noses and still not be caught. The Pilgrim's to be a symbol of freedom, as I said."

"In that case—"

"Just a moment," said Shane. "Let me add something to that. You'll notice that when tomorrow's newspapers come out, none of them will mention the incident. That'll be because what I painted on the clock was the Pilgrim symbol, and the newspapers are sensitive to anything that might offend our masters or make them look bad. But I'm willing to bet that the news of what I did has spread through half of greater London by this time tomorrow, by word of mouth. I'll also bet that the mark on the clockface won't last two days—and that no one will be seen removing it. Which means that it'll have been removed by the Aalaag, as soon as they learn about it—which they will in due time from someone like an Interior Guard or some member of the London police. But by that time too many people will have seen it to hush up the fact it was there, and put there by the Pilgrim.''

"Now we ask the obvious question," said Anna ten Drinke. Her English was heavily accented. "Perhaps you are a spy for the Aalaag—that was why you were allowed to do what you did and not be stopped by the alien on guard at the Houses of Parliament.''

"I'm not," said Shane. "But that's something you're going to have to gamble on, because there's no way I can convince you I'm not without giving away information that would mean I'd end up being caught by the Aalaag; which, aside from the fact I've no intention of letting it happen, would be self-defeating to all our prospects. But I'll give you one question to ask yourselves whenever that particular doubt comes up in your minds—and I've got a hunch it's going to be coming up again and again—and that's whether anything I do or anything about me could be so valuable to the Aalaag that it'd outweigh the cost to them of fostering a legend of a human who could do what he wants in spite of all their power—and get away with it every time."

"Why do you want us to build a worldwide organization ready to take action?" said Wilhelm Herner.

"Isn't that what you've always wanted to do anyway? Now, I'm giving you a reason. As the Pilgrim, I can be the focal point for such an undercover force; and I'm also going to be able to get you information about what the Aalaag are going to do, often even before your local Aalaag knows it. Basically, you're to start the resistance of the world's whole human population—so that if eventually the day comes to rise against the Aalaag, and you give the word to rise, everyone could, at once—or so close to everyone that those who'll hold back'll be too small in number to make a difference.''

"That's all?" asked Georges Marrotta heavily. He had sat smoking his pipe in silence up until now.

"Secondly," went on Shane, ignoring him, "I want you to foster the legend of the Pilgrim and the hopes of humans everywhere so that the organization you're going to build will have some hope and faith going for it.''

"And just how are we going to rise against the Aalaag when the time comes?" Marrotta took his pipe out of his mouth.

"Peter will tell you what I told the London people," said

Shane. "I told them you can't fight the Aalaag and win. Repeat—
you can't possibly fight the Aalaag in conventional terms and win.
But given things the way I want to set them up, we might be able
to make them fight against themselves. In brief, it may be possible
to make them decide to leave our world and go look elsewhere for
servants."

No one in the room said anything to that; but skepticism was
like the smoke cloud from Marrotta's pipe, in the air over them
all.

"Third," said Shane, "I want you to use these ordinary people
you recruit and others to make this new idea of the Aalaag's for
improving production work. Peter's told you what I originally told
him and the people he introduced me to here in London—that
the so-called Governor Project that's being tried out here is a pilot
project. If it works, they'll be trying it all over the world. There'll
be an organization like it set up in each one of your cities; and
these have got to seem to work. Unfortunately, that means they
actually will have to work. Production of materials the Aalaag want
for their own use has got to increase."

There was something like a universal, quiet groan of negation
about the room.

"You want us to push people to actually increase production?"
Anna ten Drinke demanded. "Even if we could get to the ones
concerned—and they're ordinary people not working for the Resistance—how do we get them to increase what they're producing
now?"

"Very simply," said Shane. "Part of the fall-short in production
is simply caused by nothing more than individual foot-dragging on
the part of those doing the producing. There's nothing organized
about it. It's simply a case of the farmer, the mechanic, or whoever,
saying to himself or herself—'why should I sweat myself for those
bastards?' Just get them wherever possible to stop the foot-
dragging—stop even only part of it—and what the Aalaag'll see will
be a statistical improvement for which the Governor Units will get
the credit."

He looked around the room at all of them.

"Think of the advantages in just that, for a moment," he said.
"Once their production goes up because of what you did, you can
get in touch with the humans they've got the Units staffed with,

and break the news that the only reason they're getting the improvement is because of Resistance help. Which means that from then on they work with you unless they want the statistics to go back to looking bad. Don't you see the power this can give you?"

Desoules shook his head.

"It sounds like a pipe dream," he said.

"Not a pipe dream," said Shane. "A possibility. A good possibility; and all I'm asking you to do at this moment is consider it. Think about it until you see me tonight and we'll talk more about it then. Meanwhile, I've got to get going. Peter, will you take me where I need to go?"

Shane got up from where he was sitting and started toward the front door of the apartment.

"Let him go," said Georges Marrotta. He had the pipe back in his mouth. "I don't think we need him. I don't think we want him."

"That's up to you," said Shane, still on his way out. "Peter? Maria?"

Outside the front door, in the small corridor that led to the stairs, Shane noticed that Maria was looking at him oddly. But he had no time now to ask her why.

"Is the car ready?" he asked Peter.

"Yes. We can go right away," said Peter, beginning to lead off.

"I think I'll stay here and listen to how they react in there," Maria said to Shane. "Unless you need me to come with you for some reason?"

"No," said Shane. "I'll see you back at our suite in an hour. I'll just be showing up there long enough so that I can sign out normally, as if I'd never been gone."

"I'll be there," she said.

Shane went.

He arrived back at the Unit at a lucky moment. One of the Interior Guard officers—a captain—was just exiting his car as Shane turned into the courtyard. Invisible, Shane followed him closely, slipping into the building just behind him when he opened the front door and going past him as he stopped at the desk with the duty corporal behind it, to sign in. Shane hurried up the stairs, almost blundered into the Lieutenant Governor as the other turned into the top of the stairs and started a descent, then made it the rest of the way back to his office door.

No one was visible in the corridor. He opened the door, stepped in with a sigh of relief and closed the door behind him. He stripped off his robe, hid it in his attaché case, and sat down at his desk. It was not until then that he noticed the hard copy of a message, left in the center of his papers, on top of everything where he could not miss seeing it when he came in. Some Aalaag had evidently tried to get in contact with him and been frustrated.

The print was the boldface print of the Message Room's automatic translator. The breath that Shane had held unthinkingly on seeing this evidence that someone had come and found him missing during his absence went out of him with a gush. It was unlikely that the human having the delivery duty in the Message Room today had wasted time searching for another mere human. For one of the Aalaag he or she would of course have combed the building from top to bottom. If Shane did not get the message in time to react properly to it, that was his look-out, not the messenger's.

Shane read the message itself, which was brief.

"Beast Shane Evert. You will report to the First Captain without delay."

It was signed by Molg Ema, who gave his title as Adjutant for the Day to Lyt Ahn.

Shane's responses were almost automatic. That message was a command that would override any other Aalaag command or order—not that any of the officers left behind by Laa Ehon were likely to give him counterorders. But it did require instant response. He must leave for the House of Weapons immediately.

Only, before that, he must make sure the tools he had taken from the arms locker were back in place, and to do that safely, he must first make sure that the three Aalaag officers still in the building were occupied elsewhere, so that he would not be caught entering or leaving the locker.

He decided to risk using the privacy tool. It would be good only for deceiving any other humans he should meet—an Aalaag, given light enough to notice the apparent distortion of air—would immediately know what was going on. The devices, both of them, were still in the pockets of his jacket. He put on his robe once more, on the faint chance that, if caught by one of the Aalaag, he could yet talk himself out of trouble that would arise. If he was discovered with such a device—he could gamble, for example, on the fact that the Aalaag would not check, and make the claim that Lyt Ahn had authorized his carrying it for protection from other humans who might be inimical to a servant of the Aalaag. His robe on, he checked the corridor once more, found it empty, and slipped out of the door to check the various places where the three officers might be found.

He found them in the first place he checked. The officer on duty was at his desk, with the other two in conference with him. Shane got a good look into the office as a message was carried in by a bucktoothed young messenger who was very probably the same one who had delivered the one to Shane's own desk. Now Shane slipped away, still invisible, made his way as silently as possible down to the arms locker, opened it and replaced the two items he had taken.

He made a silent prayer that no Aalaag should ever check the items for evidence they had been handled by a human. Shane had no positive knowledge that the Aalaag could find such evidence on items handled hours or even days before, but he had learned to think of nothing as impossible where the Aalaag were concerned. He went back out again. Visible now whether he might have wanted to be or not, he went back up the stairs to the main floor, saw no one, ascended to his office—and a moment later came out, banging the door behind him like an individual in a hurry, and clattered down one flight of stairs to the duty officer's office.

He rapped on the door, waited for the human voice to tell him to enter, then spoke in English to the Interior Guard lieutenant on desk duty there, as protocol required—as if the three Aalaag officers were not in the room.

"Please inform the duty officer," Shane said, "that I have just received a message from my master the First Captain ordering me back to his presence."

He showed the message to the human and was about to turn and go when the duty officer spoke in Aalaag. Clearly, he was one of the few aliens to recognize a word or two in a human tongue.

"Hold! That beast there that just came in. What is this about a message?"

Shane turned toward the three officers and took the one step forward that was permitted.

"I am ordered to return to my master, the First Captain, untarnished sir," he said in Aalaag.

The officer looked at his fellow officers, who in turn looked at Shane.

"You will be the liaison-beast from the First Captain, then. That will leave us with no beast here who can speak the true tongue," said the duty officer. "It is regrettable—but of course, unavoidable. You may—"

He checked himself. The ritual phrase for dismissing a beast in this case came perilously close to sounding as if he was giving Shane approval to obey the order already given him by the First Captain—an unwarrantable impertinence on the part of a junior officer like himself.

"I have no wish to see or speak to you further," he amended.

"I thank the untarnished sir."

Shane made one backward step and turned once more to the Interior Guard lieutenant.

"Do you know," he asked in English, "if a courier ship is ready for me at one of the airports?"

"Heathrow," said the human officer. "Alien area. Regular procedure. We got that message without explanation about two hours ago."

"Somebody on his toes, someone off his," said Shane lightly. "One of the Message Room people in the House of Weapons must have got the order about the transportation off before another one got around to messaging me. Well, that's the way it usually goes."

"Right," said the lieutenant. "We'll be seeing you again?"

"Oh, I'll be back," said Shane. "I just won't know when, until I'm on my way here."

He left. In theory he was headed directly for Heathrow airport. In fact, the moment he was beyond the courtyard and out of the sight of anyone there, he found a phone and called the hotel suite he shared with Maria. The sound of her voice coming back at him over the wire was like a lungful of oxygen to someone suffocating.

"Thank heaven you're there," he said. "Look, I've been ordered back to the House of Weapons by Lyt Ahn. I'm going to stop off, pretending I've got some clothes to pick up. I'll have just a few minutes to talk to you, so when I get there, just listen. If there're questions you absolutely have to ask, wait until I'm done, then ask them as briefly as you can, and I'll do what I can to answer you as time allows. You understand the situation?"

"I understand," she said.

He left the phone and went in search of a cab.

No more than fifteen minutes later, he was unlocking the door of the suite and she was in front of him, wearing a blue, quilted bathrobe as if she had just stepped out of a shower. The scent of the soap she had used was like an invisible aura around her; and he had to fight back the instinctive urge to put his arms around her.

"I'd hoped to take you with me when I went," he said in English, "but a sudden summons like this gives me no time to ask Lyt Ahn for permission at long distance. Maybe it's better this way. I can talk to him personally about you; and you can use a few more days' practice. Concentrate on that short list of most important phrases I gave you and work with the voice tapes I made."

He paused. She nodded.

"I will," she said.

"And concentrate even more on the protocol actions I showed you. There're people who've been servants to Aalaag for a couple of years now without being able to speak or understand any Aalaag at all, except the sound the Aalaag makes to call them by what the Aalaag thinks is their name; and they get by beautifully by just knowing what physical move to make, and certain motions and movements by the Aalaag when he or she signals to them to do something. In case of doubt, don't try to speak at all. Just concentrate on making the right physical moves. They don't expect you to be intelligent, only obedient."

"Yes," Maria said.

"Stay here in the suite as much as possible, so I can reach you in a hurry if I get the chance. If and when you do have to go out, see if someone can't buy you a phone-answering machine in the black market first. If that's not possible, try to get one of your Resistance people to steal one for you, so you can leave a phone message of where I can reach you if you're gone."

"The black market has them, I'm sure," she said.

"Finally, don't be alarmed if you haven't heard from me, if a couple of Interior Guardsmen simply appear without warning and pick you up. It'll mean that Lyt Ahn has agreed to send for you; and the Guard'll be pulling their favorite trick of not telling anyone anything. They'll probably take you directly to an airport and put you aboard an aircraft. I've no idea whether it's likely to be a commercial aircraft, or if they'll be tucking you aboard some Aalaag ship already headed for the House of Weapons. If it's an Aalaag ship, just stick to your movements protocol with the pilot or any other Aalaag who's aboard and you'll be fine. Remember, they're far more likely to forget you're there than they are to pay attention to you. Above all, even if you're afraid, never let them guess it. Fear, even in a beast, disgusts an Aalaag. You follow me?"

"Of course," she said.

"Now," he told her, "any questions?"

She hesitated.

"You won't be at that meeting with the people from the Continent tonight," she said.

"No," he sighed, "that's right. It's just this bad luck of being called back suddenly. But something like that could always happen. It's why I told Peter to get them here as soon as he could. He'll just have to fill them in as much as possible on what he knows and whatever he hasn't yet told them about what I told his people when I met them earlier. Is there something about my not seeing them you wanted to talk to me about?"

"Why do you always challenge people?" she said.

He blinked.

"I don't follow you," he said.

"Yes you do," Maria answered. "I asked you why you always had to challenge everyone. You do it even to Peter. You treated those Resistance leaders from Europe as if they were a handful of servants—or children. Why?"

"I was angry with them . . . I guess," he said, the first words coming out quickly, without thought, the last two slowly.

"Angry? Why?"

"I don't know. Because they don't understand the Aalaag the way I do. Because they've got these foolish notions about what can be done because they don't understand what they're up against. Not that all of them were all that ready to listen anyway. Your friend Georges Marrotta, from Milan, for example."

"Yes," she said, "he's a good example. I know Georges. He

likes to make up his own mind, but you didn't give him a chance. Something about just seeing them makes you angry, you say. What is it? It's got to be more than just the fact that they don't know what they've never had a chance to learn.''

"Look!" he said. "I don't have time to worry about that now. I was supposed to be going directly from the Unit to the airport. We'll talk about this some other time. Is there anything else you want to ask me about before I go? You've got plenty of English money?''

"You know I have. How can I call you after you leave here?" she asked.

"You can't," he said. "You'll just have to wait for me to try to call you; and there's no telling when I'll have a chance to do that. Anything else?''

"No.''

"Good-bye then," he said. His body cried out at him to take her to him and hold her. There was a force like that of some great magnet that seemed to be pulling the two of them together. For a moment they merely gazed at each other, an arm's length apart; then she almost hurled herself forward and flung her arms around him.

"Don't touch me!" he shouted, pushing her back. She stood at arm's length from him as his hands dropped from her shoulders, staring at him.

"What is it with you?" she almost screamed at him in Italian. "You look at me with eyes as if you were drowning in Hell and I was the only one who could reach out and save you! But the moment I come close to you, you pull away from me! What is it? What is it?''

"The—the Aalaag," he stammered. Never had his mind worked so quickly. "I can't let them guess you mean anything to me as a person, or I'd never get Lyt Ahn to agree to my taking you on as an assistant, and into the corps of translators—''

"How could they know—''

"I don't know. I don't know for absolutely certain they could. But I've learned not to underestimate them. They can do things you wouldn't believe. There was a prisoner—a House of Weapons servant the Interior Guard couldn't question physically because he was so old and sick he'd have died on them. They told the Aalaag so, and for once I saw the Aalaag take a hand themselves. They went to the place the prisoner had been accused of going to—it had been a year before, and it was in a part of the House of Weapons a human servant should never have been. They came back after just spending a few minutes there and told the prisoner not only when he'd been there, but everything he'd done on his visit—and he'd only stepped in there that once in his lifetime. He broke down and confessed; and I—I had to translate for them. I don't know if they could find evidence on me of the fact that you and I'd been close physically, but perhaps they could. We can't risk it—not yet."

They stood, an arm's length apart once more. On her face was a look like none he could ever remember seeing on anyone.

"I didn't know," she breathed after a long moment. "Oh, be careful with them. Take care of yourself."

"You," he said hoarsely, "you take care."

They stared at each other nakedly a moment longer. Then he turned and went away from her.

FIFTEEN

ONCE IN A SMALL COURIER SHIP IN WHICH, THIS TIME AGAIN, HE WAS the only passenger, Shane settled back into his oversize seat with a sense of relief. It was not that he was happy to be leaving London and Maria, particularly now; but so much had happened in the past few days that he felt the need to stand back and look at it. It had gone well, he told himself. In the case of Maria, it had gone better than he had dreamed. At least she knew how he felt. He would no longer have to pretend indifference to her, although evidently his pretense had never fooled her.

Then, abruptly, as so often happened to him, the pendulum of his emotions swung the other way as he remembered standing in the hot and crowded sitting room and the anger he had felt toward the Resistance leaders gathered there to hear what he would say. Without warning there was an empty feeling inside him.

Maria was correct. What right had he to be angry with them? They had all taken considerable risk in coming there; and it had been only natural that they had expected to learn who he was and what his plans and intentions were. Not that alone, but he had stood there, showing them nothing but a path that he alone knew would lead only to their deaths and the deaths of those who followed them—a path he had originally laid out only for the benefit of Maria and himself—and he had had the arrogance to get angry with them when they hesitated to take him at his word without further information and without qualifications.

Now that he had cooled down, the truth was easy to see. He had lost his temper with them because of the guilt he was feeling. Their hesitation reproached him for what he planned to do to them—even though they had no idea that he had any such plans. But he knew. He had been aware of his own guilt; and he had lashed out at them for making him feel it.

If only, he told himself now, there was some way to do what he wanted without sending them all to the slaughterhouse. If only the best of all possible outcomes was possible.

For a moment, his mind toyed with the wild notion that perhaps the false solution he had offered them might actually be made to work. Perhaps it might actually be possible to set up a strong and organized Resistance, to tie all the ordinary people in the world to it, so that they would move when the word was given, as one person, in defiance against the Aalaag. Perhaps, if this was properly managed for the maximum effect, the Aalaag might be so impressed that they would yield somewhat the iron grip they now held on the planet Earth and the human race, at least to the point where life for everyone here could become at least bearable again. . . .

The daydreams that came to him so easily in moments of travel like this summoned up a picture in his mind, a picture of armies in pilgrim cloaks, with staffs, marching a dozen abreast against all the metropolitan cities of the world and the Headquarters buildings of the Aalaag within those cities. He let himself imagine those buildings surrounded, besieged by a sea of pilgrims, their presence speaking the outrage of a whole world. Faced with that, he saw the Aalaag at last understanding the people with whom they had chosen to deal. He saw the Aalaag at last willing to compromise. . . .

The daydream dissolved like a soap bubble in midair. The practical front of his mind laughed jeeringly at the daydream. Even if the impossible could be made to happen and the world's humans would react as a body, the notion was insane. The Aalaag compromise? With beasts? They would die where they stood first; and there was no need for them to die—there was need only for the death of the humans who dared to stand up against them. And if these turned out to be all, or practically all, of the beasts on a particular world, so that it was no more use to them, why then the slaughter would become an object lesson to other worlds that might also dream of throwing off Aalaag authority. No, even less than the excuse of an object lesson was needed. The fact that in defying them the humans would be doing what was unlawful and forbidden would give the Aalaag no choice but to destroy them; or else in their own eyes the Aalaag would become less than they must always believe themselves to be.

He pushed away the wild, momentary dream, but it would not entirely vanish. Once hope had been raised, his foolish emotions refused to let go of it entirely. It clung to a corner of his mind until the ship was at last set down on its landing area atop the House of Weapons.

It went, however, quickly enough when he was once more walking the floors of the corridors below, the heels of the boots he wore under his pilgrim's robe echoing back from the hard, tiled surface underfoot and the equally hard surfaces of the walls and ceilings. Trotting was a more apt word in this case than walking, for that was what he had to do to keep up with the Aalaag junior officer who was accompanying him. The orders had evidently been that he was to report to Lyt Ahn immediately, wherever the First Captain might be; and they were in the wing of a floor containing the quarters of Adtha Or Ain, an area normally forbidden to members of Lyt Ahn's Courier-Translator Corps except by special invitation, or with escort. In this case, it was with escort.

They reached a door and the Aalaag with him touched it with a heavy forefinger.

There was a fairly long moment with no response, and then the voice of Adtha Or Ain sounded over their heads.

"Come."

They entered.

Lyt Ahn and Adtha Or Ain were standing facing each other in what seemed to be primarily a lounge or sitting room, in Aalaag terms. Adtha Or Ain frowned at the officer.

"What's this?" she demanded. "I commanded no one here, person or beast. I'm in private conference with the First Captain."

"Your pardon, immaculate dame—," the officer began, but Lyt Ahn cut him short.

"This is my responsibility," he said. "I left word that this beast was to be brought to me the moment it arrived. I didn't intend that it should be brought to me when I was with my consort, however. I should have been more precise in my order. You may leave untarnished, young sir. This is no fault of yours—oh, and you may as well leave the beast with us, now that you've brought it here."

"I obey, immaculate sir."

The officer went out.

"I don't wish to take undue advantage of being your consort to urge you beyond the limits of what any of your other next senior officers would feel duty bound to do." Adtha Or Ain was speaking to Lyt Ahn, with Shane forgotten, before the door had fully closed behind the escorting officer. "You may remember that I was one of your peers among the officers prior to coming here who voted for you to be First Captain of this Expedition. Also, I have discharged my own separate duties as an officer since and given no one any reason to doubt that I am unique in my right to share with you the administering of this planet."

"None of this is doubted, nor have I ever questioned it," said Lyt Ahn.

"But I feel you no longer use me as an ally, as a consort should be used. You find none of my advice helpful."

"Of course I find it helpful."

"But you will not use it."

"We see two different ways of handling a situation, that's all," said Lyt Ahn. "Laa Ehon is a most immaculate officer."

"Did I say he was not? But in being ambitious, he puts his own welfare before that of our race."

"You forget," said Lyt Ahn, "I was also ambitious."

"But properly so. Within correct channels—to make a name for yourself so that someday you might be voted, as you have been, to the position of First Captain. You did not wait until an Expedition was in place and then plan to make use of its troubles to further your ambition."

"I do not think, in his innermost thoughts, that Laa Ehon thinks of displacing me as a matter of personal ambition. I believe he thinks of what is best for the Expedition in terms of doing well on this world."

Adtha Or Ain made an impatient gesture with one large hand, one of the few emotional gestures Shane had ever seen made by an Aalaag.

"The fact that he is capable of self-deception, no matter how innocently," she said, "makes no difference. You would be wise to find some reason for disengaging yourself from agreement with him on this Governor Unit idea of his."

"That is not the way to handle such ideas," said Lyt Ahn. "If indeed his plan is a good one, the Expedition will benefit and I should therefore support it in any case. If it is bad, then by pushing it harder and faster, I hurry it toward the moment when it will fall apart of its own innate flaws."

"That is a risky course to take, where beasts are concerned. Rather you should do as I suggested with the beasts—"

"One moment, my consort," Lyt Ahn interrupted her. "This, waiting for me right now, is Shane-beast, of whom you know."

Adtha Or Ain cast a startled glance at Shane.

"I had not recognized it. Send it outside."

"If you'll forgive me," said Lyt Ahn, "I am overdue to deal with a number of things right now. Let's leave discussion of the matter as it is and finish it off later, if you'll show me that courtesy."

Adtha Or Ain looked at him for a long moment.

"I see I've no choice in the matter. We'll talk later, then."

"We will, indeed. I promise," said Lyt Ahn.

He turned toward the door. Striding past Shane, he glanced at him for a cold, impersonal second.

"Come," he said. Shane followed him out.

Hurrying to keep up with the long strides of the First Captain as the two of them headed for Lyt Ahn's office, Shane found his mind suddenly filled with worry over what Adtha Or Ain could have been suggesting as a solution to the Aalaag problem of insufficient production. Whatever it was, it was not likely to be palatable to humans—and if further evidence of this was needed, there had been Adtha Or Ain's demand that he be sent out of the room, when Lyt Ahn had reminded her that Shane could understand what they were saying.

Unfortunately, he could not even guess. Frustratingly, he did not even know the areas in which the humans, by Aalaag standards, were falling short of required production levels; and he needed this information when the situation resulting was such as to threaten the internal structure of the Aalaag high command, including that of his own master and therefore himself.

But that information was locked up in the minds and records of at least several hundred thousand human accountants. The Aalaag had machines that would let them know what and where these shortfalls were. But, like the Aalaag weapons and certain other protected devices, these machines would not work for a human, even if Shane could find one and figure out how to operate it.

The trouble with Aalaag technology was that it was so far advanced over that of humanity that there was no tracing back from the point at which a device worked or did not work, until a gap was met which could be figured out. The gap that was encountered was the result of innumerable advances, all piled on each other and spread over all the Aalaag areas of technology, so that there was no visible connection between apparent cause and result—as there would have been no visible connection, to a Stone Age savage, between a video receiver and the sounds and pictures that were produced by it.

Perhaps he could somehow lead Lyt Ahn into mentioning what production lines had fallen in short supply. Or perhaps—as the Governor Unit proliferated with other centers around the globe— he could get information from each one about its own area, giving him a general image . . .

But they were already at the entrance to Lyt Ahn's office and going in. Lyt Ahn went immediately to the chair behind his desk and sank into it, staring at the large screen on the opposite wall where Shane had once seen imaged Adtha Or Ain's conception of what might be happening to their son. But in this case as Lyt Ahn looked at it, the screen came alive with a landscape showing a bowl of rock, a valley in mountains. A lake formed the foreground of the picture and a thick finger of dark green jungle grew down one of the rocky slopes that were otherwise of bare, red stone.

Shane, having been given no orders otherwise, had checked himself, following his first two ritual steps inside the office door. He stood where he was, watching the First Captain, who was apparently completely absorbed by the image on the screen.

At first glance, except for that strip of jungle at what seemed to be altitudes too high and barren for such flora, the scene shown could have been someplace on Earth. But then certain wrongnesses intruded on the eye. The color of the sky was too light a blue and the still water of the lake had an oddly glowing, greenish cast to it. Finally, when the image was looked at more closely, it could be seen that the finger of jungle grew not only down to, but also some little distance out into, the lake.

The jungle itself was so thick as to be almost a solid mass of greenery, trunks and limbs. But as Shane watched, an upright, two-legged figure with its body and limbs wrapped in some white material like cloth, materialized from the green tangle, gazing across the lake, directly out of the screen. It was too far to identify the figure by its face, but it moved like an Aalaag. It lifted one arm and waved.

Behind the desk, Lyt Ahn half lifted one massive hand and forearm from the desk as if to answer the wave, then dropped it back on the desk's surface again. The picture vanished, leaving only a gray screen surface; and Shane suddenly realized that the First Captain had turned to his picture-viewing as a human might pour a stiff drink and down it after a trying moment was past. It was the first time he had been more than a momentary spectator of this commitment, or addiction, or whatever you wanted to call it, of viewing scenes from their lost home worlds by the Aalaag; and he shivered inside suddenly, thinking how many thousand years back in time had been the actual moment of the wave from the figure on the screen that Lyt Ahn had automatically begun to answer.

"Sit, Shane-beast," said Lyt Ahn's deep voice now; and Shane, starting into movement almost as automatically as the First Captain had begun his wave, walked over to the couch on which he ordinarily sat and seated himself there.

"Tell me of this Project of Laa Ehon," said Lyt Ahn.

"It is in place, staffed, and already beginning its work, immaculate sir," said Shane.

"And your opinion of those humans chosen to staff it?"

"I found them all very competent, immaculate sir," said Shane. "At the time you recalled me, their number had risen to thirty-four, all intelligent beasts with experience in the type of work they are required to do as part of the Project. They appear to work harmoniously together; and the principle of the Project appears to be in process of being carried out as envisioned in their hands."

"Would you say they are successful?"

"Successful?" Shane floundered. "This beast begs the forgiveness of the First Captain for its lack of ability and inefficiency, but I had not yet seen enough of the work to know whether it was at all successful or not."

Lyt Ahn nodded slowly. He got up from behind the desk and came around to the single large chair opposite the couch on which

Shane was perched. But before he sat down he put his hand gently on the top of Shane's head.

"Your master occasionally makes mistakes, and this was one of them, little Shane-beast," he said. "Of course it was too soon for you to be able to answer such a question."

Shane held himself, as always, in tight self-control under the touch of that massive hand on his head. As always, it evoked a welter of emotions. Foremost of these was a searing hatred of Lyt Ahn for the unconscious condescension of the gesture. If Shane's mind had not been able to dominate his emotions, he would have risen from the couch and tried to kill the other with his bare hands. But at the same time, underneath the hatred and fury there was a strange understanding and sympathy. It was an understanding of something almost wistful regarding this leader of a race of conquerors, who had no one to unbend with, no one to unburden himself to, but a creature that in his own eyes was no more than a pet dog. He held his breath waiting for the moment when Lyt Ahn would take his hand away and sit down, but the hand stayed there.

"Shane-beast . . . ," said Lyt Ahn in a musing voice, "if that small head of yours could only produce the answers I need. . . ."

At that, he did take his hand away and sit down opposite Shane.

"There are at present three true persons on the staff there," he said. "Is that correct? Laa Ehon himself and three junior officers?"

"That is correct, immaculate sir."

"And those who act as officers of the top rank among the beasts, there are three?"

"Yes, immaculate sir."

"Tell me of them—these three beasts."

"First," said Shane, "is the beast with the rank of Governor. It is a male who has experience of being in authority, being before the landing of the true race here an individual acclaimed to a position of decision and power over its fellow beasts on that island."

"Ah?" said Lyt Ahn almost absently. "What was its occupation then?"

Shane hesitated.

"Immaculate sir," he said, "there is no word in the true tongue that describes what it was, because its occupation was one which does not exist among the true race. It is best described as one who

215

seeks the confidence of its fellow beasts, more with words than acts, in order to be voted into a position of power over them. This beast apologizes that it cannot describe that occupation more exactly."

"Nevermind," said Lyt Ahn. "If any of my translator-beasts could do so, it would be you, Shane-beast; and since you can't do it, then I'm making an unreasonable request. What do you think of this beast?"

"I think well of it," said Shane. "Particularly, I was impressed with the fact that, as I mentioned to Laa Ehon when he asked me for my opinion, this Governor-beast is very interested in the Project, seeing it as a means by which we beasts may in the long run serve the true race better."

"Yes," said Lyt Ahn. "And the other two beasts?"

"The beast with the rank of Lieutenant Governor is very competent, having been trained and worked for some years in the keeping of records and the overseeing of the written signs in which these are normally recorded among us. The colonel of the Interior Guard appears to have acceptable officerlike qualities."

"I see," said Lyt Ahn. "Shane-beast, in all this, in all the qualities owned by the three you have just described and their subordinate beasts, as well as in the overall plan and program for the Project, do you feel any lack? Does anything seem to be missing, either in cattle or in structure, which you feel is necessary for the whole to work harmoniously?"

"Nothing that I so sense during the short time I had contact with the Unit, immaculate sir."

"Good," said Lyt Ahn. "Having had the assurance of Laa Ehon, therefore, that all is proceeding satisfactorily, I propose to begin immediately the setting up of like Units in other Districts, without waiting for this pilot Unit to fully prove itself. This is, of course, somewhat faster than Laa Ehon himself had anticipated and will require the assignment of more of my own translator-cattle to duties away from those of my own government; but it seems to me that considering the fall-short of supplies in certain areas, the less time wasted the better, as I am sure Laa Ehon himself will see when I inform him of this decision."

Shane, suddenly, saw more than that. In one lightning bolt of illumination he understood that Lyt Ahn was taking a bold and very risky gamble. In spite of what Shane had overheard him say to his consort, Lyt Ahn must have privately concluded either that the Governor system proposed by Laa Ehon would not work, or that it could be made not to work by rushing it. Laa Ehon could hardly object strongly to a desire of the First Captain to fall in with his wishes even more strongly than the Milanese Commander himself had proposed. Any weakness the plan had would be multiplied by its being put into action too swiftly. Lyt Ahn would share some of the blame—but only to the extent of trusting too strongly in a subordinate officer. Laa Ehon would carry the load of failure and perhaps even be crushed by it.

On the other hand, if the plan did not fall apart, if it succeeded in all its branches, Lyt Ahn would have effectively shown himself playing second fiddle to Laa Ehon in solving a problem vital to the Aalaag here on Earth, an action that would be sure to raise the question of his fitness to lead—and the mere fact that any such question existed would amount to an open, if silent, invitation to him to yield up that leadership to a fitter officer, who, in this case, would obviously be Laa Ehon. Shane remembered how he had learned, on the last occasion he had witnessed a conversation between the First Captain and his consort, that any such yielding up of leadership would require the equivalent of a ritual suicide by Lyt Ahn.

It was ironic, thought Shane, that the First Captain had an ally in Shane and did not know it. Must never know it—for the good reason that the very thought would be not only unbelievable, but insulting to an Aalaag. Nonetheless, it was true. Shane had his own reasons for wanting Laa Ehon's plan to appear to fail; though he, himself, privately believed that its failure was immaterial. One way or another, in the long run, the Aalaag would still get what they wanted from the human race, if they had to destroy it to do so. Still, Lyt Ahn's gamble had given him an opening for his own purposes.

"If the First Captain will allow this beast to tell him something which may be of interest, in connection with this decision of his . . . ?" he said.

Lyt Ahn stared at him from the chair opposite with a steady look that was not one of approval. The First Captain had not exactly been interrupted, since he had paused after the words he had just said, and a simple beast could easily have assumed that he was through speaking. But in fact he had been about to lay out for Shane the connection between this decision just taken and Shane's own activities in the months to come, and a beast of Shane's experience should have realized this. Shane, however, had been engaged in a small gamble of his own; that the Aalaag would not admit to himself that what a beast did could disturb him.

"What?" said Lyt Ahn.

"If the immaculate sir will remember the Council meeting to which I was summoned, there was talk there among the immaculate sirs and dames present of the need for more translators; and a plan was advanced that those of the true race should take young of the cattle into their own homes so that they would learn to speak and understand the true tongue during their best years for doing so—"

"Well?" broke in Lyt Ahn.

"This beast implores the First Captain's forgiveness if it has been presumptuous; but while I was away from this House, this time, it occurred to me to investigate among those of my kind who had seemed to me to show signs of learning something of the true tongue on their own and without being taught—those with either the will or the aptitude to do so. As a result, I found one beast which, entirely by itself, had learned to understand and even to try to speak a word or two of the true tongue, as well as learning on its own some certain rudimentary actions of civilized behavior. I experimented with this beast and although I am only a beast myself and can only guess, I came to the conclusion that given time, even adult cattle could be taught to act as translators of the true tongue—provided they were properly coached in their learning."

Lyt Ahn sat absolutely motionless. Shane had dangled bait before him; bait tailored as best Shane knew to the way the Aalaag mind, and in particular the mind of Lyt Ahn, worked. It was impossible for the human translators not to know, as every Aalaag knew, that Lyt Ahn's virtual monopoly of the only effective humans who spoke and understood Aalaag gave him a tremendous advantage over his subordinate—but also innately equal—officers of the senior rank.

Neither Shane nor any other human he knew had found or overheard any hard evidence of the fact, but there was a strong suspicion among the servants to the aliens that the life-span of the Aalaag was much longer than that of humans. If this was so, then the time required for a generation of human babes to be raised to maturity and usefulness as translators did not imply an event so far in the future of the present senior officers that dealing with such extra translators could be regarded as someone else's problem.

Laa Ehon's production plan, therefore, posed an immediate but lesser threat to Lyt Ahn's possession of the position of First Captain. The prospect of translators for all Aalaag who could use them was a long-range threat, but a much more serious one. If, however, Lyt Ahn could produce more translators now from mature humans, by using those who already belonged to his Corps, he could undercut the effectiveness of the waiting for a generation of humans to grow into usefulness. Even evidence that translators might be produced this other way could have a strong effect on a Council that had greeted the suggestion of young humans being raised almost like young Aalaag—who were normally kept if anything isolated from other races in their childhood—with strong distaste.

Shane held his breath. If Lyt Ahn took the bait, the question he would want to ask would be obvious.

"I assume," said Lyt Ahn, after a moment of silence, "that you consider yourself capable of such coaching. Am I correct?"

"In all humility, this beast believes so, immaculate sir."

"Who else among your Corps would also be capable of such teaching, do you think?"

"I have no way of knowing, immaculate sir," said Shane.

It was, of course, no less than the truth. He could only guess who among his fellow translators would make good teachers and who would not. But he was betting that Lyt Ahn would jump to another conclusion; and, sure enough, the First Captain did.

"Your modesty does credit to a creature who is only a beast," said Lyt Ahn. "But as you are the best of my translators and can only hope that you would be successful, it would be foolish to assume that others of your Corps could be so at all. Where is this beast you refer to?"

"I left it in England when I came back here," said Shane.

"Its location?"

Shane gave the name and address of the hotel in London where he and Maria had shared the suite.

"—if the First Captain permits, I could call it by our beast communications system and make sure it is there now," he added.

"Call, then," said Lyt Ahn.

The First Captain did not move, but the sound of a phone ringing was suddenly sharp on the air of the office. It broke off and out of that same air came Maria's voice.

"Hello?"

"Maria, it's me," said Shane swiftly in English. "I was just ordered by my owner to call and make sure you were there. Stay there. He's bought the idea and undoubtedly those Interior Guards I told you about are going to be there in an hour at the most. Now I've got to stop talking English before I offend him. Good-bye."

"Good—" Maria's voice was cut off after the first syllable.

"You may go," said Lyt Ahn. "You will be recalled when this beast arrives."

It was nearly fourteen hours later, however, before Shane was again summoned to the First Captain's office, from which he deduced that other matters had taken priority over Lyt Ahn's desire to see this beast Shane had spoken of. He reached the office, touched the door and was bidden to enter. Within, Lyt Ahn was alone. No junior Aalaag officer with him and—sudden uneasiness assailed him—no Maria.

For a moment Shane felt the familiar sickening emptiness of fear—for another besides himself, this time. Could Maria have said or done something that had caused her already to be dismissed— or, even worse—destroyed? The Aalaag, contrary to what most humans believed, were by their own standards extremely tolerant of the mistakes a beast could make through ignorance, or merely through the unfortunate accident that it was only a beast.

But there was always the danger of stepping across some line that separated the fit cattle from the unfit. And if Maria had for some reason been judged unfit . . . the hell of it was he might go for days without knowing for sure what had happened to her. He might even never find out, since it would be impossible for him to ask Lyt Ahn directly about such a matter. It could even be dangerous for him to raise the question; if such asking should cause him to be suspected of whatever taint had caused Maria to be discarded or put away permanently.

Happily, in this case, Lyt Ahn relieved his fears almost at once.

"Come stand here by my desk, Shane-beast," said Lyt Ahn. His thumb pointed to a spot at his own long, arm's length from the edge of the desktop. Shane obeyed. "Now turn around so that you face the entrance from the hall."

Shane did so. There was the momentary silver flash about him, temporarily blotting out even the First Captain.

"If you look down," Lyt Ahn said, in typical Aalaag fashion forgetting he had used a privacy tool with Shane several times before this, "you will become aware that you can no longer see your body. Do not be afraid, little Shane-beast. It's merely that I wish to observe this other beast you spoke of without its being able to see you. You will speak to it when I direct you to, but you will speak to it as someone who does not know it. You will not use its beast-name or any other sounds which might cause it to identify you."

"This beast will obey, most immaculate sir."

"Good."

It was additionally typical of the incredible blunders that the Aalaag could occasionally make, for all their technology and experience with underraces, Shane thought, that it would not occur to the First Captain that Maria might recognize his voice, no matter what words it spoke to her.

"Send it in," said Lyt Ahn; and the hall door opened to produce two Interior Guardsmen with Maria between them.

"Wait outside," said Lyt Ahn, looking at the guardsmen. They turned and went. The First Captain turned his attention to Maria, on whom Shane had had his attention riveted from the moment she had appeared.

It was easy to feel secretly superior over the fact that Lyt Ahn had not thought that Maria might recognize the disembodied voice speaking to her. It was even easier to let a minor blunder like that lead a human into underestimating an Aalaag. The large aliens were both intelligent and shrewd; and Lyt Ahn was, by definition of the fact that he had won the highest position among all of them on this world, one of the most—if not the most—intelligent and shrewd of them all.

Plainly, he wanted to make sure that Shane would be unable to give Maria cues about how to act, or even the moral support of knowing there was another human in the room, one she knew and who was a friend of hers. To a much greater extent than when he had spoken rapidly in English on the phone to her, fourteen hours previously, Shane would have to watch what he said in any human language as well as what he said in Aalaag. Lyt Ahn would be having the conversation recorded and translated by other members of the Corps, one or more of which might have no reason to cover up any mistakes of his or Maria's, or even to do him any kind of favor or kindness in the translation.

Happily, he had noted, Maria had taken only the two ritual steps inside, then stopped; even though the Interior Guards, who must have been given special orders to that effect or they would not have done it, had taken a full four steps into the office before halting. Also, when they had left on being dismissed, Maria had made no move to turn or follow them out, as an uninformed—or, as an Aalaag would say, an "uncivilized"—beast might instinctively have done.

So far, so good. Lyt Ahn was now making a long, silent inspection of her. She was passing that test, too, in the proper manner, neither staring directly back into the First Captain's eyes nor looking down or away in embarrassment or confusion.

"I am told," said Lyt Ahn at last, speaking to her slowly and distinctly in Aalaag, with heavy emphasis on each word, "that you understand something of the true tongue. Is this true?"

Maria was slow in answering, and Shane could guess the reason. The question had been put in far too long a sentence for her to follow.

"This beast 'fraid—'maculate sir," she said at last, in stumbling Aalaag.

"There is no need," said Lyt Ahn slowly. "Do you understand me? There is no need to be afraid. Why are you afraid?"

This time the short sentences and the repetition of certain words clearly allowed Maria to understand them and guess at the general import of the sentence; and the repetition of "afraid," together with the construction of the final sentence that indicated it was a query enabled her to understand that question in its entirety.

"First 'maculate sir," she said.

Lyt Ahn stared at her—the sort of stare that was the Aalaag equivalent of a frown.

"Of course I am the First Captain; therefore, the first among those called immaculate," he said. "But that has nothing to do with the question I asked you. I wonder if you understood me? Shane-beast, did it not understand me, or is it that it cannot explain itself properly in the true tongue?"

"If the immaculate sir will forgive what is only an opinion, I think it is the latter," said Shane, with deliberate lack of inflection in his voice. "I believe it is attempting to say that it is afraid because you are the first of *immaculate* virtue it has ever seen. Naturally, a beast like this would have encounters, even at the most opportune moment, only with those true persons of *untarnished* quality. The beast may think that because you are of such virtue that something great and possibly terrible is going to happen to it."

"Ah," said Lyt Ahn. "I see."

He considered Maria again.

"Do not be afraid," he said.

This was a common phrase used by Aalaag to humans generally, and it was known and even imitated and satirized by people who had never had anything to do directly with one of the Aalaag. Shane relaxed. Lyt Ahn had begun by talking above Maria's level of comprehension and her capability for speaking Aalaag. This was more like it. Maria would probably have recognized this last phrase even if she had never met Shane.

"Come," said Lyt Ahn.

Another command in the alien vocabulary generally understood by humans. Maria responded at once, coming forward as Shane had taught her and stopping the equivalent of three Aalaag strides from the outer edge of the First Captain's desk.

Lyt Ahn said nothing, but his moment of silence was as good to Shane as a word of approval would have been from a human in a similar situation.

"They tell me you are a healthy beast—does it understand these words, Shane-beast?"

"I do not think so, immaculate sir."

"Then tell it in its own tongue."

"The First Captain says he had been told you are a healthy beast," said Shane in English.

"I have always been healthy," answered Maria, also in English.

"This beast, immaculate sir, says it has always been healthy."

"Good. Get it to give me some examples of what it can say in the true tongue."

GORDON R. DICKSON

"The First Captain orders you to give him a demonstration, saying some of the things you know how to say in Aalaag."

"May this beast be useful, 'maculate sir?"

"Good. Have it go on," said Lyt Ahn, for Maria had paused after the first phrase, evidently waiting for some kind of response.

"Just keep talking in Aalaag until you're told to stop," said Shane in English.

"This beast is an innocent beast, untarnished sir. This beast is going immediately. This beast does not understand the true tongue. This beast hears and obeys. This beast does not know the beasts here and has never seen these beasts before. This beast does not know the way to where the 'maculate sir would send it. The only wish of this beast is to obey its master and all true persons. . . ."

"That will do," said Lyt Ahn. Maria, to Shane's joy, understood immediately and fell silent. "It is an interesting display from one of the cattle which has never received any training in speech and proper behavior. What would it do if we simply put it back where we got it, Shane-beast?"

"I do not know, immaculate sir. It will work, I suppose, as it has always done, among the cattle which have no direct contact with true persons."

"That would be something of a waste." Lyt Ahn sat in perfect silence and immobility for a good thirty seconds. "It raises a problem, however. I had been about to inform you yesterday that you will immediately begin to investigate in other areas around this world, sites and staffs of units comparable to those of Laa Ehon's pilot project in Great Britain. It would be difficult for you to do that and at the same time continue to coach this beast to see if it could indeed be brought to a proper understanding and speaking of the true tongue. Unless . . ."

Lyt Ahn fell silent once more. Shane stood, a match for his master in expressionlessness and motionlessness.

". . . unless, of course," said Lyt Ahn, "you took it with you and coached it as you went. I could name it as a special assistant to you. But perhaps such coaching would take too much time from your primary duty of examining the sites and staffs for me? Give me your opinion, Shane-beast."

"This beast can and will do anything that the immaculate sir desires. There will be no problems."

224

"Ah. Good," said Lyt Ahn. "You'd best take it back to your own quarters with you now, then; and I'll give orders for all the rest, including any necessary extra housing and feeding that will be entailed. I'll be rather interested to see how it improves its skills with the true language—if indeed it is capable of doing so. You may both go. Tell it so, Shane-beast—oh, and perhaps you should be made visible to it."

The waviness in the air before Shane disappeared. Maria had already taken the single ritual step backward, but not yet turned toward the door. She took Shane's sudden appearance without any betraying change of expression, turned and started on her way out.

"You will leave behind me," Shane said hastily to her back in English; because while her understanding of Lyt Ahn's words and the rules of civilized movement was calculated to win favor in the First Captain's eyes, Shane himself had been given an order and that order was not for him to disregard simply because it had become unnecessary. He moved quickly to Maria's side, therefore, as she paused, and she followed him out.

As they entered the corridor outside, the two Interior Guardsmen who had brought Maria to the office stepped forward from the farther wall of the corridor.

"This individual's been released into my custody," said Shane quickly. "The First Captain's giving the orders right now; you ought to be getting confirmation on your ear receivers any moment now. Just to put your minds at rest, though, I'm taking her to my personal quarters, and if there's any question, you can follow us there."

The two wavered. They had been told that Maria was their responsibility, and that had the force of an order from one of their own human officers. But the First Captain had also given them an order—to wait outside; while this little bastard, who seemed to be one of the favored translator bunch, had just told them of other orders that certainly eventually would be checked, so that they could hardly be less than the truth. They hesitated, but the thought that their last order had been from an Aalaag—the Aalaag of all Aalaag, so to speak, was the deciding factor. To disobey Lyt Ahn was inconceivable.

They stood back and watched Shane and Maria go.

"What is it? What's going to happen?" Maria whispered in Italian when they were out of earshot of the guards.

Shane frowned at her, hoping she would read the expression correctly as the warning not to talk that it was, and cursing himself for not thinking to tell her that, unlike the general practice in most Headquarters and even in most areas of this one, in the First Captain's area the corridors had ears and eyes.

"I have been charged by the immaculate First Captain to give you a great deal of instruction," he said in English, as pompously as possible. "We will begin once we are at our destination."

Maria's face lit for a fraction of a second with understanding, in acknowledgment, then was once more as studiedly expressionless as it had been in Lyt Ahn's office. They went on in silence until they came to the door to Shane's room. He opened it and ushered Maria in.

"Surprise!" said Sylvie Onjin, jumping up from the sofa. "I heard you were back and thought I—"

She broke off, looking at Maria. Maria, who had taken only a couple of steps into the room, came to a dead halt and looked back.

SIXTEEN

For a moment there was an awkward silence in the room.

"Maria, this is Sylvie Onjin, one of our Corps of courier-translators," said Shane. "Sylvie, this is Maria Casana, who's just been named by Lyt Ahn as my special assistant in the runs I'm going to be making next."

Maria and Sylvie examined each other. To Shane's eye, they threw each other into sharp contrast. Compared to Maria, Sylvie's narrow-boned frame, small hips and breasts made her look fragile, almost overthin. While Maria's dark hair and full body made her appear almost lush in contrast to the smaller woman. There was no doubt that Maria had more natural beauty; and this, combined with the rest of her comparative size, gave her an air as if her mere presence there overrode Sylvie's.

"Things do happen around here when the First Captain gets an idea," Sylvie said, offering her hand to Maria. "It'd help, of course, if they just once allowed us some warning in advance."

Maria took the hand.

"Now you've given me one more thing to worry about," she said. "I've never been in one of these places before."

Their grasp parted.

"Oh, it's really not so bad," said Sylvie. "We all like to complain about our working conditions. Where are they going to put you?"

"I don't know—," began Maria; but at that moment the door was knocked on and opened without any waiting for an answer; a squarely built, middle-aged woman in coveralls with a tool-hung belt around her wide waist came in.

"Maintenance," she said. "You're supposed to get an extra doorway here—whose room is this?"

"Mine," answered Shane.

"It'll just take a minute." The woman had already turned away from him and was examining the wall on his right. She produced a measuring tape and marker, made a few marks, then produced what appeared to be a pen or pencil from her tool belt and began to draw from the floor up as high as she could reach, standing on her toes, then across a width a little less than a meter, and down once more to the floor again.

An inhumanly straight brown line had appeared in the wall following the moving point of whatever she held in her hand. Looking more closely at it, Shane suddenly realized the line was a cut clean through the wall. When the woman was finished she made some further adjustment on the tool and, holding it out before her toward the door-shape she had just outlined, made a scribbling motion.

All that was wall within the line vanished, leaving a door-shaped opening.

"What the hell!" exploded a hearty female voice beyond the new opening, and Shane's next door neighbor, a gray-haired woman of about the age and body shape of the Maintenance worker but considerably taller appeared in the gap. "Shane, what's going on?"

"I guess they're moving you someplace else," the Maintenance woman answered her. "We just got orders to change these two rooms into a suite."

"A suite? Using my room? What in God's name, Shane . . ."

"Don't ask me, Marika," said Shane swiftly. "Ask the high and mighty."

"You've got to know something more about this than I do!" said Marika Schulerman. "Tell me what you know!"

"Only that Maria here's to be my special assistant in a series of runs I've got coming up." Shane was beginning to feel definitely out-womaned in the small, if efficient, room that now held four human bodies in what was something other than a pleasant social gathering. "Lyt Ahn's orders."

"Well, where do I go then?" Marika turned on the Maintenance worker, who shrugged.

"Not my department," she answered. "They'll probably tell you. Sorry, didn't occur to me somebody might be in there."

"If that thing cuts through walls, you might have killed her!" said Maria unexpectedly to the Maintenance woman.

"No, no! No chance!" The woman held up the pencil-shaped tool. "It only works on walls, nothing else—one of the alien gadgets. Perfectly safe. Look!"

She put the point of the object against the palm of her left hand and pressed what seemed to be a sliding control stud on its barrel with the thumb of the right hand, with which she was holding the tool. "It goes through any wall, thick as it is, but it won't do a thing to anything else. It's programmed somehow. That's the best guess—but who really knows?"

She turned and went out into the corridor, to return bearing a door, carrying it with a muscular ease that made Shane envious. She placed the door in the opening she had made and did some things to both one edge of the door and the corresponding cut face of the wall.

"Marika, this is Maria Casana," said Shane. "As I say, she's to be my special assistant on a set of runs that're presently secret."

"Oh? Glad to meet you," said Marika, turning to Maria. "So you're the reason they're moving me. What's your area?"

"Area?" echoed Maria, staring at her.

"Orient? Middle East? Romance?" said Marika impatiently.

"Maria's not a linguist—at least in the Corps sense," said Shane quickly. "As I say, the whole thing's presently a secret."

"I wonder why?" said Sylvie. "Usually when the Aalaag don't want us to know something, they just don't tell us."

"They're just not telling you, now," said Shane. "But the thing is, they've told me; and I'm the one who's supposed to keep it secret."

"Bet you it's something we won't like—something nobody but an Aalaag'll like," said Marika gloomily. "Well, I'm going to look up our own Corps First Officer and find out if he knows where they're going to put me and whatever else he knows about this. Pleased to have met you—"

She nodded at Maria and went out.

"I should be going, too," said Sylvie. "I just dropped by to welcome you back, Shane. So pleased to have met you, Maria."

"I'm happy I met you," said Maria.

Sylvie went out. Maria stared at Shane but said nothing. The worker from Maintenance was still busy fitting the door into the opening. She finished in a few more seconds and stood back, looked over her work critically, then opened and shut the door a couple of times.

"That should do it," she said. "See you both again sometime." She turned away.

"Just a minute," said Shane. "Are you issued that door-making device, or do you have to draw it from someplace each time you need it?"

"It's issue," said the woman. "If something goes wrong with it, of course, we turn it in and get a new one at the central Supply Shop. Why?"

"Just that I'd hate to see a drunken party some night get hold of one of those and start making their own doorways into my quarters," said Shane.

"No danger," said the worker. "I said it's issue, but we have to account for it, like all the other alien tools we're issued at the beginning of each work shift. Of course, after that, it's simply hung up on your own peg in the ready room of the Supply Shop, where anybody could go get one. But no one with any sense is going to risk getting hung on the hooks for misusing a tool like this. Believe me! I'll see you."

And she, too, finally left. The two of them were alone at last.

"It is all right, then?" Maria said to Shane as the door closed behind the worker. "The First Captain thought I was all right?"

"Of course," said Shane. He had forgotten that Maria would not have understood Lyt Ahn's last words in Aalaag about Shane continuing to tutor Maria in the alien language while she accompanied him around to the places on the globe where Governor Projects were to be set up. "Things couldn't be better. You heard what I told Sylvie and Marika. You're to go with me on a series of runs—that secrecy bit was something I came up with on my own—and I'm to go on coaching you in Aalaag, as we travel. Things couldn't be better. I wanted you with me and both of us out of here, if possible; and Lyt Ahn wanted a way of making translators without waiting for a whole new generation to grow up. Since we were both after the same thing, it was a shoo-in."

"Shoo-in?" echoed Maria—for Shane, like all the rest who had been in the room, had been talking English.

"Absolute certainty," explained Shane.

He told her about the Council meeting to which he had been summoned and the plan to raise human children in Aalaag households. Having done this, he found himself getting deeper into explanations of the explanations; as to why Lyt Ahn preferred the quicker method of making adult translators that Maria's case offered, and why the Aalaag had been so revolted at the idea of human children being raised like their own, and in the same quarters.

When he was done, he became aware that Maria was standing with both arms wrapped around her body, as if she was cold.

"What is it?" he said.

"It's just that there's so much I don't know," she said. "I'm all alone here, except for you. I'm frightened."

"There's nothing to be afraid of," said Shane. As when he had left her in London, it required an effort not to put his own arms around her. He found he had folded them across his chest in instinctive self-denial, so that they faced each other almost like adversaries. "And in any case, we'll be out of here in a day or two."

He was optimistic. Nearly a week went by before he was again called to Lyt Ahn's office.

"You'll leave at once," Lyt Ahn told him. "Taking that small beast you are training with you. Laa Ehon was interested to hear that I wished him to set up other Governor Units immediately at other points on this world. He did, however, suggest that the first additional one be set up at Milan, which—being his Headquarters city—would render him particularly knowledgeable about staffing it without delay. I gave him that order, accordingly; and therefore you will go first to Milan, in three days, by which time he will already have begun to set such a Unit in action."

Shane blinked grainy eyes. He had had a little more than four hours' sleep the night before and not much more than that on the preceding nights. He had had to report for duty daily at the regular hours, even though there had been nothing to do; and although he had been idle, he had needed to stay visible and in attendance— in no situation to catch up on his sleep.

The sleeplessness was the result of living with Maria in even closer quarters than they had in London. Maria had accepted his story that they dared not touch each other for fear the Aalaag would find out. The result had been that they had sat up and talked, night after night until late hours—in fact, into the early morning hours—after having talked themselves far beyond the point where they were saying anything of much import to each other, but continuing to put off the moment when going to sleep would require them to part. He would sit facing her, in a separate chair, a couple of arms' lengths distant, feeling the need to go to her like a steady hollow ache in him; and barred by the situation between them, the true dimensions of which she knew nothing.

And all the time he was being ridden by the knowledge that the empty days and the talk-filled nights were even harder on her than they were on him. Shane at least had his daytime duties to take him out of the two connected rooms. Maria, under any ordinary set of conditions, could have gotten out, could have found people to meet and things to do. There were recreation areas, from lounges to swimming pools, for the Corps members. But to go to any of these, to meet others there, was to invite the curiosity that would arise when it became clear she was no linguist—by Corps standards, nowhere near one. Those she met might accept the story that Lyt Ahn had his own reasons for attaching her to Shane, but they were sure to be curious about all other matters concerning her background and her life.

Nor had Shane wanted the word to filter back, innocent as it might be, to any of the Aalaag that there was secrecy involved in Maria's connection with Shane. Not having ordered secrecy, Lyt Ahn, if the word got back to him, would want to know why Shane should use it; and inviting questions from any Aalaag at any time was not wise. In this case, it could be even more unwise than usual.

So now Shane made an effort to pull his wits together. He had been so stimulated by fear in his first few months of working in the House of Weapons, and particularly in moments of facing Lyt Ahn, that his mind had never been in less than top gear whenever he was with the First Captain.

With time, the fear had receded. But by then the habit of an almost unnatural alertness had been built into him. Never until now had he had to prod his brains to do a swift job of assessing what the other had told him and searching for the possibilities it uncovered. Sluggishly, therefore, but not so slowly as to attract Lyt Ahn's attention, Shane's mind worked.

"Since it will be three days before I am required to be in Milan," he said, "may I suggest to the immaculate sir that I and my trainee-assistant go first to London to take another look at the Governor Unit there? It may have developed in the time since I last saw it; and the immaculate sir will remember that except for the last day or so, when I was there, Laa Ehon was himself present and in command. It might be interesting to see it at a time when he is not so."

Lyt Ahn sat in silence, his gaze unfocused upon the imageless wallscreen opposite him.

Shane's mind, forced finally into top gear, raced, building upon the possibilities of what had just occurred to him. His short hours of sleep and his concern with Maria had given him other things to think about, so he had not made his usual estimate of what was likely to happen next. He was fully aware of the Aalaag habit of expecting something to be done immediately, once a decision had been taken and a command uttered. It was the other side of the coin from their tendency to leave things hanging in midair when something of greater importance summoned them. A servant who had been told to cease a certain activity could be forgotten and left for months, not merely in idleness, but in enforced inactivity, holding his position and waiting until some further order put him back into motion again, like a powered toy.

On the other hand, in the case of a decision made and a command given, literally no delay was expected or tolerated. Therefore, Shane told himself, he should have had his plans made for an order to move ever since the First Captain had told him that he intended to command Laa Ehon to start setting up other Governor Units. But Shane had never expected, of all things, to be sent to Milan first; and he suddenly realized he needed a great deal more information about the European Resistances, which Peter was the ideal person to give him—in a face-to-face situation.

London for three days would be perfect. He could tap Peter for necessary information and at the same time set up a worldwide system of communication with the other man. He would also be able to introduce Maria as his assistant to the junior Aalaag officers in the London Project and she could practice her Aalaag on them, without fear of word about her slow progress getting back to Lyt Ahn.

"No," said Lyt Ahn. "It will be better if you leave immediately, rather than in three days, but I desire you to go directly for Milan. You will be in position there to report to me later how Laa Ehon put together the staff and other necessary matters for the Project there, from the earliest possible moment."

Shane's plans came crashing to the ground like a building razed by demolition experts. Now that the chance had been snatched from him, he was realizing how very useful to him it would have been to talk face-to-face with Peter.

Well, if he could not go to Peter, the Resistance man would somehow have to manage to come to him, in Milan.

"This beast hears and will obey."

"You may go."

Shane returned to the area in the House of Weapons that housed the translators. Almost as soon as he stepped into the cross-corridor that led down past the recreation areas to the private rooms, he found Sylvie waiting for him. She was dressed in what plainly were off-duty clothes of a navy blue skirt and eggshell blue blouse under a blue and white checked jacket. She had changed the way she wore her hair, so that two light-brown wings now swept down on either side of her face, making it seem unnaturally white, with all the blue about her.

"There you are, Shane!" said Sylvie brightly. "Come and talk to me for a minute."

"I just got orders to make a run," said Shane. "You know how it is. I can't stop."

"You can stop for a few minutes, you know you can," said Sylvie. "Come and sit with me in Lounge One. There's almost no one in there right now."

There was a feverishness about her, in spite of the whiteness of her appearance. A turmoil of emotions churned inside Shane.

"All right. For a minute," he said, and followed her into the first doorway on the left.

The lounges had been originally designed by the Aalaag, but they had made no objection to a series of alterations at the requests of the Corps people. The result was that these places now had party areas, mixed with other corners that were filled with semi-enclosed booths where a certain amount of privacy was possible.

"Do you want a drink?" said Sylvie, as they slipped into one of these booths and sat, one on each side of its table.

"No, thanks," said Shane. "But go ahead, yourself."

Sylvie's hand dropped from the coding plate of the drink dispenser in the wall, toward which it had been reaching.

"So you're leaving," she said. "You know, I haven't seen you even for a second since the first moment you got back."

"I've been pretty well tied up," said Shane.

"Oh, I know," said Sylvie. Her narrow face was framed by the two wings of hair. In the shadowiness of the booth she seemed to look at him out of some depth of shadow, as a person trapped in a well might look up at a possible rescuer. "With your new assistant, and all."

"Well . . . yes," said Shane. "You see—"

"Please!" said Sylvie suddenly, almost violently, "don't explain." Her voice had begun to shake on the last two words. "I don't want to hear you explain. It's just the way it is. That's the way it is, for all of us, here. . . ."

Tears glittered suddenly in her eyes, welled up and overflowed down her cheeks.

"Damn you!" she said. "Damn you! I wasn't going to do this. I wasn't going to do anything but tell you it didn't matter to me what you do."

"Look, there's nothing the matter—," said Shane.

"Nothing the matter? You bring her back with you, and all of a sudden—" The tears were coming faster now, but under them the expression of her face was still unchanged, still fierce. The voice was still held low and tense but under control. Then the voice did break. "Shane, what'll I do without you? The only way I could live with all this was because of you. You know what it's like, day after day! I need someplace to go, someone to go to; and there's no one now—no one in the whole Corps. There was only you! And you had to go outside to find someone who doesn't even need you!"

"You're talking about Maria," said Shane. "It's a different matter than you think—"

"Damn you, Shane!" she said tightly. "Damn you! Damn you! Damn you!"

She hid her face in her hands. With all this, she had kept her voice low. No one else in the room could have heard her but him.

He felt torn inside. Part of him was churned by guilt—although why he should feel guilty, he had no idea. Another part wanted to shout at her in fury. What did she know about it? A woman he had never touched. A woman he never would touch until the day Maria found out what he was really doing, after which she would not be touching him if her life depended on it.

"—Sylvie, listen to me," was what he actually said, out loud, "just listen a minute. I can't explain it now, but if you'll be patient, I swear to you the time'll come when there simply won't be any Maria there; and you'll understand that nothing ever happened between her and me. But I can't tell you about it now. You just have to trust me."

"No," she said, her hands still covering her face. "No! It's no use, Shane! I knew it was no use. I shouldn't even have tried to talk to you—"

She fumbled blindly out of the booth, with her hands still hiding her wet face, but parted enough to let her see a little of where she was going; she turned and hurried away from him.

He heard the heels of her shoes on the uncarpeted floor, tapping away into silence, and sat, mired in his sense of guilt and anger and unhappiness. After some minutes, he sighed heavily, got to his feet and made his way out of the lounge, turning toward the rooms where Maria waited for him. By the time he got there he had almost succeeded in pushing Sylvie into the back of his mind.

So it was that Shane and Maria came into Milan five hours later. He had encountered no objections to dressing her, like himself, in pilgrim garb. But so swiftly had orders moved them from their two rooms to a courier ship, which by that time was waiting for them on the rooftop of the House of Weapons, and from there directly to the airport in Milan, that it was not until they were away from the airport terminal that he had a chance to consider how he might phone Peter in London for directions on how to reach the Milanese Resistance people.

"But you don't need to do that," Maria had said, when he finally mentioned his oversight to her. They were sitting in a taxicab on their way into the city. "I can find them."

He felt extremely conscious of his own stupidity. Maria's ability to find her former associates had been right under his nose all this time and its very obviousness had made it invisible to him.

"But they may have moved since you were here."

"I can still find them," said Maria. "This is my city."

And of course it was. After they had settled in a hotel room, Maria slipped out still dressed as a pilgrim and returned in half an hour.

"I spoke to Georges himself," she said. "He still doesn't like you any better than he ever did, but he'll cooperate. You didn't tell me when we could meet him, so I said I'd have to phone that word in to him when I got it."

"I won't know until I've reported to Laa Ehon," said Shane, "which ought to be immediately, if it wasn't the middle of the night. Luckily, as it is, we can wait until morning. You'll have to come with me when I report."

"To meet him?" Maria seemed to shrink inside herself; and Shane knew she was remembering how Shane told her Laa Ehon had watched her without her knowing it, through the vision screen. She had never forgotten the hours of being a prisoner at the Aalaag Headquarters here in Milan, and facing almost certain questioning and execution.

"Possibly not Laa Ehon himself. He may prefer to see me alone," said Shane. "But you'll certainly be meeting the junior Aalaag officers. It's a chance for you to practice talking to them," he added, remembering what had occurred to him when he had been hoping that Lyt Ahn would let them go to London first. "Laa Ehon may have orders for me, though this time I don't think he'll consider me detailed to him by Lyt Ahn. After seeing Laa Ehon, I'll know when we can see Marrotta. But meanwhile I've got to get Peter here to Milan as quickly as possible."

"I don't suppose I should ask you why?" she said.

"No." He sighed. "There're all sorts of things I could tell you that would make it easier for both of us, but we shouldn't risk it. Can you find me a phone outside the hotel this time of night?"

She took him out into the streets and to a bakery, which was brightly lit in its back sections and where people were busily at work preparing foods that would be hungrily consumed under the sun that was yet to rise. Maria evidently knew one of the men in authority there, and after a quick, private talk between the two of them, Shane was shown to a phone in a tiny office.

"We'll have to pay them for the call, of course," said Maria.

"We'll pay it three times over," said Shane. "But they'll have to take gold. I didn't have a chance to trade for any local currency at the hotel. Did you?"

"Yes," she said, "of course. I've got it with me.

"But there's no hurry," she added. "He's one of our people—the man I talked to."

"Good."

Shane began in Italian the business of working through the long distance operator. After more than a little delay, he heard a ring. It was some time before the phone was answered.

"Smith and Smith, Exporters," said a surly male voice. "We're closed."

"I want to speak to Mr. Smith—the old Mr. Smith," said Shane swiftly.

There was a long pause at the other end, so long that Shane began to wonder if whoever had taken the call had not been briefed on the code he and Peter had originally worked out together.

"It better be important, this time of night," said the voice.

"It's vital," said Shane. "If it wasn't, do you think I'd be calling at this time of night at all?"

He was beginning to get angry.

"I'll have to go wake him up. He'll call back. Where are you?"

"I'll have someone give you the phone number," said Shane. He passed the phone to Maria. "They've got to call back. Tell them this number."

Maria spoke in English into the phone. Something brief was replied at the far end, and then Maria hung up.

"It'll be half an hour, at the soonest, he said," she told Shane.

It was, as it turned out, nearly two hours before the phone rang and brought Peter's voice to Shane's ear.

"When did you get to Milan?" Peter said, still thick with the sleep from which he had clearly been roused. "Is Maria with you?"

"A few hours ago. Yes, she is," said Shane.

"Well, it'll be all right. Marrotta'll cooperate. Do you need to know how to find him?"

"No. Maria's seen him. She brought back word he'd work with me. That's not my present problem. I'd hoped to get to London to see you before I came here. We've got to talk. I need you to come to Milan immediately, and then go on with me to Rome before going home again to England. How soon can you get off; and who's the Resistance leader I'd work with in Rome? Have you got money to fly? I can give you all the funds you need once you get here."

"Bloody hell!" said Peter. "You don't want much, do you? Just wake up in the middle of the night and fly immediately to Milan and Rome! What'll I use as an excuse for the trip if anyone asks?"

"You can think of something. Who's the Roman leader of Resistance?"

"Well, I suppose I can do it, if there's room on an early plane. I'll have to get word to you of when I'll be coming in. How do I do that?"

"Phone our hotel and leave a message for me, making an appointment for lunch, dinner, or drinks—whatever fits the time of day. Tell them you're Mr. Smith. Here, let me give you Maria to tell you the name of the hotel and the name of an eating or drinking place where we can meet—"

Shane passed the phone over to Maria, who gave Peter the information. She handed the phone back to him.

"That all?" asked Peter.

"You didn't tell me if you've got the funds for an air ticket and you still haven't told me the name of the Roman leader."

"Yes, I can buy a ticket. I don't know the leader in Rome personally. Maria can find out for you there. I'll tell you more about the situation when I see you. Now, goodnight."

"Wait," said Shane. "You'll definitely be on the first plane out in the morning you can get on?"

"Yes, yes—and yes again!" said Peter. "Goodnight!" He hung up.

SEVENTEEN

It turned out that Laa Ehon did indeed want to see both Shane and his assistant, in spite of the fact that Shane had explained to the Aalaag who was Officer of the Day that his assistant could neither speak nor understand the alien language to any useful degree. They were admitted to the Milanese Commander's presence by another junior officer whom Laa Ehon sent almost immediately out of the office, leaving himself alone with the two humans.

"This other beast with you," said Laa Ehon to Shane without preamble, "you say it does not understand the true tongue at all?"

"It understands a few sounds only, immaculate sir," said Shane. "Also, it can say a few sounds, but not well."

"Have it say something in the true tongue for me."

"Maria," said Shane in Italian. "The immaculate sir would like you to say something in his own language to him. I suggest you tell him you are at his orders."

"This beast at 'maculate sir's orders, 'maculate sir," said Maria to the powerful shape behind the desk. Her voice was thinned by fear, but Shane felt sure that no Aalaag could pick out such a fine distinction in human tones—even if the Aalaag in question happened to be listening for some such evidence of emotion.

"You're right," Laa Ehon said to Shane. "It is barely understandable. And it comprehends no better?"

"It does not, immaculate sir," said Shane.

"I see. In any case it makes no difference. It is you, Shane-beast, that I have ordered in to be talked to. I am informed Lyt Ahn wishes you to observe the formation here of a Unit similar to the one I had set up in London."

"That was the command I received, immaculate sir."

"I am pleased it is you whom he sent," said Laa Ehon. "As I may have mentioned before to you, Shane-beast, I have been interested by your command of the true tongue as well as your other qualities. The Governor Unit will be put together here in the next few days and, as before, I'll be interested in hearing your report on it before you leave. When were you ordered to leave?"

"This beast was given no specific orders as to its departure date," said Shane.

"You will be returning to the House of Weapons when you go?"

"This beast may, or it may be ordered on to some farther place before returning to its base Headquarters."

"Very interesting," said Laa Ehon. His large-boned white face with its black eyes and snowy eyebrows showed no more expression than any Aalaag ordinarily did. "One of the cattle who is as bright as you are, Shane-beast, should be aware that among the duties of a senior officer like myself is the readiness to assume any necessary command post, particularly one that requires him or her for the good of the Expedition. Also, seeing Lyt Ahn in his post of command, you have no doubt become aware that often he does things that are generally not done, or not permitted to lower ranks. It follows that as one of the officers who might, if conditions should suddenly require it, be called upon to take up the duties of him who is presently senior to us all, I also must occasionally—though rarely—do things not ordinarily done."

He paused.

"Do you understand me, Shane-beast?"

"This beast understands the words, but not the intentions of the immaculate sir in saying them to me." Shane had never encountered quite this sort of conversation with an Aalaag, even with Lyt Ahn; and uneasiness moved in him.

"The import would naturally not be understandable to a beast in any case. It is not necessary that you understand anything but the words I say to you and reply or obey as ordered. Do you understand that?"

"This beast understands, immaculate sir." Relief flowed in to replace the uneasy feeling. Unless there was something very strange in the offing, Laa Ehon had effectively notified him that all responsibility for the conversation about to ensue was that of the Milanese Commander; and Shane need not worry about being in any way responsible himself.

"Better." Laa Ehon's eyes looked directly into his. "Tell me then, is Lyt Ahn a good master?"

The shock was so great that Shane had no words with which to answer. He was literally dumbfounded. He strove to think of something to say, but the agility of mind that had pulled him out of potential hot water innumerable times before seemed dead within him.

"You have not answered me," said Laa Ehon. The tone of his voice was no different but nothing could have been more loaded with threat than the question itself.

"This beast," managed Shane finally, "has known only one master, and cannot conceive of any way in which that master could be better."

His words seemed to echo in his own ear as Laa Ehon continued to stare back at him in a silence that lengthened and lengthened.

"It is true," said Laa Ehon at last. "You have known only one master. You and your fellow beast may go."

Shane touched Maria's arm to alert her in case she had not understood the final sentence. According to the proper ritual they withdrew from Laa Ehon and left the Milanese Commander's office.

"These two beasts have been ordered by the immaculate sir to go," Shane reported to the Officer of the Day in the outer office.

"Go, then," said that alien.

Shane and Maria left the room. Shane's mind was still in such a whirl after what had happened that he said nothing, but led Maria out of the Headquarters building and back to their hotel. Maria, clearly reading the emotional upset in him, did not speak until they were in their hotel room.

"Did something go wrong?" she burst out there, in Italian. "Was it what I said? I said something wrong, didn't I? Tell me—"

"No, no . . ." The expression on her face finally registered on him—and there was the ache again, the ache to put his arms around her and shut out her fears. "You did exactly what he expected after what I'd told him about you. It wasn't you at all."

"Then what?"

Shane opened his mouth to answer and found himself at a loss to explain. The answer that had come to his mind was impossible—but there was no other explanation; and it was an answer that could mean ruin to everything he planned. For a moment he wondered if he had not become in some way infected by Lyt Ahn, from being close to him this long; because something in him was boggling at saying what he was about to say as an Aalaag might boggle at saying it.

"Maria," he said. "Maria—he's insane."

"Insane?"

She stared at him.

"Who's insane? You mean him—Laa Ehon? How can he be? How can you tell? You're not making sense!"

"In Aalaag terms, he's insane. Did you hear what he asked me?"

"Hear? Of course I heard everything, but you know as well as I do I didn't understand any of it. Shane, what're you talking about? What do you mean by 'in Aalaag terms, he's insane'?"

Shane found a chair and sat down in it. Maria dropped into one facing him. He was still searching for words to make the explanation in human terms, as much for his own benefit as for hers.

"I don't know how to explain it to you." He looked at her, frustrated. "You need to know the Aalaag the way I've come to know them. Laa Ehon did something so inexcusable, it's unthinkable; something no Aalaag would do unless he was insane."

"You still aren't making sense!" she said more gently. "Just tell me what it was that upset you this way. What's so bad you even have trouble saying it to me? What did he ask you?"

Shane blew out a heavy, defeated breath.

"It won't mean anything to you unless you know the Aalaag. He asked me if Lyt Ahn was a good master."

Maria frowned.

"Yes?" she said, when he did not go on speaking. "And what did that mean? What about that makes you say he's insane?"

"Insane by Aalaag standards—and that may not mean the same thing as it would if you called a human being insane," said Shane. "That's what's terrible about this. Suddenly he's a question mark to me. Maybe none of the rules hold for him, if this doesn't . . ."

He saw she was staring at him, patiently, stubbornly still waiting for a decent explanation. He made a great effort.

"I know all this sounds like a lot of gibberish to you," he said. "That's because of the differences between humans and Aalaag. I'm sorry. Let me try to sort my mind out, and come up with something that makes more sense. The trouble is, just as with any language but more so here, there're meanings among Aalaag that simply don't exist for humans. They don't exist in our languages because they don't exist in the human picture of things."

He paused, thinking.

"I told you, didn't I," he said finally, "that unlike humans, where the individual thinks of himself first and the race second, the Aalaag, through genetics or custom—God knows which, or both—always thinks of his race first, and himself or herself second?"

"You said something about that. I can't remember just what or when."

"All right, then," he said. "Put it this way, then. With the Aalaag, just like us, let's say sanity can be described as following certain self-evident rules for living and doing. Step outside those rules, start doing what doesn't fit them, and you look to people of your own kind as if you're acting against nature. For example, for a human to try to kill himself because his life was unendurable makes some kind of sense, according to human rules. You can be sane, maybe, and still be a suicide if you had that sort of reason. But try to kill yourself for . . . say . . . a joke, and your fellow humans are pretty sure to call you insane. Do you follow me?"

"Yes," she said. "Actually . . . no, I was going to argue the point. But for now, let's say it's so."

"Well, then, don't you think it's at least likely that if you knew for certain some human you knew had tried to kill himself for a joke—for a joke only—you'd assume he hadn't been quite sane?"

"All right, I would," she said. "Go on."

He hesitated again.

"You know," he said slowly, "the more I think of it, the more I think you'd have to have gone through all I've seen and heard among the Aalaag to understand what I'm talking about. You're either just going to have to take my word for it, or not."

"Tell me what you can," she said, "and if I can believe it, I will."

He nodded.

"You see," he said, "there's several things wrong here. Not just one. For an Aalaag to ask the opinion of one of his own beasts about other beasts—what's a beast's opinion worth in an Aalaag's eyes, anyway?—makes no sense, but it's just barely conceivable. But for one to ask any kind of opinion from someone else's beast makes no sense at all. How could he trust a beast he didn't know and didn't control, to tell him the truth? It gets beyond imagining that he'd ask the opinion of a strange beast about another Aalaag—let alone about the owner of that strange beast. Finally, it gets completely unimaginable when it comes to him asking such an unthinkable question of a beast about another Aalaag who was superior to him in rank, as Lyt Ahn is superior to Laa Ehon. Aside from anything else it's an unbelievable insult to Lyt Ahn."

He shrugged; he had run out of words. She sat without saying anything, and he also did not say anything, for what seemed to be a very long time.

"I believe you," she said. "But I still have trouble understanding it—just a few words being that bad."

He gazed at her, helpless.

"Just take my word for it," he said. "Believe me, it's something as bad as . . . as bad as . . . there's no way to describe it. No human equivalent. To ask someone else's beast! And to ask him that!"

There was another long moment in which neither of them said anything.

"You see," Maria said finally. "It's not as if Laa Ehon had been guilty of murdering another Aalaag, or anything like that. But you make it sound as if it is—or worse."

"It is. Far worse," he said. "At the very least, Laa Ehon's just signed his own death warrant. Don't you see? If he's sane, then the insult to a superior officer requires Lyt Ahn to kill him, or have him killed. If he's insane, then any Aalaag would agree he needs to be put to death as unfit."

"But how do you know they do these things?" she burst out. "Have you ever seen one Aalaag killing another? Do you really know they pass sentences of death on each other when they think one of them is unfit? How can you be so sure?"

He stood silent.

"You're right," he said at last. "I haven't seen—or even heard—one of them talk about killing another of their own kind; and I've never known of a sentence of death to be passed on one of them—even in the official documents that I've seen on Lyt Ahn's desk."

He stared at her.

"But I tell you it's true!" he said. "Everything I've told you about Laa Ehon's true! I know the Aalaag well enough to know it!"

Maria shivered.

"I do believe you," she looked up at him. "I don't know why I should, but I believe you. It's horrible. You can think like them, feel like them . . . it's almost as if you've become part Aalaag yourself, from being around them so much."

It was like being hit in the face. He hardly heard her as she went on and her voice softened.

"But you could never be that," she was saying.

"No, no, of course not!" he answered. The words tumbled out of him, too hastily it seemed to his own ears. "How could any human be like that—come to be like them—of all . . ."

He ran out of words suddenly, and in desperation he reached for her without thinking, as someone drowning might reach for a lifeboat just barely within arm's reach. She came to him and clung to him.

"I shouldn't have said it," she whispered into his ear, holding him. "I should never have said it. Don't think of it, Shane! Please, dear one, forget I said any such thing."

"I'm not like an Aalaag!" he said hoarsely into her thick, black hair. "How can any human be like an Aalaag? Nobody can. Nobody! It's crazy to say something like that!"

"Yes, yes," she soothed him, stroking him. "It's not true. I don't know why I said such a thing. Of course you aren't. I know. I know you aren't. Shane, you aren't . . ."

. . . And by some miracle they were no longer standing, but had moved—he was hardly conscious of how—to a bedroom of their suite and a double bed there; and he lost himself in her, finding at last relief, at last a place to hide from all the never-ending terrors and nightmares of the past two years.

It was a long while later, when they lay side by side on the bed and he was at peace, unthinking. The day had waned, and the late afternoon was deepening in shadow toward twilight. The window of their hotel bedroom was open and a warm breeze from time to time stirred the semitransparent curtain that had shielded them from the hard, direct, hot rays of the morning sun earlier, as they had prepared to go and report to Laa Ehon. Then the curtain had hung straight and still. Now it waved inward over them, reassuring as a blessing, as the gesture of another living human being, to tell him that the world to which he had been born still waited for his return and claimed him.

"You are my Shane," she had said, sometime in the period just passed. "No one else's." And the words had comforted him as nothing had ever done in his life before that he could remember.

"We have to get ready soon to go meet Georges," she said now.

"Yes," he answered idly. At the moment Georges Marrotta and the Milanese Resistance people seemed very far away. He did not move, and neither did she.

"How soon will they find out about us?" she asked. "I mean— how soon will they know we've been together?"

The question shocked him suddenly back into all he had escaped from in the past few hours.

"Find out?" he said harshly. "Why should they? I don't even know if they can and they wouldn't be interested anyway—in the coupling of a couple of cattle. I lied to you when—"

He broke off, aghast at the full truth he had been on the verge of revealing to her, all his plans and their inevitable outcome. If he told her—now more than ever—she would recoil from him forever. And if he had not been able to face the loss of her before, how could he stand it now? Now, she was more vital to him even than his heartbeat.

"You lied?" She propped herself up on one elbow to frown down into his face. "About what?" The darkness of her hair fell about their two faces, making a small confessional space between them. She must have seen the look he wore, because she added swiftly. "It's all right. You can tell me now. It doesn't matter what you tell me. Everything'll be all right."

But it wouldn't; and he knew it would not. Fear scrabbled in him like a drowning animal.

"I . . . didn't know how I'd act. I've been alone so long and I love you—"

The last words amazed him as he said them and realized he meant them.

"—I thought . . ." He turned his head, hiding his face against her breast so it would not betray him to those eyes of hers. "I thought you might be disappointed, somehow; and I couldn't face it . . ."

He left the rest of the sentence unsaid, partly because there were no more words in him he could safely say and partly out of the cunning of an animal-like instinct that told him his silence would lie for him more effectively than his tongue.

It was deep dusk when they finally entered the building that housed the office of the trucking firm which Georges Marrotta owned and ran. They were both wearing their pilgrim robes with the hoods pulled up and closed in front of their faces.

A young male clerk showed them into an inner office where Marrotta sat behind a desk. There were a couple of straight chairs before the desk and facing it; and it was to these he waved them.

"Well?" he said, as they seated themselves.

He was unchanged, thick-bodied and black-haired, with his pipe even at the same angle in his mouth. He looked at both of them, then fastened his gaze on the larger hooded figure who was Shane.

"I'll need some help, of course," said Shane. "That's why I'm here."

He heard the edge in his own voice. It had come instinctively in response to the tone of the other.

"Just that?" said Marrotta, ironically.

His dark eyes were steady as knife-points held at Shane's throat. Suddenly, Shane realized that a part of his reaction to this other man was an antipathy founded on fear. Somehow, in the way he was, or in the way he sat or acted, Marrotta could generate the power to make others afraid—and Shane was sensing this in this moment.

Shane was dumbfounded. For a second, even, he felt a touch of deep alarm. The Pilgrim could not afford to be afraid—particularly of someone he would eventually need to command. But that emotion was not something that would just go away because you did not want it—

Shane caught his thoughts up short, with an effort of will. What was wrong with him? He had been living in fear daily for two years, fear of those whom there was real cause to fear. What was there to be frightened of in an ordinary human, compared to them? Besides, what reasons were there for him to fear Marrotta?

But he had only to ask himself the question and understanding came, bringing a sense of shock with it. Georges Marrotta, he suddenly realized, hated him—instinctively, reflexively, not for any logical reasons. The cause could have had its roots in what had happened in London, or in Shane's being here now, or even in his having enlisted Maria—who had been one of Georges's Resistance group. But the cause did not matter. The only thing that mattered was the hate itself, and its palpable existence, here and now.

Shane had never had the experience of being hated before— not as an individual, for himself, alone. He'd like to kill me, thought Shane, fascinated, staring at Georges. If he had an excuse he'd kill me, right now, here, where I stand.

And that, he understood suddenly, was why he was afraid. There was no way around or through the hate he faced. There was no way to placate it. Marrotta wanted him off the face of the Earth and nothing less than that would satisfy him. There was nothing to be done but face the fact.

Shane had not known that the human engine was capable of such pure, undiluted antagonism. Nothing in his life so far had prepared him for it. But now, confronted with it, he found his own animal instincts responding as millions of generations of ancestors had triggered them to respond. His fear escalated into something that was no longer fear. He looked back at Georges from the hidden shadows of his cowl and knew that his own eyes were as unmoving on the other man as Georges's were on him. He found himself responding to the threat against his life with a threat as great against the other. He found himself hating back.

And I could kill him, Shane thought.

. . . A small voice in the back of his head answered—*but isn't that what you've been planning all along, for all of them?*

Time and distance seemed to move between him and Marrotta, and his hate went away, to be replaced only by a great emptiness. It was true. All his planning condemned the man across the desk from him to die eventually, and possibly under torture. This had been so, even before he had known of the other's existence.

"Well?" Georges demanded harshly. "Are you going to stand there all night? Tell me what you want from us."

"Not," said Shane through stiff lips, "until I know I've got your cooperation."

Georges's upper lip twisted.

"I'll tell you that when I hear what you want," he said.

"No," said Shane. "You'll tell me first."

He was no longer affected by the way Georges felt about him. He was too far off in emptiness. He heard his own voice, speaking almost detachedly.

"You've got a choice to make, Marrotta," he said, "and you'll have to make it now. You can follow my direction, or I'll go on without you; and if I have to go on without you, in the end most, if not all, of the people that follow you now will end up leaving you to follow me. You were in London. You saw what I did. You can't, and no one you know, can, do what you saw me do there. We need to cooperate, because we're fighting on the same side; but whether we do or not—and it'll have to be done on my terms, not yours—is up to you. Now, which is it going to be? Will you promise to give me what I need, as far as you can, without first sitting in judgment on what that is, or are you going to try to set up some kind of conditions?"

"Follow you blindly, you mean?"

"Yes."

Georges made a quick gesture with one hand.

"That'll be the day!" the gesture said, in effect.

Shane stood up. Almost immediately, Maria rose from her chair beside him.

"Come along, Maria," said Shane. His voice still sounded strangely detached and quiet in his own ears. "There's nothing we can do here."

They were almost to the door before Marrotta's voice sounded again behind them.

"Tell me what it is you want," he said. "I'll tell you if I can get it for you."

Shane turned and went back to seat himself again. Maria followed. Once more he looked across the desk at Marrotta.

"I've got to make a quick trip to Rome and back—just when I don't know," Shane said, "and I've got to travel in a way where I won't be seen coming or going, so that no one'll know I've left Milan. Laa Ehon may have had an image of me circulated among his Interior Guard—I doubt it, but it's something I can't risk. I need identification papers; and I need a car and a driver to drive me to Rome, wait for me there as long as necessary—which shouldn't be more than twelve hours at the most—and then drive me back immediately."

Marrotta did not answer immediately.

"I suppose," he said at last, "something like that could be done."

"It won't be as easy as perhaps I make it sound," said Shane. "There's more to it. I don't know when I'll be going. It'll probably be several days from now. But it could be yet this evening. Also, I won't know when I'm going to want to leave until a few minutes, or hours, before I'll need to go. As soon as I do, I'll want to leave as quickly as I can and get back just as quickly, so I'm gone a minimum of time. You'll have to find a car for me right away and start right now having at least two possible drivers ready on twelve-hour shifts—better have four in case one of the original two falls sick—and keep them standing by so I can leave any time, day or night, when the chance to go comes up for me. It goes without saying that anyone who drives me will need to know his way around Rome—because I don't—and be able to give a good excuse to local police there, or Interior Guard, for being there with the car."

Marrotta hesitated a trifle longer this time, then nodded.

"It can be done," he said. "What's the outside number of days it could be before you need the car and driver?"

"Probably not more than a week. I'll go as soon as the Governor Unit that Laa Ehon's been ordered to set up here's been running at least a few days."

"My God!" said Marrotta. "That could take them months."

"As I told Peter's people in London," said Shane, "you who

don't deal with them everyday don't understand the Aalaag. They've got technology we can't even imagine; and that, plus the way they do things, means that an order—any order—is executed immediately. If an office is to be set up, in theory it's set up and responsible for what it will do from the moment the order to set it up is issued. The order in this case probably went out the day before Lyt Ahn sent me here. By the time I landed, there were undoubtedly both Aalaag and humans handling at least some documents of the kind that fall under the authority of the office. Tomorrow, or the next day at the latest, Laa Ehon will tell me where the Unit is and let me go to see it. I'll have to spend anywhere from one day to a week with it to get ready for my trip. So, figure up to a week, but not much more."

"The drivers will want to know what kind of danger they're going into," said Marrotta.

"None, on the trip down," said Shane, standing up, with Maria imitating his actions again, "as long as they can account for their presence. On the way back, there might be a watch being kept by police and Interior Guard along the way for anyone dressed like a pilgrim."

"You could try not dressing like a pilgrim on the way back," said Marrotta.

"You know better than that," said Shane.

"What if something comes up to make you take off your Pilgrim disguise?" Marrotta said. He smiled thinly. "And your driver gets a look at your face after all?"

"The driver should try very hard not to see my face," said Shane. "If I thought he had . . ."

Shane did not finish.

He heard the words he just said as if someone else had just spoken them, in that same calm, detached voice. Something within him stood amazed that he could say such a thing. Something else knew that he was saying only what must be said.

"I'll tell the drivers that."

"Yes," said Shane. "They ought to be warned. Maria'll bring you word when I find the chance to leave, so the car and driver can be waiting and ready."

He turned and went out with her.

They took a cab back to within a few blocks of their hotel and got out. In the cab they did not speak; but when they were walking along alone together, Shane broke the silence.

"Does he love you?" Shane asked.

"I think he might have once," Maria said. "But not for a long time. No, it's just that I was one of his people, once; and now I'm yours. It's the way he is."

"Should I trust him?" asked Shane bluntly.

"Yes," she said, "at least as far as not doing anything behind your back."

They returned to the room; and, since there was now no need to sleep apart, they shared the same bed and he found his sanctuary again in the loving of her.

The next day, as he had been almost sure the Aalaag Commander would, Laa Ehon sent him to the Milanese Government Unit. It was only a few streets away from the Headquarters building and was remarkably similar to the building housing the Unit in London. As in London, there was nothing displayed to mark the structure as being in alien hands. There was also a courtyard before the building enclosed by walls and used as a parking place for human and Aalaag vehicles.

Although the interior physical layout was different, the resemblance to the London Unit was striking. Again, the humans had offices on the lowest floors, the Aalaag had theirs on the upper ones. An elevator existed for Aalaag alone to use. Shane had no doubt that the arms locker would be down in the basement—either that which the building had originally possessed, or extra space created by the Aalaag.

But once more there was the ritual of the first evening, when he had dinner with the new Milan District Governor, the Lieutenant Governor, and the colonel commanding the Interior Guard. Since these were all Italian rather than English, the meal was more of a social event and the three wore their personal ambitions more gracefully.

Nonetheless, it was an occasion on which Shane ended by parrying questions about himself, the Governor plan generally, and the exact amount of cooperation the other three might expect from him during his future official visits of inspection if any.

He returned to the hotel a little more drunk than he had intended to become, very much more tired, and unaccountably depressed. It did not help his mood that Maria was not in the room when he got there and a note on the writing table in the parlor of the suite told him she had gone to see a woman friend of long standing and would be back before an unreasonably late hour. He kicked off his shoes, lay down on the bed they had occupied earlier—somehow it seemed more friendly than the unused one—and found himself falling asleep.

He had intended to stay awake until Maria returned. He was far from easy in his mind about the security of his hidden identity with her being out by herself. But the exhaustion that claimed him was powerful. Wearily he got up, undressed, got back into bed and fell immediately, deeply asleep.

EIGHTEEN

". . . THERE WASN'T ANY DANGER," MARIA TOLD HIM THE FOLLOWING morning as he was dressing to go to the Governor Unit and she was still in bed. "Pia's not in the Resistance, but she knows I am. She also knows enough not to ask questions. She's an old friend of my mother's—in fact, the last few months before she died, my mother lived in Pia's house and Pia took care of her. But she thinks I've been gone the past few months in Bologna on Resistance business, that's all."

"Still . . ." said Shane doubtfully.

"Listen to me!" Maria sat up in bed. "I wanted to find out how Georges really felt about you—she knows him, too, and most of the others. It's all right. He does hate you, but he won't betray you; it's not that kind of hate. She also told me other things you should know. Do you realize that what you did in London is known all over Milan, all over Italy, already? I mean, by everybody, not just those in the Resistance?"

He must have looked skeptical, because she nodded vigorously.

"Yes!" she said. "It is! I don't think you realize the way the Pilgrim symbol was reaching and changing people, even before you marked it on that clock in London. And since then—to have a real, live Pilgrim—anyway, Pia'd heard of it already from at least a dozen people who didn't realize she'd already been told. And there're Pilgrim drawings everywhere—more out of sight than they used to be, but a lot more than just the ones those of us in the Resistance had put up. Everybody's using the mark now, your little drawing of a figure in a cloak with a staff; and all sorts of people are starting to wear the cloak. Do you know what the story they're telling now has you doing at the clock in London?''

"What?" he asked, sliding his arms into his jacket.

"According to the way it's told now, you first walked up to the alien—"

"The *Aalaag*," he corrected automatically. "Practice saying it in Aalaag every chance you get until you've got the pronunciation down automatically; and remember, it isn't the Aalaag who're alien—we're the aliens. Learn to think in their language the way they think in it."

"Yes, yes, the Al—the Aa—" This time she got the opening sound correct. "—laag on duty at the clock, guarding it. You walked up to him first and he started to point his weapon, the one like a spear with knobs—"

"Long arm," he said in Aalaag.

"Long . . . long arm," she repeated in Aalaag with difficulty. "He started to point it at you and you raised your hand and he froze in place. He stayed frozen while you walked to the tower, disappeared, appeared in midair by the face of the clock, marked it, and floated to the ground. You walked away, and as you walked away, the Aalaag started to come out of his frozen state, but you held up your hand again and he backed away from you and let you go."

"Good God!" said Shane.

Maria looked at him shrewdly.

"You're not pleased. I think it's wonderful."

"But . . . the idiots!" said Shane. "If they start believing an Aalaag can be paralyzed or backed off with just a wave of the hand, some nut among them wearing a pilgrim robe in imitation of me's just liable to try it and be cut down for it!"

"But the important thing is they believe that somewhere there is someone dressed like a pilgrim who can get away with it," said Maria. "Wasn't that the whole point of your doing it? All this time they've wanted someone to believe in who can snap his fingers at the Aalaag—" This time she said it correctly in the alien tongue. "And they've found it. In you. That's what counts. Not whether someone or other gets himself killed trying to imitate you."

Shane stared at her. Her practicality shocked him—and at the same time he was astonished that he, of all people, could be shocked, considering his actions and his secret plans.

"I've got to go," he said.

He was fully dressed now. She was out of bed almost immediately; she held him and kissed him hard.

"Be careful," she said.

"I'm not going anyplace dangerous, or planning to do anything risky," he answered, although dealing with the Aalaag was always risky. "What's there to be careful for?"

"Be careful anyway," she said. "Be careful even of the traffic. The traffic is terrible here, nowadays."

"All right," he said. "I'll be careful."

They kissed again, and he left.

Colonel Arturo Leone, the Unit's Interior Guard commanding officer, was the only one of the three top human administrators who was in his office when Shane arrived. Shane sent word through the Interior Guard Officer of the Day that he would like to see the colonel if the other had time to talk at the moment. He was invited into Leone's interior office, which was smaller than the offices of the three Aalaag assigned to the Unit but somehow—it was hard to say how—less spartan.

They had talked at dinner all the evening before, in Italian; but here in his office, Leone spoke in almost accentless English. He saw Shane settled in a comfortable chair facing Leone's desk, and given the chance to decline coffee or anything else to drink, before asking him his business.

"I've got to talk at some length with each of our Aalaag superiors here," answered Shane in Italian, "and it'd be best if I could catch each of them in his or her off-hours, preferably at a time when whoever it is isn't busy at something personal—you understand what I mean."

Leone nodded. Most Interior Guard were aware of the limited but serious recreations of the Aalaag—the aliens' home-world picture viewing and their incomprehensible game-playing.

"I understand," he said. "You show your experience with the Aalaag, Mr. Evert."

Shane rejected the implied flattery almost sharply.

"You know as well as I do," he said, "human servants who don't learn Aalaag ways don't last."

Some of Leone's business-hours punctiliousness relaxed. He switched to speaking in Italian himself.

"You're very right," he said. "Well, then, let's see. Ahm Or Ayla's on duty right now, but she's due to come off in a couple of hours and a few minutes. Then Cono Ra takes the main daytime shift until approximately two thousand hours, then Sem Arail relieves Cono Ra. The trouble is we haven't been together with these particular Aalaag, any of us in the Guard unit, here, long enough to learn much about their off-duty habits. . . ."

He and Shane discussed the matter and finally settled on the fact that the most promising time for Shane to try to find the three Aalaag least annoyed with the necessity of talking to him would be an hour or so before each was due to go on duty. Normally, the aliens neither gamed nor picture-viewed in the time immediately before their duty times. Leone apologized for the absence of the Governor and Lieutenant Governor, who had been called to a meeting with Laa Ehon, and then took Shane around the other human-used rooms of the building to meet each of the junior staff, whom he had not had a chance to meet the day before. Finally, with something of a flourish, the colonel installed Shane in the office Shane would have to himself for the duration of this visit and, presumably, on future ones.

Shane settled in, pretending to immerse himself in copies of the documents dealing with the activities of this Government Unit so far. Actually, he began the compilation of a record of where everyone, human as well as Aalaag, was at all times during the twenty-four hours.

He had had time to realize how much he had trusted to chance on his visit to the arms locker of the Government Unit in London, without knowing more about the movements of the human staff, as well as the Aalaag. There was no telling whether the Aalaag had taken any particular notice of the incident of a figure wearing pilgrim robes who had marked the face of Big Ben in London.

That they must know of it, through the Interior Guard, and the ordinary British police forces, if not otherwise, in spite of the fact that no newspaper would make more than the most noncommittal mention of it, was certain. That they could reconstruct exactly what he had done if they became suspicious, he believed utterly. But with some justice, he could still hope that the incident would be buried among hundreds of other episodes of defacement of property, which was what most pilgrim markings were classed as, according to Aalaag ideas of propriety. In which case, it would merely be left to their human servants to handle.

Furthermore, if that had happened, he could reasonably hope that those human servants—even those in the police and the Interior Guard—would tend to discount as imaginative exaggerations the more unusual elements in the popular account of his ascent to and descent from the clockface. The Aalaag Guard on duty there, who had seemed to notice him only on his way down or after he was already on the ground, had probably seen nothing—to an Aalaag—out of the ordinary about it, or he would have stopped Shane then and there.

Therefore, those Aalaag concerned with such human criminal acts were not likely to guess that some of their own tools had been used, let alone make the further mental leap to the unthinkable possibility that some of those tools might have been stolen from an arms locker. It should simply not occur to them that a human could have gained entrance to an arms locker and made use of some of their own tools.

With any reasonable luck, then, there should be no special watch kept on arms lockers in the new Government Units—yet. This time, and perhaps the next one or two times, he could borrow from such storage places with relative safety.

But he must still guard against the accident of either an Aalaag or a human catching him in or near a locker.

It was three full days, accordingly, before he had the movements of the alien and human personnel of the Unit charted to his satisfaction. In the process he had talked to all three of the assigned Aalaag and found them typical alien junior officers, none of them unusually clever or perceptive. There were two periods in the normal twenty-four hours, he found, when all three could be counted on to be occupied and safely out of the vicinity of the locker. One of these was midmorning, the other was just as the human staff was about to end office work for the day. The later time was obviously preferable for his purposes, when many of the humans in the building would be moving around its corridors and stairs in their normal course of activity.

When he remembered how unplanned and unthinking his raid on the locker in London had been, a coldness seemed to touch the back of his neck.

On the evening of that third day he returned to the hotel room to find Peter there with Maria.

He had unlocked the door of the parlor of their hotel suite with his room card and let himself in without thinking. He halted abruptly and at the sight of him Peter got hastily to his feet, followed by Maria, who came on to kiss him. The sudden movement on both Peter's and Maria's parts would have had an almost comic guiltiness to it, he thought, if it had not been so clearly the product of great excitement in both of them.

"Peter!" Shane said, smiling.

"Yes," said Peter. "I just got in here about twenty minutes ago. Maria said you'd be coming at any minute."

"And he's got wonderful things to tell you!" Maria shepherded him over to a seat on the couch on which Peter had also been sitting, before a long coffee table holding a tray with Scotch whisky, soda, ice, glasses, and wooden stirring rods, clearly ordered up from room service. Peter had a half-full drink before him.

"Well, that's good," he said, looking at Peter. "What is it?"

"Well, I—look here, why don't you have something first—," said Peter, reaching for the tray.

"No. No!" said Shane, and then realized he was speaking too sharply. He made his voice more reasonable. "Thanks just the same, but when you live with the Aalaag, alcohol's too risky most of the time. I've lost my taste for it. Just tell me what this news is."

"Ah. Well." Peter picked up his own glass and sat back against the cushions of the couch, still smiling at him. "You've no idea what that clock-marking trick of yours started in London—started everywhere, I'd say."

"I've been telling him how people had been reacting here," said Maria. "He doesn't realize how they're reacting—everyone who's human."

"Oh, the general populace," said Peter, with a small wave of the glass. "That's true enough. The Pilgrim symbol was already having a large impact before you marked Big Ben. But the great thing about your trick there is that it triggered off something even we in the Resistance hadn't more than suspected. Something beyond our wildest dreams—so to speak."

"What are you talking about?" said Shane.

"Well, it's a bit of a story, as I've been telling Maria," said

Peter, settling himself even more comfortably against the back of the couch. "You see, in the Resistance, we always suspected—knew, actually, though we'd no proof, of course—that there were other anti-Aalaag groups around that believed in keeping to themselves. Each military force in every country, of course, had at least one. The old Intelligence outfits almost automatically either housed an antialien group, or went completely over into being undercover anti-Aalaag organizations . . . and so on. None of these people would contact us, naturally, since they thought of us as a bunch of rank amateurs and wanted to keep their own existence secret in any case."

He paused to drink and then refill his glass. Shane and Maria sat in silence watching what was obviously a staged wait.

"So," he went on, "since they wouldn't contact us and since they none of them found anything they could do except collect data on the aliens and talk plans for some sort of possible action if this happened, or if that turned out to be true, etc. . . . we had no real way of knowing they were there. Oh, the police everywhere also had their own antialien groups, even some of the large corporations did—and of course there were free-lance paramilitary groups of the sort that tried to get at the aliens in the first few months after the conquest and found that not only couldn't they touch even a single alien, let alone kill one, just showing themselves on the horizon got them wiped out—"

"Get to the point," said Shane.

"Sorry," said Peter. "I'm afraid I'm enjoying it too much, being the bearer of glad tidings. The point is, there were all these groups lying low and now they've come out and acknowledged their existence; not only to each other, to us! They had to come to us, because we're the only ones who'd had any contact with you!"

Peter broke into laughter. The whisky he had drunk was not enough to make him boisterous, but it was undeniably enough to take some of the normal restraints off him.

"And guess what we learned, as they all began to report in?" he said.

"All right, what?" said Shane.

"That they wouldn't talk to us, their own compatriots, all this time, but every group, cell and organization of them had been in close contact almost from the beginning with their opposite numbers in other countries. That is, the Intelligence Resistance group in London knew the French Intelligence gang headquartered in Paris. The Royal Air Force group knew all the other groups in air forces in other nations. To a great extent Intelligence groups in the military knew those in civilian Intelligence and the police. . . . And so on—all over the world."

"All right," said Shane, "so the numbers of seriously involved Resistance fighters against the Aalaag have turned out to be a lot larger than anyone thought. That makes no difference to me. I've still got to do what I've got to do."

"No, no! Don't you see?" Peter sat up so abruptly that the liquid in his glass came perilously close to slopping out on the couch cover.

"Where we had no worldwide organization before, we've now got one," he said. "For example, remember how I could only call to London for you a handful of people from some of the larger European cities, when you wanted to show them the clock trick? But now we've people everywhere—and nearly all of them used to acting under orders. Don't you see what that means?"

"I can see it means easier access to help for me in more places," said Shane. "But I'm still going to have to—"

"But you're not," said Peter. "For example, we can now have the Pilgrim appear at the same time in two different places—or have him appear only minutes apart, as if he had split-second transportation to any point on the globe—"

"Hold on," said Shane. "There's only one individual who can do what I can do—so far at least."

"Actually, yes," said Peter. "But these people have resources—all the arts of the stage magician and more. They can produce people to play Pilgrim who seem to appear out of thin air, who seem to be able to float down through the air, and so on. When a real miracle is needed, if it really ever is, then you can come out and baffle the experts."

Shane looked at him, suddenly thoughtful.

"Why do you say 'if it ever is'?" he asked.

"Why, because you're too valuable to risk unless it's absolutely necessary; and there's no need to now, except in unforeseen circumstances. All the general run of people really wanted was a legendary figure to believe in, and you've already given them that. Even if you disappeared off the face of the Earth, tomorrow, most of the world's population would still cherish and keep spreading the story of the Pilgrim who could make Aalaags back off."

"In other words I'm not necessary from here on out?" said Shane softly.

"I didn't say anything like that!" answered Peter swiftly. "The mere fact all these groups exist doesn't get rid of the Aalaag or give us any new weapon to get rid of them with. The only real hope so far is the one you held out to the local Resistance leaders in London—confront the aliens with a planetful of people who're no use to them and get them to leave. We need you to get that message across to them, no matter how the message is put. We need to know that the aliens will understand. And you're our knowledgeable, articulate body on that. Of course, you'll have to work with this new organization, if you want it to work with you; and there's already been some good suggestions made by these professional people—"

"Wait a minute," said Shane, still quietly. "What new organization?"

"But I told you!"

"No."

"Well, it's very simple," said Peter. "I told you the military antialien units of one nation's military or police, or whatever, knew their opposite numbers in the other nations. In effect, even before you came along, there were actually three large networks of antialien professionals already existing. One was essentially that of the Western world, one of the Soviet, and one primarily Oriental."

"The Third World was rather overlooked, wasn't it?" said Shane.

"Not at all. Most of the so-called Third World countries were connected with one of the big three networks I mentioned—sometimes with all three of them. Of course, there were also internal differences—the Chinese and the Japanese outfits never did warm up to each other as much as others thought they might. At any rate, the point is all it took was for the three networks to combine; which, effectively, they've now done. There's a sort of quasitemporary—call it whatever you want—directorate for the whole thing already operating; and it's already come up with some ideas about what the Pilgrim ought to do next—"

"That's what I thought," said Shane.

Peter stared at him, the glass in his right hand held suspended in midair.

"Pardon me?" said Peter.

"I said, that's what I thought," repeated Shane. "You can leave now. Go back to London, get in touch with this directorate you talk about, and tell them that they can run off and play at anything they feel like; but as far as the Pilgrim is concerned, they don't exist."

Peter stared at him. Slowly, the Englishman lowered his glass and set it carefully upon the coffee table in front of him.

"In God's name, why?"

"Because I'm not interested in their ideas about what the Pilgrim should do. Because I know that any idea they come up with is bound to be wrong."

Peter still stared at him.

"How can you say that," Peter asked, "when you don't even know what those ideas are?"

"For the same reason I knew none of you Resistance people realized what you were up against in the Aalaag. These people don't either. And because they don't, they're guessing. I don't guess—I know. And one of the things I know is that they're bound to guess wrong because they don't know. I'm not going to risk everything I know I can do because of the blundering of people who don't."

Peter stared at him.

"You need them," said Peter flatly, at last. "What's more, they can find out who you really are if they really want to, by running down and questioning those Milanese Resistance people who saw you when you were kidnapped, then using that information through their own police or military contacts with the Aalaag to find you by a process of elimination. Even if that didn't work, they'd find you when they started to track down Maria. They're not like us—they can pull the strings of governmental machinery, right up to the alien level, to get what they want. Then, once they find you, they'll give you a simple choice. Follow orders from them or they'll betray you to the aliens. They'll know how to do that, safely, too."

Shane sat still, with the expressionlessness he had learned in more than two years within the House of Weapons; but inside him there was a shakiness—a shakiness made up of fear and rage. Fear of what ignorance could do to him and his plans, rage at the stupidity of humans who could still think simple answers would work with the Aalaag. Somehow, he told himself, he must come up with some kind of response to what Peter was saying, a response that would also convince this organization the other man talked about. Think! The command to himself burned in his brain.

"They can try to trace me," he said slowly, "and identify me; though if I catch any of them at it, I'll betray them to the Aalaag. I know how to do something like that safely—they don't. If they betray me, I'll tell the Aalaag all about the fact they exist—and that's all the Aalaag will need to know to find and destroy them. And I'm not just making a blackmail threat, I'm stating a fact. It's a logical development that'll follow inevitably if they betray me. If the Aalaag distrust me, the first thing they'll do is question me—and I'm not someone who'll stand up under torture."

He stopped, telling himself to calm down. He went on more soberly.

"Besides, even if I had reason to, and even if I could stand up to questioning by the Interior Guard at their orders, it wouldn't matter. The Aalaag have more sophisticated ways of getting at everything I've ever known, if they have to use them. The day I come under suspicion from the Aalaag, everyone in those organizations—and the Resistance, as far as I've come to know the people in it—are as good as dead, headed down the same route I'll already be following. The only choice this network, or organization—or whatever you call it—has, is to sit back, leave me alone and be left out of what I'm going to do; or accept the fact they're the ones who've got to take orders—blindly, and from me. Go tell them that."

The silence when he stopped speaking was almost cruel. Peter finally broke it.

"Christ!" he muttered, staring not so much at Shane as through him. "Christ . . ."

He stirred and his eyes came back to focus on Shane.

"All right," he said heavily. "I'll tell them. You've got us all by the balls—"

The harsh ringing of the phone interrupted him. Maria, who was closest to the instrument, reached out and lifted its handpiece off its hooks.

"Hello?" she said, and her face paled as she listened. She put her hand over the mouthpiece.

"Shane," she said to him. "It's a man's voice asking for Shane Evert. Shane, we've never mentioned your name in this hotel—"

"I'll take it," he said, picked the handpiece out of her grip and spoke into it. "This is Shane Evert."

—And Lyt Ahn was suddenly in the midst of them, standing, towering between rug and ceiling with barely inches to spare. His face was turned in Shane's direction.

"Shane-beast," he said in Aalaag. "You will conclude your duties in Milan within three more days. You and your assistant will proceed then, in that order, to Cairo, Moscow, Calcutta, Shanghai, Buenos Aires, Mexico City and New York, where new Government Units are being set up. You will observe each one in that order, calling in a report to me here after each one, then return to me here."

He vanished.

Peter and Maria were sitting absolutely motionless in their seats, staring at where the First Captain had stood.

"It's all right," said Shane to them. "That's only a recorded message—a projection of him. He simply spoke the order to me in his office back in the House of Weapons, it was automatically recorded and human servants traced me and set up a link through the phone system."

The other two looked at him with nothing to say.

"So," said Shane, "it turns out neither this organization of yours nor I make the decision what I do next. The First Captain has spoken."

NINETEEN

THAT NIGHT THE BAD DREAMS BEGAN.

Shane woke to find himself tightly wound in Maria's arms, his pajamas soaked, his face wet—and a devastating, ugly feeling, as of something unbearable just experienced, filling him.

"What is it?" he gasped.

"You're awake!" said Maria. "You're awake now?"

"Yes . . . I think so." The inner feeling began to recede a little from him. "What happened? What was it?"

"You were dreaming. You were saying something I couldn't make out and crying . . ." She wiped the damp skin under his eyes and at their corners with soft fingertips.

"Crying . . ." he echoed dully. He had no idea of what the dream had been. He tried to recover it, but it was as if it hid from him. "You say you couldn't make out what I was saying. Was it in Aalaag?"

"I don't—" She hesitated. "I don't think so."

"Not in Aalaag," he muttered, blocked and baffled.

"It was in English, maybe," she said. "But you were talking so thickly I couldn't understand you. You didn't really say the words out loud."

The escaped memory of whatever he had lived through in the nightmare was fading fast now, although it still hung about him like an invisible aura in the lightless bedroom. He put his arms around Maria and pulled her close to him, burying his face in her hair and deliberately shutting his mind to everything but her presence. Peace moved in; and he slept again.

In the morning he woke with his mind clearer than it had been the night before. The hotel they were in had claimed it was full, with no more rooms available; and Shane had not wanted to draw undue attention to himself in the establishment by trying bribery. Peter had accordingly spent the night on the same couch in the parlor on which he had sat with Shane the evening before. They ordered breakfast up to the room and Shane talked to the Briton as they ate.

"I've had a chance to sleep on it—and it's a good thing," he told Peter across the breakfast table. "I forgot that you're the one who's got to do the convincing of this group drawn from the organizations, the people who had ideas for what I ought to do. I don't want even to meet with these people. Make them see that's for their protection as much as mine. Anyone I meet is certain to land in the hands of the Aalaag if the Aalaag ever start suspecting me."

"Hmm," said Peter. Shane thought he saw a glimpse of that ambition in the other man he had suspected earlier. "You want to pass on all your orders through me?"

"That's right."

"I think I can make them see the sense of that," said Peter. "It's the idea of taking orders from you instead of giving you suggestions that I'm going to have trouble selling them."

"Lay it on the line," said Shane. "What I said last night still holds. They can come in under my orders or stand aside. If they get in my way, they'll deliver themselves into the Aalaag's hands."

"But to make them believe it—," Peter began.

"You had a good example last night of why they've got no choice but to believe it," answered Shane. "You saw for yourself. They can't run me because I can't run myself. Lyt Ahn pulls the strings on me; and he pulls them without warning, and for reasons they can't guess and neither can I or anyone else—even other Aalaag. In short, their plans aren't only ill-advised, they wouldn't be possible from the moment they're made, if only because of the fact I belong to the First Captain."

Peter nodded, spreading honey on a piece of roll.

"In any case," Shane went on, "you heard him give me his orders last night. My time here is limited now; and there's something I have to do which is going to take me out of sight for a day, possibly two—"

He paused to look at Maria.

"I won't be in touch even with you," he said.

"It's something dangerous, isn't it?" asked Maria quietly.

He looked at her for a moment, then nodded.

"I knew it was coming," she said. "Don't worry. I'll do whatever you say. You want me just to stay in the suite until you get back?"

"It'd be best if you didn't go out at all," said Shane. He turned back to Peter. "I'd like you to stay with her, until I get back. If any going out is necessary, you can do it. Once I'm back, you can head back to London as fast as you can and contact this organization. Tell them if they want to work with me, something I need immediately is a phone number in Cairo, Egypt, and someone there I can call on for any help I need. Don't tell them anything about Lyt Ahn's orders. Let them guess if they like, but tell them as little as possible. If they complain, repeat that it's for their own safety as well as mine—though they ought to be able to figure that much out for themselves."

"Do you want me to give them any idea of the kind of help you're likely to want in Cairo?" Peter asked.

"No."

"Ah."

"Now," said Shane, pushing his chair back from the table and standing up. "It's after nine o'clock. I didn't plan to sleep this late. I'm headed toward the Unit; and I'll see the two of you again in forty-eight hours or less—if I'm lucky."

He got to the Unit at a little before ten minutes to ten hundred hours in the morning. With Lyt Ahn's orders about his leaving in three days, there could be no waiting around for the safer, end-of-the-day period to raid the arms locker. He would have to take the more dangerous moment in midmorning, which was now only some twenty-five minutes away; and if he was caught in the basement area, there would be no excuses he could give for being there, except the weak ones that he had either lost his way in searching for a particular office, or that it was part of his duty to Lyt Ahn to report back that he had observed every part of the premises. Both were bad, because the natural thing in either case would have been for him to first contact the offices of the Interior Guard for a guide.

It was tempting simply to pass up the arms locker visit entirely. But there was too much danger he might be unable to get into Aalaag Headquarters in Rome, when he got there.

So he went to his own office, waited out the slow crawl of the minutes until the time of ten-fifteen, then went out into the empty corridor and quietly descended the back stairs of the building to the basement. Here, as in London and elsewhere, the layout was essentially the same. As in London, the door to the locker dissolved immediately at the touch of the key of Lyt Ahn.

He helped himself to another of the invisibility instruments. This time, also, he hunted for tools like that he had seen used by the Maintenance woman to cut the doorway in the wall of the House of Weapons. He had carefully taken note then of what the instrument looked like; but even with that image in his mind, it took him an uncomfortably long time to find one here.

However, he finally managed, and left the arms locker with the door once more fastened behind him. He slipped upstairs again to his office, drawing a deep breath of relief once he was above the basement level and could give a satisfying answer to anyone who questioned his presence—not that on the ground floor anyone would have a reason to question him. He returned to his office, waited until the noon lunch hour filled the corridors with human servants, then boldly mingled with them and signed out in ordinary fashion.

Outside, he refused a couple of invitations to join some of the others for lunch. Even if time had not been a factor, he would have still done so—their curiosity about him was to be expected and normal, but dangerous. Better to be known as unsocial than to have something known that you later wished was unknown.

He walked far enough off to lose any visible co-workers and took a cab back to the hotel. There, he put on his pilgrim robe, took his staff, then caught a taxi to the office of Marrotta.

Marrotta himself, he discovered when he got there, was out to lunch—and he had left no orders for people to do anything for Shane in the business owner's absence. And no, the two men at work in the office had no idea where Marrotta might be eating.

Shane produced and displayed a large wad of lire.

Both the workers in the office were shocked and insulted.

Shane went out, walked down the front of the building far enough to be out of sight of the office windows and leaned against its wall, waiting. After only a few minutes, the younger of the office workers appeared around the corner of the truck gate farther down the street, and came rapidly up the sidewalk to Shane.

"You wanted to know where Signor Marrotta is at lunch?" the young man asked.

"I want you to take me there. When I get to him"—Shane produced the wad of notes again—"you get this."

"I can't be gone that long." The pale, pointed-chinned face was damp with perspiration, the voice was highly nervous.

"Suit yourself." Shane put the notes away. "I suppose you know you and that other man in the office are going to be in deep trouble with your boss when he comes back and I tell him how you kept me from finding him."

"You're one of the two people in pilgrim robes who were in the other day?"

"That's right."

"All right."

Marrotta, it turned out, was lunching by himself in a small neighborhood restaurant, at a table for one by a wall. Shane identified him through the glass window fronting the restaurant.

"I've got to go," said the clerk. "Let's have the money." Shane shook his head.

"Not yet," he answered. "First you go in and tell him I'm out here."

"That wasn't the deal! You just wanted to get to him. He'll go through the roof if he sees me away from the office here."

"Tell him I made you bring me. As for the rest—I haven't got to him yet. Not until you bring him out here. If you want your money, get moving."

The clerk scowled at him, hesitated, but went in. Through the window Shane saw him speak to Marrotta. The trucking firm owner put his fork down, wiped his lips on a napkin and followed the younger man out.

Shane had kept his hood pinched shut from the moment he had left the hotel. Through the narrow parting in the two edges of cloth now, he could see Marrotta's face. No enmity was visible there this time. No particular friendship, either. Merely the readiness of a man in business to do that business with another member of the general public.

"You ready, then?" asked Marrotta in Italian.

"Yes," said Shane. "As soon as you can get me on my way, I need to be headed toward Rome. When I get there, I'll have to buy another staff, or a piece of wood approximately like this—"

He shook his own staff.

"Also a white bedsheet, black paint, brushes and nails. I'll also need something to make the flag stand upright, like a flagpole. Can you see to it that the driver knows where I can buy those things without making anyone curious?"

Marrotta nodded. He jerked his head to his left.

"Come on back to the office," he said. "It's Johann's shift. He's waiting back there for you."

Half an hour later, after being dropped off by a truck in a different neighborhood and picking up a car to which Johann had the keys but which was simply parked on the street—a five or six-year-old, Simca four-door sedan, a block and a half from where the truck had dropped them—Shane and his chauffeur were on their way to Rome.

Johann was a practiced driver with good reflexes. Shane looked at him with a curiosity that he had not felt before toward any member of the Resistance. What did a man like this think? What made him involve himself in a risk to life like this? Had the Aalaag done something to someone close to him? Any answer was possible. For the first time Shane felt a need to know such things about these people. A small, quiet, dark man in his thirties or thereabouts, completely Milanese in appearance in spite of his first name, which was all Shane was ever to know about him, Johann drove with concentration and made it plain he was not interested in conversation. Since this suited Shane's original plans, if not his present curiosity, equally well, they made the drive to Rome almost without words, in a little over six hours.

They stopped at last before an apartment building. Johann took a small, zippered canvas bag from the rear seat of the Simca and led Shane up three flights of dark, narrow stairs in an atmosphere heavy with the odors of past meals. The Resistance man unlocked a door and let them both into a small, single-room apartment with two tiny beds, a two-burner electric stove, one ceiling light and one lamp. It was dark enough in the room, in spite of its being only late afternoon of a sunny day, so that Johann lit the ceiling light. The room looked even less appetizing in the illumination of the one weak bulb.

"But it's safe," said Shane. "Against anyone but the Aalaag, anyway."

To his surprise, Johann crossed himself.

"Are the aliens going to be looking for us, too?" he asked.

"No," said Shane. He was conscious of an irrational urge to apologize. He went to a change of subject. "Look, Signor Marrotta told you about the things I need to buy and where to buy them without attracting attention?"

Johann nodded.

"Well, I was going to get you to take me around so I could buy them myself; but, late as it is, some shops could be closed before I got around to everything. You can probably do it quicker alone. You think you can get it all bought before the stores lock up for the day?"

"Yes," said Johann.

Shane handed him a generous supply of banknotes. "I'll wait here. You'd probably better bring back some food and drink."

"I was going to anyway," said Johann. He left.

His going seemed to bring a grayness and a chill to the room. Its cause had been only the removal of one other human body, but for some reason Shane was suddenly and acutely aware of being alone. The sensation was like a sense of betrayal in him. He was conscious of exhaustion. He flopped on his back on one of the narrow beds, feeling the thin hardness of its mattress under his spine and staring up at the wavy, cracked, and dingy white surface of the plastered ceiling.

His decision to slip away to Rome like this and have the Pilgrim make an appearance there had been so that there would be a break in the direct correlation between the cities to which he had been sent, and the Pilgrim's appearances. Eventually, as Peter had suggested, others could take it on themselves to play at such appearances, with his permission or without it. Then all direct association with his travels and such sightings would become blurred beyond tracing. But until then he must protect himself.

The actual appearance, in this case, should be fairly safe and easy. The difficult part was that he had decided he needed permanent possession of tools like those he now carried—and these could only be taken from some arms locker with which he apparently could never have had contact. Also, by preference, it should be a much larger locker than that in one of Laa Ehon's Government Units, so that the stolen tools were less likely to be missed. In a word, he needed to make a raid on an Aalaag installation with a heavy complement of officers—such as the Aalaag Headquarters here in Rome.

And the danger in doing so lay in the fact that, if caught within its walls, he would be able to produce no good reason for being there. To be caught would mean his being returned to Lyt Ahn, for certain questioning and eventual disposal. His only hope of getting away with it would be to let himself in by the same sort of private Aalaag door by which he had slipped out of the Milan HQ to provide an excuse that would save Maria's life, then hope those within who saw him there would take him for a human servant with some legitimate reason for being there.

He could not make specific plans because he had no idea of what he might run into, in the way of the Headquarters' physical layout or in human or Aalaag curiosity about him, once he was inside. His mind skirted the edge of imaginings in which he was stopped, questioned, and found out . . . and fled from these into sleep.

When he woke, suddenly, and for no apparent reason, it was completely dark in the room. He looked at his wristwatch and saw that an inner alarm had roused him close to the proper time. It was almost midnight. On the bed beside him, a small hump under a blanket showed where Johann slumbered.

The Aalaag were largely indifferent to the day and night of the planet they were on. They operated on a roughly twenty-four-hour day, and a large establishment like the local Headquarters would of necessity have a fair number of human servants on duty at all hours. Shane dressed in the sort of casual slacks and shirt he normally wore while on duty at the House of Weapons, and which was the usual human dress in most Aalaag working places that did not call for special uniforms. Over the slacks and shirt, he put his pilgrim cloak, took his staff and went out.

The Roman night was cool. He felt the chill almost immediately through the robe and his thin clothes underneath. He shrugged his shoulders to signal the robe's Aalaag-technology heating system to compensate for the temperature. The streets were empty except for long lines of cars crowded against the curbs on either side, locked tight, dark and empty. The Simca would be among them, but Johann would have the keys. Unthinkingly, Shane had planned to do as he normally did and catch a taxi. But it did not look as if this was a neighborhood where he would find taxis cruising the streets.

He could go back upstairs, wake Johann and get the keys from him or even make the little man part of the expedition. But he did not want to do either. Alone, he was not only safer, but this part of his trip would remain a secret.

With a feeling of urgency and uneasiness, he turned and began to walk rapidly down the street, looking for some intersection that would show lights in the distance, some sign of activity that would signal a greater likelihood of his finding a cab.

By these means he finally managed to find a hotel with cabs waiting before it, and take one of these to within a few blocks of the Headquarters. He waited until the vehicle was out of sight before turning to walk the last few blocks.

When he reached the Headquarters building, he found, as he had expected, that it was very much like every other Aalaag Headquarters he had seen; with the exception of the House of Weapons, which in its alien way was actually more of a palace than a Headquarters. In this case, even the private door he had counted on was in almost the same location as it had been at the Headquarters in Milan. It sat, at the bottom of a flight of a dozen steps down from the street level, some fifty feet farther along the street from the Headquarters' main entrance; which, according to custom, at this hour of the night had no Interior Guards standing on duty outside it.

There were consequently no eyes watching as he stripped off his pilgrim robe and tucked it, with his staff, in a patch of deep shadow at the fool of a wall—where hopefully, they would remain safely hidden until he came back for them. Shivering in the sudden chill of the night air once the robe was off, he went down the stairs and Lyt Ahn's key opened the door for him immediately and noiselessly.

Interior warmth flowed comfortingly around him. The door had let him directly into the first basement level where the arms locker should be; something he had hoped for but had not dared to count on. He went along the softly lighted corridor the door had let him into, touching each door he passed with Lyt Ahn's key.

Most did not open, proving themselves to be ordinary doors with no alien locks to them. A few opened, but showed themselves to be storerooms with contents in which he was not interested. He came at last to a door which he was just about to touch with his key when it dissolved before him of its own accord.

A door such as this should only do that if an Aalaag was going in and out repeatedly and did not want to bother with unlocking it each time.

Every nerve in his body tensed. His stomach seemed to curl and shrink within him. Silently and slowly, he leaned forward until he could peer around the edge of the door.

He looked into the arms locker, fully lit, but he saw no living being, human or Aalaag, in it—though there were areas into which he could not see from where he stood.

Some Aalaag might have come, gone back out and would not be returning for a while. Otherwise leaving the door unlocked was a breach of security. An unimportant one, it was true; but except under extraordinary conditions, the Aalaag did not commit breaches of security. There was only the unlikely but possible chance that an Aalaag, after entering it, had been momentarily called away for some unexpected reason and, leaving, had in effect left the portal ajar in the expectation of being back within a few seconds—or minutes at most.

Shane stared and listened. He saw no movement and heard nothing. If one of the Aalaag had opened it and left temporarily, now was the ideal time for him to steal the tools he had come to take. It was simply an unparalleled stroke of luck that needed to be taken advantage of right away, if at all. Moreover—the thought chilled him—if he did not go in now, but waited to play safe and enter after the Aalaag, whoever he was, had returned and gone again, there was no telling how long the alien might be planning to spend in the locker. If he was intending to contemplate one of the weapons of his ancestors, he might be in there literally for hours. Meanwhile, every second Shane spent inside this building increased the danger of his being observed, questioned and found out. But if he went in now and got out again before the Aalaag's return, there would not even be the use of Lyt Ahn's key on the door for alien technology to trace.

In the end, Shane hardly knew what triggered his decision, but suddenly he was inside, moving almost at a run but as silently as he could toward the back of the locker, where the tools were kept.

He had visited the tools section of three lockers now, and they were all laid out the same. He knew where to look. It was hardly a moment before he was able to find an invisibility device, a levitating tool, and one of the cutting tools he had seen the woman from Maintenance use to cut the wall at the House of Weapons.

He stowed the devices in his pockets and paused for a second longer to run his eye over the neat ranks of other tools, wishing he knew what more of them did and which might be useful to him if only he knew all those capabilities.

"Halt!" said an Aalaag voice behind him. "Turn about, beast! What are you doing here?"

Shane turned. Just inside the entrance, looking down the aisle between the equipment-banked walls, was a male Aalaag in off-duty uniform. He stared, without words, at the massive body that blocked his only way out of the locker, in this moment he had been afraid of. . . .

"Speak, beast!" said the Aalaag. "What's your name?"

Shane's wits began to work sluggishly again.

" 'Tarnished sir," he mumbled in Aalaag so clumsy it would be barely understandable. "My name Hyman-beast."

He had deliberately chosen a name with two consonants the Aalaag vocal apparatus could not pronounce, and to which consequently the aliens were all but ear-blind. He had the momentary satisfaction of seeing the Aalaag opposite him start to echo the name and give up before he had started.

"What're you doing here? Who sent you here?"

"Not speak Aalaag good . . ." mumbled Shane. He reached into his pocket and brought out the wall-cutting device. "Orders. Put this back. Door open."

"Who sent you to take it back? What beast is your superior? Haven't you ever been told that no beast is to enter an arms locker except under special orders or supervision?"

"Pardon, 'tarnished sir. This stupid beast not understand."

"What beast sent you here? Or did an officer send you?"

"Not understand."

"What sort of cattle are they sending us nowadays?" said the officer. "Beast, listen—you are not to put that tool back. You understand?"

"Understand, 'tarnished sir."

"Take it and go yourself to the office of the Officer of the Day. Do you at least know where that is?"

"Know, 'tarnished sir."

"Go there and wait for me. Tell the Officer of the Day I sent you and I'll be along before his duty period ends to explain why you're there. You understand? You tell Officer of the Day that Chagon Een send you to wait. Chagon Een come soon. Understand?"

"This beast wait Officer Day. Chagon Een come soon."

"Good. Now go. Touch nothing on your way out."

"Beast go, 'tarnished sir."

Shane walked down the aisle, slipped past the Aalaag, who did not deign to move and give him extra room to pass, and went out through the door. Once out, he turned to peer back from the relatively dim light of the corridor into the brightly illuminated locker, and saw the alien had moved to one of the racks of weapons and taken down something that vaguely resembled an ancient mace, handling it carefully and holding it at last in both hands before him, becoming motionless in contemplation of it.

Shane turned and went with all quiet speed back down the corridor. Seconds later he was out of the building and putting on his robe once more. In less than an hour he was back at the hotel, where Johann seemed not to have moved in his sleep.

TWENTY

THE PLANNED APPEARANCE OF THE PILGRIM AT THE CASTEL Sant'Angelo in Rome had been considered by Shane primarily as an excuse for his raid on the arms locker of the Aalaag Headquarters in that city. It should be a simple matter. There would be no Aalaag riding sentry around the historic—but to the Aalaag—useless structure. It had been spared destruction officially because the Aalaag had classed it as a harmless part of the custom pattern of the beasts. Privately, Shane had thought that in such restraint he scented the fact that the Aalaag, with their worship of their own past, had at least a trickle of understanding for important relics of the human past. . . .

In any case, Shane had not concerned his thoughts with it much in advance. His plan was merely to get in, display the Pilgrim mark and get out. All the real attention of his thoughts and his planning had been concentrated on the raid on the arms locker—which had been both dangerous and vital.

But now as he sat in his robes, being driven by Johann to the Castel, a perverse uneasiness began to gnaw at him. A fear about what might happen when he tried to make the Pilgrim appearance.

It was ridiculous. This appearance should be a piece of cake. There would be no Aalaag. Nor would there be any reason for human police, and no reason at all for the Castel to be under any kind of surveillance for someone playing the role of Pilgrim. For that matter, not a few of the daily visitors would be wearing robes and carrying staves. Now that he watched for it out of the car window as they traveled, he saw that Maria and Peter had been right. He was startled to see how many more people were on the streets in pilgrim garb than he had been used to seeing. Their number must have been increasing daily without his noticing it.

So, why did the feeling of fear persist?

The only conceivable cause for danger could be if the officer who had caught him in the arms locker the night before had set in motion a search which went beyond the walls of the Headquarters building, and was now causing the whole metropolitan area of Rome to be combed for the beast that had been seen in a forbidden area of the building.

And that was ridiculous.

Or was it?

The very idea of such a search was, said the logical front of Shane's mind, unthinkable. Even if the Aalaag at the Roman Headquarters had later checked the number of wall-cutting tools in stock and found it one short, the fact that they could not find it, or the particular beast Chagon Een had spoken to, was hardly important enough to justify a citywide search. For one thing, the equipment automatically monitoring the main doorway to the Headquarters—which, as far as any junior Aalaag officer was likely to know would be the only way a beast could carry away such a tool—would show that nothing had gone out that way. Therefore, the tool must still be around the Headquarters, somewhere. As for the strange beast itself, perhaps it had been only in the building temporarily to do some sort of construction job . . . it would be too time-consuming a labor to search all through the orders of the past few days on the off-chance of finding some kind of clue to its identity. Whichever it may have been, that beast had certainly not carried the tool from the building. Therefore, the tool would be found, eventually, and unusual concern was unnecessary.

Shane glanced out the windshield. They were not far now from the Castel. He attempted to think of something else, but the small knot of uneasiness in him persisted and his thoughts came back automatically onto the track on which they had been stuck.

. . . Nor would it be either practical or profitable for a junior officer to devote a great deal of time in trying to solve the mystery of a beast intruder. For one thing, clearly the beast had been able to get into the arms locker only because the officer himself had carelessly left the entrance open. Even, however, if his Aalaag sense of honor caused Chagon Een to accuse himself of carelessness and make a search, there was a practical limit to the time he could spend in pursuing it.

The Aalaag thought of themselves first and foremost as warriors. But in fact, thought Shane now, what they really were, were administrators. It took the full-time effort of all of them just to run the machinery of underbeasts on each of the various worlds they used to supply themselves. Proof of this was the limitedness of their pastimes; only the gaming and the viewing of the past of their race.

Nonetheless, the closer they got to the Castel, the more Shane's concern increased. It was a million-to-one chance, but what if Chagon Een or someone superior to him had connected the beast in their arms locker with the London report of a physical Pilgrim beast? What if the Aalaag had tracing equipment even beyond what Shane imagined them to have? What if, on walking into the Castel, he should find himself confronted and trapped by an Aalaag and perhaps a platoon of Interior Guard . . . ?

Urgently, Shane felt the need to talk the possibility over with someone, if only to get it out into the open where his sensible upper mind could measure the great odds against it. But there was no one to talk to except Johann, who had just now stopped the car and was beginning to back it into a parking place at curbside, the equivalent of a couple of blocks from the Castel.

And there was no point in trying to talk to Johann about it. The other had resisted all efforts by Shane to be drawn into conversation. Shane's first assumption regarding this had been that the smaller man was echoing Georges Marrotta's dislike for Shane. But the long trip and the working together to prepare a stand for his staff to hold the cloth with the Pilgrim mark had convinced Shane that Johann's silence was due to some other cause.

Basically he seemed, if anything, shy. Or perhaps "shy" was the wrong word. Perhaps, farfetched as it sounded, he seemed to consider Shane as a person in some strange special category that put all but necessary conversation out of the question.

At any rate, they were now at their destination. With the stand they had built that would convert his staff into a flagpole under his cloak and with the staff itself in his hand, Shane got out of the car.

"Wait for me here," he told Johann.

Johann nodded.

Shane turned and joined the late morning foot traffic that was headed toward the Castel.

Among these sightseers, more than a few of whom, as Shane had expected, were also dressed in pilgrim cloaks, Shane attracted no notice. Nonetheless, as he went, the worry and fear inside him began to increase and he began to sweat under his robe, for all that alien-designed garment tried to balance the temperatures of his body surface.

He felt a sudden, almost spiteful envy of Johann, sitting safely back in the car, waiting. It would not occur to the other man to worry about him—wasn't Shane the Pilgrim? Moreover, Johann, who did not seem unduly blessed with intelligence anyway, might well be incapable of concentrating on anything but his own immediate situation. Shane forced the thought of Johann out of his mind. He must concentrate on what was to be done.

The Castel Sant' Angelo, built originally as a mausoleum for the Emperor Hadrian, and fortified by later popes, had more of the appearance of a drum-shaped fortress than anything else. Forcing himself to ignore the apprehension he felt, Shane emerged in his cloak and staff on the top level of the drum portion itself, amongst a small crowd of the tourists, picked a spot halfway to the exterior wall with its embrasures, and went to work.

It was simply a matter of taking a rolled-up and now painted bedsheet from under his robe, together with the folded stand of metal he and Johann had constructed. He unfolded the stand, set his staff upright in it, unrolled the flag and hooked the eyelets cut into its inner edge over the bent nails Johann had hammered into the staff the day before. There was not much breeze, but enough to lazily furl and unfurl the liberated flag.

Turning from it with the first sense of satisfaction and relief from apprehension that he had felt since they had left the place where he and Johann had spent the night, Shane found something he had not counted on. He was completely encircled, hemmed in by the sightseers on the platform, all staring at him and examining him in a fascinated and utter silence. Any way out was blocked unless he wanted to physically shove his way through them. Plainly they felt that they were staring at the Pilgrim of legend—or at least someone walking in his footsteps—and they all looked as if in a second they would start crowding in on him with questions, and hands reached out to touch him.

He caught himself back from his first panic-induced reflex, which was to order them out of his way. To speak at all here and now would be far too ordinary, too human. Instead, thankful that the edges of his cowl were pulled close together to hide his face, he extended one arm in silence and pointed, beginning to walk forward.

They parted before him, along the line indicated by his pointing finger. Still in staring silence, they made a way clear; and he walked through them to the balcony that guarded the edge of this level, stepped up on it and activated both the levitating tool and the privacy one. Invisible, he then stepped off into space and, controlling his descent with the levitator, let himself safely down the outside of the structure. Down on the ground and still invisible, he made his way as quickly as he could back to the car where Johann was waiting for him.

The small man's face went pale as the car door on the other side of the front seat appeared to open itself, then close again, and the seat cushions dimpled beside him. His color came back as Shane shut off the privacy tool and became visible beside him.

"You made it. Thank the Mother of God!" ejaculated Johann, putting the car into motion and joining the traffic of the street, his eyes steady on the traffic alone. A moment later, he added, "I prayed for you all the time you were gone."

The remark took Shane suddenly and utterly by the throat.

"That . . . helped," he managed to say.

It was all a farce, he thought despairingly, as the car, under Johann's skilled control, began to nose its way out of the city northward, headed back toward Milan. How had he gotten into this, anyway? Who could have suspected that a rough sketch he had made on a wall in a moment of crazy drunkenness would operate like a lit match in a house filled with loose papers? Who could have suspected that any of this that had followed could happen?

He was a juiceless grain of wheat between two gigantic millstones that were determined to grind each other to bits—the humans and the Aalaag. Neither one had the slightest idea of what the other was, or how the other thought. For that matter they had no idea of what they were themselves, or how they thought.

And yet they should have had some understanding of each other. His mind returned to his earlier thought of the Aalaag as administrators rather than the warriors they thought themselves to be. They were administrators dreaming of a long-sought goal far in the future which would be a return to something far in the past.

There was no reason the two races could not understand each other better. They shared more than they thought. The human race had lived in a constant state of war from its animal stage on up. The Aalaag, in spite of what they believed about themselves, had once been more than just a race of soldiers—and still had some traits from that earlier time, from what he had occasionally seen.

Lyt Ahn had shown a capability for consideration, if not kindness, with him, Shane. Both Lyt Ahn and his consort Adtha Or Ain, had shown a love for their son who was possibly dead, possibly captured; and they had shown something very like affection for each other, in spite of the impression which the Aalaag generally gave, that the male-female pairings among them were for reasons of procreation and team-work only.

What were humans? And what were Aalaag? Who had even thought of those two questions, let alone how these two unknowns should get along together or not get along together? The humans at least had had a future—once. The Aalaag certainly had a past and claimed to have a future. But what kind of future would it be?

Assume they could retake the worlds of their birth. Assume they could reverse any physical changes the usurper race had made in the appearance of those worlds. With everything back as it was, could the Aalaag take up life once more on those worlds as they had used to live it? If so, how?

It would be contrary to their dream to import beast-servants to run the machinery of their home worlds, to be the suppliers of food and materials for shelter, tools and all else. But after all these thousands of years how could the Aalaag change themselves back overnight into farmers and artisans, researchers and marketers, and all else required; and if they did, who among them would be ready to defend their worlds if another race attacked them?

But this was the goal they believed themselves to be working for, and had enslaved an unknown number of races to help them reach.

It was all crazy. By human standards the Aalaag made no sense. By Aalaag standards, the humans had no worth except as domesticated animals. And yet each race formed a sort of mirror in which the other, if it would, could see a distorted version of itself.

Because of those distortions the Aalaag were ready to kill any humans who did not behave as they wanted; and the people in the Resistance wanted to kill Aalaag for being what they appeared to be.

If only, thought Shane desperately, he could be completely all on one side or another. If he could be like other humans and see the Aalaag only as monster invaders; or if he could be like the Aalaag and see other humans as no more than beasts. If he could be like Maria and Peter and Johann and . . .

If only there was some real hope for the wild notion he had originally given the Resistance people for getting rid of the Aalaag. If it would work to make them want to abandon the human race and go elsewhere. If he could summon up one grain of belief in that, one particle of real hope, then maybe he, too, might be able to completely join the human camp and find the courage and will to fight the Aalaag. But he was cursed with the knowledge that that hope was groundless. The Aalaag were about as removable by human action as the sun would be from the sky.

Somewhere along the trip back he dozed and once more had, but without remembering when he woke what it was, the nightmare he had endured back in Milan. This time Johann shook him awake.

"You were dreaming and trying to talk about something," said the little man.

"I was?" said Shane.

Grimly, he set his teeth on the determination to stay awake until he was safely back in Milan, alone with Maria. It was dangerous to appear so human, so vulnerable, in the eyes of someone like Johann, he told himself; and, in fact, he did manage to stay awake the rest of the trip, although he was unaccountably, desperately tired.

Back at the hotel suite, he found Peter still there, as he had been asked to be, but packed and ready to leave.

"Well, you can go now," Shane told him. "You can also tell anyone you want that there's been another appearance of the Pilgrim, this time in Rome at the Castel Sant'Angelo."

"I guessed it would be Rome," said Peter, "and I was sure you meant to make another appearance. Why didn't you tell us what you were going to do? I could have gotten you help, if not from the professional organization I told you about, then from the local Resistance people."

"The fewer who knew about it in advance, the better," said Shane. "You and Maria would have been the first to know if I'd told anyone. Even Johann, here, didn't know from moment to moment, until I needed to tell him so he'd be in position and ready to bring me back."

He looked at the three of them now. Maria, wearing a plain black wool dress, was standing barely an arm's length from him, having run to embrace him when he had come in. She looked remarkably composed and even happy. Peter stood back by the coffee table in front of the couch and Johann had taken a position off a little to his right and stood simply waiting. For some reason probably connected with the strain Shane had been under these last thirty hours or so, all three of them seemed to stand out as if in bright three-dimensional relief against a painted scene that was the room and its furniture; as if they were more real than it, as if, he thought, they were in some way particular, unique and precious individuals.

"Well?" said Peter. "Aren't you going to tell me about it, so I can tell whoever else needs to be told?"

Shane came back from his moment of mental fixation with an interior start.

"Of course," he said. And so he told them, all three of them, in a minimum number of words. But he did not mention anything about the raid on the arms locker.

". . . Now, if you don't mind," he wound up, "I'm going to get some sleep. I didn't sleep so well while I was gone—"

"Or before you left," said Maria.

"I'll go, then," said Peter, picking up his small handbag. "Maybe Johann can take me to the airport?"

"Sure," said Johann.

"Good-bye, then." Peter took a step forward and offered his hand to Shane, who shook it, reflexively.

"Good luck," Shane heard himself say, as if it was someone else saying it from a long way off.

"And to both of you," said Peter.

He went out with Johann. Maria stepped past Shane to set the chain lock on the parlor door to the hall.

"And now, my darling," she said, turning to him. "Bed."

He slept heavily that night, so heavily that it seemed he had barely closed his eyes before he was opening them again upon the morning.

"Did I have any nightmares again last night?" he dared to ask Maria over breakfast in the parlor of the suite.

"No," she said. "You slept beautifully. Do you go right to the Unit today?"

"Yes," he said. "Would you get us both packed? I've got to report to Lyt Ahn, and as soon as I do that, he'll pass the word for transportation for us. There'll almost undoubtedly be an Aalaag courier ship ready for us by midafternoon at the airport."

Once at the Unit, he went first to his office for form's sake, and spent some fifteen minutes there killing time and assembling some completely unnecessary papers. Then, carrying these, he went to the office of the Officer of the Day.

"This beast is to make a report to the First Captain, untarnished sir," he told the Aalaag on duty.

"Go to the Communications Room," said the officer. "I'll give the necessary orders."

When Shane reached the Communications Room, the Interior Guard captain in charge there motioned him over into a cleared area in one corner of the room.

"Your request to report is already put through," the captain told Shane. He smiled. "Now you wait for the First Captain to find time to listen to you."

Shane stood in the center of the clear area. It was no different from several thousand other such waits he had made in the past two years, but this time there was both an uneasiness and a curiosity in him that made the time seem to go more slowly than training had accustomed him to experience it. He was puzzled over what Lyt Ahn had expected him to find in such a new Unit that could be of interest to someone like the First Captain. It was too soon for any results to show either in personnel or operations, much as the Aalaag might like to think that an order creating an organization such as this set things there to running instantaneously.

Eventually, the figure of Lyt Ahn, standing, appeared in the cleared space facing Shane.

"This is to be a secure report," said Lyt Ahn.

The Aalaag who was Officer of the Day had come in some few minutes before and had been waiting as Shane had been waiting. Now it was that officer who answered rather than the captain in charge of the Communications Room.

"Understood, immaculate sir," said the Aalaag. He reached out to the wall and touched something. The room around Shane vanished. At the same time, the shapes of Lyt Ahn's office appeared around both Shane and the First Captain, so that only Shane's knowledge that these surroundings were images protected him from the otherwise natural assumption that he had suddenly been transferred around the world to the House of Weapons.

"So, Shane-beast," said Lyt Ahn, looking at him. "Your report on the Milan Government Unit. Give it to me."

Shane began talking. The same memory that his job had developed in him, the memory that had allowed him to remember in order the list of cities he was to visit next which Lyt Ahn had reeled off in his message to the hotel suite worked for him now as he talked about the Unit, giving the names of all those, Aalaag and human, who worked there presently, and his assessment of them—a discreet assessment in the case of each of the Aalaag officers, for all the privacy in which he was now reporting. It would not be considered good form by any Aalaag, and least of all the First Captain, that even a very favored beast should criticize a true person.

He watched Lyt Ahn closely as he spoke, in search of some reaction that would give him a clue to the answer he sought, to the question of what Lyt Ahn might be expecting him to have learned from a Unit so newly formed. It might be that the whole matter of having him report was simply good procedure in Lyt Ahn's eyes—but in that case, why have him come here to look the place over at all?

It was difficult but not always impossible for Shane to read a reaction in the First Captain. By most humans, the Aalaag were considered to be all but expressionless, and in practical consequence, incapable of reading expressions on a human face. This inability to read human expressions was something often taken advantage of by human children, and those human adults who, like the children, did not stop to think that the faces they made might also be seen by a human servant of the Aalaag, who would have no compunction about reporting on how their looks belied their respectful tone and words.

But, in fact, the Aalaag did express themselves; not only facially but by small body positions and movements, and long-term human servants had learned to read these signals. For one thing, an Aalaag normally looked directly at whoever he or she was addressing. Not to do so was an insult, implying that the being addressed, like an unknown human beast for example, was beneath notice. It was a mark of favor for an Aalaag to look directly at a human servant as the Aalaag spoke to him or her. But there were differences almost too small to be consciously seen in how the direct look was given. A certain type of direct stare could be the ultimate in threat, a signal of approval, or a signal of something as close to fury as an Aalaag ever permitted himself to come.

Or, it could be that it merely implied an extreme interest in what was being said or heard. How Shane had come to tell the differences in implication of different expressions of Lyt Ahn, he did not really know. Physically, he could have had difficulty describing any specific differences; but he had come to be able to know what the First Captain was feeling by the way he stared.

Primarily, the particular look that Shane was seeing now was a matter of focus. Privately, Shane had named it the "pinpoint stare." An ordinary Aalaag stare was one in which the eyes of the alien seemed to take in at least the full spread of eyes in the person looked at. But in the pinpoint stare, it was as if that focus had been narrowed down to a point no larger than the head of a pin on the forehead between the eyes of the one stared at. It signaled extreme interest on the part of the Aalaag.

As Shane began talking now, he saw Lyt Ahn's eyes narrow to that pinpoint stare. But after his first few sentences, the alien eyes relaxed again, and Lyt Ahn was merely meeting him, eye to eye.

Puzzling over this, for his first few sentences had merely been a listing of those he had talked to at this Unit, Shane felt the tension and the quickening of his mind that came whenever he had to deal with a problem involving himself and one of the Aalaag;

and, as if by intuition, the idea came to him that possibly it was not what he had said first, but what he had not said, that Lyt Ahn had been waiting to hear.

If so, what could that be?

There was no good answer apparent. Shane finished his report, was told to continue on to Cairo, Egypt, on a courier ship that would be waiting for him and Maria in three hours at the Milanese airport; and the communications contact between himself and his master was broken.

Shane left the Unit and returned to the hotel to find everything packed and ready to leave, as a result of Maria's activities.

"Peter phoned—," she said as Shane came through the door—and was interrupted by the phone at that moment beginning to ring. Shane crossed the room and picked it up.

"Pronto," he said in Italian.

"Shane?" It was Peter's voice.

Fleetingly, after his experience with the executives of the Government Unit in London who had recorded his conversation with Laa Ehon, Shane found himself on the verge of hanging up. He had forgotten how wrong he had been in his first assurance to Peter that no one would dare tap his phone; and now Shane understood that there were always a few people foolish enough to do anything.

"It's all right," Peter's voice interrupted the impulse. "I'm speaking through a special circuit and over a special scrambler phone. I just thought I'd tell you our business deal was successful and I'll be seeing you in the next few days, if you'll make contact once you reach your destination."

The line went dead.

"He's more sensible than I am," said Shane aloud, slowly hanging up the phone in his hand.

"Peter? That was Peter again, wasn't it?" Maria's gaze at him was shrewd. "That's what I was trying to tell you—he called just a little bit ago."

Shane nodded.

"We'll talk, later," he said. "You didn't pack my robe and staff, did you?"

"Of course not," said Maria. "That's a stupid question."

The Interior Guard car that arrived a quarter of an hour later to pick them up found a note stuck on the door of the suite, saying that because of sudden special considerations, they had taken other transportation to the airport.

The other transportation was, in fact, simply as usual a taxi, bearing Shane and Maria, both in pilgrim garb.

At the airport they went directly to that part of it that was now exclusively kept for traffic of the aliens and—occasionally—their servants. Here, on showing their credentials, they were escorted by one of the rare women who were tall enough to be in the Interior Guard, to an eight-place courier ship down on the field. There was no sign of other passengers, alien or human, or of the pilot. They settled down to wait, but in fact it was within a couple of minutes that the pilot—a young male Aalaag—made his appearance and they took off.

Shane had said nothing except to give necessary directions and answers to those they dealt with all the way from the hotel to this present moment. In fact, his mind was still fully caught up in trying to find some reason for Lyt Ahn's unusual interest at the beginning of the report Shane had given him. But no good explanation would come. His thoughts were beginning to run in circles, so he shelved the problem for the moment, and turned to Maria.

He opened his mouth—and closed it again as the memory of how wrong he had been about anyone who was a servant of the Aalaag daring to record what he might say. They were seated several rows back from the Aalaag pilot, who could not only easily overhear them, but record their conversation for later translation; and he had been about to speak to Maria quite openly in Italian— simply because he doubted any Aalaag on the planet could understand more than a word or two of it. He knew some of the aliens in the House of Weapons could understand a little English, but it was only of the simplest and most limited variety—and had been picked up largely by accident, since the Aalaag officially disdained the tongues of beasts.

And yet, that one memory of how he had been wrong in what he had said to Peter about phones had just now cautioned him into silence in a similar situation. He laughed out loud, at himself, and at Maria's uncomprehending stare. He was beginning to doubt all that it had taken him two hard years to learn.

"I may not know people as well as I think," he said in Italian to Maria in a clear voice that the pilot could easily overhear. "But I know the Aalaag."

Maria's gaze sharpened.

"That's right," she replied.

He blinked at her, uncomprehending.

"What?" he said. "What do you mean?"

"I mean you're right," said Maria, her dark eyes still hard on him, "you do know the Aalaag—and you certainly don't know your fellow humans."

He laughed again, suddenly a little uneasy.

"I was talking about—," he began.

"It doesn't matter what you were talking about, or going to talk about," said Maria deliberately. "You've really got as little understanding of people as anyone I ever knew."

He felt a sudden irrational fear that this change in her meant that he was about to lose her—lose that closeness that had come to mean as much as survival itself to him—together with an uneasiness that was like that which he remembered some words of hers had produced in him once before; though he could not remember exactly when, and what they had been.

"Well, I've been wrapped up in study or work most of my life . . ." he said hesitantly.

"Yes," said Maria. "Your life. Why don't you ever want to talk about it?"

"Talk about it?"

"Don't you realize," she said, "you've never told me one thing about yourself, who you were and what you did before the aliens came? And even when I've given you the chance to ask me about my life, and who I was, you always turned the conversation to something else. It was just as if by not asking me anything, you set up a barrier against my asking you anything about you. Why don't you want to talk about yourself?"

"But there's nothing to talk about," he said. "I was a graduate student in languages when the Aalaag landed, so when they took over, I was one of those who had to take the language tests to see if I'd qualify for Lyt Ahn's group of interpreter-couriers. I did, and I ended up being one. That's all there is to tell."

"How about all the years before they landed? How about your

family? Where did you grow up?"

"Oh, that," he said.

"Yes. That."

"As I say, there's nothing to tell." The feeling of uneasiness kept growing inside him. "My father died before I was old enough to remember him. My mother and I went to live with her married brother. That's how I grew up—I don't really see why you should think I'm worse than anyone else you ever met at understanding other people. My uncle was a job-hopping executive—his field was production management—and we were always moving. That meant I was always having to start over in a new school, so I never did get to make any close friends and keep them. That's probably why I don't seem to get along with other people quite so well as some other people do—"

"But you did make friends in the schools while you were at them?"

"Well," he said uncomfortably, "you see, my uncle was making a lot of money when we first went to live with him, and nothing would satisfy him but I should go to some sort of private school where they let you work at your own speed. It was actually about the only school I ever liked—anyway, I could study what I liked; so I ended up being double-promoted a couple of grades and always after that I was in a grade with kids two years older than I was. You know, when you're young, two years makes a lot of difference. The other kids I spent most of my time with didn't have much use for someone two years younger. I got pretty used to being by myself, so I spent even more time reading . . . and what with one thing and another, I just didn't have as much to do with other people, even when I got to college. . . ."

He ran down. It was all true; and there had been nothing he could do about it—then, at least. But somehow, telling it to her now made it sound in his own ears as if he was trying to excuse himself.

He waited for her to say something, but she sat silent. She was still looking at him penetratingly, but there was a softening in her gaze now.

"I just haven't had the chance to get as close to people as a lot of people do," he said. "I suppose that got me into being something of a loner. That's all."

"You really do feel completely alone in the world, don't you?" she said. "You think of yourself as standing off, apart from everyone else."

"Oh, I don't think so, not any more so than anyone else does once they're grown up," he said. "Didn't you, once you were old enough to be on your own, feel . . ."

He could not think of a good word for what he wanted to say. He made a small, helpless gesture with one hand.

". . . apart," he said at last.

"Both my parents died, too, when I was young," she answered. "I was raised by relatives, too. But the house was full of my cousins, and my uncle and aunt were as much a father and mother to me as they were to their own children. No, I never felt what you feel. You're cold—as if you're standing so far from the world, out in space, that nothing from it could warm you."

He laughed once more, but his laugh did not even convince himself.

"Come on now," he said.

"You're so alone," she said, her eyes searching his face as if to pick out the human features from what was otherwise a mask. "So terribly, terribly alone; and the worst of it is when I reach out for you, you draw back."

"I don't draw back," he said.

"Yes, you do. You go away from me even when we're in bed together. Even when we're making love, you're running away and escaping from me. Do you know what it's like to have someone in your arms and feel he wants to get away from you, even when he's telling you how much he loves you?"

"But I don't do that!" he said angrily.

"You do! Every time!" Her voice, which had tightened, softened again. "It isn't as if you're deliberately doing it—it's as if you can't help running when you find yourself that close to someone."

He could think of nothing to say.

"But you're driving even me away from you, don't you know that?" she went on.

"If you feel that way," he said, suddenly reckless with bitterness, "why don't you just leave now? You want out of the Courier-Translator Corps? I can get you out. Not legally—and it'd take a little cooperation by some people like your Resistance friends—but it can be done."

"I don't want to leave you, you ought to know that," she said softly. "I said you were driving me away, that's all. I'd never want to leave you because I know the other side of you, how desperately you love people, even though you think they'll never understand you enough to love back. You loved people so much you could risk your life to save one of them—which was me—even though you'd never met me."

"I—" He wanted to tell her that was not the way it had been, but he was too cowardly.

"I'm only warning you," she said, "that if you push hard enough, if you really reach the point where you want me to leave you, I'll have to go. You've got to understand that. It'll be your doing, not mine. It'll be up to you to stop yourself from pushing that hard if you don't want to do without me. That's all."

"You'd go," he said numbly; forgetting his words of a moment before in which he had offered to help her leave him.

"If you really want it," she said. "I couldn't do anything else. So now you know. You've been warned; and I'll pray, as I've been praying, all along, that you'll never do anything like that."

TWENTY-ONE

CAIRO WAS WARM AND DRY, EXCEPT IN THOSE ENCLOSED SPACES where air conditioning made it icy; and Laa Ehon's representatives there had simply taken over a small hotel to set up their local Government Unit. It was a rambling, one-story structure that had been built just before the arrival of the Aalaag, in imitation of a motel in the U.S—all glass and parking lot. The result was that the Unit's offices were spread out through what had been a number of guest rooms, and there was a great deal of going to and fro in the corridors—particularly, but not exclusively, by the human staff.

On his first day there, Shane was surprised to pass in one corridor an Aalaag of the twelfth rank whom he recognized. The alien took no notice of Shane—which was to be expected. But Shane recognized the other as Otah On, the officer who had been with Laa Ehon in Milan as the two considered Maria through the one-way glass to the room where she had then been held captive by them. For an officer as young as Otah On to be of the twelfth rank could only be explained by the fact that he was being considered for senior position ahead of his normal time—and that could only mean that he was the Aalaag equivalent of an aide-de-camp to Laa Ehon. Which should mean that Laa Ehon was here—but officially, at least, he was not.

Otah On could, of course, thought Shane as he went on his way, have been sent out by Laa Ehon to check into the state of readiness of this new Unit. But there was really nothing to check on here, yet. Both Aalaag and humans were merely going through the motions of running the Unit, which was too new to have received, from the local, already established offices of human and alien control, the information it needed to do any effective work.

Shane finished his own perfunctory tour of inspection, left and returned to his own hotel, where not only Maria but Peter waited for him. Maria had signaled the local Resistance people three days before where she and Shane were to be found, and Peter had flown in just that morning. Peter had arrived as Shane was leaving for the Government Unit and they had had no time to talk. It was not surprising, therefore, that he erupted out of his chair as Shane entered the parlor of the suite in which he and Maria had set themselves up.

"Good! You're back!" said Peter. "I've got half a dozen urgent things to talk to you about—"

He broke off.

"What's wrong?" he asked.

Shane saw Maria also standing back and looking at him, concerned. He was at once startled and alarmed to find that these two—that even Maria—could read his expressions so correctly. He thought back uneasily to the twenty minutes or so he had spent at the Unit after running into Otah On; but he had had no extended conversations with any of the local staff, human or alien, in that time; and in any case none of them had ever seen him before and were no more likely than any other stranger to interpret the look on his face.

On second thought, he told himself, it was hardly likely that, after two years of carefully schooling himself in the House of Weapons to give nothing away, he would have wandered about the rooms and passageways of this local Aalaag institution with anything less than an unreadable face, whatever he had been showing to Maria and Peter here as he came in.

He dropped into a chair, letting fall beside it the attaché case that held his pilgrim robe.

"Nothing's wrong," he said—and now he had no doubt that his face was back under control. "What were you going to tell me?"

Peter looked at him penetratingly for a minute, but since Shane stayed unmoved, he shrugged.

"Remember how I told you the last time I saw you that the word of the Pilgrim was everywhere, and all sorts of people were beginning to wear the robes?" he said. "Well, it's still going on— even more so, it's like an avalanche the way people are adopting the robes and staff. They're even sitting in board meetings now, in robes, with staves leaning against the backs of their chairs!''

"Good," said Shane.

"In fact, those people I told you about—" Peter broke off suddenly.

"Go ahead," Shane said, and was surprised to hear a weary note in his voice. "I think we can talk safely here. This time, I checked."

"Those people I told you about, the Organization, are thinking of making a distinctive sort of robe and staff to be sold to those who want to identify themselves specifically with the Pilgrim—"

"Fine," said Shane. "Have them make four billion of them."

"Four billion?" Peter stared at him and smiled uncertainly. "You said four billion?"

"And I meant four billion," said Shane. "That's the population of the world, more or less, isn't it?"

"You're making some kind of a joke . . . ," said Peter. "How could they possibly manufacture four billion robes? And what makes you think everyone on the planet's going to want to wear them?"

He ran down into silence, continuing to stare at Shane.

"You're serious?" he said finally.

"I'm serious," said Shane; he made himself shake off the weariness that he now felt. He had slept badly again the night before, once more with the same nightmare he could not remember on waking. "It's all right. I know they can't make that many. I know they won't be able to believe that everyone would want to wear them. But that's what's going to happen. You'd better tell them— just for the record."

"God!" said Peter.

Shane, with an interior twinge of shame, saw that the other, at least, was halfway along the road to taking Shane's unsupported word for what he had just said. Shane was suddenly sick of the continuous need to mislead even those closest to him; but at the thought of opening his mouth now, before these two, and telling them the full truth, his courage trembled and retreated.

"Nevermind," he said. "What else?"

Peter went on to talk further about the "Organization." Apparently the professional Intelligence and other special groups of

a large number of nations were now setting up the worldwide network that was to be in effect a coming together of the forces of all
the major governments; plus some governments less than major to
the point of being tiny. Once more, these people had sent a message imploring Shane to meet with their representatives and discuss
a plan of action.

". . . They say it's impossible for something as massive as their
organization, no matter how well coordinated, to operate totally in
the dark," Peter wound up. "They'll meet you under any conditions you want to name. They say the people who'd come to meet
you are aware of what could happen to them at the hands of the
Aalaag as a result of their having met you, and they're ready to
take that risk for the sake of what could be accomplished by the
meeting—"

"They've got it wrong," said Shane. "I'm the one who's not
willing to take the risk. There's always more of them. There's only
one of me and I'm irreplaceable."

The last word was bitter in his mouth, but he got it out firmly
enough.

"Tell them I've got something instead for them to do," he said,
"if they're all that eager to be part of the action."

"They'll do it, of course," said Peter. "But about this business
of your meeting with them—"

"I've said no to that one too many times already. I'm not going
to talk about it anymore," Shane said. "This other is a job they can
do, though. There's a possibility Laa Ehon is meeting with some
other very high-ranking Aalaag—and maybe that meeting's taking
place right here in Cairo."

He had come to this final, farfetched possibility after exhaust-
ing all the others he could think of for Otah On's presence at the
local Government Unit. Such a meeting, of course, would be entirely reasonable—undoubtedly any other Aalaag invited were from
areas where Laa Ehon either planned to or already had begun to
set up new Government Units. It was entirely plausible that such
Commanders should meet; and that they should meet without also
inviting Lyt Ahn, whose rank would put him above personal in-
volvement with details of a project already in the hands of a subordinate officer.

"This can show me how good they are, these people who want

to meet me so badly," said Shane. "See if they can find out where Laa Ehon is, if not in Milan. See if they can find out if other Aalaag of equivalent rank are there, too; and if all those aliens get together, see if these people can bug the meeting and get me at least a sound—preferably a sound and picture—recording of that meeting."

He grinned, grimly.

"The discussion, of course, will be in Aalaag," he said. "You can tell them they have my permission to try and translate what they've recorded before they pass it on to me."

Peter looked at him strangely.

"You sound as if you think they can't find anyone to translate it," he said.

"Not to any real purpose," Shane said. "The only ones who could make anything much more than a stab at translating the talk at such a meeting are in Lyt Ahn's Courier-Translator Corps; and even the best of those would only be able to give you what's said there, not its implications for us—us humans."

"But you can?" said Maria.

She had been so silent all this while since he had come in that the sound of her voice jolted Shane. He looked over at her, sitting in a chair not two meters from him.

"Yes," he said, "because I know something of the internal politics of the Aalaag that I don't think any other translator in Lyt Ahn's Corps does. Anyway, have these Organization people of yours check into it and do what they can."

"They will," Peter said. "I'll have a recording for you inside of a few hours after any such meeting's held."

"Don't be so sure, even if they find it, that they can record it," said Shane. The weariness he felt crested within him like a wave. "There's a privacy tool the Aalaag use . . . but have them try, anyway. Now, what about the rest of those half-dozen things you urgently needed to talk to me about?"

Peter looked grim.

"They all have to do with your meeting the people we've just been talking about."

"In that case, there's no use discussing them," said Shane. "Anyway, I've got something else for you to do as well. I want to talk to the local Resistance leaders in this area, and every other area as I get to it."

"You didn't do that at Milan," said Maria.

"And I made a mistake by not doing it," said Shane to her. "I let Marrotta's attitude concern me too much. It wasn't until I got to know Johann—" He turned back to Peter. "He was the Milanese Resistance member who drove me down to Rome and back—that I got a clearer idea of what I'm going to have to do; and it means I talk to the Resistance people everywhere I go. Does anybody know you here? Could you get them together to listen to me?"

"I know someone to ask here," said Peter. "I think they'll fall all over themselves at the chance to have them speak to you. You realize, I hope, that some of the Resistance people you'll be talking to, here and elsewhere, are going to turn out to have been Organization members, too?"

"I know," said Shane. "I don't worry about Organization people who'll be doing nothing but sitting and listening to me. Now— also what I need the Resistance to do is to get together thirty or forty men about my size, all dressed in brown pilgrim robes—this color of brown—" He reached down to open his attaché case and pull out his robe. He passed it to Peter. "Let them use that as a model, but get it back to me by tomorrow evening. Thirty robes, say, like that and with staves; and have those who are going to dress up gather at a spot I'll be telling them about through you."

"For an appearance of the Pilgrim?" Peter asked quickly. "Or demonstration of some sort?"

"An appearance," Shane said. "I'll keep the details to myself, as usual, if you don't mind. The point I'd like you to concern yourself with is that they should be in the vicinity I'll tell you about until a certain time. Then at that certain time a few minutes later, I want them to gather quickly into a clump, a small crowd I can walk into wearing my own brown robe and with my own staff, and get lost. They're to gather at that time, break up the minute the word is given to scatter, and all go in different directions, so that I can go in mine and can't be traced. It'll be best if they don't know why they're dressed that way and doing what they've been told to do—better in fact if they aren't actual Resistance members but just people sympathetic to the Resistance, or even hired for the occasion—so that's all they know."

"I can tell the local people that," said Peter.

"Fine," said Shane. "Now, on another point, if I give you a list of places verbally, can you remember them all, and in order? I don't want them written down."

"I can," said Peter.

"All right, then. My next stops—as far as I know them now—are to be Moscow; Calcutta; Bombay; Shanghai; Beijing; Sydney, Australia; Rio de Janeiro and São Paulo, Brazil; Mexico City, New York City and then back to the House of Weapons. It's a list that can be changed at any time by orders from Lyt Ahn; but as far as I know it now, it sets up some more jobs for those people you mentioned. I want transportation of all kinds—air, land and water—available and waiting for me if I need them, at each one of these cities. Also, they're to contact each city's local Resistance people and help to bring in from close outside the city any other particularly prominent Resistance leaders, so that I can talk to them as well as the locals."

"They won't like the idea of acting as transport for people you're willing to meet with and talk to, when you won't meet them," said Peter.

"Too bad," said Shane. "I'm not having life exactly the way I want it, either."

"It's just that I can't understand why you'd want to go with the amateurs when you have professionals begging to help you," said Peter. "I really can't."

"Because the amateurs just want to see the planet freed," retorted Shane. "The professionals want that, and something as well for themselves in the process."

"Some of them—perhaps," said Peter. "But there have to be a lot of them—"

"Even one would be too many," said Shane. "Can't you see that if there's even one we can't trust, then anything we set up could come crashing down around our ears when he or she decided to act alone out of self-interest?"

Peter opened his mouth to speak, then closed it again.

"Besides," said Shane, fighting another wave of weariness, "there's plenty for the professionals to do. I'm counting on them to organize—and move when I call on it to move—an army of part of that four billion, in pilgrim cloaks and carrying staves."

Peter frowned suddenly.

"Do you mean—," he began and checked himself. "Is there some way you know of turning staves into weapons?"

Shane laughed . . . and his laughter continued until he recognized the hysterical note in it and cut it off with an effort.

"That's right," he said, "they'll be weapons. The fact is, they're already weapons. Except on this last trip to the House of Weapons with Maria, I've spent at least an hour of every day there in fighting practice with the staff. There's half a dozen different martial arts schools for use of it as a weapon—if you don't believe me, get a staff of your own some time and try me out."

Peter stared at him with a puzzled expression.

"But that sort of use isn't what you've got in mind, surely?" he said. "Besides, didn't you tell us all in London that the last thing we could do was meet the aliens head-on, force to force, and expect to win?"

"That's what I said," answered Shane. "I didn't say we might not have to meet them head-on and take a few million casualties, just to convince them we meant what we said."

He laughed, without pleasure, at the look on Peter's face.

"You think it'll come to that?" said Peter, after a long moment.

"It well may," said Shane. "Did you think that somehow I was going to give you a bloodless victory?"

Peter stared at him.

"God help me!" said Peter. "I think I did."

He dropped into a chair himself, his face very still; and with lines noticeable between his eyes and around his mouth that Shane had never noticed there before. Shane felt a sudden spasm of guilt, combined with sympathy for the man. It was followed by a rush of anger at the fact that these emotions should have to be awakened in him simply because Peter had not thought the present situation all the way through to its inevitable consequences—consequences to Peter himself, as well as others like him.

"Well, now you know," he said harshly to the Englishman.

"He's only human, you know!" said Maria to Shane. Her voice and her eyes were angry.

"I suppose so," said Shane wearily. "But a tiger in the road is a tiger in the road. You can't just wish it away. Look, Peter, you'd better get busy setting up that gang of imitation Pilgrims for me."

"When do you need them?" Peter's voice was remote.

"Tomorrow afternoon, if possible," said Shane. "Call me as soon as you find out if it's possible, and I'll give you a meeting time."

"Very well." Peter rose from the chair, a little slowly, like an aging man. "I'll be calling in an hour or two, I think."

"Good." Shane struggled briefly with his conscience and lost. "I was wrong about the safety of public phones and bugged rooms. When you call me up, talk about this as if we were planning lunch tomorrow."

Peter nodded.

"Good evening then," he said to Maria, going out.

As the door closed, Shane turned to look at Maria in his turn, and found her expression still angry.

"You expect too much of other people," she said.

"Perhaps I do," he answered exhaustedly. He got to his feet and headed on leaden legs toward the bedroom. "I've got to get some sleep."

The next afternoon, just past 2:00 pm, Shane got off the bus which stopped at the circular area in front of the main entrance through the outer wall of the Citadel, and was pleased to see a large number of other figures standing or moving around the general vicinity in brown robes and carrying a staff, as he was. In spite of their relative numbers among the more ordinarily clad people near the entrance, they did not look out of place with the gold buff color of the outer wall as a background for the earth color of their robes. The area was only lightly crowded. He went across the street toward the wall to the right of the ramps leading up to the entrance.

Here, as it had been in Rome, there was no alien riding sentinel about such a politically unimportant structure. The Citadel in Cairo, Egypt, had been built by Saladin in the year 1176 of the Christian Calendar; but that date was the equivalent of the day before yesterday in terms of Aalaag history. There was, however, a human police guard at the entrance—or at least a man in blue uniform with a machine pistol slung by its carrying strap over one shoulder. Moving to his right until the curve of one of the round towers that flanked the entrance hid him from the man's view,

Shane turned to face the wall.

His intentions this time were as simple as his approach had been. Out of the corner of his eyes he saw the robe-clad imitation Pilgrims beginning to gather into a crowd at the bus stop and reached in under his robe for the cutting tool that was the equivalent of the one he had seen used by the Maintenance woman in the House of Weapons, the one he had stolen from the arms locker in the Aalaag Headquarters in Rome.

He had experimented with the tool since, and found that the depth of its cut could be varied—which was well, since apparently the tool was capable of cutting clear through a wall like the one before him. He had preset it before leaving the hotel, to a depth of one inch. Activating it now, he cut into the wall before him, forming the outline of the Pilgrim with staff in hand. Then he turned and—hiding the tool under his robe again—walked leisurely toward the crowd of robe-clad individuals at the bus stop.

He had covered perhaps a third of the distance before a voice cried out behind him. He had calculated on such a delay in reaction from the people nearby. The tool itself was silent in its operation, and the cut was only visible against the identical color of the wall in which it was incised by the shadow of its depths. Theoretically, most of those now looking at it would have no reason to connect it with him, rather than anyone else at the scene who was clad as a pilgrim.

But he had underestimated the reaction the figure would generate, together with the fact that he was the only one who had not turned to look but had continued walking away from the wall. He realized his mistake when he saw the eyes of those in front of him all swing to focus upon him—and the guard came running around the curve of the building with his machine pistol unslung and ready. He stared at the figure cut in the wall and his eyes turned like the eyes of all the rest to Shane.

Then to Shane's complete dismay all those around him, including the guard and more than half of his imitation Pilgrims at the bus stop began to go down on their knees, bowing to him.

Shane felt a sudden sickness in his gut. Unexpectedly, painfully, he remembered Johann.

"Get up!" he cried furiously at them in Egyptian Arabic. "Never kneel to me! Do you hear me? Get up, get up!"

Gradually, at individual rates of speed, they began to get back to their feet. Shane forced himself to continue to pace sedately forward as the rising people around him began to hide him from sight of the guard.

Reaching the bus stop, he stepped in among the standing, pilgrim-robed crowd there.

"Now, go!" he ordered them. "*Imshie!* In different directions—at a walk!"

They obeyed him immediately, going off in all directions except back toward the Citadel. He himself continued on around the curve of the circular central area, looking for Peter and some kind of transportation. He was almost ready to keep walking until he was out of sight of those behind him, and then make a run for it, when he saw a somewhat battered gray, four-door Chevy Nova coming slowly down the street toward him with, not Peter, but Maria behind the wheel.

It drew level. Peter swung the back door open and Shane jumped thankfully into the hot, shadowed, interior. Reaching across him, Peter slammed the car door closed again as Maria accelerated away from the Citadel.

"What're you doing here?" he shouted at the back of Maria's head. He was violently angry with her. After all he had done to protect her and save her life, for her to involve herself in something like this . . .

"Someone gave you away," Peter said beside him. The English accent made the matter-of-factness of the other man's tone of voice seem somehow actorly and unreal. "Your driver heard of it and backed out. I couldn't be sure but what they had my description, so I had to stay out of sight. We'd just heard at the last moment and there was no time to find another driver, one we could be sure of trusting. Someone else had to drive so I could stay out of sight in the back—and there was really only Maria available."

He felt abruptly humbled.

"Maria . . . ," he said. "I'm sorry."

"For what?" she called back cheerfully over her shoulder.

"You'd better get out of that robe now, just to be on the safe side if we're stopped by the police," said Peter.

"The police? What about the connections those other people you've been talking to me about so much?" demanded Shane savagely. "Can't they be of some use in a situation like this?"

"They already have," said Peter. "It was one of their people in the police who slowed down the machinery when word came through about your visiting the Citadel. Otherwise there'd have been a small army of police there waiting for you. As it was, the order went out just a little too late—thanks to these friends you won't talk to."

"Unless it was one of them let out the word that I'd be there in the first place," said Shane.

"They'd have to guess it," said Peter. "Only Maria and I knew. Your words were that even the imitation Pilgrims weren't to know what they were there for—"

He stopped speaking so abruptly it was as if the sentence had been chopped off.

"Maybe it was me," he said suddenly and bitterly. "It wouldn't take much imagination to deduce what a crowd of Pilgrims like your imitation gang might be needed for. The local Resistance here is like any in Europe, only more so. People of all religions and politics, working together. One of them could have been a police spy or have his own reason for wanting you caught."

"If it was that," said Shane, "then the fault's mine, not yours, for asking for a crowd of people in robes in the first place. In any case, the question is why someone in the Resistance would want to give me away."

"As Peter said," spoke up Maria from the front seat of the car without turning her head, "one of the local Resistance could have been a police spy—even one of the people got to dress up could have been a police spy."

Her voice altered suddenly.

"Police roadblock ahead," she said.

"It's all right. I'm out of the robe." Shane put the robe down under his feet and Peter's. "When we're stopped, let me talk to them."

Maria pulled the car into line behind those already stopped by the roadblock.

"No, no!" said Shane. "Drive up to the head of the line. Force your way into first place—"

He was clambering over Peter as he spoke, in order to get to the other side of the car. Arrived there, he rolled the window down just as a policeman ran up to them, pointing his gun.

Shane leaned out the window, waving an opened wallet in the air, and shouting in Arabic.

"What's the matter? Can't you see I'm on Aalaag business? Don't you know an official identity card when you see it? I don't have time to waste here! Let us through!"

The police officer had reached them now. He gaped at the glowing, three-dimensional rectangle that showed Shane's image and some lines of Aalaag script. As the man watched, these dissolved and reformed into Arabic script.

"THIS BEAST IS ONE OF THE CATTLE OF THE FIRST CAP-TAIN, LYT AHN, OF FIRST RANK. YOU WILL ASSIST AND NOT IMPEDE IT, IN ALL CASES."

The policeman blinked, stared and turned, calling for someone whom Shane guessed to be the superior of those in charge of holding this roadblock. A nattily dressed officer with a small mustache came over and stared at the unprepossessing vehicle and then at the card. His thoughts were all but printed on his face. He teetered uncertainly between profuse subservience and authoritarian suspicion.

Then his face darkened with a scowl. Clearly, he had decided on the latter.

"How did you come by this?" he snapped at Shane.

"I've no time to waste with you!" Shane snapped back, and broke suddenly into Aalaag. *"Obey! You hear me? Obey!"*

The officer had probably never seen one of the type of cards Shane carried in his life, although he would have heard of them. Plainly, also, he did not speak Aalaag nor understand it—except for one set of sounds that were familiar to anyone whose work might at one time or another bring them into contact with the aliens—and that was the Aalaag order to *"obey."*

His face changed. He saluted and stood back. Maria drove on through the opening in the roadblock, out and away.

TWENTY-TWO

HE WOKE IN TERROR.

In that first moment both the reality of darkness around him and the remnants of the dream were mixed up so that he did not know which was which. It was the same dream he had had for months and always been unable to remember after waking; but somehow he knew in these first few seconds that this time he had it, this time he would remember. And he did.

So he came back to himself, once more in bed, holding fiercely to Maria and being held by her in turn. He could not see her in the dark, except in his mind's eye; but in that eye he saw her face and knew it was one of those he had seen beyond the point of his lance in the dream. He remembered other familiar faces seen there, also. He was clammy with sweat and he could feel the thudding of his heart through the wall of his chest.

Then, as full realization that he was once again in the waking world spread through him, he relaxed with a great sigh of relief, loosening his drowning grip on Maria and sagging back to lie on his spine, staring straight up into the darkness that hid the ceiling of their bedroom.

"I did it again," he said thickly. "Didn't I?"

"It's all right. It's all right . . . ," Maria's voice murmured in his ear as she continued to hold him; and he realized she had been speaking to him, soothing him, all the time he was coming out of his nightmare.

"I remember, this time," he said to her and the ceiling. "It was the same dream it's always been, but this time I remember it all."

There was silence in the darkness. Then Maria whispered.

"Do you want to tell me?"

"I was in armor," he said. "It was a dark, cold night. There was a wind whipping the flames. We were all in armor and on horseback, with lance, sword and mace. And we were burning a village and killing the people, who had only pointed, fire-hardened, or stone-tipped sticks for spears and no armor. They couldn't stand against us. We killed . . . and we set fire to their brushwood huts. We killed the men, the women and the children, all by the light of the burning huts as we rode through; and not one of us was hurt, not one was scratched. . . ."

His voice ran down. With one hand he searched up her closest naked arm to her shoulder and patted it clumsily when he found it. "Let me go. I've got to get up and take a shower."

She let him go. Once on his feet he realized that the room was not wholly dark. Nighttime lighting of the city outside made ghostly rectangles of the thick curtains drawn over the windows all along one wall of the room; and by the illumination that leaked through, his darkness-expanded gaze could make out the shape of the room and the door to the bathroom. What city was it? At the moment, he could not remember. He went toward the bathroom door, stepped inside, closed the door behind him and groped on the wall for the light switch. Light came on, blinding him.

Under the steady flow of hot water from the shower, he began properly to wake. The heat of the cascading liquid flowing over him sank into him and became the heat of life replacing the cold half-death of sleep. His mind began to work. Beijing, China, that was where he was now—the word chimed oddly in his memory against the fact that he had first learned to call the city "Peiping." His area was western and near eastern languages. Among the oriental ones he stumbled like a stranger, although his innate ability had led him to a low-level working knowledge of Mandarin and a pidgin level in a few of the other Chinese and other oriental tongues. He had been able to speak well enough to the Resistance people in Shanghai, when he had met with them.

Thought of that brought back a flood of memories of such meetings, not only with the faces in Shanghai but other oriental and dark-to-light faces he had spoken to since that first meeting with Peter's group in London. It seemed unbelievable that more than eleven months had gone by since his first sight of Maria in the vision screen of Aalaag Headquarters in Milan. Most of that time, the last ten months or more, he had been involved in the inspections of Government Units; and meanwhile winter had passed into summer and then back toward winter again in the northern hemisphere. Here in Beijing, at the moment, it was no season at all, merely pleasant daytime temperatures and slightly cooler nights.

Since London he had met with other faces under many widely different conditions, from palatial rooms to structures of cardboard and cloth. They had become real and individual, those faces, as Johann had suddenly become real. Each one had developed into an individual human universe in itself, linked by relationships to brothers, sisters, fathers, mothers, children—each one with a universe of possibilities and life experiences, good and bad, happy and unhappy. Each had revealed himself or herself as something more than just one of a number of cattle which could be sent to the slaughterhouse without empathy, without realization of what life would mean to them.

And meanwhile, his own role had changed—as the world had changed, even in these months while he had been moving about it. The word of the Pilgrim had swept around the globe like wildfire.

Robes and staves were to be seen everywhere now. He no longer made an appearance in each city as the Pilgrim. Someone from the Resistance made it for him—helped if necessary by the group that had contacted Peter, the Organization, made up of the former national army Intelligences, secret service units and others.

He had come to think of these latter groups as the Professionals; and of the Resistance fighters as the Amateurs. Little by little, the two groups had drawn together, in spite of his own continued stiff refusal to have any meeting between himself and the Professionals. Still, the Professionals were capable of being tremendously useful—and they had been so. Gradually, they had worked their way into the activities of the Amateurs and into partnership with his own activities as the Pilgrim. Undoubtedly, he had admitted to himself, a long time since, they had inserted at least some of their own people into his meetings with the Amateurs; and seen as much of him as the Resistance people had been permitted to see.

But it was the Amateurs he clung to in spirit. There had been a gradual wakening in him to them as individuals, unique and precious, as companions-in-arms; in effect, that development he had first thought had begun only with his experience of Johann, on the trip to Rome, but which he had now come to realize must have roots going back further than that, to Maria and even to Peter. Now they had all taken on substance, like friends; and their numbers were multiplying by the hundreds of thousands, perhaps by the millions, daily. They were putting on the uniform of the Pilgrim and announcing themselves in opposition to the Aalaag publicly.

It was as if he had pulled a twig from some snowy slope and unthinkingly started an avalanche. The Aalaag were indifferent to much their cattle did in personal matters—but not that indifferent. Not even they could ignore a change as noticeable as this. In a few weeks more he would be face-to-face with Lyt Ahn again, and Lyt Ahn would want to know what was afoot amongst the beasts.

The image of them all, dead, like those he had killed and seen killed in his dream, came on him; and he shivered, even in the hot water of the shower, under the thought of the weight and coldness of the would-be corpses who were now still living beings. He could stand it no longer—and, at the same time, there was nothing he could do to stop what he had started. The impossible was happening. He had begun it, and he was now as much a prisoner of its inexorable momentum as any of the rest of them. Four billion humans marching against the strongholds of a race that could destroy them all in a single breath, marching against those strongholds with only wooden sticks in their hands, were ridiculous, bitterly funny. And he had been the cause of it all.

Desperation clawed at him. He had searched and searched his mind, over and over again, for some chance, some real way, or even some trick that would allow a human uprising to show just enough muscle so that the Aalaag would be willing to make even the slightest of concessions to avoid or end it . . . his mind went around again over the hopeless hope and the undeniable. Their road led nowhere but to destruction.

He could not stand it any longer, carrying this impossible load of lies. Something had broken in him, during this last dreaming of the dream; and there was now a collapse he could almost feel like a physical break inside him. He could not fight the problem any longer. Like a condemned prisoner headed toward the place of execution, he turned off the shower, dried himself, turned off the bathroom light and went out into the bedroom, groping his way back to the edge of the bed and seating himself on it. He stared into the darkness where Maria lay.

A warm hand came out of the darkness of the bed and rested comfortingly on his thigh.

"How are you now?" Maria's voice asked softly.

"All right," he said; and his voice was dull and remote, even to his own ears. "Yes, I'm fine."

She said nothing; but he could feel the disbelief in her. He could not lie successfully to her anymore, in any case.

"What did you hear when I was dreaming?" he asked.

"It was the way it always is," her voice answered. "You didn't make much sense with what you said."

"Said?" he echoed. "Be honest, Maria. I wasn't just talking in my sleep, was I? I was shouting."

"Yes," she said on an exhalation of breath. She could not lie successfully to him anymore, either.

"I've always been yelling when I have these dreams, haven't I?" he said. "What was it this time?"

"That it was too big. Too big. You kept shouting that, over and over."

"And it is," he said.

He blinked. He was suddenly conscious that his face was wet. He put a hand up to it and found that tears were leaking from his eyes and running silently down his cheeks. He wiped them away with his hand—it was useless, for others came to replace them. He gave up and dropped his hand.

"Maria," he said, "did I tell you about the butterfly?"

"You've never told me anything much," her voice answered. "Nothing about yourself."

"That's right. It was Peter I told," he said. "But I didn't tell him all of it. I'll tell you now."

So he told her. About the butterfly and the Aalaag father and son and the man in Aalborg, Denmark that they had hung on the hooks. He told her all of that, including his drinking the illegal liquor, his fight with the Nonservs and his marking of the Pilgrim image on the wall under the hooks holding the dead man.

She said nothing. He told her about being in the Milanese Headquarters and seeing her, that first time in the vision screen. He told her about going out and acting as decoy to confuse the Aalaag and about the conversation Laa Ehon had had with Otah On about her.

"... It was just seeing you there, that first time in the vision screen," he said. "I couldn't bear to let them have you. That was all, then. Later, I got to thinking of it happening to you again, when I wasn't around to help you; and I decided I had to get you out of it, into someplace safe. I decided the only way to save you was to get you into or under the protection of Lyt Ahn, with me, and the only way to do that was to get you into the Corps and buy safety for you by turning in to the Aalaag the Resistance people I could find and claiming you had helped me find them. I was going to say that your being one of them had only been part of the business of finding them. It was just a way to solve things. Then I found out I love you; and I saw what it meant to turn in people I knew, now that I knew them. Only now it's run wild, this Pilgrim business and there's no way to stop what I started. And it's all a lie, Maria, it always was a lie. What I said might work against the Aalaag won't work; and I knew so from the first."

He ran down.

"Say it again." Her voice came at him out of darkness.

"Say it again?" He stared into the obscurity.

"You never said you loved me, until now. I want to hear you say it again."

"I love you," he said.

"And I love you," she answered.

"But don't you understand what I told you?" He wanted light to see her face and at the same time he was glad that there was no light so she could not see his. "I'm a traitor, Maria. I'm a spy. And I'm a coward. I'd never have the courage the rest of you had, who went into the Resistance, knowing how you were risking your lives. I'm everything that people like Georges suspected. I did it all for myself, just to have you with me and safe. To have that I was willing to turn your friends in to the Aalaag and to what the Interior Guard would do to them."

"No," said Maria. "You wouldn't have done it."

"But I would!"

"You're not doing it now," said Maria. "Don't you understand, by telling me, you're making it impossible to do it?"

That had never occurred to him. Not that it mattered now.

"But don't you understand?" he said. "It makes no difference, anyway, because this Pilgrim business has got out of hand. It's a juggernaut now. I can't stop it. And they're all betting on what I told them; that if the whole world demonstrates against the Aalaag, the Aalaag will give up and go away, leaving our world alone. But it's not true; and I knew it wasn't true from the beginning. Only nobody can stop it now—not even me."

"Are you sure?" said Maria.

"Of course I'm sure. The Aalaag's way of thinking wouldn't ever let them give in to any kind of pressure from beasts, as they think of us. They'd die first—and there's no need for them to die. Just for us. Just for the whole world to be incinerated with the human race on it."

"Then there's another answer. You'll have to think of it."

"What do you suppose I've been doing for weeks?"

"Think some more."

"But there's nothing else to think of! You don't understand. There's no answer—just no answer!"

"Dear one . . ." she said, and her hand came out of the darkness to rest softly and warmly on his knee. He jumped as if she had pricked him with a knife.

"How can you touch me," he said, "knowing what I was going to do? Knowing what I was capable of?"

"Hush," she said. "I said you'd never have done it, and you haven't. And you can think of a way to actually do what you promised, if you'll try."

He shrugged his shoulders in the darkness, wild with defeat.

"If I could only make you understand—," he began.

"No," she interrupted. "Let me help you understand. I know you better than anyone ever knew you. You were a little boy, left all alone with no one who wanted you; and you grew up trying to make a plus out of a minus by saying to yourself that it just proved how different you were, which was good because you didn't really want other people to be close to you. But all the time you did; and so you kept denying and denying, while inside you were hoping and hoping that somewhere there were people you could be close to, people you could belong to and be like. But you never found them; and then the Aalaag came along."

She paused. Somehow, there were no words in him to tell her she was wrong.

"Do you understand?" she went on. "You couldn't find anyone to be like, among humans, so unconsciously you tried to be an Aalaag. You found things to like in them. And you felt equal to them, in spite of what you knew about them, because you could always think fast and come up with an answer that pleased or satisfied them. You practiced saying the right thing and learning how to handle them; and in the end you got to know them better than any other human knows them; better maybe than they know themselves, in some ways."

She paused again. He sat there, with her words echoing in his mind.

"Maybe . . ." he said at last. "But knowing them doesn't change the fact they can burn this world to a cinder at a whim. We're not talking about little things, we're talking about one big thing—one big destruction everyone in the world is running pell-mell into, because of a lie I told them."

"No, we aren't," she said. "We're talking about the Aalaag and the way they think. You're human, so you know how humans think. You love humanity, even though you'd never admit it to yourself; so you were able to sell them your story of how to get rid of the Aalaag. You like the Aalaag—you do! I know you hate them, but at the same time there's some of them you like, like Lyt Ahn. Oh, call it admire them, if you can't stand the word 'like.' But because you like them, you understand them; and because you understand them, you can find what's needed to drive them away from us. You can, Shane!"

"I can't," he said hoarsely. He felt as if he had been caught and was held forever immobile, like Adtha Or Ain's vision of her son and Lyt Ahn's in the hands of their enemies. He knew now why that image in the vision screen had shaken him so strongly. He was like that, himself. Enclosed in the amber of his solitariness; forever held away from the outside world, forever helpless.

"Yes, you can." Her voice was like a gentle but persistent rain tapping on the colored transparency holding him prisoner. "You tried to deny the human part of you and love the Aalaag and it

316

didn't work. Now all you have to do is admit that you've finally realized your love for the human part of you and break clear of the Aalaag part. You're the one who finds answers. Always, you've found answers. Find the answer now. You can."

"But there isn't any."

"There must be, or you wouldn't have let the world go this far with the Pilgrim symbol. You just don't want to face the fact there's a solution because—just like you didn't really want to betray any humans to the Aalaag, you don't want to do to the Aalaag what you know can be done to them."

"What makes you think such crazy things?" he said dully. "There's no way of changing the way things are going now. I tell you. No way."

"There has to be," she said. "And you can find it—it's hidden in something you know about the Aalaag. It has to be. And all you have to do is find it."

He did not answer her.

"Why don't you try to sleep now," she said. "Maybe the answer'll come in a good dream instead of a nightmare. It's almost morning, but you don't have to go anywhere today unless you want to. Lie down and try to sleep. I'm right here with you."

He shook his head.

"No," he said.

He got to his feet.

"I can't sleep now," he said. "I've got to get up. I've got to walk awhile."

"All right, then," she said, still gently. "Then walk. I'll wait for you here."

TWENTY-THREE

SHANE DRESSED, NOT IN HIS PILGRIM ROBE BUT IN HIS REGULAR OFFICE clothes, tucking into his pocket the Identification Pass that had seen them through the police roadblock in Cairo and would see him also past any local authority on the streets outside. He went down in the elevator and emerged into the wide and gleaming lobby.

It was deserted except for one sleepy-eyed clerk who looked up dully at Shane as he passed on his way toward the rotating glass panels of the front door. Evidently, however, the clerk decided that if the westerner was going out, he could probably be assumed to know enough about the streets at this hour to take responsibility for himself. In any case, it was not a specifically assigned duty of desk personnel to volunteer warnings to guests.

Shane barely noticed the clerk. At the moment he would hardly have noticed a tornado passing by him at half a block's distance. He was drunk on the realization that he had told Maria the worst there was to tell about himself and, unbelievably, she had not immediately withdrawn from him in shock and loathing.

Outside, the air was chill on Shane's hands and face and no one was in sight. It was not yet dawn, but a gray light from a gray sky faintly lit the bare sidewalks and the silent fronts of buildings. The Aalaag, who occasionally did strange things and who never explained themselves, had literally levelled a section of downtown Beijing and on a strict grid pattern of streets had built a cluster of hotels, shops, pharmacies and other service enterprises as a quarter for foreign visitors. They had done the same thing in all the large cities from Calcutta to the west coast of North America, including such unlikely places as Sydney, Australia and Honolulu, Hawaii—where the buildings wiped out of existence would have been all but indistinguishable from the buildings that replaced them.

The streets were deserted—this was what the clerk might have warned the departing guest about if he had chosen to do so. But in Shane's case, the warning was unnecessary. The Aalaag, in their stern crusade against all crime, had arbitrarily decreed that there be no unauthorized traffic in the streets of such a quarter as this between the hours of midnight and six a.m. And, sure enough, within a couple of blocks, Shane was confronted by a uniformed woman who stepped out of the recess of a dress shop entrance, her left fist upheld and her left arm bent at the elbow in the Aalaag-decreed international gesture that demanded identification papers.

Shane produced his Pass. She nodded briefly and stepped back out of his way. In the next five minutes he was stopped and checked two more times.

But he was as little aware of these interruptions in his walk as he had been of the attention of the desk clerk on his way out of the hotel. He had no doubt that those who stopped him would recognize and give way to his Pass, and his mind was too full for him to pay more than a minimum of attention to those who stopped him.

It was unbelievable that Maria should understand him so well, should know so much more about him than anyone else had ever known—more than he had known about himself—after so little time together. How could she have learned so much? The only people she had met who knew Shane at all had been other members of the Corps, during the time she had been with him at the House of Weapons—and most of that time she had been alone in their rooms.

Or had she? There had been some visitors, of course. That he remembered. But she had done little of the talking on those occasions, letting him carry the conversational ball as he had warned her to let him do, for fear she would make some mistake. The rest of the time, while he was gone, she had been alone there.

Or had she been alone? There had been a good deal of curiosity about her in the Corps, which had been the reason for the unusual number of visitors he remembered having. Marika, who had lost her room to give them their suite, had dropped by several times on the excuses of tiny items lost, perhaps forgotten and left behind at the time of her move. She and Maria, now that Shane stopped to think about it, had ended up chatting together more than Maria had with any other guests.

There had been nothing to prevent Marika from coming back when he was on duty and Maria was alone. Or for others to have come by when he was not there. Maria had never mentioned any such visitors; but then, if she had been interested in finding out about him from them, she probably would not want to risk his reaction to her seeing anyone without him.

She could, in fact, have learned a lot from such people. As a group, the members of the Corps were intelligent and perceptive. They undoubtedly had noticed many things about him which offered Maria a chance to form her own conclusions.

But even given that kind of input, she still must have an ability to deduce what lay under the human surface with an acuity he had never known in anyone but himself; and in his case it had been a sheer, raw instinct for self-preservation that had taught him to do what he did. Her ability must spring from other sources.

But whatever those sources were, she had been right in everything she had just said to him—except perhaps in her unwarranted faith that he could find a solution to the world situation that his own actions had helped bring about. He began to sober down from the exaltation he had been feeling, remembering that part of their talk. She had sent him out to find precisely what he had spent all these months trying to find with no success. The fact remained that the human race and the Aalaag were on a collision course, each fueled by its ignorance of the true capabilities of the other; and there was nothing to be done about it.

But Maria wanted him to try once more. And somehow, the hope in her had been so certain that he found it infecting even him to some extent. Perhaps there was something, some little thing, anyway, that could be done. Walking the empty dawn streets of Beijing, he put his mind to the problem once more.

It may have been the infection of hope from Maria that did it, but out of nowhere he remembered one of his own rules that he had temporarily forgotten. The rule was that when in a situation that seemed to have no solution, so that he found himself going around and around in a circular search of ways already tried and found useless, then it was time to use dynamite.

In short, the rule was to throw out everything and start from scratch. Discard all failed answers, even those that had seemed to come close, and attack the problem all over again from the starting point of pure ignorance.

And the first step in doing that was to throw the problem itself out the window. Forget it.

Just forget about a world about to go up in flames? He grinned wryly.

But the conscious mind could only really concentrate on one thing at a time. He made himself think about the argument behind what he wanted to do.

Solutions were creative. Creativity was a function of the unconscious part of the mind, which was dominated by the conscious part, in situations like this. Let these two parts of his mind represent a man on horseback, lost in the desert, out of water and desperate. The horse is capable of smelling water at a distance and does so now; left alone, it would take them both to it. The rider, however, feeling that he must always guide the horse, directs it first in this direction, then that, all of them wrong, until he ends up riding in a circle. Meanwhile, they come nearer and nearer to dying of thirst, and the water they need is just over the horizon.

The answer for the rider is to have the courage to let go of the reins, let the horse wander, and it will bring them both to water and life.

The rider was his conscious mind. The horse, his unconscious—which did not stop to reason why it should head toward the smell in its nostrils but only knew it must, to live. The necessary part for the rider was to trust the horse.

It was, indeed, the hard part. He had made himself do it before in situations like this, however, and he could do it now. For a little while as he walked he struggled with himself; but at last his conscious mind relaxed and let his thoughts run in whatever wild direction drew them. Past experience had taught him that always, somehow, the route they took in the end turned out to have been on the way to the solution he searched for.

Now, images apparently unrelated to each other flitted through his head as he continued at random through the streets. To begin with, the images were mostly concerned with his earlier years after his mother and father had died, leaving him alone with his aunt and uncle. When his mother had been alive, he and his aunt had been fairly close; but, alone, he felt he had little in common with either aunt or uncle—particularly his uncle, whom he saw only briefly and at long intervals when the man was home from work, or from trips that had either been required by his current job or made necessary by his search for the next one.

His hours in the schoolroom had been neither pleasant nor unpleasant—he remembered them only as a sort of void. He could get good grades by doing nothing more than listening to what went on in class. Rarely, for a test, he would delve into a textbook; but years of reading had given him a reading speed that let him cover the necessary pages within a very short time and the knowledge had a way of sticking, at least until the test was over.

His real life had been spent with the books in the local library. He had become fascinated by the foreign language shelves and taught himself to read French, German, Spanish and Italian, first by a process that he was to recognize only later—an unconscious recognition of Latin and Germanic roots in words of those languages which were cognate with English words of roughly the same meaning—then with a foreign language dictionary in hand. Early, he came to appreciate how much more there was to be felt and understood about the characters in Dumas's novel, *The Three Musketeers*, for example, when he read that novel in its native French rather than in English translation.

This had led him to elect numerous language courses even in high school; and his capabilities there attracted the attention of his teachers. Eventually, they had led to a scholarship and a university major in linguistics. All this came back to him in bits and flashes of remembered scenes from those past years—and for the first time he began to realize how right Maria had been, how strongly he had built a life for himself apart from family, from any friends he might have made, even from his teachers and fellow students in the areas he studied.

But how had he got from there to here—to this moment in a Chinese metropolis, facing a holocaust he himself had created for the human race?

Clearly, his unconscious mind was suggesting that his solitariness was a key to the answer he needed to deal with the Aalaag.

But why that, in this moment, in this place?

The question brought him back to recognition of his surroundings.

He was aware that for some time he had been noticing that the dawn had strengthened. A still gray, but clear, light now showed his surroundings. In that light, he saw that on the sidewalk at the four corners of every intersection he passed were one or two cats, simply standing or sitting and staring at cats on one or more of the other three corners.

They stared at him also, as he passed, but only briefly. He was almost as beneath their notice as if they had been Aalaag. They did nothing and made no noise. Nor were they together in any sense. Even when there was more than one on a corner, they were spread out from each other and acted as if the others occupying the corner with them were not there.

Perhaps it was some sort of territorial statement they were making to each other. But if so, he saw no territory being challenged or defended. Only the silent waiting and watching.

It also could be, he thought, that it was not so much that they were like Aalaag as that he himself was like an Aalaag, and they were like humans—engaged in some ritual incomprehensible to an Aalaag; which he, the Aalaag, ignored because there was no reason for him to understand or interfere with it.

How could Maria have come up with the idea that he admired the Aalaag and wanted to be like them? He had always believed he hated the Aalaag with a secret hatred that he was sure not even his fellow translators could approach. He hated them more than others did because he feared them more; and he feared them more because he had studied them more closely and understood them better. Oh, there were things for which he gave the Aalaag credit—a more than human passion for order, cleanliness, honesty and moral uprightness. But it could not be true that he unconsciously wanted to be like them; that he was, in any sense, imitating them.

As far as he could see, it was what he had encountered in high school all over again. He could never be a part of what the Aalaag were because they would never accept him. He simply was not an Aalaag and never could be. He had survived with them by using his wits, as Maria had said. Also, by being invisible as much as possible; and by giving them no need to demonstrate that they were superior to him in their own ways. Those were tricks he was good at. . . .

It hit him, suddenly, like a body blow, where he had learned such tricks. It had been in those same high school years when he had been double-promoted twice and so thrown into close contact with young human males and females two years older than he was. They had been like the Aalaag, as far as he had been concerned. In no way would they accept him. Two years at that age made for a tremendous social difference. No one of them, male or female, wanted friends of their own age to see them in friendship with a kid two years younger. Such a friendship would label them as different, at a time when everybody most wanted to be alike. Also, outside of the classroom he could no more compete with them physically, socially, or emotionally than he could compete with the Aalaag in their special alien areas.

And he had hated his classmates for it then, as he believed he hated the Aalaag now.

No—trudging the dawn-lit, empty streets with the silent cats on each corner, watching, he faced the fact that his hate was not all of it. Maria was right. He had yearned to be accepted by the Aalaag, to be one of them, since he could find no acceptance in his own race. But as there had been no acceptance possible by his classmates, there was no possibility of acceptance by the Aalaag; and in each case he had pretended not to care, to be outside it all—while inwardly he both hated and yearned to belong.

He felt a sudden kinship with the cats.

They're like me, he thought of the cats, they live alone and they'll die alone.

He stopped dead.

It had burst upon him with devastating suddenness that he had just done what he had accused the Resistance people in London, and others since like them, of doing. He had lectured them for anthropomorphizing—for interpreting the different actions of a different race as if that different race had been humans like themselves; and thereby come to erroneous conclusions and beliefs.

So, he with the cats, just now.

As a human in a cat's body he might live alone and face dying alone. But what gave him the right to assume that aloneness was the same thing for a cat? Maybe aloneness meant something else to a cat. Maybe it was an incomprehensible term, with no place in a cat's universe—something a cat was blind to, and did not react to, because, for them, it was not there. A shock went through him. He stopped suddenly and simply stood still, facing what he had just realized. The Aalaag must indeed have an Achilles' heel, which he could find if he tried hard enough; and indeed there had to be one. They had one because there was no way they could not have one. It was implied in the understanding he had just stumbled across with the cats.

He felt a tremendous excitement.

TWENTY-FOUR

ELEVATED BY THAT EXCITEMENT HE HEADED BACK TOWARD MARIA, the one person with whom he could talk over the ideas that were now swarming through his head. Walking rapidly toward his hotel through empty streets that now were beginning to show themselves in full daylight, he was astonished to see how many people were already on the street and how the sun was now noticeably above the horizon. It was going to be a clear day. He had evidently walked and thought much longer than he had imagined.

He found Maria awake when he got back to the hotel suite, up and in a robe. He grabbed her up into his arms.

"You were right!" he said. "There's a way to get rid of the Aalaag. I haven't found it yet, but now I know there has to be! Come into the sitting room with me so I can talk it over with you, and maybe sort out my own thoughts about it."

"Can we order up some breakfast at the same time?" She covered an enormous yawn with her hand.

"Ten breakfasts!" he said exuberantly.

While they waited for the food to come, he told her about the cats.

". . . You see," he was going on, once the food was before them and they were eating—at least Maria was eating. Shane had so much talking to do that he found food getting in his way. "What I suddenly understood from watching those cats was how little an individual of one species can fully appreciate what moves another species, let alone another race. What works for one kind of being can be something that doesn't even exist for another. In fact, it may effectively be invisible and inaudible. There comes a point, as

I came to it with the cats, of ignoring what can't be understood. Even if I could get myself to the point of intellectually understanding that what was moving those cats was a matter of territorial rights, I still couldn't know, the way a cat would know, what it meant in the mind and muscles and guts, to take up such a position on a corner, at that time—and hold it."

She stopped eating to stare curiously at him.

"I thought you said now you were sure there's a solution?" she said. "You sound as if, even if there was, you'd never be able to recognize it."

"Maybe not—directly," he told her. "But indirectly—what I said about knowing what things were like for another species or race was true. But while maybe duplications of awareness aren't possible, there can be parallels. Human mothers love and protect their children. Mother cats love and protect their kittens. I remember thinking once—I don't know if I said anything about it to you—that the Aalaag race and the human race were like images in different distorting mirrors of each other."

Maria frowned.

"Distorting mirrors?"

"I mean," he said, "that a member of one race sees one of the other race distorted from what he or she actually is—as if the one seen was a reflection of the one looking, in the sort of funny mirrors you see in amusement parks. There're things, in the one seen, that the one looking can't see or understand, so to make sense out of the picture, they adjust it to fit what they know about themselves. You see, the trouble is we and the Aalaag are so damned alike to start off with."

Maria nodded.

"They're humanoid."

"They're remarkably humanoid," said Shane. "Or we're remarkably Aalaagoid—depending on your point of view. It's almost unbelievable that the first completely separate race to find us should be so like us—well, maybe it isn't so surprising after all. Similarities make for the same requirements, the same sort of prehistory and social history—and the same sort of needs. Just like we'll go looking for worlds like Earth when we get out in interstellar space, so the Aalaag've gone looking for worlds like the ones they knew to begin with; and similar worlds make for other similarities.

But that's the point. Similarities—not identities. We look at the Aalaag and see a race we haven't any cause to love, so we call them aliens. They look at us and see a sort of distorted Aalaagoid which makes them uncomfortable—and so they call us beasts. But on the unconscious level we go on thinking of them as sort of distorted humans and they can't help thinking of us as a shrunken and weakened variant of Aalaag. So that when the chips are down, members of both races take it for granted those of the other see what they do, feel what they do, and ought to act the way they do."

She shook her head slowly.

"I can't believe that," she said, "that they'd go so far they'd even expect us to feel like them."

"I think they do. I think it goes so far that, down deep, they feel that we'd even prefer their home worlds to ours, if we could see them as they were before they were driven out of them. Consciously, they know we've never seen anything like that and there's no reason we should be deeply moved by their crusade to get those worlds back; but unconsciously, they simply can't imagine anything Aalaag-like who wouldn't be happy to die to recover those worlds. Because that's the way they feel."

Maria shook her head again, this time wordlessly.

"I know, I know," said Shane. "It's crazy; but I'm making a point. I tell you they don't see us as we are—and we don't see them as they are. We can't. I can't—but from my position of thinking of myself as outside both races, I just might be able to see something in human beings from which I can guess at a parallel in the Aalaag that isn't visible otherwise, but which can give us a lever to drive them away."

"If anyone can, you can," said Maria soberly. "But how are you even going to go looking?"

"I'm going to get as far away from my own prejudices as possible," said Shane eagerly. "That's where you come in. I want you to help me. You weren't at the House of Weapons more than a little time, but you met Aalaag and you've got a different slant on them than I have. I want you to start telling me what you think of them, what you believe about them. Start now. Tell me everything that comes into your mind about them; and I'll tell you where I think you're wrong. We'll discuss the difference; and the two of us together may get to looking at the Aalaag enough from the outside to begin to see where their vulnerabilities lie."

Maria stopped eating.

"I don't know where to begin," she said.

"What do you think of Lyt Ahn? Tell me."

"He scares me."

"What do you think of Laa Ehon?"

"He scares me, too."

"In the same way? Or is there a difference between them?"

"In the same way," said Maria. Then checked herself. "No, there's a difference. Lyt Ahn is more . . . terrifying, but Laa Ehon makes me shudder, in some way. I can't describe it."

"As if he was more unpredictable?"

"Yes, and . . . oh, I don't know," said Maria. "Dear, I don't know if I'm going to be any real use to you in this."

"Give it a chance. Wait and see. I think you will. What do you think an Aalaag feels; say, one who's just riding his beast in full armor through a town, when some human goes off his head and attacks him. . . ."

They kept it up for a couple of hours, at the end of which Maria was showing signs of exhaustion and flashes of temper that come with exhaustion. More and more she was answering questions with an "I don't know. I just don't know!"

"All right," said Shane at last. "Let's take a break."

They took a break by going out for a walk to burn off some of the excess nervous tension built up over the previous two hours. They strolled through the visitors' area, ended up sitting in a sidewalk cafe—for the day had now become comfortably warm—playing with drinks and watching the people go by. In the process they came back to calmness and love. They ended by returning to the hotel suite, where the maid had already been in, and going to bed again.

Refreshed, they started out the afternoon by once more getting down to work. This time Shane let Maria tell him in her own words about her experiences with the Aalaag and their government, from the time they had landed, a process which was easier on her.

With all this, however, by the hour it became time for Shane to head off alone, he had turned up nothing that made him feel he was on the track to uncovering an Aalaag vulnerability.

He was going to have to be content with putting the matter

out of his conscious mind once more, and hope his unconscious would work on what Maria had told him and come up with something. This was the evening that the local Beijing Resistance group had chosen to meet him, under the guise of a local business group having a restaurant meal with a North American exporter.

He had fallen into a pattern in meetings like this, in which he would first ask for any questions they might have; and then talk to them, using the questions asked as a cue to what he thought they needed to hear. In this particular case, after this enlightenment of the last twenty-four hours, he decided simply to speak first. But he found that apparently his chance to talk was scheduled for the final event of the get-together.

Each Resistance group was different and no two meetings went the same way. In this particular case the dinner apparently had to involve a number of courses of food and liquor, which he was careful only to taste, and what seemed a totally unnecessary number of speeches by others at the table. He tried to follow what was being said at first, but his limited knowledge of the language made the effort wearying. Finally, he simply sat back and waited silently, his cowl fastened close in front of his face.

When his turn came at last, preceded by a flattering introduction in English, he followed the example given by rising to his feet, saying a few complimentary words, then launching into a speech of his own in Mandarin.

It was a case in which his limited knowledge of that tongue could show itself to its best advantage. However privately those listening might deplore the clumsy way he spoke it, they showed visible signs of being pleased with the fact that he could speak it at all. He had, he found, a receptive audience.

Drawn by this, he found himself saying things he had not said to previous groups. He found himself telling them about the cats.

". . . we know from our own experience," he told them, "that even fellow humans can misunderstand each other if they come from different cultures. We know that people of one language may be ear-blind—they literally do not hear certain sound differences from those they are used to in their own language. The French have two ways of sounding the letter 'r' in their own tongue. The born English speaker, who has never learned any other language, has trouble hearing the difference between those two sounds. The difference in English between 'l' and 'r' occasionally is not immediately apparent to some speakers of your own tongue when they first attempt to pronounce words in that language.

"In many of these cases," he said, "the untrained ear literally does not hear something obvious to native speakers. In the same way, culturally unique actions—gestures—can be misinterpreted or literally not noticed by strangers. It's impossible to have a culture without some such unique elements—and the Aalaag's culture has them, just as ours have. By taking advantage of those elements, which I've been lucky enough to have a chance to study, I believe the Aalaag can be forced to withdraw from our world. If your people will move when the word is given . . ."

They were obviously receptive, but did they really understand? It was impossible to tell. He finished and sat down. There was a polite spatter of applause and someone else rose to acknowledge his speech. Finally, the dinner and the meeting were over.

Usually there was an individual or two who lingered behind the rest to talk to him. In this case, no one did. They moved out in a body. They had not understood. They had only been polite and taken him on faith.

Fatigue was once more beginning to drag heavily at his feet and dull his mind. He wanted to be back at the hotel and in bed. He returned to the hotel in a daze, hardly noticing the streets and the people that were now beginning to move about on them, as he went. But when he got back to his suite, thoughts of solutions were wiped out of his mind the moment he stepped through the door. Peter had caught up with them again.

The Englishman did not bound to his feet this time on seeing Shane enter. He looked thinner than before and his eyes had dark shadows beneath them; but there was tightness to his lips and a jut to his jaw that was new to his appearance.

"No," said Shane, closing the door behind him and coming to take a chair before the sofa on which Peter and Maria were sitting, "I won't talk to that organization of yours."

"I didn't come to ask you that," said Peter sharply. "I came to tell you about a meeting of high Aalaag officers with Laa Ehon. You remember asking me to have that looked into, when you were in Cairo?"

"Yes," said Shane. He looked at a coffee pot and cups on the low table before the sofa. "Is that coffee still hot? And if it is, would you pour me some?"

Maria moved forward, but Peter was already pouring. Shane took the cup and tasted the dark liquid. It had a friendly bitterness after the liquor and tea of the restaurant dinner; and some of his tiredness seemed to evaporate with his first swallow of it. "All right, what did these people of yours learn?"

"There was a meeting, all right. Fifteen high-ranking aliens from all parts of the world," said Peter. "It was held in an empty, former Egyptian army base, outside Cairo. One the aliens were evidently thinking of using for their own purposes. But our people weren't able to record what was said and done there."

Shane smiled, a bit sadly.

"I was afraid they wouldn't," he said.

"No one has any idea why," Peter said, in a tone of voice that was almost angry—as if the failure to record was because of some unfairness on the part of the Aalaag. "The aliens came singly, most of them by air in those small personal ships of theirs. It looked like they all flew or drove themselves in. At any rate, only one got out of each vehicle. The meeting apparently was held in what had been a conference room of the base Headquarters building. We were all set to film and record everything that went on in that room—"

"How did we find out that room was the one they were going to meet in?"

"I wasn't told." For a moment Peter looked uncomfortable. "But I was told the recording team was all set to get anything said or done in that room. Only, they got nothing. As soon as each Aalaag came into the room, he or she vanished—from the view of the people watching, not just on tape."

Shane laughed.

"If you think it's all that humorous—," Peter was beginning heatedly, "when they'd gone to all sorts of trouble to do this for you, after you'd refused to do anything for them—"

"All right, all right . . ." Shane made himself sober up. "It's just that it's what I was almost sure would happen—only I'd hoped against hope, somehow, that a recording could be made. Well, it was worth trying. The Aalaag technology was just too much for us."

"How?" demanded Peter. "And if that's so, why didn't you warn us ahead of time?"

"Because there was no way of knowing until we tried it. Because, as I say, I hoped in spite of everything—nevermind. I'll show you someday, maybe, how it might have been done—if I'm right about that. But who knows if I'm right, come to think of it? They could have a dozen ways of making themselves seem to vanish to human eyes. The question is, did they do it because they knew your people were there?"

"You tell me," said Peter bitterly. "You seem to know more about it than any of the rest of us."

"I don't know," said Shane, putting his empty coffee cup down. His weariness was back in full force. "Well, there're two possibilities. No, I take that back. There're infinite possibilities; but making themselves invisible to human machines and eyesight because they knew humans were about to record what they said and did isn't one of them. They would have simply destroyed the humans concerned, instead. No, I don't know what the reason was . . . but it was a reason having to do with the Aalaag, not with us. So we don't have to worry about that."

"At least," said Peter, "we know they didn't know we had people in a position to record."

"Not necessarily," said Shane. "The Aalaag might just have ignored your recording crew—like the mice or insects in the walls. But on second thought I don't really believe that. Or maybe they just haven't gotten around to destroying them yet. Again, there're any number of possible nonhuman answers. It doesn't matter. What I wanted to know was whether the other officers there were joining with Laa Ehon in whatever Laa Ehon's got in mind, or were just invited to come and consider joining—and now I don't know that."

"I see," said Peter. "That's the tragedy, of course, your not knowing. The fact that the men and women who tried to record that meeting for you may still be in line to be chopped by the aliens is hardly worth thinking about."

Shane looked at him grimly.

"My not knowing may end up costing millions of human lives," he said. "How many were there in the recording crew?"

"Why?" Peter leaned forward. "Why might it end up costing millions of human lives?"

"Because the Aalaag have politics, too," said Shane sharply.

"And there's a move afoot to replace Lyt Ahn as First Captain with Laa Ehon. If that happens, we're in trouble. Laa Ehon is unwell—"

"What do you mean, 'unwell'?" interrupted Peter. "Why don't you say what's wrong with him instead of trying to translate some alien term?"

"Because there's nothing that translates 'unwell' the way the Aalaag mean it," said Shane. "It covers more territory than any human word. It means 'anything other than well'—literally; and their definition of 'well' is different from ours. But in this case what it means is that by Aalaag standards Laa Ehon isn't sane. That means he doesn't react the same way well Aalaag do; and everything I know, everything we can use in handling that race is based upon well Aalaag. With Lyt Ahn, I know what reaction a certain action or word'll bring. With Laa Ehon I can't be sure. So I want to do what I can to keep him out, and knowing what went on at that meeting—if it really was a political meeting under the guise of a business meeting—might have told me."

He stopped, even more exhausted than before.

"All right," said Peter. Suddenly the tightness was gone from his mouth and the jut from his jaw. His face looked discouraged and old. "All right, all right. If you say so. But, oh hell! What can anyone do with you, Shane?"

Shane felt a sudden rush of revulsion against himself. It was followed by the same sort of feeling he had felt toward Sylvie Onjin in the House of Weapons, after his first annoyance with her for waiting to surprise him in his quarters when he returned from Milan. He looked from Peter to Maria now and saw expressions on both their faces that were much alike, as they looked back at him.

"By God!" he said softly. "You do believe in me—both of you!"

There was a moment of strange silence in the room.

"What else can anyone do, Shane?" Maria asked.

"That's right," said Peter. "You don't give us much other choice, do you?"

"I suppose not," said Shane. He could not stop himself from staring at them as if he had never seen them before. "But you see, until—until just lately—I've never really believed in myself."

Peter stared back at him. But Maria smiled.

"And now you do," she said, almost as softly as if she was speaking to herself.

"What's the matter with you?" demanded Peter furiously. "Did you think what we've been saying was all talk? That everything about people putting on robes and taking up staves was—by Christ, you've even been doubting all this business of the professionals getting together in the Organization, and everything I told you about them!"

"Yes," said Shane, "I guess I have. But mainly I didn't believe in the Pilgrim—so I couldn't bring myself to believe in people reacting to him the way you and everyone said they were—I didn't even believe when I saw them in robes myself. I kept on believing they must all have personal, selfish reasons for doing what they did."

"In heaven's name, why?" Peter said.

"Because, you see," said Shane, "I'm not the Pilgrim. I'm just a body the Pilgrim's using—the real Pilgrim. What the Pilgrim really is, is something entirely nonphysical who only exists in the minds of the people who believe in him—or her; and the more who believe, the more powerful the real Pilgrim is."

His voice died off suddenly. He stared at them.

"My God," he said, "that's it. All the time, my unconscious was doing the right thing and I didn't know it. Of course, that's their blindness, their vulnerability. They don't have a Pilgrim—I mean they don't have a real Pilgrim, the Pilgrim I've been talking about!"

Peter and Maria stared back at him.

"All right," Peter said finally. "Assuming that makes any sense at all—what does it all mean, according to you? What's got you so excited about coming to such a conclusion, anyway?"

"You don't see what it means?" Shane said. "It means they're blind in that area—they're lacking in that area. They've got nothing to handle the Pilgrim; and my unconscious knew it all the time—all our unconscious minds knew it all the time, that's why we've been doing what we've been doing. The Aalaag really don't understand why, when we deface buildings, we always do it with the same mark. Don't you understand? The universe as they see it doesn't include anything like the Pilgrim—to them he doesn't exist."

"You exist," said Peter.

"But I've just been telling you—I'm not the Pilgrim. Oh, I'm part of him. But the Pilgrim's you, Maria; and he's you, Peter, and Johann and even Georges Marrotta, and all the people in the Resistance, and all the people in this Organization of yours; and millions, billions more. He or she's everyone who's human!"

They were both watching him.

"What good does that do us?" said Peter.

"All the good there is!" said Shane. "It means I can let the Pilgrim run things from here on out. Maria was right. She said I thought too much like an Aalaag; and I did—so much like an Aalaag I couldn't see the Pilgrim. But now I can. I can let myself be human, let the Pilgrim speak through me, from now on. Peter, how soon could you get some representatives of this Organization to meet with me, after all?"

"You mean it?" demanded Peter.

"I mean it!"

"In about fifteen minutes, if you really mean it; if you really want to!" Peter exploded. "There's a couple here with me, now. They were in Cairo, too, when you were there, if I could just have gotten you to talk with them. What changed your mind so suddenly? Just this business of finding out the Aalaag aren't on to us?"

"That, and some other things I've come to understand in the last twenty-four hours," answered Shane. "Fifteen minutes, you said? Good. Get them over here."

"I'll be back before you can turn around," said Peter, and left them.

"I'm not sure I follow you either," said Maria quietly to Shane, after the other man had gone. "Have you got the answer now—the one you went out looking for?"

"I still don't know just how I'm going to do it," he said. "I've only got an inkling. But I know I'm going to confront the Aalaag with the Human race; and I'm going to confront Lyt Ahn with the Pilgrim. And the Pilgrim's something I don't think they can take. They'll go. How they'll go—I don't know . . ."

Shane, still staring at the closed door through which Peter had disappeared, turned to her. She came to him and he held her.

"It's so strange," he said to the top of her head. "I was doing the right thing all along and didn't know it."

"Not strange at all," said Maria.

He held her off at arm's length with his hands on her shoulders and searched her face, marveling at her.

"Come and sit down," she said.

She led him to the sofa she had been sitting on when he came in, and pulled him beside her onto it, nestling up against him. They sat together in silence until, suddenly, less than fifteen minutes later, there was a knock at the door. Maria jumped up.

"You haven't got your robe on!" she said. "I'll answer the door. You go get dressed!"

"Damn!" said Shane.

He ducked into the bedroom, closed the door to it behind him and swiftly threw on his robe over his jacket and slacks, with the cowl's front edges fastened together up to a point just below his eyes. He went back out into the other room.

Peter had returned with two men, both of them dressed in business suits and looking to be in their late forties or early fifties. They were unremarkable appearing individuals; one, Caucasian, fairly short and balding, with straight sandy hair. The other, Oriental, taller and slimmer, with an erectness and a neatness that could imply a military background.

"Pilgrim," said Peter, "may I introduce Mr. Shepherd and Mr. Wong?"

TWENTY-FIVE

THEY ALL TOOK SEATS, SHANE IN THE CHAIR HE HAD SAT IN BEFORE, this time facing the almost certainly pseudonymous Shepherd and Wong, who now sat side by side on the sofa Peter and Maria had occupied. Peter and Maria had found themselves chairs each to one side a little back from Shane, so that they were out of the narrow slit of view his closed cowl gave him, unless he turned his head, so that his field of vision contained only the two new visitors.

These men were not what Shane had expected. He had been expecting a couple of hard-sell characters who would come on strong from the standpoint that they were here to gift him with the enormous favor of their help. But—just the opposite—these two seemed self-contained enough, but if anything a little unsure and hesitant at meeting him in person. He reminded himself once more of how he had been underestimating the commitment of his fellow human beings to action against the Aalaag.

Until these two gave him some cause to doubt them, he told himself, he would take them on faith.

"Tell me," he said abruptly, "why do you think people all over the world have taken to the idea of the Pilgrim in such numbers?"

They did not look at each other in silent consultation before deciding who was to answer him; but there was a perceptible pause before Mr. Wong spoke. His accent was American, rather than British.

"There've been studies made," he said. "A number of good minds have looked at the phenomenon; and what they mostly seem to conclude is that the Pilgrim is two things—one, a particularly appropriate symbol of the human feeling toward the aliens and, two, that as a symbol he came on the scene at just the right time."

"You say 'he,' " said Shane, "taking your cue from my voice, I suppose. But how do you know I'm the real Pilgrim?"

"We don't, of course . . ." answered Mr. Shepherd. But his voice ended on such a note of uncertainty that it was almost an appeal; and this time he did turn frankly to his taller companion for help.

"I think Mr. Shepherd is referring to something I feel myself," said Mr. Wong firmly. "Of course you're right. We've no way of knowing if you're the real Pilgrim, or someone standing in for him—or her. But I feel very strongly myself that you're the real Pilgrim; and clearly Mr. Shepherd does too. But you wanted to know about why people had taken so to the Pilgrim symbol?"

"That's right," said Shane.

"According to the opinion of these scholars and others who've studied the matter," said Mr. Wong, "the Pilgrim's as close to being a symbol common to most cultures as you're likely to get. The image has religious overtones; and—in spite of other differences in individual or cultural attitudes—the idea of someone on a pilgrimage is in the folklore or history of many peoples. Along with it goes the idea of the Pilgrim being under the protection of a higher power, gifted—or perhaps blessed would be a better word—with a special purpose; and of course the robe and the staff are common to the ancient dress of many peoples. In short, it's easily identified as a symbol of untouchable good which may conquer and overcome whatever evil there is. An attractive symbol."

Shane laughed, a little bitterly.

"What's funny?" said Peter behind him.

"Nothing," said Shane, without turning his gaze from Shepherd and Wong. "I was just remembering how the Pilgrim had been born. Nevermind. Next question. Since you've had the Pilgrim explored as a symbol and realize he's a symbol only, how can people like yourselves commit yourselves to working with me—except with your tongue in your cheek?"

Both Shepherd and Wong stared at him. Wong's face seemed unemotional, but Shepherd was clearly registering shock.

"It—it may be possible to make logical explanations for why the idea of the Pilgrim has caught on," said Shepherd. "But that's not the point. Sooner or later we're going to have to fight the aliens, even if we end up doing it with only our bare hands and no plan of battle at all. From somewhere there'd have to have come someone to lead us, someone to direct the outrage in all of us. You happen to be the one who has, Pilgrim. You're real, you're there, and people are going to follow you, whenever and wherever you want to lead them. And those people include me—"

He glanced at the man beside him.

"And I think Mr.—Mr. Wong, too, is ready to follow you anywhere you want to lead him."

"That's right," said Wong calmly. "Not to follow you—even if you seemed to be taking us all to nowhere but death—would be unthinkable, to me, at least."

Shane took a deep breath. This was what he had encountered with Johann, in a slightly different form. But the last thing in the world he had expected had been that there would be true believers among the professionals. Then he remembered what he, himself, had said to Maria and Peter just shortly before—that he, himself, was not the Pilgrim, but something used by the Pilgrim, which was a being made of the substance of human belief. A coldness washed through him and he was glad of the cloak and the closed cowl that hid his reactions from the others in the room. He was as much in the power of the Pilgrim as any of those here. It controlled him, now, rather than the other way around. It had become too big for him to control. He felt like someone held prisoner, invisible and undetectable, inside a ghost.

He shook off the feeling.

"Tell me," he said, "and bear in mind I'd be spreading the word through the Resistance as well as through you, how long would it take to set things up so that in twenty-four hours we could have every Aalaag Headquarters in the world surrounded by people dressed in cloaks and carrying staves?"

Wong and Shepherd looked at each other, then back at Shane.

"Surrounded by how many?" Shepherd asked.

"As many as possible—but at least enough to make it seem as if the whole countryside had come marching against the Aalaag," he answered.

"You're talking about thousands," said Wong.

"Tens of thousands. Every one of those Headquarters is in one of the great cities of the world. I want it to look as if all the city and all the countryside around it are moving in on the Headquarters building.''

"We'd have to study the situation—,'' began Shepherd. Shane interrupted.

"I don't have time for studies!'' he said. "All I want from you is a guess; but I need it now. Give me an estimate—I don't care how rough it is. The important thing is that all over the world people dressed like the Pilgrim should gather around Aalaag Headquarters buildings as if they were going to attack them. The two things that have to be is that there has to be an overwhelming number of them in each case, and that it has to happen all over the world at the same time.''

"You mean you don't want to announce this generally ahead of time?'' said Wong. "You want men and women ready to dress and march, but not to know when or what for?''

"That's right,'' said Shane. He thought he heard Maria draw a sudden breath behind him, but he could not be sure.

"If anything like that happens, they'll send the Interior Guard out against them with the strongest weapons the aliens let them carry,'' said Peter's voice behind his other ear.

Shane kept his gaze on Shepherd and Wong.

"Ah, I see,'' said Wong. "That's what you want. You want them to let themselves be shot down by the Interior Guard and still keep coming. The sort of thing Mohandas Karamchand Gandhi used against the English in India.''

"Not at all,'' said Shane. "The Aalaag wouldn't understand nonviolence. To them it would only mean the people involved were sick beasts. No, I want them to fight back—but only with what they have with them—their fists, their teeth, their staves. I want them to fight back, and by sheer numbers eventually kill all the Interior Guard sent out against them.''

This time there was no doubt in Shane's mind that he heard an indrawn breath from Maria.

"But why that, rather than nonviolence?'' said Wong. "In the end it makes the same sort of statement, and what you're suggesting sounds bloodier and worse. . . .''

"You're right in one thing,'' said Shane. "The people involved will be making a statement by what they do; and I don't like what'll happen any better than you do. But the Aalaag are only going to pay attention when they see there's no more of their Interior Guard left.''

"Then they'll come out themselves with their own weapons,'' said Shepherd. "They may wipe out everyone in sight, clear to the horizon.''

"They may,'' said Shane. "But first they'll want to know why we beasts are acting in this unusual way. The Pilgrim will tell them.''

As he said the words, he felt as if some great change took him over. He had just stepped across a line into territory from which there was no retreat. He had never intended to come this far; but already he was here. He had ended by completely accepting what he had believed was a fairy tale, when he had started out telling it to Peter's Resistance people—that the Aalaag could be convinced to leave the world, leave the human race to itself, if the proper statement was made to them.

"I see,'' said Wong. "You—''

"Not me,'' said Shane emptily. "The Pilgrim will tell them. I wouldn't know how—but the Pilgrim does. He's known from the beginning.''

The two men on the couch were staring at him; and, out of sight behind him, no doubt, Peter and Maria would be staring, too.

"I see,'' said Maria, proving him wrong. "Yes, I see.''

"I don't,'' said Shepherd. "What do you mean—talking about the Pilgrim as if he was somebody else besides you?''

"He is,'' said Shane heavily. "I'm sorry if that doesn't make sense to you; but it's true. I'm just a vehicle for the Pilgrim—or rather I'm just one of the vehicles for him and the rest of you are vehicles, too, only not in the way I am. Don't you recognize yourselves that you're vehicles for what the Pilgrim stands for? I tell you, move the people against the Aalaag Headquarters as I said, and the Pilgrim will do the rest. He'll tell the Aalaag what it means.''

"And what will it mean?'' said Peter.

"That we won't be cattle for them anymore,'' answered Shane.

"And what,'' asked Shepherd quietly, "if their answer to that is to destroy every human being and wipe the surface of the world clean with fire—since they're going to lose the use of us anyhow?''

"They may do just that," said Shane. "The Pilgrim has hopes they won't."

"But there're no certainties," said Peter.

"That's right," said Shane. "No certainties. None."

He was suddenly angry with them.

"I shouldn't have to tell you that!" he said. "There's no choice in this. We do what we have to!"

He made himself be calm. It was not their fault they did not understand.

"We have to go on faith in all this," he said. "As I know the Aalaag, if they don't see any hope of keeping us, they won't just destroy us, out of spite. They'd consider doing something useless like that too petty and beneath them. But they'll have to be absolutely sure we're no use to them at all; and that's my job."

He took a deep breath.

"You still haven't told me how long it would take to get the people gathered around the Aalaag Headquarters," he said.

Shepherd and Wong looked at each other.

"A month?" ventured Shepherd. "Just to get the word out. And then—"

"Too long. Far too long. It has to be no more than two weeks from today. No more," said Shane. "The time is now. The Pilgrim knows it. Don't tell me word can't be passed in a few days—I've seen rumors travel faster than I did—when I was flying around the world with Aalaag help. And don't tell me it'd take any healthy human being more than a night to make an acceptable robe and staff for himself or herself."

"You're completely forgetting such things as food and shelter," said Peter. "Thousands coming into a city on foot; and what are they going to eat? Where are they going to stay?"

"Those who come must understand they're probably coming in to die. Food and shelter are beside the point. If they escape alive, that'll be the miracle."

"My God!" said Shepherd in an appalled voice. "And you think they'll come on those terms? Maybe some like us might, but—"

"They're part of the Pilgrim, too," said Shane, "all of them." He felt strangely certain of himself. A sort of exaltation had him in its grip. "You just do the job I gave you of getting the word to them. I'll guarantee they'll come. They have to come. Time is shorter than any of us think—"

"But—," began Wong; he was interrupted by the ringing of the phone. Maria picked it up.

"Who? Shane Evert—," she began; but before she could say anything more, Shane felt something like an invisible static spark that leaped from her to him, and suddenly, in the middle of the room, was the nine-foot figure of an Aalaag in white suit and black boots. His face turned toward Shane.

"Shane-beast!" The deep voice, speaking in Aalaag, seemed to push outward the confines of the small room that was the parlor of their hotel suite. "You are ordered to report at once to the First Captain. At once!"

The figure vanished.

"—And that time," said Shane, with bitter humor, "has just grown even shorter. I've just been ordered back to my base Head-quarters."

He pushed the cowl of his robe back from his head, revealing his face to them all.

"It doesn't matter any longer if you see me," he said to Wong and Shepherd. "The Pilgrim himself is here to stay now."

He stared at the uncomprehending faces of everyone there—except Maria, who looked at him with an expression in which something like joy and fear were mingled. The words of the broadcast officer-image had not, of course, been understood by any of the others.

"Start spreading the word to get ready immediately," he told the other three men. "I don't know when I'll give the word to move, but it'll be soon. Peter—I'll probably phone you, so leave a phone number where you can be reached. I leave it to you, after that, to get the word on to these other people. Get going now—"

He got to his own feet as the rest rose automatically to theirs.

"Maria," he said, looking at her. "We're leaving for the House of Weapons. At once."

TWENTY-SIX

SOME OF SHANE'S EXALTATION SEEMED TO HAVE TOUCHED MARIA AS well. In the plane on the commercial flight to which they had been assigned to return to North America, she wrapped her arms around his left arm and hugged him to her.

"You really are the Pilgrim," she said, "now."

"Well . . . part of the Pilgrim." He turned his head to smile at her smile. "The Pilgrim is everybody, you, as well."

"But you're the most important part," she said, still holding him firmly.

"Perhaps," he said. "For the moment."

But he knew what she meant. A remarkable peace had come over him. He had not tried to sleep since earlier in the day, but somehow he knew there would be no more nightmares. His mind felt clear and light and sane; and he was no longer afraid—of anything.

"No perhaps," she said. "The rest of us were fumbling around in the dark. You knew."

"Knew?" he echoed. He felt strange with the word in his mouth. "What I really know is almost nothing."

"But it's more than anyone else does. It'll be enough. You'll see."

"I hope so," he said, from the uttermost depths within him.

For the first time in three years, he realized, he had stopped trying to understand—either the Aalaag or his fellow humans. What drove him now was a racial reflex, no more to be understood by the prehistorically recent logic of his forebrain than it was to be resolved into neat equations. And what drove the Aalaag was a like element, equally old and racial. These two forces were headed for a collision that was made inevitable by the very nature of the instincts themselves.

It did not matter if he was brave or cowardly. It did not matter if he was right or wrong. All that mattered was that the deep, unthinking mainspring of his being committed him inexorably to a meeting with another mainspring-driven race, and that one of them must turn the other aside when the time of meeting came. The potential terrors he had known of for three years were still there, waiting for him in due course. He could not avoid them and they had grown no easier to think of in the interval. But they no longer mattered because now he had accepted that there was no alternative but to go up against them.

He slept, accordingly, on the plane during the long flight over the Pacific Ocean—a deeper, quieter sleep than he had had in months. The plane landed in San Francisco in the darkness of a spring-like night; and an Aalaag courier ship was waiting to take them the rest of the way to the rooftop of the House of Weapons.

"You were ordered to return by the First Captain," said the Aalaag Officer of the Day as Shane and Maria stood before his desk in the hall leading to Lyt Ahn's offices. "Nothing was said about your being accompanied by other cattle."

"Forgive the stupidity of this beast . . ." The alien words flowed automatically from Shane's tongue. "This other with me has for so long been included in my orders as my assistant that it did not occur to me but what the immaculate sir wanted us both to return to him."

"Perhaps. It may be that the wording of your orders was at fault. Otherwise, the fault is yours. The First Captain will make all clear. You may proceed now to his offices."

"We hear and obey, untarnished sir."

They went up the long avenue of black and white tiles between the walls hung with long arms.

"He wants to see us right away?" Maria asked in Italian.

"Evidently. The Aalaag don't routinely think of night as a sleeping or even a nonworking time, you know. Just let me do the talking, as usual."

They reached the door of the offices, touched them and were ordered inside.

"What is this?" said Lyt Ahn from behind his desk. "I wish to speak only to you, Shane-beast."

"Forgive this beast, immaculate sir. This other will withdraw—" He spoke to Maria in Italian and saw a flash of mixed concern and relief in her eyes as she turned and went out, closing the doors behind her.

"Shane-beast!" Lyt Ahn stood up behind his desk and walked around it to the couch where he usually sat during their informal talks. He sat down. "All that is to be said at this time from this moment on is to be private between us."

As he said so, the silvery grayness like mist flashed momentarily around them, then cleared to reveal walls, furniture, ceiling and floor—everything, including the couch where Lyt Ahn sat and one chair facing it. Without waiting to be ordered to do so, Shane walked over to the empty chair, and at Lyt Ahn's nod, seated himself in it.

"This is a thing that should never be done," said Lyt Ahn to him somberly. "It is a thing for which there should never be a need. But matters are not as they should be. A beast should never be allowed a glimpse of the private matters of the Aalaag."

"I have no wish to see or go or hear where I should not, to where my master may not want me to be," said Shane—and for a moment he almost meant it. For some reason the situation, Lyt Ahn's tone of voice, or both together had touched a deep feeling that was like understanding and pity in him.

"If I did not wish it, you would not," said Lyt Ahn. "I do wish it, out of my duty as First Captain of the Expedition landed on this planet. Listen to me, Shane-beast. I have decided to give you to Laa Ehon on a permanent loan."

The last words rang in Shane's mind for a moment without sense. Not only were they the last thing he had expected to hear, but all his plans had been based on the fact that he would have access to Lyt Ahn. It was not for a beast to protest an order of one of its own superiors and unthinkable in it to protest the order of an Aalaag; but too much was at stake here for him not to speak.

"If the immaculate sir would listen for a second," he said impulsively, "there are reasons why it would be much preferable if I could stay with the First Captain. I—"

"Silence!" said Lyt Ahn.

GORDON R. DICKSON

His voice was not raised, but his eyes for a second were fixed on a pinpoint of surface between Shane's eyebrows.

"I was approached by Laa Ehon on this matter," he continued, "since my favor was involved in any purchase of you from me, and matters being as they are between us at the moment, it was not practical that he accept the duty of a future favor to be made to me. Therefore, he asked that I simply make a gift of you to him."

Lyt Ahn paused. This time, Shane wisely said nothing.

"Laa Ehon," said the First Captain, "is a senior officer of immaculate record. He has had marked success in improving production in certain areas already where his Government Units have been at work for at least a few weeks. In courtesy I could hardly refuse him a gift, unusual as it was for him to ask it of me, rather than I, myself, volunteer the offer of it to him. Still, there are precedents. . . ."

For a second Lyt Ahn's thoughts seemed to go elsewhere.

"In courtesy," he repeated, after a moment, "I could hardly refuse him. At the same time, it was only reasonable that under our present circumstances I might not wish to make of you an outright gift to him. Accordingly, I have done what amounts to the same thing—made you available to him on a permanent loan."

He paused. The sharp focus of his eyes had relaxed.

"Do you understand what a permanent loan is, little Shane-beast?"

"No, I do not, immaculate sir."

"It means that you are his for as long as either of us shall live. On his death, you would be permanently returned to me. On my death you would be permanently returned to my heirs. Also, on a permanent loan, it is understandable that some conditions be made. Since you are actually still my property and part of my Corps of Courier-Translators, one condition I made was that you should be free to return whenever you considered it necessary to inform yourself of changes in your Corps, so that if necessary you would be able to resume your duties there. This need to return is written into the understanding covering the permanent loan between Laa Ehon and myself; and it takes precedence over any other order, any emergency."

Lyt Ahn paused. Again his eyes were focused on a pinpoint area of Shane's forehead.

"It is understood that you will not abuse this privilege," he said.

"I understand, immaculate sir," said Shane.

"At the same time there is more at stake here than appears on the surface. . . ." Lyt Ahn hesitated, as if it was painful for him to continue. The silence stretched out between them. The First Captain's eyes were focused on the nothingness of the gray that surrounded them.

"I am always at my master's service," murmured Shane finally.

Lyt Ahn's eyes came back to him.

"I know that, little Shane-beast," he said. "I know that. That's why I'm choosing to speak to you now about things that—things that are not normally talked about between Aalaag and beast."

Once more there was a long silence on the part of Lyt Ahn. Shane waited patiently for it to pass. A part of his mind was in turmoil, trying to adjust to the thought of life as a beast of Laa Ehon's, trying to fit this in with the plans he had announced to Wong and Shepherd.

"I do not know," said Lyt Ahn at last—and Shane, watching, understood that the Aalaag was speaking more to himself than to any beast that might be closeted with him. "I do not know if we will any longer be worthy of our worlds, once we regain them. They will have to be rebuilt, of course. They will have made slag-heaps and mud catacombs of our forests and prairies. They will have fouled our lakes and streams and oceans. But there are ways to repair such things. We will have to replace our flora and fauna; but we have carried all these years the germs of the lives that will do that, once the land is again ready for them. . . ."

He turned his head to look at Shane; but he looked blindly, more through Shane than at him.

"All might be made the same. But ourselves? We are no longer what we were when They came. Time—the thousands and thousands of your years, little Shane-beast, have made us into another people, of necessity. What will we be like, back on our own land, but with no beasts to be our servants, and only ourselves to hold to the code that the necessity of survival has kept alive in us?"

He looked away again from Shane.

"No," he said, in a musing tone, "we are not the same. This long time has been an unnatural time for us, and we, even we, have become in some ways unnatural. We are not all that we were—all that we could be; and this affects some of us more than others."

He looked directly at Shane; and this time he was seeing Shane.

"It is unthinkable that an Aalaag should ask a beast to report on the behavior of another Aalaag," he said—and hesitated.

"If the immaculate sir will permit," said Shane quickly, "I was asked a question by Laa Ehon, which as a beast of the First Captain I should perhaps report to him."

"A question?"

Lyt Ahn's eyes drew together once more to focus on the single point between Shane's eyebrows.

"What was this question?" asked Lyt Ahn.

"The immaculate sir who is Laa Ehon," said Shane delicately, "inquired of me how well I liked my master."

Lyt Ahn's gaze tightened and tightened, until Shane could almost feel the focus of his gaze burning like the light of a laser into the skin of his forehead.

"This is the truth, Shane-beast?"

"Even if I should be questioned by my masters, they would find out only that it is the truth and all of the truth," said Shane.

There was a terrible silence.

"And what did you answer?"

"I said that I had had no master but one and wanted no other."

"I see."

The focus of Lyt Ahn's gaze moved off Shane. The silence came back. But this time it did not last long. Lyt Ahn looked at Shane.

"You are not only wise, but a kindly small beast," he said. "Perhaps I may be forgiven in that I have been easier on you than on some of my other beasts. You've made what I have to say to you easier; and I think you knew that you were doing that; and I appreciate the effort."

"My master praises me too highly," murmured Shane.

"I praise neither too highly, nor not highly enough!" said Lyt Ahn sharply. "I only note the fact and the truth. Now listen and remember what I tell you."

"Yes, immaculate sir."

"Good. What you are to understand and remember is that it is possible—rare, but possible—even for an Aalaag to become less than perfectly well. You must also understand and remember that, although I have lent you to Laa Ehon on a permanent basis, you remain my beast. The time may come when you may wish to return for a visit to me—that has been provided for, as I explained to you earlier. Be sure of that. There can be no moment when you are in service to Laa Ehon that you cannot say to him, or to those who are officers under his command, that you must return to me. And there cannot be any thought in the mind of any of them, including the immaculate sir Laa Ehon himself, that you should not be permitted to go."

The heavy voice stopped speaking.

"I understand, and I will remember, immaculate sir," said Shane.

"When you return to me, in no case will you make a report to me," said Lyt Ahn strongly. "You will only answer what questions I may put to you. You understand this?"

"I understand, immaculate sir."

"Good."

The gray flashed once again about them and they sat in the office of Lyt Ahn facing each other.

"You may go," said Lyt Ahn. Shane rose.

"One more thing—," he said quickly, daring greatly. "The beast who is my assistant—may it go with me?"

Lyt Ahn stared at him.

"I have lent Laa Ehon one beast, not two," he said at length. "It will be found duties here."

"If the immaculate sir pleases—" Shane left the words hanging.

"You have some special reason for wanting this other beast with you?" demanded the First Captain. "What is it?"

"Most immaculate sir, it is a female and we are contemplating mating. As the immaculate sir has perhaps heard, among certain of us beasts—and it and I are such ones—matings are for life. I would prefer not to be parted from it."

Lyt Ahn sat still, thinking.

"I cannot give another beast to Laa Ehon," he said at last. "The beast you refer to, however, will be placed on indefinite leave and sent home to Milan, Italy, from which it came, as I understand. You will therefore be able to see it from time to time."

"Yes, immaculate sir."

"Go."

"Yes, immaculate sir."

Maria was waiting for him outside in the hall. She opened her mouth as he came out of the doors of Lyt Ahn's offices, then closed it again at his sudden frown. In silence they went back to their quarters; but once in them she turned and threw her arms around him.

"What is it, Shane?" she burst out. "In the name of God, I can tell something terrible's happened! What is it?"

Gently he took her arms from around him and made her sit down. He sat down beside her with his arms around her.

"It's not that bad," he said. "We're going to be separated; but we'll be in the same city and, depending on how liberal Laa Ehon is with his beasts, I may be able to see you every day when there isn't some special work or emergency going on."

"Laa Ehon? The same city? You mean Milan? Why?"

"I had a talk with Lyt Ahn," he said. "It was a talk under a seal of secrecy, so I don't dare repeat it to you. But what it boils down to is that he's giving me on permanent loan to Laa Ehon."

"But why? I thought they didn't particularly even get along."

"Because Laa Ehon asked for me as a gift. Lyt Ahn could refuse to make a gift, but he couldn't refuse Laa Ehon entirely—no, hush now, and listen to me. I don't understand why, myself. It's got something to do with the Aalaag mores. The tricky part is, I'm to go to Laa Ehon, but he wouldn't lend you along with me."

"Shane, couldn't you think of some reason? Couldn't you do something? Didn't you argue with him?"

"As far as I could. When that didn't work, I told him we were about to mate. The mating of beasts they think of as valuable is unofficial Aalaag policy. So he made a concession. You're to go on indefinite leave from here to Milan; and—well, the rest is up to me and to what I can get Laa Ehon to agree to."

"If it's policy, Laa Ehon'll have to give in, too, then."

"Maybe," said Shane, staring at the floor before them. "I learned a lot from this talk that I didn't understand before. It's pretty clear that that gathering the Organization people couldn't film or record was a political meeting and Lyt Ahn knows it took place. I made a mistake—that reminds me. I daren't go out of the

House of Weapons now. If word of it got back to Lyt Ahn, or if he called for me and I wasn't here, it might look strange to him. You'll have to do it."

"Do what?"

"Sign out of the House of Weapons on some pretext of your own, for just an hour or two. Find a pay phone in the city and call Peter. Tell him things are at a crisis point and we have to move as quickly as we can. I want a specific date for that gathering—as soon as it can be held—that I mentioned to him when we talked to Wong and Shepherd in Beijing. He's to send the answer to me through the Resistance people in Milan; because we'll be there, you and I, possibly in hours. Also tell him to get me the name of some representative of the professional group in Milan who I can get in touch with in a hurry—and one more thing. The business of the Resistance and others helping the new Government Units Laa Ehon set up is to be reversed. Have him pass the word to do everything possible now to slow the Units up and make them not work."

"All right." Maria got to her feet, suddenly wiped clean of emotion. She was decisive. "Have you got time to tell me what's going on?"

"Not now. As soon as you get back. Tell them at the gate you may be gone a couple of hours, but get back here as quickly as you can. Lyt Ahn may have already issued the orders to take us to Milan. Now tell me, so I'll have the same answer you will if I'm asked— what excuse will you be using for wanting to go out?"

"I need a kind of soap I can only get in your stores here."

"Good." He caught at her hand. "Be careful!"

She squeezed his hand and then pulled free.

"Don't worry about me. I ought to be back in twenty minutes at the most."

He watched the door close behind her.

There was nothing to do but wait and worry. He took a firm grip on his emotions and told himself that if he had to kill twenty minutes he might as well kill it constructively by replaying in his memory the conversation he had had with Lyt Ahn and seeing what more he could read from it about Aalaag ways and the present situation.

Once more, he told himself, he had made the error of simplifying the Aalaag and all that pertained to them. He had assumed that the question Laa Ehon put to him—the same question he had told Lyt Ahn about—reflected an "unwellness" of Laa Ehon in Aalaag terms. But he had been basing his opinion of Aalaag reactions and judgments on what he had seen of the reactions and judgments in Lyt Ahn. What if Lyt Ahn belonged to a highly conservative group or party among the Aalaag; and Laa Ehon belonged to a much more liberal one, where such a question was not unthinkable in terms of ordinary Aalaag manners? Also, what if there were a number of other high-ranking officers among the Aalaag on Earth who thought as Laa Ehon thought, and would be ready to league with the Milanese Commander against the First Captain? If those things were so, it would explain why a number of such officers were willing to meet semi-secretly with Laa Ehon.

He was still exploring the implications of that possibility when the door opened and Maria was back with him. Even as she stepped through it, an Aalaag voice spoke from the wall communicator.

"Shane-beast and Maria-beast, you will report in fifteen minutes to the landing area on top of the House for your transportation to Milan."

"You reached him?" Shane asked her, as the voice stopped speaking.

She nodded.

"Let's go then," he said.

For once, the courier ship that carried them was full; with young officers of high-number rank taking with them their full equipment, including complete battle armor. Shane frowned slightly at this, and at what he seemed to sense as an air of unusual excitement among their Aalaag fellow passengers—who, he gathered from overheard conversation, were going beyond Milan to places in the Middle and Far East. All seats were filled. Shane and Maria were left to perch upon the piles of gear in the open cargo area behind the seats in the back of the ship.

It was probably the safest possible place they could have found to talk privately. Even if one of the Aalaag in the rear seats might recognize a few words of Italian, the general level of talk and other sounds in the plane would be enough to cover the sound of Shane's and Maria's voices to the point of unintelligibility. And here there was absolutely no possibility of their conversation being bugged by human agencies. Shane said as much to Maria as soon as the ship took off, and she nodded.

"You don't even trust our rooms in the House of Weapons anymore, do you?" she said.

"I can't," he said. "Just about anything's become possible. But I can't see anyone, human or Aalaag, having time to bug the storage area of this ship on such short notice. What did Peter say when you called him?"

"That he'd take care of everything and see you personally in Milan."

Shane frowned.

"If he's lucky," he said.

Maria looked at him narrowly.

"I'm to pass word where I am through Resistance channels as soon as I'm settled," she said, "and he's to contact me to find out when to contact you. You did say you thought you'd be seeing me daily, didn't you?"

"If Laa Ehon's agreeable," said Shane. "He should be. But— too many things are turning out not to be as I thought them. I've been wrong more often about the Aalaag than I thought I ever could be, particularly as far as underestimating how other people fear and loathe them. I thought my own feelings were greater than most peoples' because I had to live so close to them. In fact, I thought I was almost alone in that much feeling; and I didn't wake up to the fact that it was almost universal until recently."

"I hate them!" said Maria, in a low, intense voice. Her fingers had tensed and curved into the shape of the talons of a bird of prey. "I've always hated them, from the first. They've got no right. They never had any right to take this world, no right to take over everything on it, no right to treat us—all of us—like property!"

"In their own minds they have a right," said Shane somberly. "They honestly believe they're superior, and that the superior has a duty to rule and control the inferior."

"They aren't that superior!" said Maria.

"You'd have a hard time convincing any one of them of that," said Shane. "They could point to their weapons alone to prove it. Actually, they believe they're superior in all things—science, technology, morality, mental ability—anything you want to name. Anyway, even if they were a lot more like us in many ways, how could you ever compare two races? It's oranges and apples. What's a sign of excellence in one could be a blemish in another.''

"You still admire them in some ways, don't you?" said Maria.

"There're things about them to admire, you know," he answered. "Even by our standards. Wouldn't you admire someone you could trust to always tell you the truth, no matter what the personal cost to him or her, no matter what the personal consequences? But let's not waste time on that. I really do think I'll be able to see you every day, in Milan. But just in case I don't, just in case something happens to me, there're things I want you to know, so that you can pass them on to people like Peter. Because I see now that, with me or without me, the human race is never going to stop trying to get rid of the Aalaag or any race who tries to take them over.''

"I'm listening," said Maria.

"One of the things I made a mistake about was to assume the Aalaag were all alike—that if I found out something about how Lyt Ahn reacted, then every other Aalaag would react the same way. You remember when I came back to you and said that Laa Ehon was insane—that he'd asked me a question no Aalaag would ever ask another Aalaag's beast to answer?''

She nodded.

"Well, maybe he isn't insane—unwell, as the Aalaag put it—," he said. "Maybe Laa Ehon's one of a group of Aalaag who wouldn't be shocked the way Lyt Ahn was when I told him about it.''

"So you did tell him," said Maria.

"Yes, but it almost wasn't necessary," said Shane. "Listen to me carefully now, and remember this. Lyt Ahn had already begun to have suspicions Laa Ehon was unwell—but there seems to be some reason he couldn't just declare Laa Ehon so and take away his authority. I think it's because Laa Ehon does belong to this other group of Aalaag on this world of ours I just talked about—a group that thinks like Laa Ehon and doesn't think like Lyt Ahn; and, more than that, includes individuals in high positions, probably even on the Council of Area Commanders—maybe even a majority on that Council.''

"You mean that Lyt Ahn might be agreeable to the Aalaag pulling away, off of the Earth, but the others wouldn't go?''

"I don't know," said Shane. "Somehow I think that whatever's decided, they'll all do it together. But maybe the others could have enough weight in any decision so that even if Lyt Ahn was ready to order all the Aalaag to leave, he wouldn't because the others were against it."

Maria looked at him sharply.

"I see now why you were so upset when Lyt Ahn suddenly decided to lend you to Laa Ehon," she said.

"Yes." He nodded. "I had arguments I thought the Pilgrim might be able to make work on Lyt Ahn. Aalaag arguments, according to how I thought I understood the Aalaag thinking. But I'm not so sure now they'd work on Laa Ehon or one of the other aliens who think like him—if I'm right and there're others who think his way."

"But if Lyt Ahn already thought Laa Ehon was unwell, why did he back this business of the Government Units, which was Laa Ehon's idea? More, why did he shove it forward even faster than Laa Ehon looked like he was ready to?"

"I think," said Shane hesitantly, "he thought that the plan couldn't possibly work; and pushing it faster than Laa Ehon had planned would make its faults show that much sooner. You see, if it had worked, Laa Ehon would have gained authority in the Council at Lyt Ahn's expense. And, of course, the plan shouldn't have worked—only I had to tell the Resistance and others to make it look like it was working."

"So now," said Maria, "the other senior Aalaag officers think Lyt Ahn's showed a failure in judgment; and he's lost authority because Laa Ehon saw things more clearly than he did. So that's the reason for all this."

"It could be worse than that," said Shane. "What I'm afraid of is that Lyt Ahn himself actually believes he was wrong, and therefore he's less than he should be. It could be it wouldn't take much more for him to offer to step down as First Captain and let Laa Ehon take over. You have to look at it the way an Aalaag's mind would look at it. So what I'm really afraid of is that Lyt Ahn's taken a last-resort chance by sending me to literally spy on Laa Ehon, to see if I can find anything that will help him make up his mind if he should step down or not."

"You just finished telling me Lyt Ahn was the honorable type of Aalaag; so how could he do that?" said Maria. "Or isn't it dishonorable to make you into a spy on a brother Aalaag?''

"I'm not really sent out to spy. Lyt Ahn's just going to ask me questions when I come back for a visit to the House of Weapons. But, you're right, of course. Even that's not right—except that I gave him an excuse—deliberately. I told him what Laa Ehon had asked me. That brought out into the open the point that Laa Ehon may actually be unwell. If so, then it's not only a duty but a kindness—again in Aalaag terms—to establish the fact; and means that he couldn't in conscience use against someone he believed to be a well officer would be excusable to establish the fact of Laa Ehon's sickness.''

"I don't see anything in all this you've told me," said Maria, "that's so critically important to pass on to Peter and others if you couldn't. What is it you were going to tell me?"

"What's important is just that I'm going to report Laa Ehon as unwell, whether he is or not," said Shane. "If I'm right about Lyt Ahn, at least, as long as he's First Captain, until he resigns or is voted out of his command position, he can give the rest orders and they'll obey. If nothing else, it'll create a leadership crisis that Peter and the rest can take advantage of; and it might stop Laa Ehon and his group long enough for me to play the issue out with Lyt Ahn the way I planned to.''

"You've never told me how you planned to.''

"Yes, I have," he said. "We set up a demonstration with thousands of pilgrims surrounding each Aalaag Headquarters and then the Pilgrim will tell him that we will die, if necessary, but we'll not serve the Aalaag anymore.''

"You mean you'll tell him." Her face was pale.

"No, I really mean the Pilgrim will tell him—through me.''

"But it means you'll be there, facing him.''

"Yes," he said. "You knew that.''

"You never really said it, until now.''

"There's no other way," he said as gently as he could. "When I say we'll all die rather than go on being cattle to the Aalaag, I have to be ready to do it, too.''

She did not say anything for a moment.

"So this is what you want me to tell Peter," she said, and her voice was bitter. "You should tell him yourself when you see him in Milan.''

"I will—if I can."

She stared at him.

"He'll be here in a day, two at most—and you say you're practically certain Laa Ehon will let you come to see me."

"I am. But there's always the possibility . . ." He let the sentence end itself.

"What you mean," she said, "is that when you leave me in Milan to report for the first time to Laa Ehon, it may be the last time I ever see you."

He took a deep breath.

"Yes," he said. "There's that chance."

They sat looking at each other; and after a moment he put his arms around her and held her closely to him. But it did not help.

TWENTY-SEVEN

"So," SAID LAA EHON, "YOU WERE UNABLE TO TELL ME HOW WELL you liked your master because you had only had one and had no basis for comparison. Perhaps you can tell me now how you feel about being on permanent loan to me, Shane-beast."

Shane stood at attention before the office desk at which Laa Ehon sat. It was his third day in Milan and he was seeing Laa Ehon for the first time since his arrival. They were alone in the Aalaag's office, which was furnished much like the one in which Shane had been used to having his talks with Lyt Ahn. But Laa Ehon had made no move toward any of the more comfortable furniture that would signal an "unofficial" mode to the interview.

Shane was grateful now that Lyt Ahn had refused to let Maria be lent to Laa Ehon as well as himself. Maria had no experience with this sort of Aalaag, no experience at standing, if necessary, for hours while being questioned.

"I am very interested to find myself lent to the immaculate sir," he answered now.

"Yes," said Laa Ehon, "it was both kindly and generous of Lyt Ahn to make you available to me. You mirror your master's nature, as a good beast should. But of course, now, you must come to mirror mine. I understand you were also allowed to bring your assistant and mate-to-be to this city with you. I take it you have established it in quarters not too far from here, so that you may see it with the least possible difficulty when I give you freedom to do so?"

"Yes, immaculate sir."

"Such an arrangement is agreeable to me, as well," said Laa

Ehon reflectively. "I am interested to see what kind of offspring you will sire. But of course, your main interest will be in the work I wish you to do."

"Of course, immaculate sir."

"Indeed, you will find it most interesting. I will not, of course, rank you first in the Corps I wish you to build—and which will bear some resemblance to the Corps to which you belong with Lyt Ahn. It is far too soon for me to decide who should have first rank in that. But you may consider yourself in this Corps which I now create as one of second rank, acting as First Officer until further notice. If you satisfy me that such a promotion is deserved, it could be that rank will become permanent for you. But that remains to be seen. Have you any questions?"

"I should prefer to think before putting questions to the immaculate sir, so as not to burden him with things I might find out otherwise."

"That is intelligent of you," said Laa Ehon. "Nonetheless, I am interested in hearing now what you might wish to know. Say whatever questions come to your mind, even if later you find that they were unnecessary."

Shane's mind, in fact, was racing. He had achieved his first objective, which was, effectively, to be commanded to enter into open conversation with Laa Ehon. The next step would be harder. What he dreamed of doing was to lead Laa Ehon into some statement that could possibly be reported to Lyt Ahn as evidence of instability—in Aalaag terms.

"I am grateful for the consideration of the immaculate sir," he said. "Perhaps I might ask then if the sir foresees all Commanders eventually having their own Corps of courier-translators?"

"I see no need for that," said Laa Ehon. "My own need for such a Corps is all that interests me at the moment. But—I did invite questions from you, so I will answer this one, somewhat frivolous as it is. No, I do not see other Commanders needing such a Corps. I am one whom events might bring to become First Captain, sometime; therefore there is a use to me in the experience of having such. I am curious that your first question was not where the other potential member-beasts that would work with and under you might be found."

"The immaculate sir is entirely correct. That should have been my first question."

"But was not. I will recall that," said Laa Ehon, "when the time comes for weighing your merits as First Officer. To answer that question, I have had a search going on for some time to find teachable beasts with abilities; and that search has so far produced eight of them. You will be directed to the place where they are even now waiting to be examined by you, on leaving me."

"I am grateful to the immaculate sir. Is it the wish of the sir that I immediately begin to test them as to these abilities, so that I may report to the sir my opinion of them as future Corps members?"

Laa Ehon's expression, of course, gave nothing away; but Shane was certain he had scored a point by coming up with the exact question the other had wanted him to ask next.

"Yes, you may do that, Shane-beast," Laa Ehon said, "and report to me with your findings as soon as you have them on all candidates."

"May I then ask the sir what sort of use those qualified among them are to be put to first?"

Once again, Shane had the feeling that he had scored with the right question in the right order. Laa Ehon sat for a good two minutes without answering; but indications too fine for Shane to identify individually in the other's face and attitude made Shane suddenly sure that the delay was mere show, that the Milanese Commander had had his answer ready for a long time. If he had been a human, he would have adopted a thoughtful pose.

"That is, of course, something to be decided," said Laa Ehon, "and I will be interested in your own ideas on the subject, when the time for that comes. Perhaps you might be thinking about uses for these candidates, yourself."

It was abruptly very obvious to Shane that he had not been the only one trying to bring the other to say certain things. Laa Ehon had also been leading Shane to utter words that, if said by Shane, would justify what he, as an Aalaag, might safely reply. Shane decided that the best way to handle this was to walk directly and openly into the trap.

"If I am to do that, immaculate sir, it would be of considerable help to me to know under what conditions the immaculate sir foresees this Corps being used."

Again, Laa Ehon went through the motions of taking time out to think.

"That is difficult to say right at this moment, Shane-beast," he answered finally. "The future is always full of possibilities."

He fell silent abruptly; and his gaze, which had been on Shane, was suddenly not seeing him anymore, but looking through him to something apparently visible only to his own alien thoughts.

Laa Ehon sat, wordless. To Shane, who had lived through so many Aalaag conversational silences that he was by way of being a connoisseur of them, there was a difference about this one, following as it had upon a speech, oddly interrupted. It was, he thought, as if Laa Ehon had been about to say something more, but had not. Aalaag did not trail off their voice as a human might, on leaving a sentence unfinished. All speech ended on an emphatic note that was an effective period to whatever was being said. But there was a clear feeling in Shane that the Milanese Commander had suddenly changed his mind about putting whatever it was into words. Shane was searching his mind for possibilities of what that unspoken thought would have been, when Laa Ehon unexpectedly returned his attention and voice to Shane at once.

"I am, of course," Laa Ehon said, "thoroughly in agreement with Lyt Ahn's stipulation that you be allowed to return to the House of Weapons at any time you feel it necessary; and I have given orders that you be allowed to arrange transportation through the Officer of the Day without notice. But it could happen that some inconvenience might be produced at this end by one of such trips without notice. Have you any idea when you might need to so travel?"

"None, I regret to say, immaculate sir," answered Shane. "Possibly not for months, but perhaps even within the week. I came immediately I was notified that I had been lent to the sir. My sudden departure could have left unattended to some matter that might call me back, as I say, within a week or two. I regret that I have no way of knowing so that I could notify the sir in advance."

"It might be inconvenient," repeated Laa Ehon, in a tone so low it was the Aalaag equivalent of a muttered aside to himself. His gaze, which had once more become unfocused, refastened itself on Shane. "We will not concern ourselves with that now, however. You are clear about your immediate duties?''

"Forgive this beast, but I am not, immaculate sir. You wished me to examine these candidates for a Courier-Translator Corps that you mentioned. What beyond examining them does the sir wish me to do?''

"Teach them, of course.'' Laa Ehon's gaze sharpened on a point between Shane's eyebrows.

"This beast understands. They are to be taught what the duties are of a courier-translator.''

"Not at all. What you are to teach them is the true tongue, teach them to speak it well as you are speaking it now. For what other reason would I have borrowed you from the First Captain?''

"Forgive the stupidity of this beast, immaculate sir. Not everyone can be taught—''

"I think such failure unlikely in this case. These are all beasts who speak a number of beast-tongues, already. Granted that there is more to the true tongue than any beast-noises, they should all be able to learn it. If there is one—or even two—who actually does not have the capability, you can reject them. You may go.''

"I thank the immaculate sir and obey.''

Shane turned and left the office, his mind whirling. The odds that any of the human linguists he was about to meet would be capable of learning to speak Aalaag even at median level for Lyt Ahn's Corps, let alone at Shane's level, were minuscule, to say the least. Lyt Ahn's present Corps members represented a beginning body of students from all over the world that had been nearly two hundred times their number. Almost all the rest had failed because of their inability to speak—not a failure to understand, but to *speak* the alien tongue. As Shane himself had explained to Maria, the human vocal apparatus was simply not capable of forming certain of the Aalaag speech sounds; and those like himself who gave their masters the impression that they could speak "the true tongue" with some facility did it by linguistic trickery and imitation of the stumbling pronunciations of the very young Aalaag, who were equally in process of learning to speak it.

At any other time, Shane would have been in deep shock at this order to do the impossible. But it happened that he had other and greater things to think about at the moment—also, he should be well away from here before Laa Ehon had a chance to check on whether the candidates selected had been successfully taught, to the extent the Milanese Commander clearly expected him to teach them. Maria had called him over the local phone lines into the Headquarters building to say that Peter had gotten into Milan the night before. But Shane, required by Aalaag custom to wait on the spot for Laa Ehon's arrival, had not been able to leave the building since early on the day when he had first reported in to that Command.

Now, at last, once he had made some sort of show of examining the candidates, he would be free to go to the apartment in which he had established Maria; and learn from Peter what was happening as a result of the message he had asked her to phone him from Minneapolis.

He already knew in what part of the building the courier-translator trainees Laa Ehon had mentioned had been assigned living quarters, classroom and relaxation lounge. He made his way to the last of these places, accordingly, confident that was where they would have been required to wait, for as many minutes or days as it took him to get to them.

They were all well enough acquainted with Aalaag ways to scramble to their feet the moment he appeared in the entrance. He might have been someone from Housekeeping come to clean the room, for all they knew, but it paid to take no chances.

He looked them over. There were no women among them, which might indicate some fanciful notion of Laa Ehon's—or it might simply be a matter of chance. They ranged in age from what looked like the late teens to the middle fifties and were of all shapes, sizes and appearances.

"I'm Shane Evert, acting First Officer for this Corps," he told them in Italian. "I'll see you no later than midmorning tomorrow, and in the meantime you're to write me up your personal histories, with lists of the languages you can speak, and how well you speak each one. That's all for now."

He turned and left, like them following ordinary Aalaag custom, which made no provision for hellos and good-byes, or get-acquainted speeches. He was there to give orders, they were there to take them. Each side had now acted as was proper and he would see them tomorrow.

Still, as he walked away, he found himself worrying how best to deal with them. At the very least he would have to keep them occupied; and he had probably better find some way of appearing to show progress to anyone—but specifically to Laa Ehon—who might come to check on how he was executing his orders.

It was as he left the Headquarters building for his walk to the apartment where he had left Maria that the inspiration came to him. He had already had the experience of trying to teach Maria enough Aalaag to make it appear that she not only knew some of the alien language, but would be quick to pick up more. He had already discovered phrases composed of sounds that were easiest for her to say. He could begin by teaching these trainees the same phrases. Being talented to at least some extent, linguistically, they should pick them up even more quickly than she had. They would not really be able to speak Aalaag, but they could be brought to appear to do so—and they also should be faster than Maria at learning to understand the Aalaag questions that would cue such answers.

Happily, a human's main contribution to conversation with one of the masters was simply to say "yes" politely to whatever he or she had just been ordered to do. Ordinary beasts were not asked questions, as Lyt Ahn, and now Laa Ehon, had asked him. Even if the language problem had not been there the average Aalaag would assume that any response one of the cattle might make to a request for information would be either not understandable or unreliable.

He breathed deeply of the cool outside air as he began to walk the four blocks which were all that separated the Headquarters building from the apartment. It was perhaps an hour or so past dawn. A sunny morning, but with a new crispness to the atmosphere now in his lungs that reminded him suddenly that it was November and that the day was, if anything, warm for this time of year.

It came as something of a shock to realize that winter was once again moving in on the Northern Hemisphere of Earth, which was his main area of travel. Time was going fast. It had gone fast, in fact, with all that had happened, since the day on which he had rescued Maria and met members of the Resistance for the first time. He looked about him, seeing things with a curious clarity of vision like that of someone just released from prison. Above, the sky was an empty blue that seemed to reach up to infinity beyond the tops of the surrounding buildings. The wind was not cold, but it had a sharp edge to it which swirled the robes of those among the large number of those walking by him who were dressed as pilgrims with robe and staff. It was still surprising to him to realize there were now so many of them. He found himself walking more briskly and feeling a sense of urgency for some reason he could not at the moment identify.

He reached the apartment building where they now lived and climbed the three flights of stairs to the apartment. When he unlocked the door and let himself in, he did not see or hear either Maria or Peter; but since it was hardly possible that they would not be here, he went toward the back of the apartment which, like the others above and below it, had an open balcony overlooking a small walled garden behind the building.

He came down the long corridor that gave access to the row of rooms that made up the apartment and looked out through the door at its end. He paused at the murmur of voices. He smiled. They were there.

He looked out. The morning sun, striking in at an angle as it rose, had evidently made a pool of warmth at the far end of the wind-shielded balcony. There, on rather uncomfortable wicker chairs, Peter and Maria sat across from each other at a small, round-topped glass table, talking. They were both clad in dark-colored, bulky sweaters, thrown in bright contrast by the sunlight against the green-painted concrete that made up the wall on one side, the floor beneath them and the waist-high barrier between them and the open air beyond. Above that short wall, the concrete had been extended upward to form arched openings, so that both Peter and Maria looked strangely out of place, like people transported back in time.

Their talk was too low-voiced for him to make out the words; but it was a very intent conversation, for their arms were extended across the little table and both hands of each clasped with each other's in a single grip. Still smiling, Shane went in.

"Well, here I am!" he announced in English.

They broke their grip and straightened up, putting a space between them as he came up; and Maria jumped to her feet, throwing her arms around him and kissing him almost violently.

"Hey," he said after a moment, gently disengaging her grip, "you're going to squeeze me in half. I know I was kept longer than we expected, but I haven't been gone that long!"

It was then he noticed there were tears in her eyes.

"Why, what is it?" he asked, cupping a hand around her chin and lifting her face for a closer look. "What's got you upset? I'm all right."

"It's nothing," she said, breaking away from him and brushing the dampness from her eyelashes. "Peter and I were just talking about how life used to be—before the aliens came—and how it's been since; and when I saw you I remembered that, bad as it is now, if it hadn't been for their coming, we'd never have found each other. . . ."

"My fault for bringing the subject up," said Peter from his chair at the table. "No point in dwelling on the dead past, anyway."

Shane pulled another chair up to the table and sat down. Maria sat down again as well. They all looked at each other across the small tabletop and he turned to Peter.

"What's the answer?" he asked. "How soon can I expect gatherings of Pilgrim look-alikes around the Aalaag Headquarters buildings?"

Peter made a wry face.

"You realize what you were asking?" he said. "You not only wanted thousands—millions, possibly—to gather in robes where you want them, but you wanted them to do it simultaneously all over the world; and you're talking about people who aren't under orders, or even mostly in direct communication with either the Resistance or the professional group."

"All right," said Shane. "I know it was a tall order. The thing is, it's got to be done. All I expected you and the Organization to do was pass the word and give me an estimate of how quickly it might produce results."

"Nonetheless," said Peter, "I want you to understand how impossible it was—what you were asking for."

"I understand!" said Shane impatiently. "What have you got to tell me? That's what I want to hear now."

Peter gave him a lopsided smile. It was the kind of smile evoked from someone who has finally shrugged and given up on argument.

"All right then," he said. "Here it is. What you asked for was effectively impossible. We decided to pass the word right away for people to start coming into the cities—just into the cities, they weren't told any more than that. They were to wear Pilgrim garb and gather in the cities, and wait.''

"Wait?" Shane stared at him.

"Wait for the Pilgrim, who would have a message for them very soon now,'' said Peter. "This leaves it all up to you. When you think there're enough of them gathered, when you're ready yourself, you pass the word to me and it'll be passed to everyone everywhere— where to go, what to do and what to expect. And if you want our guess as to how long it'll take you to get, say, fifty thousand people to fill the streets around the alien Headquarters in each city, it's that anywhere from another five days to another ten days will do it. There, now, you have it—as much as we can give you.''

Shane heard the words echoing in the cavern of his mind. The moment of silence that followed seemed to stretch out forever. His physical ears, in the silence that followed Peter's voice, recorded the distant sounds of the city, traffic and far-off street sounds of voices.

He felt once again as he had felt on the way here, when he had noticed the blueness of the sky and the brightness of the morning. It was not so much a clarity of vision like that of someone released from prison, he thought, as that of a prisoner who at last with a sort of relief hears announced the day and hour of his execution. That execution itself his mind refused to picture. His thoughts went forward until the moment when he would stand and speak to Lyt Ahn as the Pilgrim—but beyond that point they would not go.

Instead, inside him, there was a strange sort of peace. He could feel the warm-bodied, three-dimensional nearness of Maria and Peter along with the three-dimensionality of the world about him in this moment and they were like members of his own family. Maria was a part of him; the part he would leave behind to go on with the world after . . . after Lyt Ahn. Peter was like a brother, or some other close, loved relative.

They had never been together like this before. They would never be again. But it was not something to regret in its passing, for one such moment was enough for a lifetime.

TWENTY-EIGHT

HE TOOK MARIA WITH HIM TO HIS TRAINEES AT THE HEADQUARTERS building. But first he went through the channel of command, deliberately, to get permission.

He had been given no authority to approach Laa Ehon directly, therefore he went to the office of the Officer of the Day—or rather to the senior human underling of that office, the equivalent of a Chief Clerk—who told him that the OD was very busy and that Shane must compose himself for a wait of an unknown length of time. Meanwhile, what was the subject on which Shane wished to talk with the Officer? They began their conversation in Italian and Shane changed almost immediately to German as he identified the other's accent.

"... Actually," said Shane, "there's no need for me to speak personally with the Officer. You can simply relay my request to him. Tell him I need to bring in my assistant to help me demonstrate the conversational use of the Aalaag language to the trainees I'm educating in that tongue; and will he therefore honor us by issuing permission for her to be admitted with me to the building here?"

"Oh?" said the Chief Clerk, suddenly agreeable. "Perhaps after all you should speak to the Officer directly about something like that. I'll see how soon I can get you in to him."

"I hope indeed it won't be too long," said Shane wistfully. "Laa Ehon was most emphatic about my getting these trainees to speak Aalaag as soon as possible—"

"Wait just a moment," said the Chief Clerk. "I think the Officer may have just come upon a free moment unexpectedly, just now. Just a second...."

He vanished into the inner office of the Officer of the Day and returned a moment later to usher Shane in.

Standing at attention in the customary manner, Shane politely repeated to the Aalaag his request to bring in Maria. The Officer of the Day stared at him, going into a silence. Shane smiled inwardly. He had no way of knowing what the alien mind of the other was thinking; but he knew he had now presented him with a problem.

As Officer of the Day, during his hours of duty the other was a little like the captain of a flagship on board which the admiral was sailing. The admiral—in this case, Laa Ehon—might make the large decisions as to the overall use of the Headquarters building and its occupants, human and Aalaag; but the general operation of the building was the prerogative and responsibility of the Officer of the Day. Laa Ehon would have given no specific commands about allowing Shane to bring in any otherwise unauthorized human. On the other hand, the Commander would have ordered that Shane be given all facilities needed. Bringing in Maria was not clearly covered by this command; on the other hand to refer so small a matter to Laa Ehon himself would be to make the authority of the Officer of the Day himself appear petty.

It was not that the Officer feared Laa Ehon's anger if he made the wrong decision. When on duty his own right to decide was unquestionable. Rather it was what he would think of himself if he made the wrong decision.

"If it is of interest to the untarnished sir," volunteered Shane, "my assistant is, of course, like myself, a member of the Courier-Translator Corps of the First Captain. . . ."

"I see," said the Officer. "Certainly, in that case, I cannot doubt its worthiness to be admitted to this place. The permission is given. Chief Clerk, you will attend to the necessary orders of record for such admission."

"At once, untarnished sir," answered the Chief Clerk, who had been standing back a pace, deferentially. He spoke a simple and somewhat blurred, but passable Aalaag, at least as far as these common phrases went.

"You may both go."

"We obey, untarnished sir," said the Chief Clerk, and led Shane out.

So it was that Shane brought in Maria; and put her through a series of answers in Aalaag to questions which he made to her in that tongue, for the edification of his small class. The trainees listened as if their lives depended on it—as it could be they did—and Shane was left with the feeling that at least some of them were reassured that they had not been put to an impossible task of learning.

But he was most pleased by the oldest of the group, a man named Julio Ramarco, a short, grizzled man of fifty-eight whose list of known languages had shown only eleven known intimately, but over twenty known to some extent. At the bottom of the list had been an apparently reasonless note: "I also have perfect pitch."

What had impelled Ramarco to mention this apparently irrelevant musical ability, Shane did not ask. But the note had started him thinking. He himself had perfect pitch, as it happened, and so did a sizable minority among the courier-translators in Lyt Ahn's Corps. It had not seemed to give the ones having it any greatly noticeable advantage—but there might be some connection. Meanwhile, the long list of partially known tongues was evidence that Ramarco was likely to have a real interest in languages in general.

Accordingly, Shane had given some special attention to the man, and this had paid off. Ramarco was by far the surest and fastest learner in the class. Shane had named him acting Second Officer and trained him to run the rest of the class through a drill consisting of the easier phrases in Aalaag, repeated over and over in an attempt to improve their pronunciation. As a result, Shane now had a sub-teacher who could fill in for him in his absence.

Shane was now able to retire Maria from the classroom and the Headquarters building; and, in fact, it was only the day after he had done this that they received an unannounced visit by Laa Ehon.

Shane had been expecting it, but not this soon. It was the reason he had maneuvered the Chief Clerk into letting him speak directly to the Officer of the Day. While the latter had been effectively compelled to give Maria permission to enter the building, he had been almost as obligated to mention his decision to Laa Ehon—unofficially submitting the decision for his superior's judgment.

That Laa Ehon would be drawn to visit the class as a result, to see what was going on, was not so certain—but fairly sure. So it was that the door to the classroom opened one day and Laa Ehon walked in.

The class was on its feet in an instant and, like Shane, at automatic attention. It was not on them, however, that Laa Ehon's gaze settled first, but on Shane.

"I am informed you have brought an assistant into this matter," he said abruptly.

"That is correct, immaculate sir," answered Shane. "I made use of my former assistant in the Courier-Translator Corps of the First Captain, who is also my mate and of which the immaculate sir will remember we spoke on my arrival."

Laa Ehon considered him for a moment.

"Yes, I remember," he said. "I would like to see this mate-assistant of yours. Have it step forward from the rest."

"This beast regrets, immaculate sir," said Shane, "the beast to which the immaculate sir refers is not here. Having finished its most recent duty, it now sleeps in its lodging elsewhere in the city."

"Ah," said Laa Ehon. For some reason even Shane had never been able to understand, the Aalaag were extremely punctilious about not disturbing each other on their off-duty time; and this punctiliousness extended to allowing even their human cattle rest and sleep when these were due them—although nothing other than the most alert attention was tolerated when a beast was on its job. "You will bring it, then, for me to view at the first convenient opportunity."

—Which would be never, thought Shane to himself. He had been overjoyed that Maria was already gone when Laa Ehon had chosen to make this visit to the class.

"You are now, then, conducting the teaching of these cattle yourself?" Laa Ehon asked. "I would like to hear how well they have approached a workable use of the proper tongue."

"At the moment," said Shane, "I am having my second officer practice teaching the others. If the immaculate sir wishes to watch and hear it on such duty, I can give the necessary command and the demonstration will be made."

"Do so."

Shane spoke to Ramarco in Italian. Ramarco, who was already down in front of the class, turned about and began obeying. Laa Ehon listened.

"They speak as well, or perhaps a little better than, some of the cattle who have been in supervisory positions for a year or more, here at this Headquarters," he remarked, interrupting after half a dozen questions and answers had been made. He turned to the trainee standing closest to him.

"What are you called?" he demanded.

"Immaculate sir," stammered the trainee in Aalaag, "this beast is called Luciano-beast."

"Well enough," said Laa Ehon thoughtfully. "That one understood me and answered correctly, if barely understandably—"

He touched the belt around his waist and there was the momentary gray flash of a privacy tool going into operation around the Commander and Shane. The trainees could be seen staring into the space where, to their vision, Shane and Laa Ehon had suddenly disappeared.

"I would not wish to compliment you in front of these lesser cattle, Shane-beast, such being prejudicial to discipline," Laa Ehon said, "but you are doing properly and I find it interesting that you have made this much progress so quickly."

Shane had been lying awake nights trying to think of a way to lead Laa Ehon into saying something he could report to Lyt Ahn as evidence of "unhealthy" thinking. The best idea he had come up with had not been planned for a moment such as now; but it was as if the psychic entity that was the real Pilgrim of whom he had spoken took control of him. He found himself replying almost before he had time to think.

"I am honored that the immaculate sir is pleased," he said. "May I say that I am pleased with the trainees that the immaculate sir has caused to be selected for me to work with. I can see them learning much more quickly than I would have imagined. It will be only a matter of time until the immaculate sir has his own working Corps of courier-translators. I can see them moving to and fro to the lesser offices of the immaculate sir's Command; and when one of those lesser offices is faced with the problem of dealing with a beast that knows no Aalaag at all and speaks a tongue none of the local sirs' cattle can speak, I can see them becoming available to the Officers in those lesser offices—"

"Silence!" said Laa Ehon.

As Shane had expected, there was no change in the other's tone of voice; but, as Shane had also expected, the focus of Laa Ehon's eyes were drilling a single hole between Shane's eyebrows. The Milanese Commander towered over Shane, motionless, as Shane was motionless. Like predator and prey, frozen, they stood confronting each other.

Shane said nothing. Laa Ehon said nothing for a long moment.

"It is not for a beast to make plans for the use of my cattle," said Laa Ehon finally. "It is not for a beast to exceed its orders. I, myself, will make plans for these cattle. Their use is already in my mind, and you will learn of it when you are commanded to play your part in that use. Do you understand me, Shane-beast?"

"This beast understands, immac—"

"You can have no conception of what would be a proper use of such. I have told you, you are not to teach them the courier-translator tricks that you yourself learned under the eye of Lyt Ahn. As one who may become First Captain myself, if need arises, I have my own uses for cattle, my own view of the future. Do you understand this, Shane-beast?"

"This—"

"That is good, because my needs and envisioned uses vary greatly from what another's might be. Indeed—" Laa Ehon's gaze was still focused on Shane's forehead, but now he seemed to be looking through the flesh and bone at something far beyond— "what I have in mind has never been envisioned before. In fact, I will tell you this much, that those you train may find much of their time spent in my Government Units around the planet, as I radically alter the structure of relationship between Aalaag and cattle. It is true that in the last few days, the last week or so, there have been some small problems with the efficiency of these Government Units, yet the concept is too sound to be so impeded more than briefly."

He stopped speaking; and, as once before, Shane was left with the clear impression that the Commander had meant to say more, but had interrupted himself. He found Laa Ehon's eyes plainly upon him, and him only, once again.

Laa Ehon touched the privacy tool on his belt and without

warning they were visible to the room and the trainees, these gaping at their appearance. Then, as suddenly as he had appeared among them, Laa Ehon turned and walked out of the room.

"Ramarco," said Shane, staring at the door to the classroom, which, having opened itself before Laa Ehon as he exited, had now closed again behind the Aalaag, "take over the class. I may not see you until tomorrow, or not even for longer than that. But in any case, until you do see me next, you're in charge of the daily classes and the Corps."

He went out himself.

He signed out of the Headquarters building and began the walk to the apartment. It was afternoon now, and the sun was out, with only a few clouds in the sky; but the temperature had lowered and the wind had even a keener edge than it had had the morning a few days before when he had come home to find Peter and Maria on the back balcony. He was grateful for the Aalaag-designed temperature controls built into the business suit he wore, as into his pilgrim garb.

He noted the greater proportion of people in robes, however, as he went. There were even more than he had noticed yesterday, but they were still far from numerous enough for him to imagine them gathering around the Milanese Headquarters in the numbers he would need. On the other hand, there were enough of them so that it was not impossible to imagine the Aalaag taking some notice of their presence, even now. While his permission to leave Laa Ehon for the House of Weapons took precedence over every ordinary order that could hold him here in Milan, there was one situation in which it could be denied.

That would be if a state of military necessity was declared by the local Aalaag authorities—in effect, by Laa Ehon himself. It was unreasonable to suppose that Laa Ehon would declare a state of military necessity merely to stop him from leaving, considering all the extra duty complications which the order would entail for those Aalaag serving under him; but it was not completely inconceivable that the presence of so many pilgrim-dressed cattle could become a reason for declaring such a state to exist. Now that he had something to report to Lyt Ahn about Laa Ehon, Shane must get out of Laa Ehon's area of authority as soon as possible. He reached the apartment and bounded up the stairs.

"I'm leaving Laa Ehon," he told Maria abruptly, as soon as he gained the apartment. "I'm going to check out on the basis that I have to go back to the House of Weapons—I told you about that."

"Yes," said Maria. "And we leave tomorrow?"

"I leave tomorrow. You leave tonight, separately," Shane said. "I want you on a plane for someplace other than Minneapolis, so Laa Ehon can't find you and use you as a lever against me."

"Could he?"

"Could he what?"

"Use me as a lever against you."

"Of course he—" Shane broke off suddenly. He took one step to her and held her. "You know that."

"Sometimes," she said. "Sometimes I don't know anything. Sometimes I wonder."

"Well, don't wonder anymore. And please get on the phone right now. Find a flight out tonight—use the names on those fake papers Peter's Organization got us, to make the reservations both for you and me."

"Where should I go, then?"

"To . . ." Shane hesitated. "I'll tell you what. Peter went back to London when he left the day before yesterday, didn't he?"

"Yes," she said.

"Well, go to London. Stay with Peter. I'll follow tomorrow by commercial plane, too, and find you there."

"All right. We'd better hope there's a flight to London tonight with a seat available."

But there was. That night, alone in the apartment, Shane lay in the darkness on the bed, newly large with emptiness, staring at the ceiling and unable to think. It was not that his mind would not let him sleep. His mind was empty, but sleep would not come, did not come, until well after midnight.

He woke early to the alarm, dressed and went out to the Headquarters building. It was barely dawn as he entered and signed in at the desk just inside the entrance.

"Now that I'm here," he told the Interior Guardsman on duty behind the desk, "I'm going right out again. I'm signing out for an unknown number of days to make a necessary trip to the Headquarters of Lyt Ahn, the First Captain. If you check your orders, you'll find my permission to do that."

The Guardsman—a subaltern—keyed the screen set in the level top of his desk and read the message it returned to him.

"Yes, here it is," he said. "There's an additional insert from Laa Ehon ordering you to leave word of when you'll get back, if you know when that is."

"I don't," said Shane. "Note that in your record."

He signed out, and left the building again. Two hours later he, himself, was on a plane to London, traveling with a ticket in the name of William Anderson which Maria had bought for him with cash before leaving the terminal, and left for him to pick up at the British Airlines desk.

Once at Heathrow, he got through customs and immigration with a minimum of delay. He had been traveling up until now in ordinary business clothes and for a moment, seeing the large number of pilgrim-dressed people around him, he was tempted to find a private corner long enough to take his own robe from his attaché case and slip it on over his ordinary clothes.

On second thought, he decided that for the moment anonymity lay more in seeming to be apart from the Pilgrim movement. He took a cab into the city, to Peter's address, which was a house in one of those semi-circles of dwellings in parts of London that surround a small, fenced area of park. He paid off the cab, walked up to the door, suitcase in hand, and rang the bell.

Maria let him in.

"All right?" he asked—in English, in case someone else should be in the house and listening.

"All right," she answered.

He held her tightly for a moment; and during that little time, the absurd thought crossed his mind that they could avoid everything that was due to happen, simply let it pass by without ever touching them, if he just continued to stand like this and hang on to her, forever. Then common sense returned and he let her go.

"Is Peter here?" he asked.

"He'll be home in an hour or two," she said, taking him by the hand. "Come into the sitting room."

The warm comfort of the sitting room—Shane would have called it a "living room"—with its thick blue rug, its fireplace, over-stuffed armchairs and the heavy red-blue drapes at the windows, moved him deeply, suddenly, almost to tears. The still air of the place enfolded them both like a pair of comforting hands. A room like this might have been part of a home the two of them could have had together—once, in ordinary times, when things had been different.

He sat down numbly in one of the chairs flanking the fireplace. She sat down on the floor at his feet, leaning against his leg, and they both gazed into the fireplace, though there was no fire in it.

"I love you," he said, his fingertips moving over her dark hair. She looked up at him.

"And I love you, dearest," she answered in Italian.

The early winter afternoon twilight darkened as they sat there, the light coming through the windows with the heavy drapes. Coming in to land at Heathrow, Shane had seen the sun like a red ball dim enough to be looked at directly and not far above the horizon, although it had been only early afternoon. The outdoors had been colder here, too, than in Milan—clearly winter was upon this more northerly land—and the pilgrim robes were more numerous. There was also an excitement in the general atmosphere, a strong current of feeling in the crowds of people he moved through, that he had not noticed in Milan.

Now, however, the room was quite dark and they were becoming conscious of its chill. Maria knew where the makings of a fire were kept in the house and they built one in the fireplace. The flames of this, plus the lamps they turned on, drove the darkening of the day back into the corners of the room. A little over an hour later, there was a sound of a key in the front door lock and the sound of the door itself opening. Footsteps came into the hall outside the sitting room.

"Anybody here?" called Peter's voice.

"We're in the sitting room!" Maria called back. She was seated decorously in the armchair on the other side of the fireplace from the one where Shane sat. The footsteps came toward them, loud and sounding oddly multiplied on the bare, wooden floor of the hall and muffled suddenly by the blue carpeting as he entered the room.

"So you made it all right," he said to Shane, coming in. "I've brought some people to see you."

Before Shane could answer, two more people entered the room. They were Mr. Shepherd and Mr. Wong.

Shane smiled.

"I thought you two might be along," he said, watching as the three men pulled up other chairs into a rough semi-circle between his chair and Maria's.

"It's good news," said Peter, "the Organization's got a definite date for you now."

He stopped and looked at his two companions.

"You can have your crowds ready to storm the gates of the alien Headquarters five days from today," said Mr. Wong. "We began passing the word two days ago that the Pilgrim would have a message to all those who gathered at the nearest alien Headquarters in seven days from then. That leaves five days almost to the hour from this moment, in Minneapolis—if you want it. We can trigger the exact moment for you with people of our own in the crowd that'll be surrounding the Headquarters there, if you'll tell us just what exact moment you want."

"What makes you think I'm headed for Minneapolis?" Shane asked.

"Pilgrim," said the tall, upright Mr. Wong, his voice deeper than Mr. Shepherd's, "there are ways of calculating answers. Crowds have their natural boiling points. It varies from culture to culture, but it's calculable—it goes back to the moment when one tribe of savages, after jumping up and down and yelling for half an hour, would suddenly begin the attack on the enemy tribe it was facing. Also, how can the Pilgrim speak to the Aalaag as a whole, except when the Aalaag as a whole is represented by the person of Lyt Ahn, First Captain of Earth, and owner of the beast Shane Evert, who talks face-to-face with that alien from time to time?"

There was a pause in all conversation.

"I see," said Shane thoughtfully. "Five days, you say?"

"Yes," said Shepherd, "so you see we need to know things. For instance, do you want to set a time to trigger the crowd at the Minneapolis Headquarters? Or do you want to trigger it yourself? If so, how are you going to let our people in the crowd know when?"

"I'll trigger it," said Shane. "If what I'm going to do is going to have any chance at all of working, I'll have to be the one to trigger it. You don't need a signal to your people in the crowd. They'll have no doubt about the time, when the time comes."

"We'll go ahead in any case," said Wong, "but just for the information of those of us who've worked for this moment, what's your estimate of how the Aalaag will react—and the odds? Our own figures are forty percent odds that you get rid of the aliens, forty percent that they leave, but incinerate the surface of the world before they go, and twenty percent they come up with some solution that negates the crowds and you; and leaves us right where we are, their slaves—those of us that're left—but wearing heavier chains."

"I've never thought of odds," said Shane slowly. "They don't matter to the Pilgrim; and, for myself, I can't think beyond the point when I face Lyt Ahn. After that whatever happens is up to him, and the other Aalaag; and while I think I know more about them than any other human, the truth is I could live a thousand years and probably never understand them. Their minds are in some other universe than ours—guessing what they'll do is useless."

"You must have a hope of success, surely," said Shepherd.

Shane shook his head.

"I'm only going to do what I have to do," he said.

"Well, then," said Wong, "is there anything we can do to help you?"

"Not that I know of," said Shane. "Oh, come to think of it, the crowd will already be thick around the Headquarters by the time I get there. You can see that I get safely through the people there. I'm supposed to be en route to there now, and I left the Headquarters in Milan today—as you probably know. I'm going to have to report to them that I was held up somehow getting there, and hope I'm believed; but I don't want to report in until just before I see Lyt Ahn, to speak to him as the Pilgrim. Maybe you can arrange my flight by commercial airline to Minneapolis, so I arrive at just the right hour."

"We better not take chances with a commercial airline. We'll send you across as part of the crew on a cargo flight, on a plane of our own," said Mr. Wong.

"What puzzles me," Mr. Shepherd said, "is why the aliens don't seem to have noticed what's going on. Pilgrims multiplying under their noses and they don't seem to pay any attention."

"They've noticed," said Shane emptily. "They've been taking

over worlds like ours ever since they lost their own, thousands of years ago."

"But then why haven't they done anything?" demanded Peter.

"How do we know they haven't done anything? Maybe they're watching and listening to us talking here, right now. Whatever their usual procedure is in such cases, they'll have done. Maybe it is nothing. They can't imagine us doing anything to hurt them—and of course, they're right. We had our chance with our weapons and our armies when they first landed. You remember how many days that lasted. But, even if they didn't think of themselves as invulnerable, they wouldn't be moved to do anything from what they've seen so far because the Pilgrim is inconceivable to them."

"Inconceivable?" echoed Mr. Wong.

Shane nodded.

"The Pilgrim's an instinct, a reflex in us, that the Aalaag don't have. Humans are moved to go on pilgrimages to touch something invisible and untouchable that's shared with others of the race. In their case, the Aalaag don't have to go to find such a thing; they're already where it is. That's also why they don't have any religion or understand the idea of religion except as superstition or magic in the minds of underraces. What they worship is the race they already are. Even to be First Captain is relatively unimportant to Lyt Ahn. But to be an Aalaag is all-important. While, to us, to be our own individual selves is the most important thing in existence. Imagine what makes you, you—different from anyone else in the world. Don't you think that if that vanished, you'd effectively have ceased to exist? While an Aalaag'd find the yearning to be an individual ugly and repugnant, if it wasn't for the fact that they can't imagine such a thing in the first place."

Mr. Wong looked at him curiously.

"But how does all that tie in with this entity you talk of as the real Pilgrim?" he asked.

"The Pilgrim is the ability in each of us to be what makes us our unique, individual selves. The Aalaag would take that from us—without even realizing what they're robbing us of. So the idea of the Pilgrim has come up, up, up from thousands of fathoms deep in our unconscious history and prehistory, to be the symbol of the right of each of us to be what we are—not some other's idea of what we should be."

"But just that—," broke in Shepherd. "If that's all he is, this Pilgrim of yours, what makes you think he can make the Aalaag back away from us; when the best of our armies together couldn't?"

"Because the Aalaag can't face him. As long as he doesn't exist for them, they can deal with us. But once I can make Lyt Ahn see him they'll have to turn their backs on us to shut out the fact that something like him could exist—"

Shane broke off.

"I shouldn't call him 'him,' " he said. "The Pilgrim is neither male nor female. What the Pilgrim is, is spirit—a great, invisible living existence that can't be touched—by humans or by Aalaag."

He looked at the expressions on the three men's faces; and he tried to look at Maria but somehow he could not manage to turn his head.

"But he's real," Shane went on. "As real as that fireplace. I can feel him here in the room with me now. Maybe you can't, but I can." In fact the hairs were standing up on the back of Shane's neck and a chill ran down along his spine.

"I feel," he said, "that he's so close here, and so real, that if I pointed at that curtain there and told it to move, as if a wind had stirred it, it'd move."

He pointed as he spoke—but the curtain did not move. Still, he felt the presence of what he had named the Pilgrim. He looked again at the faces of the other men and laughed.

"You think I'm crazy, don't you?" he said. "At least a little crazy. But if I'm crazy, why did you come to me? Why are you working with me? Because I didn't come to you or ask you for anything. I'll tell you why you came. You came because there was some of the Pilgrim in you, as there is in every human. He brought you to me, and he moves you, as he moves me and all of us."

He stopped speaking. It was a moment when the others could have spoken, but none of them said anything. It was so still, he could hear his own breathing in his chest.

"Do you know how I see him?" Shane asked them. "I see him as a great towering shadow, thousands of feet high, standing over the House of Weapons in Minneapolis. A great shadow in the shape of someone in a robe, with cowl closed to hide both head and face and the hand that holds his staff. He's only a shadow. You can put your hand through where you see him, but he's real—maybe, in some senses, more real than we are, who only live a hundred years at most and then get replaced by someone else as vessels to hold him.''

He looked at the other men and laughed again, this time a little sadly.

''But most, I think, don't feel him the active way I do,'' he said. ''So you do think I'm crazy, don't you?''

''Not I,'' said Peter, his voice oddly thick. ''I don't think you're crazy, Shane, at all. Tell us more about him—about the Pilgrim.''

''There isn't any more,'' Shane said. ''He's just a part of every one of us, a part that means nothing until it starts to gather together out of a very large number of people.''

He paused, but as they sat still, saying nothing, he went on.

''Because he's what he is, he can't endure the kind of slavery the Aalaag want to hold us in,'' Shane said. ''That's all. One on one—or even several on one—we can enslave each other because there's part of him in the slavers as well as in the enslaved, and only the little piece in the slave fights against it. But when even a whole tribe is enslaved by another tribe, the parts of him in those enslaved gather together and grow into a being with some powers. Here, the Pilgrim is made up of all the people in the world; and he's through serving the Aalaag.''

He paused again. They still listened in silence.

''That's what I have to get Lyt Ahn to see,'' Shane said. ''If I can just make him see that . . .''

His voice died away. Even now, no one else spoke.

''Well, tell us at least this much,'' said Wong. ''What do you plan to do, once you have your pilgrim army at the gates of the alien Headquarters building and yourself face-to-face with Lyt Ahn? I think it's time we knew.''

''I plan to tell him about the Pilgrim,'' said Shane.

''But you just said he couldn't conceive of the Pilgrim.''

''No, but he can believe in the Pilgrim, without conceiving of him, if he sees that humans are ready to die for what the Pilgrim stands for—you see, that's something the Aalaag do understand. They're born, live and die, to do something for their race. The worst torture an Aalaag could conceive of . . .'' The vision of an amber block with a figure held motionless inside it came back to his mind. ''. . . would be to be forced to live forever while being held back from doing anything at all for their race. To die for their race, to die for any purpose considered good by the one who dies, makes sense to an Aalaag."

"I see," said Mr. Wong. "And so you'll prove this to Lyt Ahn—how?"

"I'll suggest that he try to remove the humans from the square in front of his Headquarters," said Shane emptily. "He'll send the Interior Guard out to do it."

He stopped speaking. The others waited.

"And then . . . ?" said Shepherd.

"What will happen will happen," said Shane. "If what I think of as the Pilgrim lives, Lyt Ahn will be convinced by what he sees. Then his choice will be to take his Expedition from Earth, or destroy Earth and then take his Expedition from it."

"And you think he won't destroy Earth before leaving?" Wong asked.

"I think there're reasons why a sane Aalaag wouldn't," answered Shane. "But that's all I know. There's nothing more I can tell you."

He took a deep breath.

"Now," he said, "you told me the point of action was five days away. That means there're at least four days before I leave here. If this house is a safe place for me to hide in that time, I'll just stay. Otherwise, you'd better find some safer place for me to wait."

"You'll be perfectly safe here," said Mr. Wong. "Also, as I said before, does it matter much now if you're recognized?"

"Only if Laa Ehon or Lyt Ahn has posted me as a deserter for not showing up in Minneapolis within twenty-four hours after I signed out of the Headquarters in Milan," said Shane. "But Lyt Ahn, I think, wouldn't do that until a lot more than twenty-four hours had gone by; Laa Ehon might, just to put the machinery to work to locate me. But—you're right. As long as I stay away from Aalaag, it doesn't matter where I go or what I do."

He turned to Maria. She was looking at him strangely.

"What about it, Maria?" he said, smiling. "How'd you like to enjoy the next four days? What would you like to do?"

"I'd like to go to some museums, some churches—to old places that have things that were part of people over the centuries before this," she said, immediately and seriously. "I want to look at things that show us what we were once. When I was in England by myself before, I was too young to want to spend my time in museums—and churches were only for Sundays and confession. But now I want to see and touch what the race was, before the Aalaag were ever dreamed of."

"All right," said Shane. He swung on Mr. Shepherd and Mr. Wong. "I suppose you can help us, with a car and English pounds, directions, if we need them?"

"Of course," said Mr. Wong gravely.

TWENTY-NINE

THEY STARTED OUT THE NEXT MORNING WITH THE DARK GREEN SEDAN that had been lent them and a pile of guidebooks and street maps. But the first place Maria insisted on going to was a flower shop, where she considered a number of small potted plants but ended up buying a cineraria, which they took back to the sitting room and she put on a small table before one of the windows.

"Now," she said, standing back to look at it, "this place is ours."

It was merely one of the vanguard of a flood of such plants, prematurely forced by greenhouses into bloom for the Christmas season that would come later; but as Shane looked at it, it did seem that its small, red-white blooms on the eight-inch plant stood out bravely in the stuffy, heavy-furnitured room and brought it all to life.

They went out again, to Westminster Abbey, the Tower of London and the British Museum, as well as to a number of other such places both in the London area and outside it. In between they ate in restaurants, went for walks and generally behaved more like two people on a honeymoon than anything else.

It was clear to him that this was what Maria had had in mind, a time-out, during which they could pretend that everything was ordinary and what was just ahead of them did not exist. The places they chose to visit and walk in were places that were largely deserted these days; and it was easy to pretend.

It was in the early afternoon of the third day, in one of the museums, that they ran across the suit of plate armor—turning a corner and encountering it so suddenly that they both stopped short, as if they had come face-to-face with all they had been trying to forget.

Indeed, at first sight it could have been an Aalaag because of its very size. But even this shrank as they recovered from the first shock and came closer. The fact that it was on a pedestal that added to its already considerable height, and shone under the tall window some feet behind and above it, had contributed to the illusion of an Aalaag in full battle gear.

It was no such thing. It was a complete suit of sixteenth-century plate armor—from somewhere in Germany, the plaque on the stand informed them—erected in a standing position with tilting helm, right-hand steel glove holding upright a short stabbing spear, butt to the ground. The spear was about the length of the Aalaag weapon, the long arm, and the strong in-pouring of early winter sunlight reflected from the metal plates with a gleam not unlike the protective, silvery shine of alien armor.

Even now that they had recognized it for what it was, the sunlight flooding over the figure lent it a radiance of its own and made a sparkling in the seams between the armor parts as if precious gems had been fastened there. For a moment, even for Shane, it took an effort to realize the figure was not alien and alive. But when he tapped its breastplate with his knuckle, now, only a drumlike sound returned. It was hollow; and the one who had worn it had been dead for centuries.

The hair on the back of Shane's neck rose and he felt the shiver within him like that he had felt when he had sensed the presence of the Pilgrim. But in this case it was caused by the thought of the person who must once have owned this metal casing. Whoever he was, he would have had dreams of what he might do, wearing it. He would have thought of things to be accomplished in it, things that could leave his mark upon history and time. Once this armor had clothed such a living being.

But now, according to the plaque, not even his name was known. And the breastplate, when Shane had tapped it, had given back only the sound of emptiness. Centuries had passed and the wearer was dust. It seemed to Shane that he could even smell that dust, now coating the inside of the armor. Nothing else remained of dreams and ambitions—of what once had been a man. He, whoever he had been, was long dead and all that remained was the smell of the dust of time.

Only, for a moment the unfeeling armor that was left had once more owned the power to terrify—though in no way the original owner could ever have imagined. It was merely that the size had been so convincing; and the sunlight, so effective upon it—and the suddenness with which they had encountered it. They stood still, looking at it with the wordlessness that had suddenly come upon them.

Even now that they knew it for what it was, only an artifact, and a human artifact at that, it could create a powerful feeling in them. Once, its owner had been as they were now.

—And even this remnant of him, like they themselves, might be nothing but ash in two days if the Aalaag should choose to destroy the world and everything on it. It was a sudden reminder of all they had been pretending did not exist; and in mutual, silent agreement, they turned and walked away from the great tower of empty armor, leaving it to the silence and equal emptiness of the gallery in which it stood.

It woke them out of the dream in which they had been successfully living for the last few, short days. They were conscious once more that there was only what was left of this day and one night and then they would be going to Minneapolis. Shane, because he must; Maria because she had insisted on accompanying him as far as she could, which would be almost to the threshold of the House of Weapons.

They finished their tour of the museum, took the car that had been provided for them and drove for several hours, out of the city far enough so that flat open fields stretched to the horizon; and above that same horizon the winter sun, going down, was the same red ball Shane had seen as his plane had landed. Then Shane turned the car and they drove back to a restaurant in the city for dinner.

But there was little appetite and almost as little speech in either of them. Shane felt simply empty, as if his soul had already left his body; and he was unable to sense how Maria must be feeling, where normally he would have been quick to touch her mood with his own.

They went back to their house. The air in it was slightly stale-smelling, and as they passed the sitting room on their way to the stairs up to their bedroom, Shane noticed that nearly all of the petals of the cineraria had fallen, and the sprig of plant, itself, looked shrunken and dying. Maria had fussed over it daily, giving it water and moving it to take advantage of the best window to give it sunlight, but there had not been enough light after all for it to survive, and the blooms were gone.

They went up to their bedroom on this last night and to bed. They would have to be up at two in the morning to get to the cargo plane that was taking them overseas, and neither could sleep. Shane lay on his back, completely empty now, even of words, watching the ceiling and letting the slow minutes march by in his mind. Sometime during this long watch, he felt Maria take his hand.

"You know," she whispered in his ear, "I believe in the Pilgrim, too. I wanted you to look at me so that you could see I did, when you were talking to Peter and the others, so that you could see I did. But you didn't look and I tried to will you to, but I couldn't."

Shane turned on his side toward her, put his arm around her and squeezed her.

"I thought you might," he said.

"I wanted you to know," she said, "that I believed. Like Peter. In the Pilgrim."

"Did you believe before you met me?"

"I think I did," she said. "But after I met you, I was sure. Then, in the sitting room there, once you told us all what he looked like, I could see him—just as you said, looming over the Aalaag Headquarters building."

"You didn't need to believe," Shane said. "He's not like Peter Pan who needed people to believe in fairies. The Pilgrim's with us whether we want him or not. As long as there's one person alive, he's there."

"And if the Aalaag kill everything on Earth, including every woman, man and child—then that ends the Pilgrim, too?"

"Except that the Aalaag would remember him," said Shane. "He'd be with them forever, then, like a ghost in their own minds."

He raised himself suddenly on an elbow, staring down into the area of shadow that was her face.

"You know," he said, "they can't afford any more ghosts. They've got too many already."

For a long second she did not answer.

"You mean the other races they've done things to?" she said.

"No. The ghosts of the things they've done to themselves. They've only got a shred of faith in themselves left, and it all depends on their keeping to their original plan of winning back their own worlds—though they never will."

She said nothing for even a longer period this time.

"How do you know they never will?" she asked.

"Because they know it. I can smell that knowing in Lyt Ahn, and some of the others; and it has to be the basis of the madness in Laa Ehon. But they've got no choice but to go on as if someday they'll walk on their own worlds again."

She sighed softly.

"And none of this helps us."

He lay down again on his back, staring at the ceiling.

"None of it," he said.

They went back into silence, lying close together.

As the small clockface on the bedside table next to Shane moved its hands within a couple of minutes of two, Shane rose, put on the light and began to dress. Maria had gotten up a moment after he did and was dressing on the other side of the bed. When her eye caught his, she smiled.

The military-looking cargo plane that was carrying them was apparently making a shipment of a large unit of some complex medical equipment; whether an actual, already arranged shipment, or one invented for the purpose of carrying Shane, he did not know and it really did not matter. He and Maria were given white overalls to wear so that they were dressed like the other four attendants who accompanied the equipment.

But they had nothing to do but sit and wait out the ride in a couple of reclining seats. Shortly after takeoff, Maria dozed off and soon was deep in slumber. Shane watched her sleep with a satisfaction he could not define. He himself had no sleepiness. He felt no desire for it, as if he would never need to sleep again.

They landed at the Minneapolis-St. Paul airport shortly after dawn of a gray, overcast November morning that promised rain, or more likely, snow. A large, dark blue, four-door sedan pulled up to the cargo hatch of the plane. Shane and Maria left their fellow passengers for the car's padded interior, grateful for its warmth after even a few moments of exposure to the wind and chill outside.

They were taken to an office building in downtown Minneapolis and an elevator carried them to its twelfth floor. From here they could look between other buildings down into the open square that had been created by the Aalaag before the House of Weapons when that Headquarters had been built. From the tall windows through which they gazed, they could see the square thronged with tiny figures in pilgrim robes and carrying staves. Above, they, themselves, were in some sort of boardroom with a long table and comfortable chairs around it. Peter was there, also, having gone on ahead of them. But, among the half-dozen other men and women in the room, none was either Mr. Wong or Mr. Shepherd.

Nor were any of them in pilgrim robes. Shane smiled a little grimly, looking at them, and he felt his hand taken by Maria. A fraction of a second later her shoulder and hip touched against him.

"It's the ones down there who count," she whispered to him.

He nodded and looked again down at the square. More of the robes of those there, made tiny by distance, were of gray—almost the gray of the concrete underfoot—than anything else. But every other color was also represented, mixed among the gray. They would be homemade, a good share of those robes.

At first distantly, then coming on him with a rush, he felt an identification with those at whom he looked. Once more he felt the presence of the Pilgrim. The hair rose on the back of his neck and head, and a chill shuddered through him. He knew that now, if he looked up from the square, he would see—or believe he saw— the shadow of the Pilgrim towering over the House of Weapons.

Someone moved up to stand beside him on the other side from Maria.

"Do you see him?" asked the voice of Peter.

"No," said Shane, still keeping his gaze fixed on the square.

"Neither can anyone else, here," said Peter savagely. "But he's there. I want you to hear something, Shane. Turn around, would you, for a moment? Sender! Milt Sender, would you step over here for a moment?"

Shane turned back into the room, Maria letting go of his arm necessarily as he did so, but staying close enough to touch him. A small, lean man in his fifties with a sharp face and hair that was black, straight and thinning over a round skull, came up to them. His voice was surprisingly sharp and penetrating.

"What is it? I'm very pleased to meet you, Mr. Evert and Miss— Casana, is it?"

"Yes," murmured Maria.

"Shane, Milt Sender is one of our crowd psychologists. Milt," said Peter, "tell Shane what you told me—about the simultaneity of the gatherings."

"Yes," said Sender, turning his gaze and his incisive voice on Shane, "it's curious, but there seems to be some sort of unconscious consensus at work around the world. That crowd down in front of the alien Headquarters is close to the boiling point. But all around the planet, wherever there's another alien Headquarters—day or night, it seems to make no difference—there's a very equal crowd at just about the same emotional point. As I say, it's interesting. As I say, it's most interesting. Almost as if they were hooked together by some sort of telepathy."

Shane said nothing.

"It's the Pilgrim," said Peter, the savagery still in his voice but that emotion now mixed with satisfaction.

Sender shrugged.

"For God's sake, tell him, Shane!" said Peter. "Make him understand!"

"That isn't my job," said Shane. "If he doesn't react, he doesn't."

"It's not my job to react," said Sender, "it's my job to observe—and draw conclusions."

"Then you're a fool," said Peter, swinging away from the smaller man. "Shane, when do you want to be escorted to the Headquarters?"

"Any time now," said Shane. "If you don't mind, is there another room here where I can talk to Maria privately for a moment, before I go?"

"Certainly," said Peter. "Come with me."

Shane and Maria followed him out of the room they were in and through the next door down on the same side of the hall outside. They stepped into the deep brown-gold carpeted private office of someone evidently earning a very large salary. In front of the window wall there was a high-backed leather armchair and a desk, looking into the room, but everything else there was expensively furnished more in the style of someone's idea of a comfortable den or library.

"Pick up the phone and push the red button on the phone stand when you're ready to go," Peter told Shane, and left them.

As the door closed behind him, Shane turned and reached out. She came into his arms; and they held tight together, without a word.

"Go with Peter," he told her, after a bit. "Stay with him. That way, I'll be able to find you."

"—When you come back," she said.

"—When I come back," he repeated.

The words went away from them and were lost against the laden bookshelves of the room.

"Whither thou goest I will go," she said.

He smiled sadly. "I'm supposed to say that."

"No," she said, "it's the woman—it's Ruth who says it in the Bible."

"But I'll be coming to look for you, not the other way around."

She gazed unvaryingly at him.

"Whither thou goest," she repeated, "I will go. Oh, Shane!"

She held him fiercely to her and they simply stood there, wrapped up in each other for a long while, saying nothing because there was nothing to say that would make any difference. Finally, he pulled away from her, having to use real strength to break the clasp of her arms.

"I'll have to go," he said.

"Yes." She let her arms drop to her sides. They did not bother with the phone, but went out of the room and back into the one from which Peter had taken them a little earlier.

"Everybody's ready," he said. "We'll take you right to the first line of Interior Guards, Shane, then it's up to you. You'll both find robes on the chairs behind you, there. You'd better get into them now—we've got one you can unzip and get out of in a hurry, Shane, when you get to the line of Guards. That is, if you need or want to."

"I will," said Shane.

He and Maria turned, found the robes and put them on. Shane's robe fastened down the front with long strips of Velcro, rather than the zipper Peter had seemed to have in mind. Shane was grateful. It would be even more certain to get out of quickly than one with a mechanical closure that might jam at the crucial moment; as easy to get out of as a bathrobe.

Their robes were gray and so was the robe Peter now put on. When they reached the street-level lobby, they saw that the six men waiting for them there wore robes of the same shade.

The first breath of outside air chilled Shane's lungs as they stepped through the glass doors of the building and onto the sidewalk. Street traffic was almost nonexistent, but the sidewalks and to a certain extent the street itself was full of a quiet river of people dressed as pilgrims with staves, and headed in the direction of the square. From them, as they passed, Shane sensed the excitement he had noticed on landing last in London, compounded by a tinge of the savagery he had felt in Peter upstairs. He felt it, and he felt the presence of the Pilgrim once more.

They were bundled into a personalized van that was equipped with carpeting and soft seats for them all. The van pulled from the curb and nosed its way among the pedestrians toward the Headquarters, until the thickness of the crowd made further traffic by vehicle impractical.

"Right," said one of the six men, sitting up front next to the driver. "We get out here then."

They left the van and joined the crowd. The robe Shane wore did not have the advantage of alien technology, and he felt the cold through it. The sky was dark and heavy with a low-hanging cloud bank solid overhead that threatened snow, and the wind blew icily in their faces. It occurred to Shane that Maria, beside him, would also be feeling the cold, and he put his arm around her as they went.

They were in the square by this time, enclosed by the pilgrim-figures already there. As they went forward the crowd became thicker, until their escorts had to ask to be let through.

"We've got one of our leaders here, to talk to the officer in charge of the Guards," they said. "Let him through, please, let him through. . . ."

They got through. Under the force of the bodies crowding in
on them, Maria was pressed ever closer to Shane until it seemed
they had become one person moving with a single will and mind.
They were very close to the line of black-uniformed Guards and
the silver-coated wall before them, unbroken now, for the protective shield had flowed down even over the entrance. The guards
were in a depth of three lines, each of which stretched the full
width of the building. They each held the latest thing in a machine
pistol that human technology had devised before the Aalaag came.
Each weapon was fed directly from a bandoleer around the large
shoulder and chest of each Guardsman, a bandoleer holding nearly
two thousand rounds of bullets, small and light, without much penetrating power but so poisoned that to have the skin broken anywhere on the body by one of these missiles meant certain and
almost instant death. Word of the weapons had been advertised to
all humans by the Aalaag when the Interior Guard was formed.

Behind the three lines and at the top of the steps leading to
the entrance to the Headquarters, now invisible under the silvery
screen extended to cover it, stood their human officers in a clump,
talking.

The six escorts, with Shane, Maria and Peter in their midst,
had pushed their way through the crowd until their leading two
men were face-to-face with the first line of Guardsmen. They could
take Shane no farther. He turned to Maria and put his arms around
her for a last time.

She held to him, even when, at last, he tried to pull away.

"Maria," he whispered to her. "I have to go. I have to!"

"I'm trying to let you go!" she whispered back. "I just don't
want to—I can't—"

Suddenly she wrenched her arms from around him and backed
away the few inches their escort had won for them from the crowd.

"Go now," she said. "No, don't touch me again. Go!"

He could not bear the look in her eyes. He felt a hand clasp
his shoulder briefly. "See you on the other side," said Peter's voice
in his ear.

He turned from that voice and Maria's eyes toward the Guardsmen and pushed his way half a step forward as one of the escorts
in front of him slipped back into the spot Shane had occupied a
second before.

"Get back there!" said the Guardsman with whom he stood now face-to-face.

Shane ignored him. Instead of answering the man, he raised his voice and shouted, in Aalaag, toward the knot of officers.

"*Officer-beasts! Attention! Come!*"

He had deliberately chosen Aalaag commands that even an ordinary Guardsman was likely to have heard at some time or other from one of the aliens; and any officer would of course understand them. The heads of the men talking came up and around. They stared at the crowd and one who wore the collar tabs of a colonel pushed past the rest to look out at the crowd.

"Who was that who yelled at us, just now?" the colonel shouted back in English. "Identify yourself!"

Shane waved a hand over his head; and a slow, swelling, angry mutter began in the ranks of the pilgrims behind and around him.

"I am a courier-translator for the First Captain!" he shouted back, still in Aalaag—and dodged past the Guardsman before him, who now made no effort to stop him. "I must get to the First Captain!"

Of these last Aalaag words the only ones he could be sure the officers would understand were the terms "courier-translator" and "First Captain," but these should suffice. And they did.

"Let him through!" shouted the colonel, as Shane slipped forward between the other two lines of Guardsmen and the mutter behind him rose to a roar.

Shane reached the knot of officers and ripped open his robe along the Velcro-sealed parting to show the white oversuit he sometimes wore when on formal duty inside the House of Weapons.

"I'm to see Lyt Ahn as soon as possible," he gasped.

"Call in," said the colonel to a lieutenant at his elbow. But the junior officer already had his wrist communicator to his lips; and was speaking into it. A moment later the lieutenant nodded.

"He can go in," the lieutenant reported to the colonel.

In the same moment the silver curtain vanished from before the doors to the House of Weapons. Shane went forward and the doors opened before him. He stepped into the interior of the building in which he had been based for three years.

He glanced back over his shoulder and the doors had closed behind him. Suddenly all the outside noise was gone. Out there, the shining protective curtain would once more be hiding them from the sight of Peter, Maria, and the rest of those in the crowded square. He turned right and went toward the wing of the structure holding the offices and living quarters of Lyt Ahn.

THIRTY

A FEW STEPS DOWN THE CORRIDOR, HE CAME TO A DIFFERENCE FROM his last visit. It was a desk with an Interior Guardsman and a sign-in "book." The book was simply a screen inset in the desktop, which—touched by Shane's finger—identified him.

Shane nodded to the Guardsman, who nodded back without saying anything further. He was one of the tallest of the humans drafted into that Corps—Shane guessed that, standing, he would be at least seven feet tall. A right leg stiffly extended in a white cast explained why he was at this desk job when his fellows were at arms. But the smallness of his head and the roundness of his face gave a youthful, innocent look to features that to Shane looked a little pale, and certainly somber.

The corridors Shane passed through on his way to Lyt Ahn's offices were empty. This was not surprising. Under the present conditions the Aalaag in the House of Weapons would all be either on duty or standing by, ready to go on. As for all the human servants, they would be taking every opportunity to keep out of the sight of their masters; in case one of the aliens should be angry because of the disturbance outside and in a mood to take it out on any human that he or she came across.

The walls about him as he went seemed to enclose him in silence and solidity, shutting out all that was happening beyond them. Here was the separateness of the Aalaag. Inside this Headquarters, the rioting of the subject race on a whole planet was nothing but a summer storm that, in a few minutes on the temporal scale within, would blow itself out and be gone.

Little by little, the familiar effect of the place began to take control of him. In his own mind once more he shrank in size, became fragile and less than those who called themselves his owners. He no longer felt the presence of the Pilgrim looming above the House of Weapons, only that little part of the Pilgrim that he carried within him and of which he was now conscious. He turned a corner and came unexpectedly upon a small group of young Aalaag officers, not in armor, but wearing the archaic harness over their ordinary working clothes that would support the armor's weight if they were required to put it on in a hurry. They were clustered together watching a large wall screen that showed the three lines of Interior Guard outside and the crowd beyond, from a viewpoint that seemed to be the equivalent of a couple of stories up, in the center of the front wall of the building. As far as Shane could read the tiny signals that marked Aalaag emotion, they radiated a pleased excitement like that of a group of humans watching a sporting event.

Their attention was all on the screen; he had every expectation of slipping past behind their backs, unnoticed, but he had barely gotten half a dozen steps past them when a bass voice hailed him.

"Beast! You there! Come here."

He turned and went back to the group.

"Did one of the untarnished sirs call me?" he asked.

"I called you." An unusually tall young officer looked curiously down at him from a position right before the screen. "You are Shane-beast, are you not? Of the Courier-Translator Corps?"

Shane felt a faint touch of surprise and chagrin. It was just his luck to run into one of the rare officers who paid attention to the individual appearances of humans.

"This beast is indeed Shane-beast," answered Shane. "In what manner can I be of service to the untarnished sir?"

"You can settle a question among us, Shane-beast," said the officer. He lifted a thumb to indicate the screen. "Tell us, do those cattle out there consider the rods in their hands to be weapons? Or not?"

"Untarnished sir and sirs," said Shane, "that is a question to which it is difficult to give a precise answer even under ordinary conditions, and this moment is not ordinary. The body coverings and the rods you mention are the traditional accoutrements of some individual beasts in our past history who traveled on journeys to places considered by us places of great magic; and virtue was thought to be gained by these travelers in going to these places. The body coverings were their only protection against weather; the rod was to assist them in traversing difficult country, but could also be used as a weapon against any other beast or lesser species that should impede their progress or threaten them. In this case, the rods are carried mainly as possible weapons."

"You hear the beast, Neath Mhon?" demanded the tall young officer, swinging about to face the Aalaag next to him. "I said they were weapons and possibly to be used as such."

"Those who carry them must be unwell, then," retorted the other. "Our own Guard-beasts can kill them all before any such simple weapons could be brought to play against them. Consider, they must reach the Guards before they can use the rods, and there is no hope of even one of them doing so."

"Shane-beast," said the tall young officer. "Are they unwell?"

"Not as we beasts consider unwellness, untarnished sir," answered Shane.

"Then do they consider there to be some magic—" there was no Aalaag word for religion and their word for magic was always pronounced, as now, with disdain, as something pertaining only to primitive species—"in these rods that would make them effective even against the weapons of the Guard-beasts?"

This was a most unusually discerning and inquisitive Aalaag, thought Shane.

"Untarnished sir," he said, "that is a question to which I have no clear answer. I can only say what I believe; and I believe them to consider that the rods are not magic in any way."

"Then they have to be unwell," said the other Aalaag. "It must be that they have a belief in magic or are unwell, one answer or another."

Shane said nothing.

"Well, beast?" demanded the Aalaag who had just spoken. "Answer me!"

"Forgive this beast, but it does not know how to answer the untarnished sir," said Shane. "I have answered to the limit of my ability to do so."

"Oh, leave the beast alone, Neath Mhon!" said the tall young officer. "It's given us what it can. Let it go about its duties—you are indeed on duty, are you not, Shane-beast?"

"Indeed, untarnished sir," said Shane. "I am on my way to report to the First Captain."

"Go then."

"Go."

"Go."

"Go." Several voices spoke hastily and simultaneously.

"I thank the untarnished sirs," said Shane.

He turned and continued on along the corridor, encountering a few other solitary Aalaag, apparently moving between offices, but still no humans. Eventually he reached the familiar doors to Lyt Ahn's offices, and touched the panel of one door.

"Come," replied an Aalaag voice that was not Lyt Ahn's; and the door opened before him. He stepped into the office and found the room empty of aliens except for the aide seated at the desk, smaller than that of Lyt Ahn, which sat just inside the doors.

"Your purpose?" demanded this Aalaag.

"Untarnished sir, I am Shane-beast of the Courier-Translator Corps, presently on loan to the immaculate sir Laa Ehon. I am returning from Milan as I was commanded by the First Captain, to speak to him."

The aide considered him.

"It is a busy time," he said. "You will wait in that corner there. You may sit or lie on the floor, if you desire."

"This beast thanks the untarnished sir."

The aide returned to his work. Shane went to the empty corner of the room behind the aide's desk and from familiarity that had bred the action into a habit, seated himself cross-legged on the floor with his back against the joining of the two walls.

He began his wait. From those Aalaag who came in to speak to the aide on business of one kind or another, he gradually pieced together a picture of what was happening within the House of Weapons and its counterparts all over the world.

Apparently, all the Headquarters belonging to the Aalaag had closed up and put out Interior Guards to deal with any problems from the pilgrim-dressed crowds around each stronghold. Aalaag in every area had also been put under orders to return to their Headquarters building, and all but a handful had already done so. The Commanders of the various areas—including, Shane guessed,

Laa Ehon—were presently gathered at the House of Weapons for a military council, over which Lyt Ahn was presiding at the moment.

The hours slid by. Checking his watch, Shane saw that it was almost three o'clock in the afternoon. Twice already, he had had to ask the aide for permission to go to the nearest human latrine. His western-educated legs had cramped several times in the cross-legged seated position and he had been forced to uncramp them by stretching out, dog-fashion, on the floor on his side.

Years in the Aalaag service had dissolved any self-consciousness he had originally felt about curling up like a dog on the floor of some room where he was waiting to speak to one of the aliens. But after some hours it occurred to him that this one time he did not want Lyt Ahn to return and find him lying down. He therefore seated himself once more, making himself as comfortable as he could in the cross-legged position and set himself to wait until his interview with the First Captain would be possible.

After a while he ceased to pay more than passing attention to the visitors coming into the office and to what he could overhear the aide saying, in his occasional response to messages from his desk-communications equipment. As on previous occasions when he had been forced to endure such endless waits, his mind withdrew from his body. He was no longer conscious of the hard floor under him, of the once again commencing cramp in his legs, or even of passage of time itself.

But, unlike previous occasions when his mind had simply withdrawn, putting him in what was something like a wide-awake doze with eyes fully open but no continuous thought process, this time his mind wandered.

Old memories came back to him, moments of large importance and small. He remembered being told he could not climb into his aunt's lap. This, which must have happened when he was still very small, he had remembered doing with his mother when she had been alive and well. After his mother's death his aunt had endured his climbing during the first few days, but the time had come when she had pushed him off.

"You're a big boy, now," she had told him. "You don't need people to hold you."

But, his soul had cried in that instant, he was not a big boy yet, still far off from being old enough for kindergarten, and he deeply felt the need of someone to run to, someone to hold him.

Other memories returned, of various scenes from his school and high school days when he was left to stand apart, shut out by his older classmates from whatever they were doing at the time. Sharply and strongly, he remembered the moment in which he had scratched the first outline of the Pilgrim on the brick wall holding the body of the man dead on the hooks in Aalborg.

He remembered seeing Maria for the first time in the wall screen of Laa Ehon's office. He remembered walking past the Aalaag sentinel on his riding beast, outside the Houses of Parliament, after he had marked the Pilgrim symbol on the face of Big Ben. He remembered the nights and days with Maria since—having her with him had changed him profoundly. He had never realized how profound that change until now.

Once, he would have laughed at the idea that he could consider dying to protect or defend anyone else. It was the limits of utter foolishness to think, seriously, that he might put his own life at stake between anyone else and death, or anyone else and serious harm.

Now, he knew better. His appreciation of what that death meant had grown no less. It loomed no less terribly in his thinking; but he knew now that he would go to it in Maria's place—that, in effect, he had made a decision to do just that, though he had not thought of it in those terms, on that first time he had seen her, and gone out into the city of Milan to create an excuse for her not being a beast that the Aalaag would wish to destroy.

Now, the idea of her death had become unthinkable to him. The suffering and death of others he had come to know, like Peter, and like Johann in the Milanese Resistance, had become things he would prevent at any cost to himself. At last, it had developed that the suffering of the race he belonged to was a thing he would not allow at any cost anymore.

It was strange. He felt no braver, though for Maria's sake, of course, he had pretended that there was a chance that not only could he bring the Aalaag to leave Earth, but that after doing so he could leave the House of Weapons, untouched.

But this last, he knew, and had always known, was the one most certainly false of all hopes. The question would not be why Lyt Ahn should destroy him, even if the First Captain could be brought, with his fellow Aalaag, to depart. The question would be what possible reason there could be for Lyt Ahn not to destroy a beast who was not only the leader of cattle who had chosen to revolt, but one who had individually betrayed Lyt Ahn's trust by being disloyal and an enemy even while taking advantage of that trust.

The strange thing was that his certainty of his own end made no difference. It was a lion in the doorway, but it was only the lion he had expected to come through that door, sooner or later. Meanwhile he had found someone to love, someone who loved him. And he had done something. Right or wrong he had not just let his life trickle away into nothingness. All humans in the end wanted their moment of living to have some use; and he had. He had *done*. The desire to do so was a feeling upon which even humans and Aalaag could have agreed, if the Aalaag had come to Earth otherwise than as overbearing conquerors.

He had *done* something and what might follow was of secondary importance. His mind did not so much refuse, as fail to picture, what would follow once he had spoken to Lyt Ahn. It was as if a room existed in his imagination, but it was a room which had been filled with concrete. There was no way of entering it, even if he had wanted to.

He thought of the short time he and Maria had had each other. The days and nights came back to him like immensely precious possessions to be counted over once again. He remembered their last few days in London. He remembered stopping in the doorway to the little balcony at the back of their apartment in Milan and watching her with Peter, their two heads close together, both the hands of both of them clasped together in something like a promise or a prayer.

It came to him then, without pain, what he should probably have guessed long since; which was that she and Peter had, at least once upon a time, loved each other. Possibly they still did; and the clasping of their hands he had seen was evidence of it. Shane could not doubt that all these last few months it had been he, himself, she had truly loved. They had been too close for any pretense to hold up.

But perhaps for her there had once been Peter instead—possibly that had even been the reason Peter had been in Milan at the time Shane had been caught and questioned by Georges Marrotta's group.

But there was nothing impossible about her being still in love with Peter, in spite of her feeling for Shane.

Shane felt a sudden sense of great relief, recognizing this at last. In the end, Maria and Peter would have each other—and if Shane was successful, they would be together in a world that was for humans alone. If the Aalaag should leave the world and leave it unharmed, Maria and Peter could live normally, marry and have children, as people had in the past and might again. If the Aalaag should destroy the world on leaving, of course . . . But if neither thing happened, and the Aalaag defeated the Pilgrim and surmounted all the reaction of a human race that was now against them, even then Peter and Maria under other names could hide among the millions of beasts populating this world and in some degree have a life together still. And Shane would in some measure have bought that future for them.

It was a relief to think they would be safely away from this place by now. The Organization people would not stay around a Headquarters that might suddenly open up its alien weapons and scorch the Earth to the horizon in all directions; and Peter would have seen that Maria and he were part of whatever evacuation the Organization had planned for its own people.

A long, long time had gone by since he had first been told to wait in a corner of the office. Hours upon hours had passed since he had even looked at his watch. Just how long, he could not say. But a different Aalaag was on duty as Lyt Ahn's aide now; and more than a few hours had passed since that changeover. He had no particular desire to look at his watch again. The time was immaterial. It would be early morning by now, at least. Possibly, it was even daybreak outside.

He thought with compassion of those who had taken their turn at standing in the cold before the House of Weapons. For himself, the discomfort of his position had been forgotten a long time ago. Even the visits to the latrine had all but ceased. Lyt Ahn's office and everything in it had become irrelevant to him. His consciousness lived in his thoughts and those thoughts were of happy moments with Maria.

Strangely, he found himself free of all self-comforting illusions;

and because he was free, happier, not sadder. Out of the same realization that Maria must have carried with her a love for Peter all this time, there came to him the further understanding that she had not at all been deceived about the fact that, whatever larger things might result, once he had come back here to the House of Weapons, he would almost surely not be leaving it again. So she had given him the courage and the reason to go, by pretending to believe his pretense that, while there was danger, his chances of escaping were good. Meanwhile, she had also given him everything else she had, to make what little real lifetime was permitted to him worth living.

She had made him happy. It was a remarkable thing. He found himself wondering if all those in the past who had been aware they were about to die, those still with the health of life in them but knowing they were condemned, had ended by feeling as he did, a resignation and sense of accomplishment. Above all, a feeling of peace . . .

The door opened and Lyt Ahn strode into the office.

"I will rest now," he told the aide at the desk. "The Council meeting is over and the Commanders are also going to rest in quarters already assigned to them. Call me if necessary, of course. There is nothing unusual, nothing important, that I should deal with before resting?"

"No, immaculate sir," said the aide. "Nothing—unless you had some urgency in your desire to see the courier-translator that has just arrived from Milan to report to you?"

"Courier—" Lyt Ahn broke off, his gaze traveling past the aide into the corner where Shane sat, once more thoroughly awake, thoroughly aware and in the present, but motionless and silent. "I did not see it there behind you. Shane-beast?"

"Immaculate sir—" Shane tried to get to his feet, but his legs had long since gone to sleep. The two Aalaag watched in noncommittal silence as he pulled himself upright with a palm of each hand on each of the adjoining walls. "Immaculate sir, this beast is reporting as ordered."

"Come," said Lyt Ahn.

He turned on his heel and walked farther into the office to seat himself at his desk. Shane tottered after him, unsteadily, toward the far side of that desk; and Lyt Ahn, as if suddenly recollecting something, turned to look at his aide.

"Cjhor Elon," he said, "I will receive the report of this beast in particular privacy."

"Of course, immaculate sir," said the aide, getting to his feet behind his desk. "Shall I prevent all interruptions?"

"Yes. Subject to your own good judgment."

"I am complimented, immaculate sir."

The aide went out.

Lyt Ahn stood up behind his desk and walked across the room to stand before the large screen where Shane had once seen displayed the image of Lyt Ahn's son, as imagined by the mother, in the hands of those who had taken over the original worlds of the Aalaag.

Once more, without visible signal from Lyt Ahn, the screen came to life. But now it looked down from the building like the screen in the hallway Shane had passed hours earlier—the screen with the small group of Aalaag officers watching it—and showed the square below with its crowd and its lines of armed Interior Guardsmen.

"Come over here," said Lyt Ahn.

Shane walked clumsily over to stand at the left of the Aalaag before the image at which the other was looking. The effect was eerie. This particular screen went from near the top of the wall all the way to the floor at their feet, and was three-dimensionally perfect in its reproduction of the scene outside. To Shane it was as if they stood one long stride from the floor's unguarded edge, some five meters above the heads of the last rank of Interior Guards, looking down at them and out at the crowd in the square. The whole scene was brilliantly illuminated by artificial lighting that seemed to come from nowhere, but left the farther buildings surrounding the square in darkness. Bright as it was, that light did not intensify the darkness of the night overhead. Looking up, Shane could clearly see the stars of a cloudless, cold and windy night. No moon was visible. He glanced at his watch finally, and saw with a shock that it was nearly five o'clock in the morning.

Lyt Ahn glanced briefly at Shane.

"It is very interesting to see such a beast as you again," said Lyt Ahn gently. "Your breed of cattle has been requiring extra attention from us lately, attention we should not have to give them at this stage of an Expedition. Do you recognize any of your own kind as those you know, in the square down there?"

Shane stared out at the sea of cowls and glimpses of faces without really focusing on any of them.

"I do not know any of these beasts, immaculate sir," he said, "and they would not know such as a Shane-beast."

"That is reasonable," said Lyt Ahn. Again he glanced briefly down at Shane. "And I did not mean to imply that you were as those outside are. In any case, we have other things to talk about. You have been with Laa Ehon since I saw you last."

"This beast has," said Shane.

"Then I wish you to answer questions which I shall put you. Do not volunteer any information beyond that for which I ask. Do you understand?"

"This beast understands."

"Good." Lyt Ahn went into one of the Aalaag silences for perhaps twenty seconds. "Little Shane-beast, you have been allowed to come closer to the machinery of Aalaag decisions than any beast is ordinarily allowed to come. To properly answer the questions I am about to ask you, therefore, you had perhaps better be allowed further into an understanding—as far as your small mind can understand, of course—of what is at stake in that which I ask and the replies you make to them."

He paused—this time briefly.

"Do you understand?" he asked.

"This beast believes it understands the First Captain. The immaculate sir wishes me to be both fully truthful, but impersonal, in my answers about the immaculate sir Laa Ehon; this for weighty reasons which may well be beyond the understanding of this beast."

"Indeed," said Lyt Ahn. "Therefore you must comprehend how all-important it has always been, is, and always will be—our need to work toward our return to retake the home worlds that were stolen from us. It is something that concerns all Aalaag during every minute of the life of each. Those who, because of some weakness or perversion, fail to be so concerned, threaten the great purpose itself. These, we call unwell. You have perhaps heard the word used loosely, used even where your own kind is concerned where one of them has deviated from what it ought to be and do. But, strictly speaking, a beast cannot be well or unwell, since it has no part in the great purpose that rules the Aalaag and which we—all of us who are Aalaag and well—obey without question, without thought."

"This beast believes it approaches understanding of what the First Captain has just said."

"Good. I ask you, then," said Lyt Ahn, still watching the Interior Guards, warm in their Aalaag temperature-controlling clothing, and the steady, uneasy movement of the robed crowd in the square as it moved and shifted under the cold that would be penetrating even through the heavy clothing which most, if not all, would have on under their robes. "I ask you if the sir Laa Ehon has ever in your presence spoken of the Great Purpose?"

"Immaculate sir, he has not," said Shane.

"Has he ever spoken to you in any manner or of anything which you might assume to be contrary to the Great Purpose?"

"He has not, immaculate sir."

"Have you seen him behaving in any manner, or have you heard or overheard from his staff or beasts of behavior of his that seems contrary to the Great Purpose?"

Shane hesitated.

"I am awaiting for an answer, Shane-beast."

"Immaculate sir," said Shane, "I am not sure what kind of behavior would be considered contrary to the Great Purpose."

"Tell me of whatever you think might be so; and I will decide."

"Immaculate sir, Laa Ehon wished to set up his own Corps of courier-translators and his wish in borrowing me was that I should teach them."

"You are right," said Lyt Ahn, "that is idiosyncratic, but not itself in any way a failure toward the Great Purpose. Do you have any other instances about which you were doubtful?"

"But immaculate sir, the sir Laa Ehon did not wish me just to train the beasts he had found to be courier-translators as I and those of my Corps in your House are courier-translators."

"In what way, then, did he wish you to train them?"

"To be primarily of use, the sir said, in his new Government Centers."

Lyt Ahn's gaze tightened on Shane's forehead.

"When did he speak of this?"

"He spoke to me of it just over a week ago."

"A week ago," said Lyt Ahn thoughtfully. "For some few weeks now, the Government Centers he originally suggested and has for some time been setting up have been producing not more, but less, in the areas to which they apply. Yet you say that only eight days ago, he was speaking of creating a Corps of courier-translators for use with them. Did he say what these new courier-translators were to do at the Government Centers?"

"He did not, immaculate sir, except to say that he might be First Captain himself, one day."

"And so he might," answered Lyt Ahn. The focus of his eyes narrowed still further. "But I told you not to volunteer information."

"This beast apologizes for forgetting that command," said Shane. "But—"

"There are no exceptions. An officer is not to have his reputation tarnished by the suppositions of a beast. I find nothing in what you have answered that justifies any doubt of the sir Laa Ehon's wellness. We will cease talk of that officer."

"This beast's apologies, immaculate sir," said Shane. He felt the urge to speak like a great hand at his back, pushing him forward, a hand that could not be resisted. "I understand that I am forbidden to volunteer information to the First Captain; but I feel a duty to say that I consider Laa Ehon unwell."

"Your opinion does not exist in this matter," said Lyt Ahn. His gaze was terrible. "Except as I request it; and I have not."

"The duty then passes from this beast," said Shane, "to his master."

Even as he said the words, he knew what reaction he invited by what amounted to an accusation that Lyt Ahn was, because of considerations of his own honor, leaning over backward to find Laa Ehon well. But he also knew that, once he had said it, not only he but Lyt Ahn were left with the unavoidable fact that it had been said.

Lyt Ahn stood silent, gazing out at the scene shown before him for what was perhaps a minute and seemed to Shane an eternity.

"Tell me, then, why you consider the sir Laa Ehon less than well," said Lyt Ahn at last, turning his gaze directly back to Shane.

"Because he spoke of causing changes in the established relationship between beast and Aalaag.''

There was another long silence on the part of the First Captain. Then he looked back at the screen.

"You are a beast of very unusual courage," he said at last, slowly. "I absolve you of impudence and of going against my orders. I will ask you a question. Laa Ehon spoke of these changes. To whom?''

"To me, immaculate sir," said Shane. "I had been presumptuous enough to speak of how his Corps of courier-translators could be put to use, once I had trained them. He stopped me and said that it was not for such as myself to plan their use, that he had plans of his own. He then mentioned what I have just said.''

"You may go," said Lyt Ahn.

Shane turned and walked back into the room while Lyt Ahn continued to stand, his eyes on the view shown in the screen. Halfway to the door, Shane's steps slowed and halted. He took a deep breath, and suddenly everything he must do lay clear and plain before him. He had hoped for something to show him the way, but he had never expected the certainty that took him now. He turned and stood, facing the back of Lyt Ahn.

Several seconds went by. Then, slowly, Lyt Ahn turned and regarded him.

"You have not gone," he said, and there was the hint of a note that could have been sadness in his voice.

Shane knew where the sadness would have come from. A single defiance of the strict orders of its master might be admirable in a beast if it turned out that defiance had been caused by the beast's wish to best serve its master. Two defiances in a row could only mean that Shane himself was unwell—and that anything he had said until now must be disregarded, and he, himself, destroyed.

"Shane-beast has gone," said Shane. "Now I am here. It is only the body of Shane-beast that you see before you; a body which I, who am the *Pilgrim*—" he used the English word, for there was no such word in Aalaag—"am using to speak to you.''

THIRTY-ONE

LYT AHN'S GAZE BECAME VERY STILL. FOR SHANE HAD CEASED TO USE the third person submissive form of address in which all beasts should address their masters or mistresses. He was speaking to the First Captain in the direct, formal mode of equal to equal, as one Aalaag to another; a mode which beasts were not even supposed to know, but which most of the translators in the Corps had picked up by ear, long since.

"I am here and I am not here," said Shane. "For I am not simply a Shane-beast who is unwell. I am an entity without form or body, but with no lack of power for that reason. I am here, though untouchable, in your private office. I am also in the square outside, in each of those *humans*"—again he was forced to use the native word, the utterance of which in any human language, the Aalaag ignored in their presence—"there. I am in all who properly belong to this world; and I speak directly to you, as the individual who speaks for those who have come without invitation among us. You may destroy this body at any time you wish; but to do so will only result in your not hearing what I have to say. And for the best purpose of you and your people you should hear that."

He waited out the silence from Lyt Ahn.

"What is this supposed to be?" said Lyt Ahn. "One of the many different magics in which you beasts so superstitiously believe?"

"There is no magic here. Nor are there any beasts, anymore. Of all people—" Shane began to walk slowly forward until he once more stood where he had stood at Lyt Ahn's side, looking down at the square. He turned to face the other, who had turned as well, to look down at him. "—the Aalaag should understand that each individual of any people carries within him or her a portion of what belongs to that people as a whole. There is no Aalaag who lacks such a portion; and likewise there is no *human* without it."

Lyt Ahn tilted a thumb toward the crowd outside.

"We do not call those a people, but beasts and cattle," he said. "And we would not use that word you use to describe them, even if it were pronounceable."

"Such refusals," said Shane, "mean nothing and change nothing. I have pointed out to you that the Aalaag have a thing in common and that the *humans* have a similar thing in common. That is all I am. Not the *human* thing itself, but one of its aspects. Normally I exist in all individuals of this kind; but—once brought to life, as your people have brought me to life—I will live on, even with your people if there were none of mine, as long as one or the other survives."

"This, as I say, is superstition," said Lyt Ahn.

"Then if it is, your people are also superstitious."

"You will not," said Lyt Ahn, "compare the Aalaag to your own cattle kind."

"I do not compare them," said Shane. "I have no purpose in convincing you that what I say is true. I only am. The comparison you feel is in your own mind only."

"If you have no purpose in convincing me of anything," said Lyt Ahn, "why speak to me at all?"

"Because of what I am," said Shane. "I am an aspect of the *human*. I must express that aspect to you because that is my nature. Once I have expressed it, you will do as you choose."

Lyt Ahn looked at him through a long silence. Then the First Captain turned and looked at the shifting mass in the square. While the Interior Guards stood still in their warmed clothing, those in the pilgrim robes were shifting constantly, not only to keep themselves warm simply by movement but also to leave the square and make room for others to take their place, when cold, hunger, exhaustion or the needs of the body forced them away. Lyt Ahn looked back at Shane.

"What aspect is this you conceive yourself to represent?" he asked.

"I represent a rediscovery in them," said Shane. "Over many centuries of civilization my people had forgotten what they were and what they could not be. Wars, conquests, dominance and en-slavements of each other had developed in them layers of trained behavior to hide what was a natural instinct, deep in them."

"You are not answering my question," said Lyt Ahn.

"I am answering it," said Shane, "but the answer you want is not one that can be given in a word. Wait and listen, and you will hear what it is."

"I will give you only a little more of my time," said Lyt Ahn.

"I am that instinct I just now spoke of, reawakened," said Shane. "When you Aalaag came to this world, you limited or ended many things that *humans* thought of as evils and that *humans* them-selves had not been able to control. You brought peace and shelter and food and medical care for all you did not consider unwell among this native race. You brought cleanliness and order, and many other worthwhile things—but you brought them all with a mailed fist, an armored fist that arbitrarily destroyed what it chose not to cure—and you did what you did for your own comfort and reasons, rather than for those of my people."

"This is not true," said Lyt Ahn. "Any well Aalaag would scorn to mistreat, or fail to care for, cattle which were not sick."

"As those you see before you now, are sick?"

"Obviously," said Lyt Ahn, looking down at the crowd in the screen, "they are sick. These at least must be destroyed. They have not been so yet because we need to learn what caused them to gather like this."

"Which is what I am here to tell you," said Shane, "and why, behind them, there are more gathering, and more. There are oth-ers on their way to each Headquarters you have built on this world, and others behind them, and they will never stop coming."

"It is an epidemic of unwellness then," said Lyt Ahn, brooding once more over the crowd. "If you have a cure for it, tell me; and as many of the beasts as can be saved will be."

"It is not an unwellness," said Shane. "That is what you must understand. It is, as I said, a reawakening of an instinctive trait in them, a trait that has been in them for millions of years and which can never be cured, suppressed, or changed. They do not tame."

Lyt Ahn slowly turned his eyes from the crowd back down upon Shane.

"Not tame?" he said. "We tamed them within one week of our

first landing here. They have been tamed for three of these local years."

"No," said Shane, "they thought they were tamed, as you thought they were tamed, because of the centuries in which they had let themselves be owned and used by others of their own kind. But that was not a deep enough subjection to waken the ancient instinct of which I am an aspect. Slowly, very slowly at first, but gradually growing more and more rapidly aware of the difference until this moment, when now it runs like a fire out of control around the planet, came the realization that you Aalaag are truly different. You are not of their own *human* kind and have no right to use them. Now they know you for what you are—strangers that do not belong here, that can be permitted to win nothing here, that cannot be permitted even to exist here without their permission."

Lyt Ahn stared at him.

"Certainly you are unwell, Shane-beast, *Pilgrim*, or whatever you think yourself to be," he said. "We came down to the surface of this world and your people had their chance with all that they possessed, to drive us off. If they had, we would not have complained; for it would have meant that we were lacking or unready to match strengths with you. But it was your people who failed— and now, three years after we have kept you and treated you well, you complain."

"I do not complain. Nor do they," said Shane, extending his hand toward the screen. "I only report what is. The *human* spirit has awakened and realized it will be no tame beast for any other people. You and yours must take the consequences of that awakening."

"You continue to speak as if you, not we, have the strength," said Lyt Ahn. "What can your hundreds down there, or your thousands, or even your billions counted on all the surface of this globe, do against us?"

"It is not what we can do, it is what we will do," said Shane. "We will drive you off, or die."

"You mean you will force us to kill you? All of you?"

"If you will not be driven off, there is nothing else." Now it was Shane that looked up at him for a long moment of silence. "I tell you, even if we had the vessels in which to flee from you, that this world here is our home, and here we will drive you out or die."

The air in the room was suddenly so charged with emotion that it was as if the two of them were enclosed in a solid medium. Lyt Ahn did not move and no expression of his face or gaze changed; but the difference radiated from him to Shane.

"You dare say this!" said Lyt Ahn.

"I neither dare nor do not dare," said Shane. "What can you do to prevent my saying what I wish? If you find what I say uncomfortable, you can only kill this body before you and then wonder, for the rest of your life, what other truth you might have heard if you had not acted too quickly."

"Hear this from me then," said Lyt Ahn. "Without cattle to work it, this world is of no use to real people such as ourselves. If what you say was true, and I do not believe that to be so, perhaps we might leave your unwell race to die of its own sickness in its own time; or perhaps before we leave, we might put you out of your pain—all of you."

"You will do what you will do," said Shane. "No one doubts that the Aalaag could destroy all life in this world. But is this the way of the Aalaag, to destroy something without sufficient reason? And is it sufficient reason that those who inhabit this world are of no use to you?"

He paused. Lyt Ahn looked back at him and said nothing.

"Moreover," went on Shane, "there is no reason to tell me this, since I am not of flesh and blood and therefore will be unaffected by what you do. If you destroy all humans, I will remain with you. If you do not, as long as there is a human alive I will be in him or her—man, woman or child. But also, is this the mind of the Aalaag that speaks to me, through you? A mind that out of sheer affront, because another people cannot be what they are not, chooses to destroy them? Is this the Aalaag mind that thinks killing a people will negate the words their spirit has said? The questions their spirit has raised? Will the fact that *humans* choose to stand and die change the fact that the Aalaag ran and survived?"

The silence was long. And it was a silence in which Shane's words might as well have been painted in the air between him and Lyt Ahn; painted there, never to be erased.

But the moment came finally when Lyt Ahn, who had gone as

hard and immobile as a mountain, relaxed. Only a human that knew the First Captain as well as Shane could have read the tiny changes in physical appearance signaling that relaxation—but Shane did read them; and for the first time since he had begun talking, a small hope crept into his mind.

"We ran, only so that we could return and win," said Lyt Ahn; but he said the words almost as if he had repeated and repeated them countless times, until the original emotion and meaning was all but lost. "Do you know why I have listened to you this long, Shane-beast? For in spite of all you say, it is as a beast called Shane that I think of you."

"It does not matter why, only that you listened," said Shane.

Lyt Ahn made a gesture with one large hand as if brushing aside some floating mote of dust in the air before him.

"I have sat for the last eight hours," he said, "listening to talk very like yours. Indeed, one group of speakers has said something very like what you have just said. I was in my Council of Captains, with the Commanders of the various Districts of this planet; and they were disturbed. As the First Captain, the one who must decide eventually, I only sat and listened; although had I not been First Captain, I would have sided with those who considered this Expedition to have failed. In other words, since I was chosen First Captain and since I give the orders, I am saying that I have failed, in leading the Expedition here."

He glanced for a moment, almost musingly, out at the crowd, then back to Shane.

"We studied you for nearly a hundred of your years before coming here," he said. "The physical world itself seemed good. Your breed seemed promising cattle. I had few doubts when I ordered the Expedition of which I had been chosen leader to settle here."

"I have told you," said Shane, "that on first contact even the *human* people did not understand what would come of it, if they and the Aalaag tried to coexist."

"There were two main bodies of thought expressed at that Council just past," Lyt Ahn went on, as if Shane had not spoken. "There were those who felt that this world and its beasts had shown too small a return for our efforts and that we should look elsewhere. Then there was the other opinion—led by the sir Laa Ehon, who now will attend only one more Council, since your report that he wishes an unacceptable change—a change that could lead to an unwell deviation from our eternal purpose to retake our home worlds. In thinking so, he, himself, proves that he is unwell. But the opinion he led at the Council was that we should set up a much stricter control of all cattle and look to a change in our leadership here—which would inevitably mean that if the other Captains felt likewise, I would offer my resignation from the post of First Captain, which post he might otherwise have been one to fill."

The dark Aalaag eyes focused on Shane.

"What you say echoes much of what was said by those who thought this Expedition should look elsewhere for a world and cattle. Though none there spoke with the words you have spoken."

He paused.

"For the first time—" Lyt Ahn's deep voice seemed to echo against the silence in the room. Seemingly absentmindedly his right hand moved slightly in the air; and a depressed but now noticeable volume of sound came from the screen, a murmur of the voices and movements of the crowd there. "Yes, for the first time, it occurs to me that this world of yours might also be a world of unwellness; a planet that it might not be good for Aalaag to inhabit."

He looked back at the screen.

"You may go," he said.

"I am not Shane-beast and I do not go," said Shane.

Lyt Ahn looked back at him.

"Must I destroy you here and now?" he asked.

"Not unless you think it wisest to," said Shane. "I have pointed out that destroying me would leave you in the future wondering what else you might have learned."

"I have learned nothing so far since you announced yourself to be other than Shane-beast," said Lyt Ahn, "except that you are subject to delusions and unwell."

"That is incorrect," said Shane. "You have learned to take into your decisions the factor that the people of this world might, after all, be untamable."

Lyt Ahn considered him.

"You speak with great certainty," he said. "I spoke of delusions and unwellness."

"But, being Aalaag, you must consider the possibility that you are wrong, and that what I tell you is true."

The silence was longer, this time.

"How did you come to know so much about the Aalaag?" Lyt Ahn said, finally.

"If I tell you, it will offend you," said Shane.

"Tell me."

"Because, in too many ways we are similar, we *humans* and you Aalaag. I think, even if we were not untamable, our similarities are so close as to bring our differences eventually into conflict; and both our peoples would come eventually to a moment like this one, no matter what any of our peoples did in their effort to live usefully together."

"You were right," said Lyt Ahn. "You are offensive."

"You asked to be told."

"Yes."

Once more Lyt Ahn looked at the screen and then back at Shane.

"You are ready to die if necessary, Shane-beast?" he said, then checked himself, something Shane had never seen an Aalaag do before. "No, I will try to call you by that unpronounceable name of *Pilgrim*, as you wish, because you show the courage that—well or unwell—is needed for a willingness to die a necessary death."

It seemed to Shane as if he looked into a great, cold emptiness; but to his own surprise, he was still not afraid. Long since he had told himself that if ever an Aalaag caught him being guilty of an offense that by their laws would condemn him to death, he would physically attack the Aalaag who caught him, in hopes of a quick, rather than a slow, death. He realized now that the quick death he had envisioned would have come, if it came at all, not because of a reflex of an attacked individual, as a human might react; but because of Aalaag approval of a creature that had the will to attack even though it knew it could not possibly win.

Nonetheless, he found a real satisfaction now in the thought that when he went out, it would be attacking the First Captain with his empty hands. He could do that much that was tangible.

"So I will do what I must, as my duty as First Captain requires," said Lyt Ahn.

He looked at Shane; and Shane believed he read tiny signals of a genuine sadness in the other.

"Why should I pay attention to anything you say?" Lyt Ahn went on quietly. "You are a beast and unwell. This I know. Your talk about your fellow beasts being ready to choose death to our kindly service—and it has been kindly, *Pilgrim* . . . I cannot make that unmanageable sound . . . it has been kindly, Shane-beast."

"I know that," said Shane, "as it is the intent of an adult to be kindly when he thinks to protect the small feet of a child by putting them into his own oversize boots. Kindly, but in error."

"Nonetheless, your words that your fellow beasts choose death to service are only that—words, and from you alone. I am not convinced that this is so. It has not been so in the past."

"In the past the Pilgrim was splintered among billions of people. Now the Pilgrim is one, here with you and in all humans who know of you."

"I do not believe you," said Lyt Ahn. "It is unwellness speaking in you; or magic, and magic is a delusion. It does not exist."

"You are in error. It is neither unwellness nor a delusion of magic," said Shane. "What I tell you is simply the truth."

"Why then have you and your kind never produced proof of it?"

Shane drew a deep breath.

"Now it is you who are right," he said. "I have been hesitating—because the creature before you is Shane-beast, and Shane-beast does not wish to happen what must happen to prove what I say. But you are right and only proof will reach you."

They had been saying all this while facing each other, with the screen beside them. Now Shane turned to look into it and down into the square—not only at the people in their pilgrim robes, but those in the three lines of uniformed Guards.

Lyt Ahn turned also, so that they looked together into the screen.

Shane drew another deep and bitter breath.

"Order your Guards to clear the square," he said with effort, on the exhalation.

There was neither sound nor movement from Lyt Ahn. Shane looked up, and saw the First Captain looking down at him.

"And why should I give such an order?" said Lyt Ahn. "I have told you that those down there must be destroyed, but they need not be destroyed just yet; and if I order the Guard to send them away and they do not go, then the Guard must destroy them. Nothing else can happen."

"You should give the order to learn the truth," said Shane.

Lyt Ahn looked into the screen.

"Colonel-beast," he said.

The face and shoulders of a lean-featured man in his midforties, with a tight, pinched look on that face, all but filled the space of the screen. To either side of him, the backs of armed Interior Guards and parts of the shapes of those in pilgrim garb beyond could be seen. The Guards Colonel would be talking, Shane knew, to a three-dimensional image of Lyt Ahn; and it was probable that only once or twice before, if at all, would he have gotten an order directly from the First Captain, instead of having it passed down to him through the chain of command.

"Yes, immaculate sir?" replied the Colonel.

"Clear these cattle from the square before my House," said Lyt Ahn. The Colonel stared at him, pale-faced. After a second Lyt Ahn added, "You may use your own native customs in the executing of that order."

"Yes," said the Colonel hoarsely, "immaculate sir."

He turned away and the view of the screen pulled back to show not only the crowd and the three lines of armed Guards, but the Colonel in conversation with a small handful of other Guard officers, all of them standing on the slight elevation that was the top step of the brief stairs to the still hidden main entrance to the building.

After a second, one of these other officers stepped away from the group and faced the square. He spoke to the crowd over the heads of the three lines of Guards; and his voice was amplified, no doubt by some alien device, though Shane saw nothing in his hands or on his person, so that his words echoed off the walls of the buildings surrounding the square.

"You are ordered to disperse!" his voice roared. "All those not accredited to be here, leave the square. I repeat. Clear the square! All of you. Clear the square!"

The crowd rippled like the surface of a sea when the first puff of an oncoming wind strikes it. A low mutter swelled up from it. It did not begin to disperse.

"This is a second and final warning!" The voice of the officer speaking, for all its loudness, seemed to Shane's ear to crack slightly on the last two words. "Clear the square at once!"

The mutter rose to a volume that approached the amplified voice of the officer.

"Leave! Leave now!" cried the officer over it. "We don't want to have to fire on you, but if you don't start clearing the square immediately, we will be forced to. There is no exception to this order. Clear the square!"

The crowd roared and rippled again, this time forward.

"Ready weapons!" cried another voice, also amplified, but with the growing noise from the crowd, possibly only barely heard by the most distant of the armed Guards themselves.

For the first time there was movement among the Guards. Some unslung their weapons and lifted them into firing position; others only made part of the motion. They looked at each other.

"Observe their faces, First Captain," said Shane to Lyt Ahn. "Look at the faces of the Guards armed with weapons."

The point of view of the scene shown in the screen changed. Suddenly they were looking from a point above the heads of the front line of the crowd at the three ranks of black-uniformed, weap-oned men.

Their faces showed every range of expression from the grim to the frankly fearful; but most simply looked pale and uncertain. None of them, thought Shane, had in all probability ever been in anything resembling a war. Nearly all had most certainly never fired the killing devices they held at anything other than a paper target.

"Why did you ask me to look at these?" asked Lyt Ahn. "I see nothing different about them. There are no marks upon them, nor any other change visible."

"The fault is mine," said Shane, angry with himself. "I had forgotten something. You are aware that *humans* claim to read—" he paused. There was no word in Aalaag for "expression." "— feelings in the shapes and movements of each other's faces."

"I have heard that," said Lyt Ahn. "Did you expect me to see such in these Guard-beasts?"

"Yes," said Shane. "I had forgotten that even an Aalaag as perceptive as yourself—as Shane-beast has found you perceptive— might not perceive such things in the faces of what you call cattle."

The scene returned to a view of the square from above and

behind the uniformed men.

"READY TO FIRE!" cried a human voice, its volume of amplification now raised again until it dominated even the ultimate roar of the crowd.

Shane made himself stand still and watch. Lyt Ahn would watch; and no Aalaag would understand the emotion that would cause a human to turn away. Shane stood, held in the grip of his own will. Lyt Ahn gazed curiously at the screen.

"FIRE!"

The scene became a heaving, disorganized mass of bodies as the crowd rolled forward. Of those Guardsmen who had lifted their weapons into anything like firing position, perhaps three out of ten actually pressed the triggers of their weapons, and of those weapons fired more than half sent their light, poisonous missiles either over the heads of the crowd or into the pavement at their feet—where, unfortunately, they splintered and their broken parts did their killing mission after all. But this was only in the first few seconds. Those in the front of the crowd fell as they advanced, but those behind clambered over the fallen bodies and kept coming until they reached and swept over the three lines of Guardsmen, and the black uniforms vanished under a pressing mass of colored robes and flailing staves.

In less than a minute there was nothing left to be seen on the screen but the crowd itself, now growling against the base of the unpenetrable, silver-coated walls of the House of Weapons.

Lyt Ahn continued to stand watching them. Shane turned to look at the First Captain's eyes, but could read nothing there, even with his nearly three years of intimate knowledge. After a long minute, Lyt Ahn turned and went back to seat himself at his desk.

"Cjhor Elon?" he said to the air before him. "Is there anything of urgency demanding my attention at the moment?"

"Immaculate sir," said the voice of his aide, "the General-beast in command of the Interior Guards wishes to send a larger force of Guards out to replace those that failed to clear the cattle from the square as you ordered."

"No," said Lyt Ahn, "that order is cancelled. Orders are to be that none—neither beast nor Aalaag—shall leave the House of Weapons. What else?"

"Immaculate sir," said Cjhor Elon's voice. "All other Headquarters report that they also have just now passed through an attack on the guard-beasts they had placed outside to contain the cattle gathered there; and in all cases the guard-beasts have been killed. The cattle remain. The officers temporarily in command at the other Headquarters ask for orders."

"The order applicable to them is the same one I have just given for this place," said Lyt Ahn.

"Did I not tell you I was everywhere at once—here and at your other Headquarters at the same time?" Shane said to him.

"What other matters are there of more than ordinary urgency?" asked Lyt Ahn. He had not looked at Shane nor shown any sign that he had heard the words Shane had just spoken.

"Just at this moment the Officer Supervisor of the guard-beasts of this House asks to speak with you."

"I will listen to him."

The projection of an Aalaag whom Shane recognized as the one having direct control and responsibility for not only the Interior Guards at the House of Weapons, but for all the Interior Guards Corps around the world, appeared before Lyt Ahn's desk.

"Immaculate sir," said the projection. "The Guards of the Corps for which I am responsible have failed to clear the square before your House as you ordered. Not only that, but they behaved shamefully in allowing themselves to be killed, when they should have done the killing and obeyed the order. This reflects on me, as the Supervisor of their Corps. May I have the First Captain's special permission to step outside alone, myself, and clear the square at the First Captain originally ordered?"

"I have given an order," said Lyt Ahn.

"Forgive me, immaculate sir," said the projection; and vanished.

"Cjhor Elon," said Lyt Ahn to the empty air before him, "you will contact all Captains who sit on the Council to gather in the Council Chamber. I leave for there now."

"Yes, immaculate sir."

"Come, Shane-beast," said Lyt Ahn, getting to his feet and striding toward the door of his office.

Shane followed.

THIRTY-TWO

IT WAS NOT SURPRISING TO SHANE THAT ONLY FOUR OTHERS OF THE Area Commanders were in the Council Chamber when Lyt Ahn and Shane reached it. What was surprising was that the other eighteen, including Laa Ehon, were there within the next five minutes.

Meanwhile, Lyt Ahn had walked the length of the room to seat himself at the head of the long table surface that floated apparently unsupported in midair; and Shane had taken the usual position of a beast who had been brought along—standing at the First Captain's left elbow.

Lyt Ahn said nothing and the others said nothing until they were all assembled. Shane, who had grown so used to such silences that he normally ignored them, found himself counting the seconds of this one until Lyt Ahn should speak. When Lyt Ahn did, the deep and measured tones of his voice seemed to come like the short coughing roar of a lion on Shane's tense ears.

"I would not normally have called you all to Council again so soon," said Lyt Ahn, "however, something of overriding importance has come up."

He looked up and down the table at them.

"It is always a moment of unusual strain when the immaculateness of a senior officer must be examined," he said. "For the information of all of you, I recently denied a request by the sir Laa Ehon to buy the beast beside me here, but agreed instead to let him take it on permanent loan with provision that it might return to me from time to time when it considered such return was necessary to remain current with its duties in my Corps of Courier-Translators. It returned for the first time only yesterday, although

it left the House of Laa Ehon some few days ago. I have not inquired into the delay, which I assume to be because of the unsettled
condition of the native cattle, worldwide. That may be investigated
later and should not concern us, here.

"As I had told this beast I would, on its return, I asked it certain
questions; and as a result of my communication with it, I learned
that Laa Ehon in speaking to it had referred to a future in which
there would be a different relationship between ourselves and the
local cattle."

He looked at Laa Ehon. Laa Ehon looked back. Both faces
were perfectly without expression.

"Allowing for the limitations of beasts, I did not, of course,
accept this information at face value. But since other matters had
caused me to concern myself about the wellness of the immaculate
sir, earlier, I felt duty-bound to ask him now about the reference
the beast reported; and moreover decided this should best be done
in full Council.

"Accordingly," his eyes stayed on Laa Ehon, "I now ask the
immaculate sir if he planned any deviance from the way laid down
by our ancestors and adhered to ever since we were forced to flee
our homes; and which calls for a specific and unvarying relationship to all beasts put to our service."

Shane stared at Laa Ehon. In his own mind, he had no doubt
that Laa Ehon was unwell. But was he unwell enough to lie? Laa
Ehon's gaze remained as steadily on Lyt Ahn as Lyt Ahn's on him.

"I did have plans for a future that in some fashion could be
said to deviate from the way chosen by our ancestors," Laa Ehon
answered. "I have come to believe that only by such minor deviance and a closer association with those we call beasts can we hope
to regain our home worlds."

The Council room was held in an Aalaag silence, until Lyt Ahn
spoke again.

"In that case, I consider you unwell," said Lyt Ahn.

He looked around.

"Does any of the Council have an opinion, a comment?"
Silence.

"Laa Ehon," said Lyt Ahn, "do you agree or disagree?"

"I disagree that I am in any way unwell," said Laa Ehon. "But
I am a senior officer of the Aalaag and will act accordingly.

Therefore, I now resign my post and my rank and will accept instead a new ranking which is one lower than that of any other Aalaag on this world. Beyond this, I stand ready to obey the orders of my superiors."

"You will, of course," said Lyt Ahn, "leave the Council Chamber now. Your second-in-command will be confirmed in acting command of the District that was formerly yours.

Laa Ehon rose, turned and left the chamber. After the door had closed itself behind him, Lyt Ahn looked back at those still seated at the table, but it was not to them he spoke next.

"Cjhor Elon," he said to the air before him.

"Immaculate sir?" responded the disembodied voice.

"Arrange communication for me with the Captain of the Fleet."

"Yes, immaculate sir."

There was a moment's wait. The Captain of the Fleet, Shane knew, was an Aalaag officer, equal in authority to the Commander of a District, who had charge of the maintenance and readiness of the fleet of the space vessels which had brought the Aalaag to this world. He or she would be a senior officer whose tour of duty consisted of several months of time, after which the incumbent was relieved and replaced by someone similar.

The Fleet itself stayed continually in orbit around the world. Shane's impression was that either the structure of the ships would not endure a landing at the gravity on the planet's surface, or the state of instant readiness in which they were always kept required that they be in takeoff position at all times.

The projection of a male Aalaag, in full armor but with his helmet's surface presently nonexistent over his face so that his features were exposed, appeared in the very center of the table, on his feet and facing Lyt Ahn.

"Immaculate sir," he said, "I am reporting as ordered."

Shane blinked. For the projection of someone who, in the flesh, would be in orbit miles above the Earth was the most remarkable he had ever seen. Where the officer appeared to stand the table surface should have bisected him at the hips, so that either the lower part of his body should have been invisible, or the tabletop would have to have disappeared around him.

But nothing of either kind had happened. By some strange

technological magic, the tabletop was still visible as a continuous surface, while the lower half of the officer was also visible, as if he was surrounded by nothing but air. It was an impossible vision, but still Shane saw it.

"You are Neha Morlo, of the fifth rank," said Lyt Ahn, "and you have been on duty as Captain of the Fleet for over four local months. Is this correct?"

"It is, immaculate sir."

"And the ships are, as always, ready to leave as soon as they are loaded by the members of the Expedition?"

"Yes, immaculate sir."

"Members will begin boarding shortly, upon concluding their duties here," said Lyt Ahn. "We will be returning to—"

He used a word in Aalaag Shane had never heard before.

"—as soon as all members and necessary equipment are boarded."

"Yes, immaculate sir."

"You may go."

"I obey, First Captain."

The Captain of the Fleet vanished. Lyt Ahn looked down the table surface at the other officers there.

"I have come to a conclusion, suggested by events in the last half of the local year, but coming to be a certainty with the events of the last few hours," said Lyt Ahn, "that the cattle of this world are not suitable for training as beasts to our purpose. Accordingly, we are returning to the planet on which this Expedition was organized; and, once there, the Expedition will be dissolved. Another may be formed; but I would recommend that our experience with this world guide those elected its senior officers to a more careful study of the new target world before settling there.

"I now resign as First Captain of this Expedition, my resignation to take effect once the members of the Expedition have all disembarked on—" Once again he used the new word.

"I do not choose to be considered for First Captain of any further Expedition, once this one is concluded," Lyt Ahn went on. "This Expedition has failed; and any such failure is, of course, the ultimate responsibility of its First Captain. My consort, Adtha Or Ain, has for some time wished to put in motion a reconnaissance of the area of our original home worlds, to acquire definite knowledge of whether the previous reconnaissance, of which our son was a member, had all the members of its team slain by those who have usurped our sacred soil, or whether our son was captured alive and is being kept for millennia on exhibit, encased by the usurpers, as we know has happened to others of our people who have fallen into their hands."

Lyt Ahn paused slightly.

"I intend to take care of this neglected duty and at the same time atone for my failure with this Expedition by making a further, solitary reconnaissance of the Home Worlds area. I will therefore be unable to accept command of a new Expedition even if I would ordinarily be required to by law, if the members of that new Expedition should unanimously vote for my services."

He stopped speaking; and the silence that followed lingered in the chamber. Shane understood suddenly what Lyt Ahn was doing. Over the past two years in the First Captain's office and elsewhere about the House of Weapons, he had overheard enough Aalaag talk about such reconnaissance missions to know that what Lyt Ahn had just announced was his own finish. A solitary adventure into the area of the Aalaag Home Worlds was certain to end, whether Lyt Ahn discovered the fate of his son or not, with the former First Captain himself encased and kept like a fly in amber.

"We will now," said Lyt Ahn, "deal with the details of evacuation from this unproductive world. I'll go around the table and I'd like each of you in turn to give me an estimate of the time it should take you to get all your officers into the ships of the fleet— also tell me of any special problems which you envision this departure posing in your area . . . ."

He and the other Captains became involved in the details of their withdrawal from the planet Earth. Standing beside Lyt Ahn and apparently forgotten, Shane found himself feeling no sense of triumph, nor indeed, any emotion whatsoever. It was merely over and finally done with, that was all—what he had set out to do. His mind slipped back to wandering in the universe of his own thoughts about Peter and Maria, which it had come to do in his long wait for Lyt Ahn to return to his office, earlier.

There was a stir about the table surface. Aalaag, including Lyt Ahn, were rising to their feet and leaving the chamber. Shane followed the First Captain and watched as he was joined by Cjhor

Elon, just outside the door.

"A general notice is to be sent out to all Aalaag," Lyt Ahn told the aide. "We abandon this planet. All personnel with weapons and other possessions in the arms locker of this House should collect them and prepare to leave. Otherwise all duties are suspended and they will have free time until ordered to assemble for transport to some ship of the Fleet."

"I will attend to this, immaculate sir," said Cjhor Elon.

Neither he nor Lyt Ahn paid any attention to Shane, following behind them with the automatic obedience of a beast still obeying the last order given it. Lyt Ahn continued to give orders to the aide all during the walk back, but Shane hardly listened. None of this concerned him and his fate still remained to be dealt with by Lyt Ahn. It was with utter stupefaction, therefore, that he watched the First Captain and Cjhor Elon pass through the double doors into Lyt Ahn's private office and, attempting to follow, found the doors had closed themselves in his face, leaving him alone in the hall.

He stood where he was, baffled.

He had fallen almost completely back into the automatic reactions of Shane-beast in the House of his masters. A beast left without orders simply waited. Therefore, he waited . . . and waited. No summons came from within the office, the doors did not open. Nothing at all happened.

Like a semi-waterlogged piece of wood, slowly ascending to the surface through dark waters, the realization dawned upon him that Lyt Ahn was through with him. He was not to be executed, elaborately or otherwise. Nothing was to be done to him. Like the Earth itself, he had simply been abandoned by the First Captain.

Unreasonably, a pang of emotion passed through Shane. It was ridiculous, but in a sense he felt as shut out as he had felt when he had been left an orphan by his mother's death. It was even as if he had been unfairly deprived of the execution he had been expecting. He felt his discarding by Lyt Ahn as he might feel the same action by a lifelong friend or close relation.

He still stood, perplexed. A massive uncertainty held him. Like a man suddenly reprieved from a verdict of death, he had the overwhelming feeling that the world around him was infinite in size, but that he had nowhere to go in it. Almost, it was as if he did not belong among the living; that having been put away for good, he should have the decency to remain there, and not re-enter the universe from which he had been permanently ejected.

With great effort, he pulled himself out of the feeling which held him, the way someone drowning in a bog might pull himself back to firm earth and life.

There was no point in his standing here.

He turned away from the two closed doors and walked away down the empty corridor, his heels clacking loudly on the black and white tiled floor and the echo of his passage bouncing back from the hard walls from which the display weapons had already been stripped. After some long distance and several turns in the empty corridors he finally began to encounter both Aalaag and humans—humans who were former servants of the Aalaag, but like himself hardly realized that they were no longer.

The Aalaag were mostly in movement from one place to another. The humans were standing around in small groups, talking; or wandering from one group to another. Corps difference had disappeared. Shane saw Guardsmen in conversation with courier-translators and members of all other corps of workers from Maintenance people to personal body-servants to the Aalaag.

He passed them all by, feeling pulled in a certain direction but not yet sure of where that was. In any case, he felt no desire to talk with these others. It was not until he reached a corridor on the ground-floor level that he heard his name called by a voice he recognized.

He turned to find Sylvie Onjin running toward him.

"Shane!" she panted, catching hold of his left arm and pulling him along with her. "Come with me. We're calling a general meeting of all the humans here. We've got to decide whether to march out in a body, as we are, or send delegates to talk to the people outside!"

He stared at her.

"Don't you understand?" she demanded impatiently, tugging at his arm. "The Aalaag have refused. They won't take any of us with them. You know what the ordinary people'll do to us who worked for the aliens, once they're gone and we're unprotected! They'll kill us all. They blame us for all the hanging on hooks and the tortures. They blame us for everything. None of us dares go outside until we've come to some agreement with the people out there—come on, Shane!"

432

"Wait," he said, stopping and forcing her to stop. He looked at her. Her close-cut brown hair retained its order, but her face was pale and tight-drawn over the bones beneath its skin, to the point of ugliness. She had been capable of raising a feeling of tenderness in him, once, and the ghost of that feeling still lingered in him; but somehow he could no longer give it life and substance. He took her free hand in his free one.

"Sylvie," he said, "a meeting's not going to do any good, or delegates either. Come with me and we'll go outside together. I'll see no one hurts you. They'll listen to me. I'm the Pilgrim, the one who got this revolution started all over the world."

She stared at him. She let go of his arm and suddenly jerked her hand out of his.

"Oh, you've gone crazy, like so many of them!" she cried. "Go out with you? You must think I'm crazy, too! You, the Pilgrim? Do you think I'd believe a thing like that? Someone like you could never be the Pilgrim; anyone'd have sense enough to understand that. The people outside'd tear us to bits the moment you tried to tell them such a thing!"

She backed a step from him.

"You'll just have to save yourself, Shane," she said. "I can't help you if you've gone crazy. I haven't got time to help you if you're crazy. . . ."

She had begun backing farther with her last words. As she stopped talking, she turned and ran; and he lost sight of her in among the other bodies, human and Aalaag, passing through the corridor.

Sadly he put himself back into motion and went on his way. It came to him finally that he knew where he was going, after all. He was going to the front entrance of the House of Weapons. Before he reached it, however, he found his way blocked by a tall, thin man in the blue overalls of the Maintenance Corps but with the collar tabs of the beast-officer who was that Corps' Commander.

"You're Shane, aren't you?" said the man. "I've seen you around and I know your reputation. You could have been in command of the Couriers by this time if you'd wanted. Look. Your own Corps will listen to you if you speak to them. You've got to help me."

"Not now," said Shane. He started to push past but the other caught him by the loose fabric of the overalls over Shane's chest.

"No, it has to be now. Don't you understand? They're going; but they're leaving behind everything of their technology they built into places like this. People who don't understand seem to think that with a little jiggering and poking we can learn how to work these things. But we can't. Ordinary people don't understand what the gap between our technology and the Aalaag's really means. It'll take years of study for us to understand what they've left behind; and even then the chances we'll learn how to use it—anyway, you've got to help by speaking to your own Corps people. Tell them—make them understand they mustn't try to monkey with the technological stuff, even those that worked with some of it under Aalaag direction. And those people outside have to be made to understand that technicians like those in my Corps have got to be protected and supported for the years of work it'll take—"

"I'm sorry," Shane broke away from him. "I can't help you now. I've got to go. Good-bye."

He kept walking. The other followed alongside him for some little distance, still talking to him, but Shane refused to answer or look at him. Finally the Maintenance Corps Commander gave up and Shane was alone when he came at last to the main entrance of the House and found it wide open.

He stepped out from it into the chill sunlight of a November morning and caught sight as he passed through it of a grayness to the outside edge of the entrance. He turned and looked up at the building and saw only the sheer rise of blank concrete wall surrounding the darkness of the entrance. No silver coating flowed over that surface.

He turned away again and looked out over the square. At its far end, some vehicles were parked, some passenger cars, two heavy, army-type trucks and three ambulances. There were people around them, standing and talking; but whatever work they had come there to do had evidently mostly been done, for there was no air of urgency about those in movement. Here and there could be seen the tall figures of Aalaag in full armor with only their faces uncovered. Shane recognized them all as junior officers experiencing that rare thing for an Aalaag—free time. They wandered about the dead bodies in the square like tourists at an amusement park, discovering and calling each other's attention to things. They and the humans around the vehicles paid no attention to each other's presence.

He blinked his eyes in the daylight, although it did not seem that strong after the day-bright lighting inside. Still, he was shocked to realize that a full, cold night had passed while he sat or stood, and waited for and with Lyt Ahn.

He looked last at the part of the square at his feet, right up against the House of Weapons, and knew finally why he had come. What was here had called him. The dead. Those he had killed.

They lay in windrows like breeze-heaped leaves all mixed together, bodies in pilgrim cloaks and bodies in the black uniforms of the Interior Guard. Those who were merely wounded, if there had been any such after staves and poisoned bullets had done their work, had evidently already been removed.

He began to walk among them, looking at their faces. He was surprised at the serenity of the features of most of them; until he realized that neither poison nor staff-blows would have brought death so swiftly that the body would not have had a chance to relax, and the expression of the features when death came would have shared in that relaxation. The charge of the crowd upon the Guardsmen had scattered the black-uniformed men, and so the dead lay in separate clumps where one or more Guardsmen had been brought down.

It was remarkable how similar pilgrim and play-soldier looked in death. Shane had not expected so many to look so young. That the Guardsmen should look so was not surprising. Those lined up before the building had been from the lowest ranks of that Corps and had indeed been young. Overgrown boys in most instances. But he had not expected so many of those in gray cloaks, men and women alike, also to show such youth.

Not that there were not older faces to be seen among them. He reached one heap and thought he saw something familiar in a cloaked body that lay on its back near the top of the heap, but with its face and upper body covered by the pilgrim corpse that had fallen on top of it.

He bent to take hold of the corpse on top and with some effort rolled it aside. The face on the body underneath was uncovered. It was the body of Peter.

He stood over it, looking down.

He should have expected it, he told himself, from the last words of the Englishman, when the other had squeezed Shane's shoulder and spoken in his ear, just before Shane ran for the protection of the lines of the Guardsmen.

"See you on the other side," Peter had said.

The words had sounded overdone to Shane at the time, almost melodramatic, and not like what Peter would normally say. He had supposed then that their unnaturalness was owing to the fact that Peter was playing up the pretense of everyone that Shane would be able to give Lyt Ahn the human ultimatum and still walk back out of the House of Weapons alive—something none of them in their hearts could have actually believed.

But Shane understood now that it had not been pretense at all that had caused Peter to speak so. The other man must have planned from the beginning to be in the first wave of those in the square, whenever the time came to clash with the Guards. Peter must have been telling only the truth when he said that he believed that Shane could see the gigantic shadow-figure of the actual Pilgrim. It would have been that sort of belief in him which had led Peter to form his Resistance group in London. He had been one of those who, from the first, had truly believed that humans would do anything rather than continue to endure the Aalaag in the long run.

Now, Shane was alive after all.

And Peter was dead.

He deserved better than to have his body lie sprawled like this, awkwardly in a pile of other, nameless corpses. Undoubtedly, there would be people along in due time to take all the bodies from the square for proper interment or disposal. But until then, Shane thought, he could at least pull Peter off the pile and straighten out his limbs decently.

He began to do so. Like the body he had to remove first from above him, Peter's lifeless form was heavy and difficult to move. As it finally came free from the pile, it exposed the bottom layer of the heap, in particular the body just beneath. Shane was concentrating on nothing but Peter; but suddenly he knew without looking.

Slowly, on neck muscles that fought against the movement, he turned his head to look at who lay under Peter; and it was Maria.

There was an end to feeling in him.

THIRTY-THREE

MECHANICALLY, HE FINISHED PULLING PETER CLEAR OF THE OTHER bodies and laying him out on the cold concrete with his legs straight and together and his arms at his sides. Then Shane went back to the heap and began to move bodies so that he could get Maria out.

It was a hard task. Some of the bodies, particularly those of two of the Guardsmen which he had to shift, were heavier than he was. But he kept at it and finally he had removed all who in any way lay upon Maria. Uncovered, she lay still, with the same relaxed face as the others, as if she slept. Only a breath of the wind stirred a wisp of her dark hair, blowing it across her closed eyes and forehead. Unthinkingly he set the hair gently back in place.

It was then he noticed that her left leg had been broken. Either Peter or the last body he had removed, had fallen on it in such a way as to deal it a blow below the knee; and the distortion of the overstressed bone was visible. As gently as if she was still alive, he drew her free to lie beside Peter and set about straightening her out as naturally as possible.

With the two of them at last clear on the concrete, he sat down beside Maria and took her hand in his. It felt waxy and there was a stiffness to it. His own hands could not warm it; and the longer he sat there, the more he became unable to endure the fact that she should lie here, like this. He could not shift Peter any distance, but surely he could carry her, say, as far as one of the ambulances that were still parked at the edge of the square, and lay her out decently on one of the stretchers inside it.

He squatted on the concrete at her side, got one arm under

her shoulders and head, the other under her hips; and, holding her, he struggled to his feet. He began to carry her toward the nearest ambulance, perhaps fifty steps away across the square, standing empty and waiting with its back door open.

For perhaps a dozen steps he had no doubt he could make it; and then swiftly—too swiftly—the weight of her body began to tell on his arms and shoulders. He would not have thought it would be so hard to carry the body of a relatively small person such as she had been. His knees, his back, his whole body began to give; and a fury took him that he could not do this last thing for her— carry her to a place where she could be laid down properly.

His knees gave finally. He sank down on them and managed with shaking arms to lower Maria gently to the concrete, rather than simply dropping her. He sat, squatting on his knees, with his head bowed over her. I'll make it, he told himself. I'll get her there if it takes a hundred tries like this.

"—Shane-beast, is that you?"

He looked up to see one of the young Aalaag officers looking down at him. It was the tall one who had helped to get him free from the questioner in the corridor when he had been on his way to the office of Lyt Ahn.

"Yes, untarnished sir," he answered automatically.

"They were warriors, were they not?" said the tall Aalaag enthusiastically, looking around the square at the dead. "Beasts, and clumsy at it, but warriors—what are you doing with that particular dead one, Shane-beast?"

"It is my mate," said Shane dully. "I was taking it to lie properly in one of the medical vehicles at the edge of the square."

"And you were too small to carry it all that distance yourself," said the Aalaag. "How does it come that someone like you had a mate who was on the side of those cattle who attacked our beast-troops?"

"It is a long story, untarnished sir," said Shane dully.

"Nevermind. I understand. It was unwell, this mate of yours, like the rest, was it not? But it also, like the rest, was a warrior. Here, I will take it for you."

The officer leaned down and scooped up Maria with one hand and arm. His armored fingertips among Maria's dark hair held her head gently. The rest of her body weight was supported on his crooked forearm. He carried her as if she was no weight at all.

"Come," he said.

Shane forced himself to his feet. Together, the Aalaag carrying Maria, they paced across the square to the ambulance with the door open.

"You wish her where? Ah, I see the surface you mean." The Aalaag slid Maria's body on one of the stretchers fastened to the side of the ambulance. Shane pushed in after him to lift her arms up and cross them on her breast.

"That is good," said the Aalaag. "Stay with your mate, Shane-beast. If the cattle had been all like you we would not have to be leaving."

He turned and went back across the square to join several others of the Aalaag there and evidently to tell the story of Shane and Maria, for he gestured with his thumb toward the ambulance as he spoke.

Meanwhile, Shane sat numbly beside the motionless form of Maria. He had taken a blanket from one of the other stretchers and covered her, all but her face, so that it was almost as if she was merely unconscious, not dead. His mind was still a void; and all he felt inside him was the emptiness that had been with him for some time now. The only thought he seemed able to manage was that he had killed those who lay about him in the square; therefore perhaps it was fitting that he should have killed Peter and Maria as well.

Some minutes passed. Suddenly there was a voice shouting at him and he was literally jerked away from the cot.

". . . stay clear, can't you?"

There were two figures in white coats. They had pulled him from the side of Maria and thrust him clear out of the ambulance. They were now bustling about Maria as if in some unholy ritual, hooking her up with electric cords to some box with a screen, across which a line of light jumped and ran, pulling away the blanket he had covered her with and wrapping her with some sort of endless, heavy bandage. One of them was pushing something into her mouth as if he would ram it clear down her throat.

"Stop it!" he shouted at them, and started to clamber back into the ambulance to stop them, when he was caught from behind and found each of his arms held, straightened out in the grip of a blue-uniformed policeman so that any attempt to move forward brought an excruciating pain to his elbows. "Let me go!"

"Keep him out of here!" said one of the white-coated figures, without turning its head. "There's a chance—aside from that broken leg I think she's only hypothermic . . ."

"Come on with us, friend," said one of the policemen, and the pain in his arm increased until it forced Shane to turn away from the open end of the ambulance.

"Wait! No!" Shane cried. "You mean she's alive? There's a chance?"

"Come on with us," said the policeman as the two of them marched him in the direction. "We've got to get you out of here."

"But I've got to stay and see if she's alive!" Shane was almost crying. "It's Maria. She's . . . she's my wife!"

The footsteps of the policemen slowed for just a second and they looked across Shane at each other.

"It doesn't matter," muttered the one who had not yet spoken. "It's for your own safety. We've got to get you out of here before some crowd comes along. Do you know what they'd do to you, dressed like that?"

Shane had completely forgotten that he still wore his indoor uniform coveralls from the House of Weapons.

"It doesn't matter," he said, as they came to a patrol car. "It doesn't matter what happens to me. I've got to know if she's alive, I tell you!"

He played his last card.

"Don't you understand?" he said. "I'm the Pilgrim—The Pilgrim!"

"Sure. Sure you are . . ." One of the policemen shoved him into the back of the patrol car and got in with him, while the other climbed behind the wheel. A moment later they were underway, moving away from the square, away from Maria, headed for downtown Minneapolis.

They held him in the jail for nearly ten hours. At the end of that time, there were footsteps in the corridor and Mr. Shepherd—still dressed in a gray pilgrim's cloak—showed up, along with one of his jailers, who let him out with a touch of apologetic awe.

"Maria!" was the first word he said to Shepherd. "I've got to know if she's alive—"

"She is," said Shepherd. "We'll take you to the hospital now. I'm sorry about this. There were supposed to be some of our own men on duty at the square at all times, just in case you were able to come back out after all; but something seems to have gone wrong. We'll find out about that later . . ."

Shane paid no attention to the rest of what Shepherd was trying to tell him. Everything, in fact, was a blur until he got to the hospital and the room where Maria lay under white sheets, with a massive-seeming cast on her left leg. She smiled palely up at him. He had only a few seconds with her before the nurse and Shepherd—for different reasons, but united in execution of them—literally pulled him out of the room again.

"Peter pushed me behind him at the last minute before they fired," she had told Shane. "I couldn't pull myself out with my leg broken. I felt sure someone would come and then, when they didn't, cold as it was . . . I just went to sleep."

"I'll be back!" he shouted at her fiercely from the corridor, as he was finally led away by Shepherd.

"Where are we going?" he demanded of the other man. They had been caught up with and surrounded by half a dozen men also in cloaks and carrying staves, some with the same faces as those who had taken him through the crowd to the House of Weapons. "Where's your friend Wong?"

Shepherd coughed dryly.

"Mr. Wong and I belong to different areas of thought," he said. "Now that the Aalaag are leaving, we more or less find ourselves on opposite sides of the table again. But nevermind that. A few others have come out of the aliens' Headquarters building since you did; and we managed to save some of them from the crowds of pilgrims roaming the streets. The word they give us is that the chief Aalaag—the one you worked for personally—is just about to leave for their Fleet, which is up in orbit; and he won't be back. We didn't expect that—I suppose we expected like a ship's captain he'd be the last to leave when the ship went down. If he does go, the question it leaves us with is—who down here speaks for the aliens until the rest of them are all gone? We need you to go back into the Headquarters building and find that out for us."

They were getting into a car—no, into several cars, for cloaked attendants were evidently once more going to escort them. Shane let himself be bundled into the back seat of one large car and was joined a second later by Mr. Shepherd.

"What on earth do you want to know that for?" Shane asked, staring at the other man. "With the Aalaag there'll always be someone in command; but what difference does it make to you who it is?"

"It's just that there could be things to discuss," said Shepherd, as the car pulled away. "The ownership of what they're leaving behind them, for example, whether they ever intend to come back, whether we'd be welcome if we ever get out into space and run into their people again—that sort of thing."

"My God!" Shane stared at him. "You don't suppose one of the Aalaag'd speak to you, or any other human about things like that, do you?"

He put his hands to his head.

"When are people like you going to understand that the Aalaag aren't like us?" he demanded. "Would you let yourself be stopped and oinked at if you were leaving a farmyard full of pigs— or stopped and baaed at if you were leaving a flock of sheep? They don't care about anything they leave behind; and they care less than that about us."

"But we need to know as much as we can, in any case, don't you see?" said Shepherd persuasively. "Knowledge is valuable; and we've still got a little while in which to learn things from them. If you could find even one who'd be willing to come out and explain just why they're leaving—"

"They're leaving because we showed them we'd rather die than go on being their slaves," said Shane. He stared at the older man. "Don't you understand that? They do!"

"Of course. But—"

"To this day," said Shane, "there isn't one of them who can make sense out of more than one or two stray sounds in any human language. You couldn't talk to one of them in anything but Aalaag; and when you talk to him or her in Aalaag, you'd automatically be talking about the universe as they see it. There's no way to describe to them the universe as we see it—or even this world and us—in any terms but theirs; and their terms automatically describe it and us the way they see those things, not the way we do. So what's the use of your knowing who's in command, or getting any one of them to talk to you? Even if you had a language in common, he'd never understand you; and you—God help you and those like you—you'd never understand him!"

Mr. Shepherd seemed to draw in on himself, sitting more stiffly.

"We thought you'd be willing to do this one last thing for us," he said. "We thought you'd want to be helpful."

"Helpful!" echoed Shane.

He thought of what it must be like now in the House of Weapons. He thought of the news that Lyt Ahn was about to leave; and suddenly his attitude changed. Maybe, after all, there were things to be done by going back in there as Shepherd wanted; particularly if Shane could talk to Lyt Ahn himself, before the First Captain took off—as he would be doing eventually, in his own personal ship from the landing area on the roof of the building.

There was nothing Shane could do about what Shepherd and his friends wanted to learn from the Aalaag; but there was just a chance he might be able to reach through to Lyt Ahn in a different way, with a different message that would be more worthwhile to Earth's children in coming centuries than anything else that could be said to any Aalaag, if Lyt Ahn would listen to it.

"All right," said Shane. "Take me there. I'll go in if they let me and do what I can."

So the car he was in, preceded and followed through the streets, and flanked once it entered the square, by the other vehicles accompanying it, brought Shane at last to a point where the scattered bodies left no more room to drive closer to the entrance. The entrance itself was still open, wide, tall, dark and unguarded.

"Wait for me here," Shane said, getting out. "And I do mean—wait!"

He went in.

Unlike the last time he had walked these halls, there were fewer humans to be seen and almost no Aalaag, but all moved with a definite purpose and none of the humans this time made any attempt to talk to Shane.

He went toward Lyt Ahn's office; but when he got there he found its door open and no Aalaag either at Lyt Ahn's desk or at the desk of his aide. His heart suddenly pumping with urgency, Shane turned and headed toward the roof landing area.

He took one of the elevators that had traditionally been forbidden humans; and it was fortunate that he did so, for he stepped out of the elevator inside the square of armed and armored Aalaag who were plainly on guard around the landing area. The back of a tall, armored figure that the years of experience had taught Shane to recognize as the First Captain in full war panoply was striding toward the waiting personal vessel.

"Stop!" said the nearest Aalaag on guard, swinging his long arm around toward Shane. Shane ignored him.

"First Captain!" he shouted after the retreating figure. "You are still First Captain and still have a duty to hear what I have to say—for the sake of your duty to the Aalaag!"

The tall figure took two more steps as if it had not heard, then checked and slowly turned. The face was obscured. The silver protective screen over the helmet was complete.

"Let it come to me," said Lyt Ahn's voice from the featureless helmet.

The Aalaag covering Shane with the potential death in his long arm moved that weapon aside. Shane walked forward toward Lyt Ahn. It had been so long since he had seen the First Captain in full gear that he had forgotten what an imposing sight the other made. It was not until he halted, an Aalaag pace from the First Captain, that the facial area cleared of its protective screen and the features of Lyt Ahn looked down at him.

"What duty to the Aalaag do you speak of, beast?" he said.

"Have you forgotten who I am so soon?" answered Shane. "I am Shane-beast. I was the Pilgrim and also in my duties to the Aalaag a faithful servant to you. I spoke the truth."

"What have the noises of a beast to do with my duty?"

"I am Shane-beast. Call me by that name."

"All beasts are but beasts to me. Answer quickly, or you will be destroyed."

"I have faced destruction many times. Now is no different," said Shane; and was surprised to realize that he meant what he said. "What happens in this moment is more important than my life—or yours, First Captain of the Aalaag Expedition to this planet."

"We will both pass away, soon enough," said Lyt Ahn, expressionlessly. "I will give you one more chance to say something that will justify my listening to you."

"You must not go on that reconnaissance to discover what has become of your son."

There was a brief but tense Aalaag silence.

"I must not? Do you use those words to me, beast?"

"You will not, for the sake of your duty."

"My duty forbids it? You are truly unwell, beast." Lyt Ahn began to turn back toward his waiting vessel.

"Your duty to the survival of the Aalaag," said Shane. "Your own knowledge that to some extent, Laa Ehon, though unwell, was correct."

"Correct? What beast-nonsense is this—even assuming a beast could know if an Aalaag was correct or incorrect?"

"Listen to me, First Captain," said Shane. "I said once in your office that in some ways the Aalaag and we *humans* were too much alike. The Aalaag would not endure conquest. We *humans* found we could not endure conquest. But we still live and grow. The Aalaag have stopped growing and are beginning to die. You know this."

Shane stopped, waiting for a reaction from the tall figure.

"Go on—while you can, beast," said Lyt Ahn.

"Laa Ehon would have taken the first step in giving up the old, old dream of recovering your home worlds; and beginning to live and grow all over again as a new race on new worlds. I would not have understood that myself a year ago, but my mate has helped me to see it. On new worlds, in partnership—not as conquerors and conquered—with whoever own the worlds they settle on, the Aalaag can begin again that growth without which a people must die. It's too late to have such a partnership here, with my people. But the Aalaag can be saved if they look for it elsewhere with a people that, like them and like us, will not be subjugated, but can be lived with."

He stopped speaking. Lyt Ahn made no response.

"That is the duty I spoke of," said Shane swiftly. "Not to go on the reconnaissance, but to stay with your people, alive and speaking out for that truth that you knew to be in part of what Laa Ehon was attempting, and the truth that lay in the fact that in the end, here, we you call beasts chose death rather than to go on being your servants."

He stopped once more.

Again there was silence. Finally, Lyt Ahn broke it.

"You are a beast," he said. "You cannot help being a beast, but you are a beast. There were times past when we were together that I almost forgot that. Listen to me, beast."

He paused.

"I am listening," said Shane.

"You told me you were aware of the useful things that the Aalaag rule had brought to your kind on this planet. You even listed some of them, such as peace among yourselves and cleanliness. Such is the Aalaag way. We improve the lot of those beasts we find on the worlds we occupy."

"In some senses," said Shane.

"In all senses," said Lyt Ahn, "though in the beginning, during the early years, the beasts are not capable of appreciating all that is being done for them. But where they endure, serviceable and appreciative, we continue also, and the time comes when the beasts fully understand and appreciate what has come to them with our coming."

He paused, briefly.

"When that time comes, they are attached to us by stronger bonds than they were ever able to imagine. Life, without us to order and guide them, becomes unthinkable. From that time on, we gradually educate them over hundreds of years in the Aalaag way, and they learn to follow it with gladness. In the end, they are such that we could rely upon them to give us what they should give us and do for us what they should do, even if there was not a single Aalaag on their world to command them to it."

He paused again.

"At last, they become small imitations of the Aalaag," Lyt Ahn said. "They can never become as we are, because they are not—cannot be—us; but they come as close as the beast-limitations of their natures allow them. And these, mark me, beast, are from then on numbered among those destined for special favor."

"And what favor is that?" Shane stared up at him.

"When the time comes that we return to recover our worlds, if they volunteer—and we would never ask them—to follow and spend their strength and their lives to help as far as they can in that great work—we will allow them to so come."

"You will allow them?"

"We will allow them," said Lyt Ahn. "If and when. That was the great possibility that you and your kind have now lost by your behavior. Listen to me, beast."

"I am listening," said Shane.

"Some of our younger officers were unduly impressed by the manner in which some of your ordinary cattle, armed only with rods, attacked and overwhelmed members of my Corps of Interior Guards, who were on duty outside this place that was once my House. In years to come, these young officers will age and grow wiser. They will be disabused of their false admiration."

"It is not false," said Shane.

"It is not surprising that you should hold to that illusion," said Lyt Ahn. "You were correct in that the impetus for it came from your primitive past. But what animated those who attacked was not courage, as you and these young officers seem to believe, but a reflex only, a reflex of unwellness. Your kind is indeed unwell, all of them."

"No," said Shane.

"Your refusal to believe it makes no difference," said Lyt Ahn. "What makes a difference is the fact that we who are Aalaag recognize this unwellness; and so, at my order we have rejected you from the chance of development we have held out to well beasts. You called after me to tell me something you believed of use to me and the Aalaag. I have just told you something that is of use to you and your kind—but you will never believe it."

Shane continued to stare at the heavy, white face looming above him. At last, he was out of words; out of arguments that would touch this one individual among all the Aalaag, whom he had imagined had an open mind.

"You understand now," said Lyt Ahn. "You conceived the conceit that we were leaving because you had shown yourself too brave and independent of nature for us to control. It is not so. We, who do as we wish, build or destroy at our pleasure, choose to abandon you. Not because you have shown that you prefer death to service, but for a far different reason."

"Because we will not be slaves," said Shane thickly.

"No," said Lyt Ahn. "Because you are unworthy."

The silver protective screen flowed back over his face. He

447

turned and strode away toward the ship. Shane watched him go.
In the cold sky above there were no clouds and his armored figure
loomed enormous. The sun gleamed and radiated from all his silver shape, sparkling in the joints that were the connections between
the various parts of the armor as if these were filled with jewels.
And it seemed to Shane that he smelled the dust of time.